Take Back the Years

Johanna was just fifteen years in the summer of 1939 and the onset of the Second World War, when she was thrust into a life of change and turmoil, suffering initially the upheaval of evacuation, and later the true horror of war in London.

Spanning almost eighteen years we are taken though the war years with authenticity. The story encompasses a particularly tender love story, whilst also exploring the division between devastation in London and the relative tranquillity and beauty of rural England.

There is fear, loss, bereavement, and the magic of awakening love. The story is rich in tenderness and spicy Cornish humour, as we watch Jo develop into a caring, conscientious young woman, who learns to live with rejection in her search for true happiness and fulfilment. Tragic consequences bring about a dramatic climax as the reader finally comes to realise their true significance.

Full of period detail and evocative story-telling, the author captures beautifully the atmosphere of the time.

MARGARET QUINN

Take Back the Years

Ellingham Press

ABOUT THE AUTHOR

Margaret Quinn has been writing poetry and children's stories since a teenager and has had many items published both locally and nationally. This is her first novel.

Born in London, it was as an evacuee in South Wales that she first found a lasting love of nature. She experienced several war years in London as a young adult, being deeply involved with the ARP and Red Cross voluntary nursing. Margaret then worked as a hospital secretary until her marriage. She had two children before embarking on a rewarding teaching career.

For Peter

British Library Cataloguing in Publication Data
A catalogue record for this book is available from the British Library

ISBN-13 978-0-9547560-5-5

Published by Ellingham Press
www.ellinghampress.co.uk
Ellingham Press, 43 High Street,
Much Wenlock, Shropshire TF13 6AD

Printed in the UK by Lightning Source

PROLOGUE

Johanna was out of breath by the time she reached the lychgate. Her hands were trembling slightly as they wrestled with the rope that looped the top bar and stopped it swinging open. She glanced back to the road. A lonely, empty road, devoid of traffic and with no sign of the usual walkers, backpacked and laughing, ready for the tramp round the headland and coastal path. Not a day for the faint-hearted, she thought, 'Just right for me though.' It was now very windy, with low clouds almost hugging the cliffs, promising rain.

Closing the gate, she stopped for a moment to still the inner excitement that this morning's news had precipitated, her hand rustling the letter in her pocket. She gave a moment's thought for her kitchen – had she left everything safe? Then she turned to plunge down the covered walk towards the open moor and the sea.

The path was slippery from overnight rain. Her feet slithered frequently, and often she only kept her balance by reaching out for an exposed tree root, or a low-lying bush to cling to. The gully was rocky underfoot. The continued damp of late summer had formed moss which made her hurrying footsteps even more difficult to control. She scarcely noticed how deep the channel had been cut overnight, for the rain had been heavy and prolonged. The culverts that converged at the top of the leafy path had disgorged their overflowing contents, gaining force until the whole of the walkway had become a running river. She felt her feet slipping, but her eyes were focused straight ahead to where the bright clear path for the headland began. The few chirrups and scurries from nearby birds didn't stop her flight. Usually Jo would have walked the leafy lane, stopping to talk to anything she heard rustling. The bramblings had become quite tame and used to hearing people in this confined space. They could often be encouraged to come near for titbits. She had nothing for them today though. Johanna was not even thinking of them, until one bird gave such a sweet shrill song, right over her head. Then she paused for a moment, gazing skywards through the branches of the overhang to seek out the little songster.

'Oh yes,' she breathed, 'oh yes!'

Her heart felt like singing too. Singing like the bird. Her step was light now, she could feel her heart pounding in her chest. Her breath caught again and she stopped, folding her hands tightly together in front of her. Jo thought she'd burst with happiness – and yet this overwhelming feeling of joy was almost like a pain. As tears formed in her eyes and ran slowly down her cheeks, she turned to open the gate, gasping as the full force of the wind caught her. She faced the view now revealed, the wide sweep of the bay, and threw her head back and laughed, laughed at the sheer joy of being alive, of being alive on this special day – this very special day!

Jo crumpled the letter once more, as if to reassure herself it was really there. Her features softened as she thought of the day ahead, her brown eyes were distant as they gazed towards the horizon, seeing and yet not seeing the wonder of the storm-tossed waves stretching away into the distance. Some strands of her light-brown hair had escaped from the wide comb controlling it, and she put up her hands to tame them. Strong, capable hands, square almost, but with tapering fingers and well-cared-for nails, and browned with the summer sun. She stood still, leaning into the wind and enjoying the buffeting. Her slender body still girlishly rounded, brown eyes clear and a face as unlined and smooth as a teenager.

Johanna lifted her face to the wind and stepped out towards the headland path as the memories came flooding back – back to the long hot summer of 1939, before the Second World War had started, and to when it had all begun! She had been fifteen years old then – happy and carefree – spending the holidays in her favourite place in Cornwall. Fourteen years ago, she mused – such a long, long time!

CHAPTER ONE

Johanna woke early on Sunday morning, stretched and yawned, but kept her eyes closed, breathing in deeply the fragrant, fresh, morning air. In the summer she always slept with her face near to the window, turning her little truckle bed round on the side wall, so that her head rested just below the sill. From here she could see the night sky, and on clear moonlit nights she would gaze at the stars as they blazed like jewels in the heavens, until they fused together as her eyes became tired. She loved to watch the storm clouds racing madly above the farm, and the lightning flashes that lit the sky and sent her snuggling down into the safety of her blankets.

She had heard her aunts get up earlier, both treading quietly on the planked floor of their dormitory-like bedroom. Jo had listened clearly to Edith's loud whispers as they discussed what the day was like, and what outfits they would wear for church. She thought for a while of the sisters' friendship. Edith and Mollie were so different in temperament,and yet they always got along splendidly. Mollie's quiet manner did nothing to restrict the ebullience of her sister. She could picture her mother joining the whispered discussions during the long nights when they were, as children, banished to bed early to conserve the oil for lamps. Jo wished she had a sister, someone to share her innermost thoughts and girlish dreams.

The room she now had at Widegates had been grandma's room years ago, but now she had moved into the 'dormitory' with her daughters. They used to tell her stories of midnight feasts, when Tom would join them, all using a form of sign language so as not to disturb their parents, for life always began early on the farm, and the adults needed their rest.

Mollie and Edith's room was long, with low windows at each end. As a child Jo had loved the ease with which she could look out onto the yard and the fields at the back, but now she found the necessary crouching a little awkward, and wondered at the need for their low placing. Three beds lined the length of the back wall, side by side and equally spaced, and all covered with bright counterpanes that grandma had worked from scraps of material. One wall, the opposite one, accommodated two heavy, dark wood wardrobes and high chests of drawers, whilst between each bed was a small locker and bookcase that housed certain personal treasures. Johanna remembered her mother saying that these were 'secret' places and nobody ever took advantage of them. Private things remained private at Widegates.

The curtains were heavy and dark, and hung close to the floor to conserve whatever warmth the house afforded, for in those days there was no central heating, and certainly no heat ever in the bedrooms. This room was placed half over the kitchen though, and Mollie had shown her where the plaster wall got warm from the kitchen range. A 'spartan' room, Jo's mother had called it, but it was home to her sisters.

Jo's room next door was small and square. Reasonably spacious with only the truckle bed and a chest for furnishings, but she often pictured it, filled almost with a brass double-bed. There would have been little room to move about in when her grandparents had it for their own. Large wooden hooks were still in use behind the door for clothes, and on the planked floor were several rag rugs, faded and flat, but affording some little comfort from the cold floor in the winter months.

Now though it was summer. Jo made a conscious effort to keep her eyes tight shut. What was the day like? It felt warm, and yes it was sunny, for she could feel the sun's gentle warmth as it fell on one arm flung up and around her head She let it fall. Immediately the rays of the sun fell warmly on her face. Jo smiled to herself as she noticed the orange light waver underneath her eyelids, sometimes bright and then fading to a pale yellow, before deepening again. Today was Sunday, and today was her fifteenth birthday.

'A very special day tomorrow,' Edith had said as they'd all hugged her goodnight. I do hope so, thought Jo, relaxing in bed and waiting for that wonderful moment when she'd open her eyes and take in all the early morning magic of the farm.

She heard grandma in the kitchen below her room. Such a clattering of pans and rushing of tap water, as she prepared the morning meal. She heard uncle Tom gently persuading his new filly to stand still while he mounted her. Tom had difficulty with mounting his horse because of his 'bad' leg, but refused help from any of them, choosing to place himself on the first step of the huge concrete block that always held either full or empty milk churns. It was his practice to tour the farm early each morning. The young farm-worker would saddle his horse and lead it to the milk stand, tying it carefully to a bar that enabled Tom to stand firmly and to mount. He hated to be seen struggling up the step, his movement awkward and with the necessary use of two walking-sticks. He had a way of swinging his body into a rhythm to produce a fairly free progress. At the top he would discard the sticks, hold on tight to the restraining bar, and then coax his horse into the right position for mounting. He'd always trained his horses to stand still for him, but Sallie was still new to this. A little young, and not yet sure of Tom.

'Come y'ere girl … come my lovely,' Jo heard him say, and much gentle coaxing ensued, until, finally, the repeated gentle, 'Good girl, good girl,' from Uncle Tom announced that Sallie was now standing near and docile. She heard him talk quietly to her.

'There, there. You're a fine lass – we'll be the best of friends … there, there.'

Johanna was half-dreaming once more, listening to the scurrying noises of little things in the eaves of the farmhouse, and the birds setting up a troublesome quarrelling as grandma threw out scraps of fat and odd bits of bread for them. Then from below:

'Darn it girl … woah … woah … bugger me. What did you do that for?' And she saw in her mind's eye, uncle Tom balancing precariously on the edge of the milk stand, with his Sallie just out of reach. At times like this she had often leapt out of bed, hung out of the window, and offered encouragement. As a child uncle Tom had waved to her and laughed at his predicament, but now that she was older, she sensed a drawing-away and some embarrassment over the many difficulties he had with his disability, so she refrained now from letting him be aware that she knew, or even noticed his many problems. The horse must have steadied once more, for she heard a jingle of reins and a cool – 'steady, steady, now', from her uncle, and then a satisfied sigh. Again the jingle of harnesses as uncle Tom readjusted his body comfortably to the saddle, and then with a quiet – 'Giddup now' she heard Sallie walk slowly over the cobbles of the yard. Tom passed the milking shed where his sisters were already at their stools, with buckets wedged tightly between their knees and their arms and hands busy in the rhythmical movement natural to long-time milkers.

'Marning Tom.' It was Edith's firm, strong voice, followed by a chuckle. 'Having trouble with that 'en already are you?' Tom did no more than grunt. Then a gentler voice, a light young voice:

'Morning Thomas. Lovely morning,' from her aunt Mollie. She heard the gate click open and then shut once more as uncle Tom manipulated the special closures with his whip handle, then a final call for the dogs, Fly and Jack to 'come on up now!'

Jo maintained her quiet listening as the horse trotted along the hard clay path at the side of the hedge. She smiled to herself again as she pictured her aunts, both hunched over their stools in the cowshed. The sunlight pouring down through the skylight roof, the cows munching their way through the special feed in the mangers, the odd rattling and clanking of the chains as they moved their heads to give a low 'moo-moo'. Almost a purring sound in appreciation of the girls as they milked them. The slosh of urine and faeces as the cows defecated; she could almost smell the warm heat of it here in bed.

The aunts were chattering now, and although she couldn't hear what they were saying, she was able to differentiate between them. Mollie's voice, so low and sweet and young-sounding, totally out of keeping with their appearance, and Edith's, shrill almost! A laughing sturdy voice, always full of excitement, yes that was it. Edith was always excited; she tackled all the farm jobs with a gusto that surprised the farm-hands. Her loud cheery laugh had made many a hard, wet day fun! She was great to be with, and today she had promised she would make Johanna's birthday special, she had said so last night!

With that thought in mind Jo opened her eyes. She blinked at the bright sunlight, bounded out of bed and stuck her head and shoulders as far out of the little window as she could.

'Morning aunt Edith, morning aunt Mollie, I'm coming now, won't be a moment.'

She heard Edith's loud chuckle and they both shouted 'Happy Birthday'. She called a laughing 'thanks' before ducking inside again, throwing on her farm clothes as quickly as she could and a few minutes later was running along the top passage, stopping for a few minutes in the small bathroom to splash her face with cold water and rub it to life with a hard towel. A quick check in the mirror to count her freckles, before trundling, at breakneck speed down the back stairs, past the cheese room with its sour, pungent smell. Slowing down a little to tread carefully through the lounge on the bright oval rag rugs, set out on the slate floor. She had learned at an early age to respect the dangers of these, having suffered several nasty head bumps as the mats had skidded under her feet. Finally she emerged into the huge kitchen, where grandma was busy over the hot range getting breakfast. A wonderful smell of bacon assailed her nostrils – bacon and freshly baked bread, and Jo was hungry!

The kitchen was large and square, with wide low windows looking out to the yard. It was dominated by a long centre table, bleached white with scrubbing, and the old black kitchen range at the far end of the room. From here emanated the smells that set Jo's mouth to watering. There was a high shelf above the range, heavy with gay pots and a remarkable china teapot, with large silver scrolls all around the sides. Below the shelf, on hooks, hung the iron saucepans and frying-pans used daily by grandma when cooking for so many hungry mouths. They were hung rather low, and often, as she bent over the range, her head would touch them and set them swaying lazily. Jo often thought they'd be better placed elsewhere, but grandma was used to them being close at hand and never noticed the little knocks.

Sometimes there would be as many as ten people for meals. The table was set simply. No cloth, just places set on the bare, clean, well-scrubbed wood. It was wide enough to hold mountains of food and a variety of dishes, with people sitting on either side on long benches, and only grandma and Tom having places at the head and foot of the table. Tom was able to manoeuvre his wheelchair into position, and grandma had a wide, high-backed wooden chair that sat so solidly on the floor that it seemed immovable. Meals were a social, carefree and happy time, and the good wholesome food was enjoyed by all.

Two doors led from the kitchen to the back of the house. Between them was a narrow white sink, which was used by family and farm-workers for hand washing before meals. One door led to the dairy. A light airy room, shelved all round with cool slate and here a barrel-like butter churn dominated the centre of the floor. Various dishes of cream sat, cloth-covered, waiting their turn to be fed into the churn. The adjoining room was smaller and darker. It housed two old, well-worn wooden chairs, and three long metal baths. The latter were three-quarters filled with milk which had been treated to form curds in preparation for the making of the round cheeses that Widegates was famous for locally.

Between the wide windows, a door led to the yard where, to the left, the strong farm gates were left open to the country lane, and to the right were shallow stone steps that led up to the doors of a low-roofed barn attached to the side of the house.

Now the early morning sun spread its rays across the slate floor as it crept round the side of the house. Soon it would reach the window where grandma's collection of copper pots set on the sills would glow warmly in the bright sunshine.

The kitchen was the hub of the house and grandma was totally in command there. She was an early riser. 'Early to bed and early to rise,' was her favourite saying. Often Johanna was admonished for wanting to stay up, particularly when she was dragged in from the back steps on some moonlit night, when the stars hung like jewels in a black velvet sky, when the owls hooted from the woodland in the valley, when she could hear the soft lowing of the animals and the rustling sounds from the eaves of the house behind her. Night time was such an 'alive' time – she was loathe to leave it for sleep!

Tom was an early riser too. He and grandma often had the first cup of tea together, whilst she sat by the range, encouraging the fire with red leather bellows, to get the oven heat correct for the bread. Here they would discuss the day ahead, for although Tom and the girls ran the farm between them, grandma kept a tight hold and interest in what went on. She would watch her son as, insular and proud, he rejected physical help. The ground floor at the farm had interconnecting rooms, with always one shallow step to manoeuvre to get from room to room. These had been adapted to slopes for Tom, so that indoors he would use his wheelchair to advantage. It was somehow part of him and not an extension. But outside was another matter. Grandma would watch her son's awkwardness as initially, he lifted himself from the wheelchair to rely now on two sticks for support. She watched as he struggled across the yard, muttering as usual, 'Bugger me … get off now,' at the welcoming dogs, and she remembered the tall and agile young man he had been and shook her head sadly. If only he hadn't contracted polio.

Breakfast was a main meal at the farm and always included the four workers who'd started their labours some two hours earlier. It was a large meal, with the table piled high with bacon, eggs, marmalade and honey, Widegates' own cheese and butter, and best of all with warm crusty, freshly baked bread, which was always grandma's first morning job. She was a mountainous woman, appearing shapeless in the loose black dress that seemed to hang from her shoulders like a tent. She had long, thinning grey hair, tied loosely into a bun at the nape of her neck. Her face was florid, but then she was always bending over the hot kitchen range. The girls used to say: 'Mum's glued to it!' Her features were large and her mouth set in a straight tight smile. Deep folds of skin at the sides of her neck and under her eyes gave her a heavy, tired appearance, but if you looked closely, the blue eyes twinkled, and the rigid mouth was always ready to relax into a smile of real beauty. It was so when she greeted her granddaughter, and now her smile was wide as she held her cheek forward for the usual morning kiss.

'Happy birthday Johanna,' she said. Jo gave her a quick hug.

'I'm so hungry, grandma, I could eat a horse, but I've got to help in the cowshed before breakfast. Today we have to get the chores done early for we are going to church.'

Very soon the milking was completed, the cows unchained and then left to wander into the yard. The cowshed was hosed down by aunt Edith and Jo, whilst Mollie measured, cooled and churned the milk. The huge metal containers were then trundled across the yard to await collection. Only then did the three of them make for the kitchen and breakfast. Tom and two of the farm-workers were already there, seated and eating. The smell of the freshly baked bread made Jo even more hungry. She rinsed her hands at the kitchen sink, wedged herself on the bench seat between her aunts as grandma said:

'Bacon or lamb, Jo?'

'Oh, lamb please,' and she watched as slices of cold leg of lamb were set on a plate for her.

'You'll make the girl fat,' observed Tom, who was amused at the amount of cold meat being piled onto her plate.

'Here lass, help yourself to pickle,' and he passed a jar to her and the platter of warm bread.

There were always eggs at the farm for breakfast, and always bacon, but the lamb was for special occasions, and she could see by the glances coming her way, that it was a birthday treat for her. The men appreciated it too and were holding up their plates to Mrs Varcoe for second helpings.

'What have we to do before church, Aunt Edith?' Jo's face was red from the warmth of the kitchen.

'Sunday chores as usual. See the cows into the far field. Gather the vegetables for dinner. Let the geese out and collect all the eggs, then, my lass, get yourself pretty. We are going to Lamellion church today.'

'But that's a car ride. I thought we'd be going to St Lowell.'

St Lowell was the parish church situated down the lane and some half a mile nearer to the river. They always went to St Lowell. Jo was puzzled at the change in routine. Now Edith interrupted her.

'It's a treat,' she twinkled. 'You'll love it!' And love it she did. Ten-fifteen saw them bouncing down the lane to Pont in the little Morris Minor, both aunts in summer dresses and Edith sporting on her head a wide straw hat covered in flowers. It looked quite strange on top of her square face and short hair and was firmly fixed with two huge hatpins, tipped in red. The hat just didn't go with her shoes either for Edith had big feet, and shoes were bought for comfort, and to last. The dress was of a dainty, soft material and her feet below looked huge and clumping in the dark brown serviceable brogues. She was happy though, and, giving Jo instructions, her blue eyes twinkled wickedly.

'You'll have to hurry – when we leave the car. The church at Lamellion gets so full that we often have to stand in the porch. Choir's marvellous too.' Here Mollie's face crumpled as she exploded with laughter, whilst a bewildered Jo looked at first one then the other.

Mollie's dress was of pale blue linen and suited her dark colouring. She looked neat and cool against her sister, her sun browned, merry face alight with fun, and her dark curly hair bouncing and catching the morning sunlight as she manoeuvred the little car through the narrow country lanes. Mollie looked elegant today. She was always neat and tidy; a round small person, with the same Varcoe blue eyes, but this morning her strong hands were encased in short white gloves to complete the picture.

'You look good enough for a wedding, aunt Mollie,' Jo remarked, whilst still wondering what was making them laugh so. The car was left at the end of the long drive, and they went through a small lychgate that was strangely painted pale blue, then stepped out onto the gravel path leading directly to the church It was small, built of grey stone like St Lowell, and nestling in a little copse of trees. The surrounding area was mostly woodland and gave a delightful closed-in feeling to the church, but occasionally Jo saw gaps in the trees, and these afforded her a distant view of the sea.

The church seemed quiet and the door, half-open, made a rusty grating noise as they pushed it aside to enter. The sun shone brightly through windows to the right, and Jo could see the dust motes dancing in the rays of light. The church was empty! She turned to Edith questioningly, but found her kneeling in prayer. She sat looking around her for a second or two and then heard steps in the porch; the door grated once more, the dust motes set up a more lively dance as a man and woman entered. He was young and tall, wearing a dark suit and a clerical collar. He acknowledged the woman with a slight tilt of his head, and quickly walked to the vestry at the back of the church. The visiting priest, thought Jo.

By now the woman had turned in front of the old, high-backed piano, situated at the side of the porch door, and was busy shuffling music sheets. Her long narrow face was entirely devoid of expression, and half-hidden under the most stupendous straw hat. Jo had secretly thought Edith's a bit too … oh, too something, but this one … well! The hat had a wide brim that dipped and bobbed with each move of her head. The crown was completely covered with large white daisies, and a butter-yellow ribbon went round the brim to fall in two stiff braids down her back. Her dress was unfashionably ankle length, made of brightly coloured cotton, the background being the same soft yellow as the ribbon on her hat. The few wisps of hair that had escaped from the confines of the hat, were mousy and curly, and she wore glasses that had a settled appearance, well down on her long nose.

Jo stared, until Mollie nudged her. 'Manners,' she said, but her eyes were full of mischief. 'This is only the beginning!' Jo went to question her, but her aunt put a finger firmly to her smiling lips in admonition. On turning, Jo noticed that three other people had entered the church. A man and woman, both in dark colours, with a young girl of about her own age. A pretty girl, auburn-haired, and with a sulky bored face. Jo smiled in acknowledgement of their appearance, but didn't have time to notice a response for the priest chose that moment to reappear, now cassocked, and took up a position half-way up the aisle. 'Strange,' thought Jo, until she heard Aunt Mollie whisper by way of explanation.

'They can't get the piano up the aisle, so all services are held at this end.'

The piano lid was slammed up. She heard a scraping chair and was aware that her aunts were now standing. The first hymn was announced and it was a favourite of Jo's. 'Lead us, heavenly Father, lead us'. She was prepared to sing her head off, not needing to search for the words in the little hymn book she'd brought with her. A huge noise, a thumping chord, was banged from the piano by the daisy-hatted lady. Jo gasped as it was followed immediately by a voice, a loud fruity voice, a loud fruity and confident voice, beginning the hymn. She exchanged a sidelong glance at her laughing-eyed aunts and joined in, but instead of a pleasure the singing became a battle. The pianist banged away noisily, increasing and decreasing the tempo to suit herself, with the small congregation trying hard to keep with her, and all the time her hat seemed to be in danger of falling off her head as she thumped rather than played the piano.

The young priest had a clear strong voice, and seemed to divorce himself totally from both piano and singer. He sang steadily and at his own pace, with a serious expression on his guileless face, as he gazed at the ceiling of the little church. The small congregation did their best. Jo noticed that the young girl continued to look bored and made no attempt to sing or even to open her hymn book. The aunts had a marvellous time, their clear voices rising in unison, and after a while Jo found that she could join them without a laugh bubbling up into her throat and threatening to choke her. The service progressed with the daisy-hatted lady answering all the responses shrilly. The beginning of each hymn remained a shock to the system, for no matter how much Jo thought she was prepared, the noisy chords, accompanied by the loud, tuneless singing, simply just took her breath away.

Finally, the service was over. The priest, with a nod to his small congregation, fled to the back to disrobe. The daisy-hatted lady, after banging down the piano lid, scraping her chair into position and gathering her gloves, sped from the church without another glance at her fellow-worshippers. Aunt Mollie introduced Jo to the young girl.

'Veronica Prouse, her aunt and uncle.' The smile given to Jo was small and tight-lipped, and very soon Jo and her aunts were striding up the path through the lychgate and making for the car, where all three exploded into laughter.

'But you said …' began Jo.

'I know, I know,' Edith hugged her niece, doing a little dance as she tried to open the car door at the same time. 'I know, but wasn't it fun to have a surprise – wasn't it?'

'Veronica was a bit stuck-up,' Mollie commented when they had more or less returned to normal.

'Strange girl. Bored I expect at having her aunt and uncle in charge.' Edith then went on to explain that Vee's parents were away in India for some months. Term-time was spent in Fowey, where her aunt and uncle set up a temporary base at Veronica's parents' home by the river, but during the holidays they all went back to Lamellion, to an old grey-stone house, situated well off the road in a damp woodland valley.

The car was stopped about half-way home and Johanna encouraged to climb a gate to a large patch of clover in the corner of a field.

'It's your birthday, Jo. See if you can find a four-leafed one.' It was a magical morning as Jo searched with her aunts, and found not one, but four! These she placed carefully in her hymn-book as they set off for Widegates and lunch.

'The boys are due home today, and we've asked them for supper tomorrow.' Mollie's voice was quiet and her face looked straight ahead as they left the winding country lanes and reached the main highway. Jo's heart lurched. Bryn and James home today for the holidays. What a marvellous birthday present!

'I'd go to the headland after lunch, Jo, and watch for them

across the bay,' Edith said. 'We'll let you off the dishes as it's your birthday.'

The wind blew through the grasses at her feet and down through the bracken as it clung to the side of the cliff. She watched as the bees flew, hovered and settled on the mounds of thrift dotting the top of the headland where she sat, some late blooms attracting them. Foxgloves, their heads brown now, the bright spring colours all gone, waved in the soft breeze. The path, easily determined, followed the folds of the cliff, dipping and turning to disappear, only to return to sight further along. She watched a hawk weaving over the headland ... bonny brown bird, so graceful in flight. It hovered near to her, its wings fluttering swiftly as it peered for some unsuspecting little creature, dived deeply, vanished for a second over the cliff edge, only to reappear disappointed, then to wheel away to continue the search a little further along the cliff.

The tide was low. The sea relatively calm, but with an edge of white water frilling the rocks around the bay, like a necklace of lace. The sea birds were quiet, a few gliding over the cliffs, silently powerful. The bracken carpeting the cliff was already browning, and the sun, hidden now behind clouds, sent a glancing bright ray far out to sea, so that it appeared emerald green and light on the horizon. Below her, in shadow, the water now looked dark and forbidding. Johanna shuddered at the thought that it was here, on this part of the coast, that a fishing vessel went down in the spring gales: the *Pretty Kettle*, manned by four men from the village. Hard to imagine that this present calm could become a maelstrom of raging seas to engulf and sweep away men and boats.

Jo sat at ease, knees drawn up to her chin, her brown eyes dreamily contemplating the middle distance. She was casually clad in dark shorts and a yellow checked shirt, with a yellow jumper slung roughly round her shoulders. Her slim leg were tanned, and her feet comfortably encased in white plimsolls. The breeze caught her long, light brown hair, whipping it round her head. The sun now played on her face, which was aglow with health, her soft round cheeks tinged pink with anticipation, and as she brushed the fine soft curls off her face, the sun caught and glinted on the blonde highlights.

She stood up and stretched herself, her face to the sun which shone brightly over all the headland once more. A small boat had come into sight round the jutting shoreline, heading straight across the bay towards where she stood. She could just make out the colours, yellow and blue, as it came nearer. It was them – at last! She waved, swinging her yellow sweater over and around her head as the boat thumped its way across the bay. She saw an answering wave from a dark figure at the wheel, then a song drifting up on the light breeze … 'On top of old smokey …' They were back. She laughed into the wind, joining in their song; waved and watched as they passed her, going out of sight round the next headland and into the estuary. They were home – home, and the holidays had just begun!

CHAPTER TWO

The blue and yellow motorboat chugged merrily into the estuary. Bryn felt excited as he edged the vessel to its mooring, and he threw James a disarming smile as he overshot, slightly bumping the jetty.

'Out of practice,' James commented, returning his grin. The boys secured the mooring lines, transferred to the dinghy and rowed into the quay at Polruan, where James's dad, Jim Trevarder, was waiting to take them to Pensilva, some four miles away. He was a tall, wide-shouldered man of some fifty years and towered over the boys as he threw his arms wide in welcome.

'Summer hols once more, lads. Time for Cornwall again!' They both chatted excitedly on the journey, asking about the farm, questioning about the animals; about the situation in Europe, and a possible impending war, until, eventually, Bryn sat back to drink in the scenery, as if Cornwall was folding its beauty around him.

'Five whole weeks of holiday,' he thought, 'and Jo is here as well!' He saw again her small figure waving madly from the top of the headland, and his heart gave a sudden lurch. 'Golly, but I've missed her. I hope James will be free to spend time at Widegates tomorrow. I'm looking forward to her birthday supper.'

As they turned into the gateway of Pensilva, James's home, he saw again the beautiful old house bathed in evening sunlight. He experienced such a feeling of excitement, of pleasure … of returning! He tumbled out of the car and stood on the driveway taking deep breaths of this clear Cornish air, sweet with the scent of late roses from the flower garden and tinged with the fresh sea smell that was, in itself, part of the summer holidays.

Jane Trevarder flung open an upstairs window as they arrived, her fair hair smooth and tidy gleamed in the sun, as she waved a welcome to both boys.

'Hello you two. Food's ready. I'm just coming.' James waved his arm in a wide arc at his mother, as he stood, tall, broad-shouldered, his straight fair hair ruffling in the evening breeze. His strong face, with its wide smile, and his sturdily built body, was a replica of his father. In contrast, Bryn was dark in colouring, his face already tanned from many hours of cricket at school. At seventeen and a half years, Bryn was a tall graceful young man, slim almost, but well-proportioned and with wide shoulders. His features were even, eyes blue-grey, and he had dark curly hair. There was a small dimple in the centre of his firm chin, and his mobile mouth smiled generously at his friend's mother.

'Good to be back,' he commented to James, as he helped collect their luggage from the car.

Bryn was to enjoy this holiday at Pensilva more than any other, for he sensed the changes that possible war would bring to their young lives and lived for each day separately, cramming everything he could into it; filling his senses with the beauty of the area, his mind with companionship, and working his body hard, whether at the farm or in leisure pursuits. He worried about the future, his future, their future, but kept his thoughts to himself. He was used to keeping his own counsel, and indeed until he met James at school had had a fairly lonely existence, spending more time with adults than with children of his own age.

Bryn's parents had been killed in a hunting accident in Africa, during their stay with Bryn's uncle, Mark Vaughan, his father's eldest brother. The old car in which they were travelling had turned over on a high rutted road, tumbled down a steep incline and burst into flames; Bryn was then six years old! He remembered well the terror of waking at night, calling and calling for them, and the deep sense of loss that even now remained with him. They had been a close and happy family, and Bryn had adored his mother. Jim Vaughan, his father's youngest brother, a bachelor living in Beckenham, had taken him in. His uncle was bewildered at first, not knowing how to cope with this heart-broken little lad; but he was good and kind. Always there to comfort him through his night terrors, Jim would rack his brains during the daytime hours to find amusing or energetic things they could both do when free of his work. He employed a housekeeper to keep an eye on the lad. She was elderly in every sense of the word and, though she looked after his physical wellbeing, was hardly the right company for a young, growing boy. So it was Jim who taught Bryn how to throw his first rugby ball, how to serve at tennis, to swim, and to kick a football clean and straight. On quiet evenings they would play table games together. Bryn soon became a worthwhile opponent at chess and joined the local school team at eight years of age! Their relationship was good, open and caring. Jim adored the lad and it was a miserable day for him when, finally he took his nephew to the West Country and to school at Taunton. Bryn was eleven years old. Jim had realised Bryn's need for young company, and he was right.

It was at Taunton that he first met James, and they were soon to become inseparable; both only children, they saw in each other the brother they'd been denied. It was natural then that Bryn should be asked back to Pensilva, James's home, for holidays. Jim was a busy man, an accountant with his own firm in Beckenham, so was happy for his nephew to have a place to go for the long school vacations, but Bryn always spent Christmas, Easter and various exeat weekends with him. The summer though belonged to Cornwall, and with the freedom allowed and the countryside, river and sea, they enjoyed every minute spent there. Both could handle boats well by the time they were sixteen. Bryn's uncle bought him a small motorboat, and, weather permitting, they would hop along the coast, visiting the little seaside towns. Jim Trevarder also taught them how to sail. Their boat was moored on the local crowded estuary, so the boys had to learn disciplines perhaps before the actual enjoyment came. They swam from the sandy bays, walked the cliff paths for miles and, right from the start of their friendship, worked together at Pensilva. Bryn was sure that he would farm when he grew up!

James's gentle sunny nature brought out the best in him. Bryn became less shy, more sure of himself, but, as Mollie was heard to say:

'That lad never lets himself go. He keeps something back all the time. As soon as you think you are really getting through to him, he pulls back. It's as if he's been hurt too much and is scared to get really close to anyone.'

It was two weeks into the holiday. Jo and the boys were quiet as they sat together on a long bench at the quay in Polruan. It was warm and still in the valley, even the seagulls seemed full of apathy and just stood on their firm webbed feet a few yards from them on the boat-yard wall. Jo threw the remains of a cornet at them, but they scarcely moved, not in the least interested in food!

'Impossible,' Bryn shrugged his shoulders. 'Impossible – a seagull that's not hungry!' They lapsed into silence once more. There seemed no need to comment further on the gulls.

Earlier that afternoon an incident had happened that had left them all feeling disturbed. It had seemed such a short while ago that they'd set out from the farm on their bicycles. Three happy carefree youngsters, with the rest of the day ahead of them for enjoyment. They were to attend a party in Fowey, and it was their intention to leave their bikes at the boat-yard, to go over the river by the foot ferry, and afterwards uncle Tom had arranged for them to come back with the pilot when he came off duty.

'No hanging about now, mind,' he'd admonished them. 'Richard Williams is a busy man and he'll have had a hard day and be wanting his supper and bed.' Richard Williams had known Tom all his life and they had attended the same school. Tom often visited the low house on the cliff, where the pilot lived with his wife and daughter. Selina was a gentle, dark-haired girl, who often joined the little group during the holidays.

'He's collecting Selina at the same time,' continued Tom 'So you'd best leave the party together.'

They had assured Tom that they would make straight for the quay at ten-thirty.

'We'll be there waiting for him in all probability, uncle Tom,' Jo had promised.

The young people had often taken the ride to Polruan. The road was straight, nursing the side of the headlands. They had left Widegates at about four-thirty. There had been a different feel to the afternoon. The wind was skittish on the hills, the high clouds wheeling away over the moors as fast as others gathered to join them, in never-ending serried ranks, like marching soldiers, or armies of horsemen. Jo had started it all.

'Let's go down Pont way. Let's not get off our bikes on the hill at all … I dare you both.' Her brown eyes shone with excitement at the thought of the ride ahead of them. She knew inwardly the dare was pretty stupid, because the road led down a very steep, winding and narrow hill, which finally came out at a T-junction on the Polruan lower road, and she shuddered at the thought of the speed they'd have to control.

'Brakes good, are they?' she queried, as the boys stood undecided. James and Bryn weren't at all sure. They knew that they should ignore the mad dare, but Jo's eyes were teasing.

'Afraid?' she queried.

That did it! The bicycle clips were placed firmly on. Brakes checked, and with a wave to uncle Tom, who was busy with the sheep in the adjoining field, they set off at a slow pace, pedalling hard, uphill past the church, and then on to the flat stretch that bordered the farmlands of Widegates. Bryn chatted with James as Johanna led the way.

'What a super holiday, James. I wonder about going back to school though, for it will be so different sharing everything with that London lot.' At the end of the term they had heard that a group of boys from London would, in all probability, come down to share their school. The head had told them how he wanted them to behave, and had added:

'Only a miracle will save this situation.'

'We've not had a miracle yet, have we, James?' added Bryn. 'The news is still very unsettled, though I know the grown-ups like to kid us along that everything is all right.'

'It's only that they don't want to think about the possibility of war,' replied James. 'It will be awful for those London boys to have to move away from home like that. To be housed with strangers too … Some of them will be only eleven years old, as we were when we started at Taunton. Remember how lonely we were at first, but at least we all shared the experience and were under the same roof. I'd not like to be thrust in with some family or other … not at all!'

'Half-day school will be fun though.' Bryn was always looking on the positive side of things where school and work were concerned, and the thought of extra games lessons whilst the classrooms were being used for educating the boys from London was a marvellous consideration.

'I expect they'll plan visits to museums and things as well.' James made a face at the thought of boring school outings.

'I heard they are thinking of starting a farm … growing crops, keeping some animals as well. Mr Jones mentioned that one of the soccer pitches might be dug up.' Bryn's voice was getting indignant.

'So long as they leave the rugby posts in position,' James averred, leaving no doubt as to where his loyalties lay.

Bryn looked up as they came to the turn in the road. He noticed how far ahead Jo was, and called an anxious 'Watch it now ...' as she seemed to swing out of sight as the road tilted downwards.

'Let's catch her up.' James was already pedalling like mad and they both soon found themselves racing helter-skelter down the narrow winding lane. They applied their brakes and slowed down just a little, but, even so, the steep hill needed all their concentration to control the turns and twists of their bikes. Jo was just ahead of them now. They could see her hair streaming out behind her, heard her excited cry as she whizzed round the next bend. They heard too a sharp squeal of brakes and then a thump! Both boys instinctively gripped their brakes and managed to control the wild surge forward as the bend came into view, the road eased out, and they came to a screeching halt. Jo was nowhere to be seen!

Across the road a white van had veered into the hedge and the driver was busily trying to extricate himself, a feat he found impossible as he was jammed right against the branches. They heard him swear, then watched as he manoeuvred himself across the seats to open the passenger door and slide himself out, grumbling and looking about him.

'Where did that darn girl come from ... now look what's happened.' He scratched his head and looked about him, his face now registering alarm as 'that darn girl' was nowhere to be seen. He paled and looked under his vehicle, just as he heard Jo's voice.

'Well, help me out someone ... please.'

The driver of the van straightened, looking first relieved and then extremely angry as he moved behind the van and peered over a small gap in the hedge, where a tousled fair head had appeared and a hand reached out confidently for help.

'For two pins I'd leave you there, miss. What were you thinking of, coming into the road like that? Like a witch sent from the devil you looked, with your hair all flying ... I might have hit you, and we both could have been killed. Whatever did you mean, girl?' His face was cross as his large rough hand grabbed at her slim one. She was pulled and lifted so that she seemed to fly through the gap in the hedge and landed tousled and bewildered at his feet.

Jo brushed herself down, her face going red. Oh, she knew she'd been wrong; how awful, and with the boys watching too ... but her brakes hadn't seemed to respond and before she had realised, she had been out into the road and straight into the path of the white van.

She looked up, her face almost bright red now.

'I'm sorry. Yes it was quite wrong of me, and I know I gave you an awful scare. Gave myself one as well,' she added with a wry grin. 'The brakes were on hard, but I just couldn't stop ... awfully sorry.' Her voice trembled. Bryn and James had appeared after slinging their bikes down at the side of the road. 'United front,' James had whispered, as they settled one on each side of her.

'Are you hurt, Jo?' quietly Bryn asked. She shook her head, but was near to tears, and in front of the boys this was unthinkable. She looked up bravely once more and held out her hand to the driver, her eyes swimming with unshed tears and her mouth trembling. The driver had calmed down a little now and was shaking his head at seeing her distress ...

'All right lass,' he said kindly. 'I don't suppose you meant it, and no harm done really. A few scratches to yourself,' he pointed to her shins which were torn and oozing little droplets of bright red blood, 'and a few scratches on the van I shouldn't wonder.' He turned to Bryn. 'Could you give me a leg up so that I can get the van out of the hedge before we have trouble with another driver trying to use this road?' Bryn cupped his hands and felt the driver's foot placed firmly in them. He heaved up as the man caught hold of both sides of the open doorway, and heard a metallic bang as the leg thumped against the sill of the van. 'Why, he's got an artificial leg,' thought Bryn. 'Perhaps he's been in an accident like this before ...'

The van was undamaged. The branches and twigs of the hedge still softened by their cover of leaves had not harmed it at all. The driver checked on Jo once more ... 'Enjoy the rest of your holiday, lass, but watch those hills and check your brakes!' Then, with a wave at the boys, he was off, taking the road towards the village. Bryn checked Jo's bike, so giving her time to collect herself and clean her leg up a bit with a spare hankie James had produced. It was a quiet trio who made their way along the towpath from Pont. Every slight hill was walked down, without comment, and all made a great do of talking about ducks, boats, and the berries on the bushes, to hide a certain embarrassment. It was Bryn who said finally:

'It was a damn silly thing to do Jo … but we are all to blame. Nothing serious happened, so let's forget it and enjoy our day … OK?' The day lightened – it had a future once more, and they all set too singing as they followed the river path to the quay. Now they sat and watched as they waited for the ferry. The river was busy. A clay ship had come to the centre of the estuary, the pilot guiding it through the lanes of small sailing vessels tied up on this side of the water. As it passed, the boats bobbed and weaved on their mooring lines, their riggings setting up a pleasant jingling as the wake from the large ship moved the water around them.

'I wonder where it's come from?' Jo murmured almost to herself. A few yards from them, a boy and girl were busy trying to tie their boat into position. It was proving difficult as both wanted to be in charge. They saw the annoyance on the face of the young girl. She was about ten years old, inclined to plumpness, and with a mop of untidy fair hair. In contrast, the boy, whom they presumed to be her brother, sported a neat mass of dark curls on his fine head. His face was boyishly good-looking, and his body lean and firm. He glanced their way and seemed embarrassed at having an audience.

'Not that way, silly,' they heard the girl call. 'Oh, give me the rope – you're useless.'

'Imperious little beast, isn't she?' Bryn commented quietly.

'Bossy I should say. Bossy, just like you were, Jo.' James grinned widely at her.

Jo was amazed – an attack on her, and now!

'I was not, and I most certainly am not.' She shouldered both of them as they exchanged glances behind her back.

'You were on the day we first met,' Bryn said. 'I remember clearly: "Boy", you said … "boy, are you strong enough to get that kite for me?" … and you looked me up and down, checking me over as it were. I was furious.'

'Well, you didn't run away did you, and you did get the kite for me. In any case, you had the most smashing legs ever … still have!'

'You'll not get round me that way. Remember James what an autocratic little thing she was. Bossyboots we used to call her on the side. I took an instant dislike, and was amazed when you said that you knew her – remember?'

James was now smiling broadly.

'I remember you both… ' "My name is Brynmau Vaughan, what's yours?" "Jo." "Why, that's a boy's name!" "It is not, you stupid boy. Jo is short for Johanna." '

'Oh yes, I remember,' laughed Bryn. 'I was jolly soon put in my place.'

The teasing continued. Jo felt an inner warmth at Bryn's tone. He was obviously settling the day back to its pleasant beginning. Hiding the misery of the crash that nearly was. Both she and James were quick to respond.

'How your mother had a little spitfire like you when your brothers are so gentlemanly, I'll never know.'

Jo exploded with laughter, for her brothers were not at all like that. Proper rather, and a little squeamish as far as the farm was concerned, Bill and Ray loathed their visits to Widegates. Holidays there had proved to be an agony for both of them, perhaps particularly so as Jo had taken to farm life, the animals, the smells and the open air, like a duck to water. Nowadays, dad took the boys camping in Cumbria. They were there now, and, she thought generously, hopefully having as good a time as she was.

Jo's mother was the second sister in the family and the only one to have married. When visits to the farm had first been made, grandma had been young and managing it all very well with the help of young men from the village.

Uncle Tom had married and bought the old, grey house down the lane, near to the covered walk to the wide bay and headland. It was a beautiful old house, standing firm and proud, with all the front windows looking out across the sea and to the coastal path. Tom had contracted polio as an adult and had been near to death for weeks. He had somehow survived against all odds, but had lost the full use of his legs. For as long as Jo could remember, he had struggled along with sticks, dragging one leg behind him, a leg that had seemed small and crumpled somehow to a young child.

'But why won't it work, uncle Tom?' she had asked him, over and over again. 'I can massage it if you like.'

So, to please her, and perhaps to afford some comfort to himself, he had let the child stroke his ankle, trying to 'magic' some movement back into his poor leg. Such moments always ended in fun, for Tom was a fun-loving person. He would produce some treasure from his pocket, or suggest a ride to look at the sheep, and the leg would be forgotten – for the time being at least.

Tom's young wife hadn't been able to cope with his illness, and had sadly left him. When grandma had started to ail a little, Tom had come back to help his sisters manage things. He had been there ever since, using the old storeroom next to the cheese room as his. It had been made comfortable with carpets. There was a wide window overlooking the sea view and he escaped there when necessary. It was of course on the ground floor, making it easily accessible for him with his wheelchair and sticks.

Tom never sold his house down the lane, but he never visited it either. It was as if he had just walked out and left all his dreams and happiness there. Shut in and not to be disturbed.

He was a handsome man, with the Varcoe piercing blue, laughing eyes, but at times one noticed the lines of pain etched upon his face, and his eyes lost their sparkle and had instead a faraway look in them.

Jo used to sense his bleak sadness, and would twine her arms round his neck and shoulders from the back of his special wheelchair. She hugged him and whispered …

'I love you, uncle Tom … please don't be sad.'

Aunt Mollie had been engaged to a young man during the Great War, but he'd been killed towards the end of 1917. She had stayed on at the farm, a bonny, seemingly happy little lady, with a gentle voice and manner, and an infectious laugh that rang out at every opportunity. She was in charge of the kitchen garden and most of the dairy work, but would help in the fields when necessary, proving herself to be as strong as her sister. Her stout little figure could be seen any day, dressed in neat ginghams, pottering over plants, rushing to and from the dairy and working over the huge kitchen range with her mother, as she talked to the cats and clucked at her ducks, hens and geese, who always seemed to crowd round the kitchen stable door. Her dark curly hair was cut tight to her head, and her blue eyes twinkled, just as her brother's did. Johanna loved her dearly.

Anyone visiting Mollie and meeting with her in the farmyard had to run the gamut of her 'quackers'. They followed her everywhere, getting under her feet as she laughed and talked to them, as they kept up such an incessant racket of quacks, clucks, honks and hisses, that conversation with her was impossible. She laughed shrilly above it all, shooed them away with her arms, and at the same time ushered her guests into the kitchen, the main hub of the house. Mollie was never lost around the farm. Her squadron of feathered friends directed her whereabouts; nor could she ever seek a quiet spot without being found, and sought after by her 'quackers'. She was not a solitary person fortunately, never needed a hideaway spot to be quiet in; the farmyard area was her domain, and she loved her particular responsibilities there.

Jo's mother, Lillian, was the beauty of the family, with her willowy figure, sweet oval face, brown eyes and long blonde hair. She had married young and had been barely nineteen when Jo's dad had taken her to live in London. They had a large Victorian house in the south-east of town. Jo was the middle child and had two brothers, Bill and Raymond. They were a happy family, and if their father didn't appear on the scene for weeks at a time, well they understood that his work was important and made the best of things. Jo knew that he worked for the Admiralty and needed to travel a good deal.

Edith was the youngest. A large, raw-boned woman, jolly, carefree and noisy. She was tall, long-legged and walked with an almost deliberate slowness, but managed to cover the ground quicker than most. Her eyes were the same piercing blue, her mousy hair was cut short, and was straight, full and bouncy. Edith's cheerful personality brought a smile to those around her, for she was always totally happy.

Jo now thought of Widegates, as she sat on the quay between her friends. So many happy holidays had been spent on the farm. Now, when she arrived, the whole house and area seemed to welcome her in a most special way. It's more like home than home, she thought. The feeling of intense excitement was always there, initially when being met from the train at St Austell, again after a short quick drive, when the car drew up at the ferry crossing, and she could look right towards the estuary. Her eyes floating over the moored yachts, the dredgers and the confusion of motor boats that crowded together there, to where the river opened wide, and where the castle ruins guarded the entrance to the harbour. Later, nearer to Widegates, she would look about her as if seeing it all for the very first time. The hedgerows, high banked, the monument guarding the wide sweep of bay, and uncle Tom's old grey house.

As the car descended the final narrow lane, through gaps in the high banks she could see the rolling hills, the river valley, deeply wooded; the distant clay hills near to the moor, and then, standing clear against the sky, the bell tower of St Lowell church. Slowly, as they dipped further down the lane, a slight curve enabled her to catch the first glimpse of Widegates, nestling in its own folds, some half a mile from the church, and sheltered by its own little copse of trees. The farmhouse was grey, as was usual in these parts. A long, low-lying house, with a sprawl of outbuildings and a silver silage container.

Jo was thinking how much she wished it was the beginning of the holidays. Wished that she didn't have to return to London, wished her father was a farmer, so that they could all live here forever. 'I wish … I wish …' she whispered to herself.

'Come on, dreamy, or we'll miss all the fun on the other side.' It was Bryn, her Bryn, and they were going to a party! She jumped up, quite herself once more.

'Race you to the ferry then …'

'She's back again!' Bryn shrugged his shoulders, and raced after her.

The party was to be held at Veronica's home in Fowey in the tiny garden overlooking the river. 'A casual party', the invitation had said. Before this summer, James and Jo had scarcely known Veronica. Jo's first impression of her at church at Lamellion was not a good one. However, Bryn knew her well. It seemed that their parents had been friends years ago, and they'd frequently met one another at the home of Bryn's uncle. This summer they had included her in several of their excursions. 'Do you mind, chaps?' Bryn had asked. 'She's having a pretty boring time with her aunt and uncle. Her parents don't get back from abroad until a little later in the month. We could cheer her up perhaps.' And so they had often been a foursome. Veronica had settled in well and Jo was to learn that under that sulky, bored expression was a young girl quite capable of enjoyment. She was friendly and open with both boys, but she had a natural casualness towards Bryn that was disarming to Jo.

They swam together. Veronica was a powerful swimmer, and often the other three would watch as she swam across the bay, her red head, with the hair tied into a knot, bobbing up and down in the waves. Sometimes she'd be lost to sight, and then Bryn would stand

and study the water, his face concerned. She rode with them round the farm, helped with the chores, with the harvest, and sometimes stayed for a meal at Widegates. Happy times, when thoughts of war were thrust aside. Grandma and the aunts watched them, and listened to their light-hearted bantering. 'Let them be happy while they can,' Mollie thought to herself.

It was four contented tired young people who travelled back across the water in the small but robust pilot's boat, with the searchlight on the front, seeking the way for them amongst the crowded estuary. They were all quiet, but James answered Mr Williams's questions about the party, with Selina filling in on bits that had specially appealed to her. Jo watched the water. The river was smooth and dark at the turn of the tide, and she could see the lights of Fowey reflected in it – deep set and far down. There was a quarter moon that travelled with them, both above in the heavens and below in the black swirl of water. It was a still night, a little cool, but with a clear, fresh breath of air that she found suddenly exhilarating. Jo was content though to sit quiet.

It had been a good party. They had met young people they hadn't seen for ages, for Vee had gathered her guests from a wide circle of friends. The carpet had been laid back in the bay-fronted lounge, revealing a perfect parquet floor, ideal for dancing. Patio windows were flung wide to reveal a fairyland of lights, suspended from anywhere strong enough to hold them. It was these they had seen on crossing the water earlier. Trestle tables had been set up in the dining-room, laden with food, where, during the course of the evening, groups of young people chatted and picked at a variety of enticing savouries and sweets.

Veronica's father, tanned from his Indian trip, made a punch which James was sure had been tinged with 'the good stuff'. Jo thought that he was probably right, for after a lively hour or two dancing to the latest popular music, she felt sleepy and was happy to sit out. A small glass of sherry always had the same effect on her.

Bryn had been popular with all the girls, loving the dancing. He had sought her side whenever he could, but was continually torn away for more 'footwork'. Jo hadn't realised that he had such a natural grace. James was a quiet companion for the latter part of the evening as they watched the fun and hilarity.

'Veronica is setting her hat at Bryn you know, Jo. Just look at her.' Johanna watched as Vee and Bryn navigated themselves around the floor and out onto the patio, dancing a lively number. 'She likes to dance and so does he. They are having such fun,' she replied. Secretly though, Jo agreed with James. She had been watching them together a good deal during the holidays, and to her dismay, at times feeling a little jealous of the attention Bryn seemed to give Veronica. She dismissed the thought; it wasn't worthy of her. They were both her friends, and after all Bryn had known Vee since they were children.

'He's not her type really,' she continued, giving James a poke with her elbow. 'Veronica is looking for someone with lots of money. Come on, James, let's dance this one too.'

The evening had ended with a rousing singsong, and then the guests began to leave, in twos and threes, some to travel by car to outlying farms and villages, others to walk Fowey's quaint narrow streets to local homes, whilst others, like Jo and her party, made for the river and a boat to cross the water.

One still, grey afternoon, they wandered down to Connington Woods and strolled along the central footpath that eventually led to the river. At the edge of the woods they came across an old derelict building, wide and sprawling, with outhouses and barns. It had clearly at one time been a flourishing farm. They explored it all, finally sitting in the walled garden and speculating on what sort of people might have lived there.

'I wouldn't mind it,' Bryn said. 'Perhaps I'll buy this when I'm older.'

Later that evening uncle Tom told them that the farm had been flourishing up to twenty years ago. The farmer had accidentally shot himself whilst cleaning his gun. There were no relatives to leave the farm to, and so it had been sadly neglected. 'They say it's haunted …' Tom puffed at his pipe, pretending to ignore six bright questioning eyes. 'They say,' he continued. 'They say, that every August, at full moon, the funeral procession is seen starting from the farm and making its way up the lane … a small procession, mind, because he had no relations. Every person who attended is dead now too…'

Of course, James and Bryn wouldn't let this alone … a haunted house. They must explore this. It was decided that they would spend the night there. The calendar was consulted with regard to the full moon and requests made to camp out in the woods. Jo cried off – she made sure that grandma would refuse her permission so that she didn't lose face with her friends. Uncle Tom's description of what had happened had unnerved her, and particularly when Edith followed it up, describing the haunting with a seriousness that was unusual for her. The boys never spoke about the night they watched for the ghosts. Suffice to say, they saw nothing strange, though they both shook their heads mysteriously when questioned. Jo was to learn years later from James, that they'd both fallen asleep, having imbibed a full bottle of cider for comfort and dutch courage.

That summer, Bryn and James were amused to discover that Jo wrote poems. 'Jingles', she called them! It was a compulsive creation for her … everything and everybody was used as inspiration for her simple and often amusing verse.

The three of them were watching the gulls one bright windy day as they sat in the shelter of a large rock, just below the headland. They could see the coastline from this point and had watched as a fisherman hauled in, and collected from his lobster pots, and then in the distance saw a large vessel approaching.

'Another job for Mr Williams,' commented Jo.

'A pilot's life must be fun,' said Bryn. 'Pretty skilful too. I should think.'

'Lots of responsibility,' returned James. 'I wouldn't like to turn out on some of the rougher nights. Awful for Selina and her mother when he does have to, for she has a clear view of the estuary from her lounge. The pilot boat must look so tiny and vulnerable from the house on the cliff.'

'Don't be silly.' Jo had been gazing out to sea, but now she turned to them. 'He doesn't go out if the weather is too bad. The ships have to ride out the storms in the bay.' Her slim arm pointed to the horizon.

'Is that right?' Bryn sounded unbelieving, but his eyes were teasing. He loved it when Jo got angry and sought every opportunity sometimes to encourage her to flare up.

'If Jo says so, then I expect it is.' James, always the peacemaker answered, and then quickly changed the subject. 'Look at the gulls … how they love the wind.'

'Let's make a jingle about them,' said Jo. 'First line for me, then you Bryn ... then me again, and afterwards James, and so on ... all right?' The boys exchanged looks, but didn't answer, so she started:

'I love to watch the seagulls,
High up in the sky'
Bryn followed ...
'Dipping, weaving and whirling ...
Showing how to fly'
This from James.
'I'd like to be there with them
That will be my goal ...
Like Icarus to soar quite free
Over the wide expanse of sea'

James finished with a flourish. Bryn slapped his friend on the back. 'Hey James, that's not at all bad ...' It was the beginning of a new game, the 'jingle game', and whenever they were together, little poems were created by all three. Unbeknown to the boys, Jo remembered them and wrote them down. Edith and Mollie were amused when she read them aloud in the evenings. Soon after they'd left Widegates that summer, whilst Mollie had been changing sheets in Jo's room, she found one jingle just for her, propped up on the window sill.

'Aunt Mollie loves her 'quackers',
and she feeds them lots of grain.
But they follow her around all day,
which can be quite a pain.
They're always on the scrounge for food,
but she doesn't seem to mind.
For they give us lots of eggs for tea,
which is really very kind.

Thanks for everything – love Jo.'

The five weeks of the summer holiday progressed all too quickly. Johanna, Bryn and James spent every minute they could together.

Uncle Tom was glad to have help on the farm, and though James had certain chores to do for his father at Pensilva, he too was often seen joining his friends, helping to clean the byre ready for the over-wintering of the cattle, or holding the ladder whilst Bryn repaired some small hole in various outbuildings. They helped with the harvest, particularly the stooking, joining the aunts and farm-workers in the fields from dawn to dusk, loving the merriment always induced by Edith's saucy wit. She was teasing now, Jo felt sure, as she watched the boys, both leaning on the farm gate near to the barn. Bryn tall, his long figure graceful and relaxed against the gate, dark head thrown back in laughter and his blue-grey eyes sparkling with life. In contrast, James's smile was gentle, to match his nature, and his fair hair glinted in the sunshine as he watched his friend.

They were gay, happy times, and, if indoors, the adults seemed preoccupied with the radio and news of Europe, the young people scarcely noticed, but fled at every opportunity to their headland, where they could weave their own young dreams for a while, ignoring the reality, and what was obvious to all three, that their world was shortly to be turned upside down. They shoved the thought aside, and during quiet moments, when conversation might have developed into serious considerations, discussions were averted by laughter and fooling.

It was David Grant who brought the matter up quite clearly one balmy evening, just before their departure. It was a beautiful warm afternoon and they had carried a small picnic, which they ate perched high on the rocks over Lansallos Bay. The sea was still and peaceful, there was a quiet about everywhere, and even the gulls were resting. Shoals of fish, feeding in flurries, darted energetically from left to right, their silver bodies glinting in the sunshine, as they leapt from the water in a voracious orgy of eating. Several gulls floated or rested lazily nearby, occasionally leaving the water for flight, only to settle once more near to the shoals of fish. They were not anxious to feed, and it appeared to Jo that they were keeping watch ... 'Almost as if they are keeping track of the fish in readiness for the next meal,' she thought.

It had been their intention to walk to the little seaside harbour round the bay, but they'd lazed away the time, so finally had turned back towards their part of the headland as the sun began to sink.

Passing the little cottage on the cliff, they heard music floating on the evening air …

'Let's call on David.' Bryn said. 'We ought to say goodbye to him as we are leaving tomorrow.' They left the cliff path, clambering over a small stile and took a steep incline towards the sea. The water was at low tide and slushing gently on the rocks. The bay looked as if it were full of steely, shining slate, rather than water, and where the evening rays of the sun caught it, the sheen was almost unbearable.

'He's playing *La Bohème* again,' Jo remarked as they scrambled down to appear breathless and in a heap, at the front of the cottage. David's home was perched on a wide ledge facing out to sea and almost at the bottom of the cliff. The views from the small patio were extensive, reaching right round the bay on the one side towards Polperro, and to Pencarrow Head, the estuary, Gribbin Head and Mevagissy on the other. David Grant sat in his battered old chair outside the door of the cottage. It was a well-used chair, they knew, for they'd seen it many times, filled with his huge figure, and unkempt and empty. The seat was sunken, the arms ragged and shaggy, but it was obviously a well-loved chair. With his pipe and a dreamy, contented expression, David would settle down for talking or listening, and this was how they found him … eyes closed, his pipe out, as was usually the case, and the music floating away gently on the evening air. He always played his records softly: 'To enhance the sounds of the sea, not to drown them,' he had often explained.

David smiled at their presence, got up from his chair heavily, selected from the cottage some old cushions, which he now threw in a scattered fashion onto the patio. He was a huge man, both tall and wide, and needed to stoop a little as he entered the doorway. His movements were slow and deliberate. Bryn always thought them the quiet movements of a man with all the time in the world. His large, square face was contented, a smile of welcome and pleasure showed now as he greeted his young guests, his sharp blue eyes merry.

'Make yourselves at home … good to see you.' He settled himself again in the old armchair.

The patio was made from huge pebbles so the cushions were necessary for comfort. They arranged themselves around him, and waited until the last strains of music had died away. David had three special records that he played regularly on his gramophone. All were recordings by His Master's Voice with the little white dog and loudspeaker emblazoned in the centre. They were the Intermezzo from *Cavalleria Rusticana*, Indian Summer, and *La Bohème*.

'Now then,' he turned as the last notes of music faded. 'Now then – what were you three discussing so avidly over on the rocks at Lansallos, and for so long?' He reached his hand to the side of the armchair and clasped his old binoculars for an instant.

'You've been spying on us,' Jo laughed, 'And suppose we'd been doing something we shouldn't?'

'And what would that be, miss, I wonder? No, I wasn't spying. There was a kestrel over the cliff path and I was following it round in its search for food. Just happened to spot you all resting, that's all – was the picnic nice?' He screwed up his eyes, made a face at them and proceeded to puff at his pipe. Getting no response from it, he reached behind him to where, on the ledge, was his old lighter, and for a while all three watched as he sucked and sucked until the pipe came to life and set him coughing, as it always did. He looked up contentedly, smacked his hands firmly on his knees, and leaned forward.

'Come on now. What were you discussing? Was it the war?' The word was out ... the word that they'd been trying to ignore amongst themselves for so long. Bryn gazed seawards and heard James say.

'No we weren't actually, but we would like to talk about it to you. At home everything is so tense, and I know that Johanna and Bryn feel the same tension around them. What do you think will happen, David?'

David Grant had first appeared into their special world some three years before. Initially, he was just someone they'd heard about. Tom had told them that Bay Cottage on the cliffs was now inhabited, and he advised them to respect the privacy of the new tenant, who was to be warden for the area. They had stopped going down to sit on the patio at the front of the cottage, or to clamber further down to the black rocks that jutted out into the bay at this point. One evening, however, shortly after he'd taken over the house, David met them on the coastal path. He was gazing down at the rocks on the foreshore, his huge body perfectly still. He put out a hand behind his back to stop them going further, and then pointed to where, far below, they could see a nest, a kestrel's nest. It was just visible in the crack or fissure of black rock ... the jagged edges creating a marvellous camouflage. Bryn was sure they'd never have spotted it themselves, not ever!

'You've got good eyes to find that,' he whispered as a kestrel left the nest and flew in a wide arc below them.

'Patience, lad, patience,' David returned. 'I've watched and heard it for days from the cottage. Finally, yesterday evening, I pinpointed his homing place.

So began a relationship that enriched all four of them. David loved anything wild and they had spent many hours during the holiday times with him, watching the live creatures on the headland. He had shown them how to watch the cormorants flying low over the waves, in small parties, line astern. They looked rather like geese. They had watched as these 'crows' of the sea dived for fish, bringing their capture to the surface before swallowing it. They had spent hours, using David's binoculars in turn watching the kestrel as it hung on quivering wings, head down scanning the ground. The shrill cry was easily recognised and never ceased to thrill Jo when she heard it.

David taught them to recognise various gulls. The deep barking, great black-headed gull, common to these parts, which nested off the cliff slopes of the headland. The terns who patrolled the inshore waters during the summer, plunging into the sea from a great height, and staying submerged for so long that Jo often thought them in danger. The razorbill, with its white winter face. They used to watch its energetic splashy dives with amusement.

He had shown them old nests used by the long-eared owls in the woodlands of the valley, inland from the coast. He taught them to search the shingle beaches for the shells of sting winkles, keyhole limpets, needle and cowrie shells. When they were younger, Bryn and Jo had made a shell garden at the cottage for him. They had bent their heads over rock pools, the small pockets of water left behind on the shore when the tide goes out. Here they would find the common limpet, tiny free-floating animals, the colourful sea anemones, small starfish, and if they were lucky, a hermit crab.

They had searched the hedgerows for evidence of weasels, and the river bank for otter. The cottage housed a small library of books on wild life, and these were continually being referred to. David was an educator, and his love of natural things enabled him to make the searching both exciting and rewarding. They never tired of it!

As he got to know them and realised that they appreciated the natural things as he did, so began a friendship that was to last. One that was to be renewed by each or all of them, time and time again during the holidays; summer, winter and spring. During the cold days of the Christmas break, Edith used to make warming soup which they carried in a large, bright green flask with a lip. This they shared with him, huddled in the tiny cottage, whilst the sea raged and tossed outside; they talked of the wild things, of music and sometimes, when David was in the mood, of his home in North Wales, of its customs and the magic of the scenery there.

It was to David that a young Johanna first explained why she called Pencarrow Head – 'Mr P'. A couple of years ago, just as she was leaving the cottage after a visit, on a sparkling spring afternoon, Jo had stopped for a moment to admire the view. The water was bubbling and bright, the air sharp and clear, blowing in straight from the sea. She had lifted her head in appreciation and her hand in salute.

'Thanks Mr P for a perfect day,' as she turned to go. David caught her arm, 'What did you say Jo? Who is this Mr P?' he asked suspiciously.

'You are looking at him, silly,' and she pointed to the headland. It was true, the area resembled the head of a man in repose, the noble forehead being the highest point, the nose a rocky prominence, and the beard was suggested by a fascinating layered rock formation. The wide grass path that weaved over the headland seemed to create a smiling mouth that completed the picture.

'Do you know, I've never noticed that before, young Jo. "Mr P" eh … mind if I call him that too?'

'Of course not. I talk to him all the time, and I feel he's real and looking after me. Even on the most awful days he seems to smile at me.'

'Does he now,' David responded, as he laid his hands casually on her shoulders in gentle affection.

'He's special too in another way, but you mustn't laugh at this.' The young Jo watched David's face, and then went on. 'He always makes the weather good for me. Sometimes it's misty and wet at Widegates, and yet, when I walk out to Mr P, then the sun comes out – he seems to make the mists roll away – just for me.

David was touched, and loathe to mention that any prominence, jutting as far out as this headland, afforded visitors the same warm welcome.

Now, this evening some two years later, it was quite natural that it was to David that they turned to ask about the impending war.

'There will be war I'm afraid, and very soon, but as to what will happen … who knows! Times are different now. Defences are different. Weapons are different, but because of the fighting in Spain, well, what we do know is that modern warfare is a terrible, frightening thing.' The young people listened, their faces tense.

'Will it be long – the war, do you think?' There was a catch in Bryn's voice.

'If you read the papers you would know that some say it will be over before it really begins. Let's hope that this is so, but I'm not sure, not sure at all, and I doubt if anyone really knows.'

'We might be able to fight, Bryn, if it's a long war!' James's voice was excited and his eyes shining. Jo looked at them aghast. Bryn and James to fight! The war to last so long that they would be old enough! A heavy weight seemed to constrict her chest, and she folded her arms around herself, feeling both frightened and vulnerable. The boys hadn't noticed her reaction, but David put a comforting arm out and drew her close.

'There, that's enough, you two. You are frightening Jo. There is no glory in war, lads, only devastation and misery. Put your minds to your studies and pray that it will be well over before you're both through school.'

'Were you in the last war?' James wanted to know.

'Yes, James, I was. That's why I say there's no glory in it … none at all.'

They sat quietly for a while, the boys gazing seawards, lost in their own thoughts, whilst Jo fixed her gaze on first one and then the other, her face registering an unbelievable sadness. David changed the subject and told them about the mink he'd seen in the water just below the cottage.

'Don't say anything, mind, or they'll be out to shoot him. Come down in the week and I'll show you.'

'Can't be done, David – sorry,' returned Bryn. 'We are all off in the morning – hols over, worst luck.'

There was silence for a while as all realised that this 'goodbye' was to be different from any they'd ever taken of David before. No 'see you at Christmas' this time. None of them knew where they'd be at Christmas … none of them knew anything anymore!

David sensed and caught their mood. He puffed on his pipe for a moment, leaning against the white wall of the cottage, his eyes had a faraway look as he began.

'It's a long, long year to my birthday. My birthday is in November, and then it's a long year to the next. Through early winter … then the long Christmas period, and the cold months of January, February and March…then the long summer and down into autumn and winter. Then it's my birthday again, in November. I'll be forty-one – I was born in 1898, sixteen years before the Great War … yes, it's a long year to my birthday …'

Johanna shivered in the now cool evening air. Everything was so sad, they were all sad, sad at the holiday being over, and frightened at what was ahead. Only David would be here … still here when they returned, but David was sad too … sad at the thought of them leaving with the lonely days ahead of him, through the last months of the year. They left him there, as the first cool winds of autumn blew in from the sea. Left him to wait.

CHAPTER THREE

The war did come as David rightly predicted, just as the young people commenced their autumn school term. For Bryn and James it was more or less a normal life at their school in Taunton, for the school from London hadn't arrived, so they were soon working to a disciplined timetable.

It was Johanna who suffered the upheaval of evacuation and had her young life turned upside down. She was evacuated from London and settled in a small coastal town, where the school was shared with the local girls' high. It was a weird arrangement, with afternoons only spent in the classroom situation, the mornings being taken up with organised walks or lectures in the Park Museum, a dim, quiet and church-like place, or in any other available hall.

She was happy in her billet, which was beautifully situated in a park, and just two minutes' walk from the sea, and where on 3 September, she experienced her first chilly thrill at the sound of air-raid sirens. The ups and downs of the wailing set her nerves jangling and sent a strange crawling sensation over her scalp. Little did she know that this frightening noise would become an almost continuous part of daily life for years!

Jo's first Christmas away from home was a good one on the whole. The school organised various functions to keep the girls occupied and together. She particularly enjoyed a carol-singing session in aid of the Spitfire Fund. The moonlight night was clear, with stars twinkling a welcome. Lamps were not allowed because of black-out regulations, but a group of some thirty girls, well guarded by six teachers and two local policemen, went from street to street singing their hearts out.

The months fled by with little of the war touching Jo. She did well in her schoolwork in spite of the difficulties and frustrations of a shared school building. She also corresponded regularly with Bryn and James. When writing to them, she was transported over and over again to Cornwall, remembering their last holiday together, and wishing those days back, back to a peaceful and carefree world.

The year 1940 was to shatter her peace, for from July onwards, apart from the isolation from her family and those who had been so much part of her life, was now added the trauma of real danger. A danger to be considered day after day, as the skies of Britain filled with enemy planes intent on devastation, destruction and death, mainly at this time directed towards London where her parents lived.

In the early months of the war, between 1939 and the evacuation of the British Expeditionary Force from France in May 1940, there was a period of 'stand-off', a waiting, generally termed 'this phoney war'. There was a complacency about life and people went about their business with an amazing air of confidence, a 'let's get on with it' attitude was most evident. This was broken by the German Army circumnavigating the famous Maginot Line (built by the French to prevent such an invasion) and sweeping across France. The British Forces fought a rear-guard action all the way back to the beaches of Dunkirk where, bombed and machine-gunned day and night, they awaited rescue. Destroyers which brought off most of the three hundred thousand men were helped by an armada of small boats manned by volunteers. Every sort of vessel helped; pleasure boats, river ferries, fishing smacks. Richard Williams, the pilot at Fowey, and several of his friends from the village were amongst those who helped here.

The British people seemed to remain on the whole unruffled, though there was a very real threat that Hitler would attempt a serious invasion at any time.

Jo and her school friends heard that church bells were to be silenced, to be rung again for an invasion only. They discussed this amongst themselves, and were generally irate about it, but adopted a certain complacency with regard to the invasion.

'Impossible. They'd never get over the Channel.' As they talked, the strip of water became wider and infinitely more insurmountable. 'No, of course there would be no invasion!' However, the possible reality was thrust home to Jo when a month or so later, Mrs Dingle produced a leaflet entitled *If the invader comes.* The warnings and advice struck terror in her heart. The adults all spoke of the reality of the situation and made provisional plans to leave London should the enemy arrive on our shores. They spent hours making lists of things to take, and even collecting some of these items, but whatever plans were discussed were always limited by the possible lack of transport. Jo buried her head like an ostrich. The thought of an invasion evoked such a trauma within her, and particularly during the day when she was away from home. She just couldn't bear to think of it! Widegates was safe and inviting, and she couldn't imagine enemy soldiers there at all. 'I'll get to Widegates somehow,' she thought – but she made no plans. The fear that it engendered made Johanna put the thought of a possible invasion to the back of her mind. It just wouldn't happen!

The Battle of Britain began on 10 July 1940 with, initially, the German Luftwaffe attacking the convoys of merchant ships travelling through the straits of Dover. In early August the enemy began its full attack on the south-east of England, with fleets of bombers protected by fighters, but the Luftwaffe were to have no easy victory as they could not hope for air superiority until Fighter Command had been eliminated. Bases in Kent came under heavy attack, but then, on 7 September, the Germans turned aside to bomb London. Hitler was in a hurry, for he had invasion in mind. He was also anxious to retaliate, for the sake of prestige, for the night bombing of Berlin and other German towns. He hoped that this bombardment of London would bring about the collapse of the British spirit. It certainly disrupted civilian life and caused many casualties. The Battle of Britain ended after a dangerous golden summer, but London was 'blitzed' almost every night from 7 September to 10 May 1941.

Two weeks before Christmas Johanna's father was killed during a hit-and-run raid in London. He had made his way from work, leaving the dark passageway that connected with his office in the Admiralty, just as a bomb exploded nearby. The blast had blown him back against a wall, and he slid down awkwardly, sitting with his knees up and yet still clutching his well-used black briefcase. A policeman came hurrying over, but Mr Dingle got himself up, dusted the legs of his dark trousers, white now with the rubble dust that was settling around them. He made to move – raising his hand as if to thank the policeman – took one step – buckled at the knees and collapsed on the pavement, flat out, cheek resting on the kerb; just as if he'd fallen asleep … perhaps after too merry an evening. He had suffered a fatal heart attack.

The funeral was a quiet one. The simple church service attended only by his immediate family, a few colleagues from the London office, and Mollie, who had travelled up from Cornwall to be with her sister. Bryn was there – Jo was thankful for that.

Since returning home she had been in a daze, there seemed so much to do. Her mother was standing up to things bravely. Bill had got compassionate leave from his army base at Salisbury and arranged the funeral. He had met Johanna at the station, and she watched him as the train drew in. He looked strange to her in his army uniform; his dark, coarse, wavy hair was cut very short and emphasised his firm square chin and deep-set blue eyes. His tall frame looked leaner, and he was peering at the train intently, his face a mask of sadness. Bill hugged her close and for the first time in her young life, Jo sensed that she was giving rather than receiving comfort from her gentle elder brother.

Mrs Dingle had made a list of things to do and look into. High on that list were clothes! She could find nothing dark to wear for herself and Jo, and this seemed to worry her, worry her unnecessarily, Jo thought. 'It's not as if Dad will be there to see!' Shopping was out of the question as there were no clothing coupons left.

'I'll borrow,' she told Bill. 'Someone will be able to help.' So it was that Jo was neatly clad in a dark skirt and cardigan, both belonging to Mrs Harris from a few doors up the road, whilst her mother had borrowed a grey coat from Mrs Jackson, Jo's godmother. It was a good coat and Mrs Dingle looked smart in it. She retrimmed a navy hat with a dark band and searched out a pair of dark gloves. Jo would have to wear her school raincoat, but that was navy and quite suitable. Having sorted out this and several other minor problems with regard to the funeral, Mrs Dingle's motivation came to a sudden halt. She sat. She sat for hours, scarcely aware of what went on around her. Raymond hovered over her incessantly, offering cups of tea, his round, usually happy face registering bewilderment, and his brown eyes red-rimmed and sore-looking. It was only when Mollie arrived that the release of tears came to her.

Jo felt a deep sadness that she'd never been really close to her father. He had seemed remote for some years now and, since the beginning of the war, had been completely wrapped up in his work, sometimes spending not only hours, but days at the Admiralty. He had always followed her brothers' activities with a light interest; had taken them on a yearly holiday, mostly to the Lake District which he loved, but Johanna's passion for Cornwall he had never understood, and, in truth, Jo thought he had resented the 'pull' that Widegates had for both the female members of his family.

When Jo had been called to the head's office at school and was told the news, she had been stunned. Her father dead – impossible! He had seemed to her to be such a permanent person. She saw fleetingly his portly body, with a wide head that grew from his square shoulders, his strong jaw and yet gentle well-shaped mouth. Her knees weakened and she sat down, bewildered and dismayed at what this would mean to her mother, for her parents had had a close, loving relationship.

'I must go home,' Jo decided, and would not be deterred. Now, with the funeral over, she had talked to her mother and Bill about the possibility of her remaining at home and resuming school at Greenwich. They had a skeleton staff at Main School and she would be welcome there.

'I'd sooner you were safe, Jo,' Mrs Dingle sat quietly, her hands clasped tightly in her lap. 'Safe from the bombing.'

'I know, mum, but you'd be all alone and I'd worry dreadfully about you. In any case I'd get more help with matriculation courses here, for Main School has so few pupils.' So it was decided that she should stay at home, and Jo's heart sang. She would be in London with Bryn, and if she felt a twinge of remorse at this happiness during such a sad time, it was short-lived. She was young, and she loved! This she knew – knew the moment she'd seen Bryn in church, heard his gentle words of condolence, and met his blue-grey eyes with her brown ones. Life will never be the same, not ever, and she hugged her secret through the miserable days ahead. The thought of Bryn coloured every moment of every day and somehow, deep inside, she knew that he felt the same.

They kept in touch and met when they could. Sometimes Bryn would cycle over to spend a few hours in Lewisham. They walked though once familiar streets, now strange and quiet and bleak with bomb damage. Occasionally a visit to the cinema was planned, and on these days Bryn stayed over. They talked, they laughed, they planned. Mrs Dingle was happy for Jo to have a young companion. She sensed her daughter's depth of feeling, but wisely made no comment. It was enough that they were happy. Bryn was now nineteen years old and if the war continued, he would be due for call-up soon.

Bryn had returned to Beckenham after leaving school and was now working in his uncle's firm of accountants, some twelve miles from Jo's home. They had met only twice since that long summer of 1939, just before the war. 'What children we were', Jo thought. At sixteen years and nine months she now felt very grown-up, for so much had happened since they'd waved their childhood goodbye.

It began, she remembered, when David Grant had first spoken to the boys about the impending war. A shadow had passed over her life then. Now 'it' had happened, she had faced her goodbyes, the evacuation, the fear. It was a much more mature Jo who had opted to stay in London, a London that had suffered extensively from continual bombing, and even now was being terrorised with hit-and-run raids during daylight hours, and often indiscriminate bombing from planes flying so high that their presence was only occasionally spotted by a bright flash as the sun caught and reflected on the windscreens. The frequent raids conditioned their way of life. Jo got used to the warnings, and though the shrill, harsh sound of the sirens always sent a thrill of fear through her, she tried not to show it. Sometimes there was no visual evidence of enemy bombers and the 'all-clear' would sound after half an hour or so, but at other times one was made aware of impending possible disaster by the 'crump' of bombs, the drone of German planes, and the intense local ack-ack fire.

At this time Jo undertook some temporary messenger duties with the local street wardens. The post was housed in the front room of a small bungalow at the end of the road. On hearing the warning, she would don a tin hat and make her way up the road, hugging the fences and hedges to avoid, if possible, the fall of hot metal from the guns which were located in the park at the back of her house. The ping-ping and rattle of it hitting the roadway and pavement accompanied her, but she felt safe under the hat – unreasonably safe, and almost enjoyed being out, and not shut in the damp, musty Anderson shelter in the garden. Her mother was getting involved with work at a children's home, so often Jo was alone, and she was pleased to be useful. As a runner, it was her job to carry messages from one post to another. She did ponder on occasions at the way of things. The warden's post was operated by three mature men – all reasonably fit, and they took their duties seriously, but it was their job to delegate, and so she, a mere girl, was sent out and about to cope with hot metal from the barrage, and the risk of bombs.

Sometimes the nights were moonlit and clear. Jo felt vulnerable then. She almost felt that the enemy could see her! The black nights were a comfort, dark, dark nights when she found her way by sense and feel. The pillar box, or post box as we call them now, was situated near to the warden's post, and made a useful landmark. Often she was relieved to find its round body. Each house along the road had a different entrance, so Jo memorised these during daylight hours to make her night life easier. Bryn hated her doing this dangerous commitment, but she was adamant. Her friend Mary also did messenger duties … sometimes they would meet and exchange messages, speak a word or two, and then move off silently into the night, alone and vulnerable.

London during the war was a strange unsettled place for youngsters. There were no gatherings of friends on street corners as at Bexhill and no groups of young people in church on Sunday. Most of the younger generation were either evacuated or in the forces, or sent out of town for useful munition work. Even the Red Cross class was made up mostly of adults, and boasted just Mary, herself and two other girls as the 'babies' of the team.

For a while London had a short respite from bombing, but nevertheless people spent sleepless nights listening as wave after wave of enemy planes made for Birmingham and Coventry. News of these cities was devastating. Mid-April saw a resumption of the bombing, and on the sixteenth they experienced one of the most severe raids ever. It was a night of heavy explosions and fires, all hell let loose as the attack progressed for some eight hours. Local shops had taken some direct hits and goods were blown all over the pavements. Jo and her mother, whilst commiserating with the owner of a gown shop, found themselves being offered winter coats from his now soiled and damaged collection. It was a dull morning, with light rain falling, and with the shop roof open to the sky soon nothing would be salvageable. They went home happily – new coats and no coupons! The shopkeeper accepted the only cash they had with them, which when counted amounted to some three pounds and a few coppers!

Despite the raids it was a settled life at home with both brothers away, Raymond at school camp in Surrey, and Bill with his army unit; it was marred only by the sad news that grandma in Cornwall had passed away. She had been ailing for some months and seemed happy to go. Neither Jo or her mother went to the funeral, which was held at St Lowell church and attended by many of her local friends and associates.

Jo's mother felt useful and needed at her work with the children's home in Beckenham, where she managed the care of children orphaned by the bombing. She arranged for their evacuation to foster homes around the country, hopefully to places of safety. Mrs Dingle hated the fact that the children had to be separated, and had now been given permission to make a trip to look at an old manor house near to Coddington, in Cornwall, with a view to opening a children's home there. It belonged to an old lady of some eighty years, who lived in one small corner of the huge, sprawling building. May or early June had been earmarked for this visit, just as soon as Jo had taken her exams.

Johanna attended church regularly, walking to the early morning service through the recreation ground that, sited between the railway and a small river, remained untouched by the war. It was a quiet oasis of peace where the river trickled slowly and ducks still nested along its banks; where willow trees hung their bright green fronds into the slow-moving water, and where the war seemed to impinge not at all, except above in the sky, for here the barrage balloons hung like silver cigars in the heavens.

Jo got used to the windowless rooms in the house. The close bombing of the past months, 'the blitz', had broken most of the glass, and that had been replaced by a harsh canvas. Some light was afforded through this, but it was a dull green light. Often the canvas would 'plop' and suck out when bombs landed too near, occasionally causing the canvas to tear, leaving ugly jagged edges to let in the elements. There was dust everywhere – no matter how much they cleaned and swept, with so much local bombing the air was always full of it. Jo's mother showed her how to hang a damp sheet over her wardrobe so that the dust couldn't penetrate to her clothes, and any left hanging over a chair at night always had that final cover of a sheet or an old towel to keep them clean.

About this time Jo acquired a kitten. She arrived on her bed one night during an air raid, having obviously entered the house through the kitchen door. Some months previously, the locks had been damaged when the door had been forced open by a blast, and now it was difficult to shut securely. Usually Jo fixed a tilted chair under the handle, but that night she'd forgotten. The kitten was welcomed and kept Jo company during the long lonely evenings, and afforded her comfort at night when they both curled up for sleep together. Jo called her Tibs.

The air raid shelter was only used when the raids became too bad, or when they had been disturbed more than twice by the sirens. Jo hated the shelter and, but for her mother's insistence, would never have slept there, for she found it both claustrophobic and damp. It had an earthy smell which assailed her nostrils unpleasantly, and she never got used to it. On the whole, her father had made it as comfortable as possible. There were bunk beds to sleep six. A table pulled out from the far wall, and a little cupboard that housed a kettle, teapot and the necessary ingredients for making hot drinks sat next to it. A tin for snacks, a torch for emergencies only, for electricity had been wired in. A drum for water stood at the entrance and hanging on the far wall several hot-water bottles – comfort for the cold, damp nights! Jo's mother changed the water regularly and made sure the food tin was filled with whatever was available, but she understood her daughter's antipathy to sleeping there, and only insisted when Ray came home for a spell. Then Jo would spend claustrophobic nights – awake and anxious! Hating the smells and the feeling of being shut in, until her nerves were so raw that she thought she'd burst. It was Bill who finally persuaded his mother to let her sleep in the house as a permanent thing.

'She's old enough to know the dangers, Mum – she'd sleep in the shelter if she could!'

Mollie wrote from Widegates. 'Plymouth was bombed last night. I know now at least a little of what you are experiencing, and my heart goes out to you both. Do think well about a future here in Cornwall, or at least until this dreadful war is over. We heard the noise of planes just as we were off to bed. Edith and I crept through the double black-out curtains at the front, and saw a glow in the sky to the east. Distant rumbles were carried on the wind, and flashes lit the heavens. We were silent, filled with thoughts of the agony the people of Plymouth was facing, and stayed by the door a long while, listening to the noise of planes as they turned near to the coastline. Tom joined us after a while and he spoke just once … "I think our sister should bring that child here Mollie. Will you write to her?"

'Tom is right, Lillian – you should be here …'

Jo never got used to the changes the war had wreaked on Main School. The bright new extension, completed just before the war, was mostly windowless and boarded now, with the hall and gymnasium both dark, dusty and devoid of furniture and equipment, most of which had been sent to Bexhill to the shared girl's high school.

Jo recalled evacuation one evening, when, sitting by her bedroom window, she suddenly noticed the smell of wood burning – cherry wood! The air was filled with it and in a moment Jo was transported back to October 1939, when she used to walk from afternoon school, back to her billet along roads of detached, gabled houses, breathing in the sweet smell of smoke from freshly lit wood fires. Almost every chimney was exuding smoke at this time of the day and she used to breathe the air deeply, loving its pungency.

After the summer holiday of 1939, Jo had returned to find London in a turmoil of preparations for war. As she journeyed on the top of the bus from Paddington station, she saw huge piles of brown everywhere, where massive air-raid shelters were being prepared. The streetlights were being capped with hoods to direct the rays downwards. Railings had been torn up along park borders, and rows of houses had front gardens opened to the pavement, their iron-railed security required for the war effort.

'We are like that at home Jo,' Mrs Dingle said. She had come to meet her daughter and was as dismayed as Jo at these changes. 'Fortunately though we still have the privet hedge for protection.' As they journeyed through south-east London, Jo's thoughts were sad; she felt depressed and the same feeling of fear shot through her that she had experienced by the little cottage on the cliffs, when David had talked to them about war.

'War is so ugly,' she thought. 'Already things are getting ugly!' She should have been prepared therefore for the same ugliness in her immediate home area, but the change and devastation was such that tears had come welling up in her eyes. The park at the back of her home had been dug up for a huge air-raid shelter to be built there. Gone were the shrubs and the trees; gone the crazy-paved path that had wound through the colourful flowerbeds; gone the strip of smooth, bright grass that from childhood she had run over, skipped over, rolled on and turned cartwheels on. All gone – and in its place were mounds of ugly brown earth. 'Yes, war is indeed ugly!'

That evening, the wireless announced that evacuation of schools from London had begun, so for four days Jo attended school each morning, armed with a horrible gas mask, and an attaché case packed tight with a change of clothes and other essentials. Each afternoon she returned home, relieved and tense. On the fifth morning the atmosphere in the school was different somehow, and the teachers seemed to be quieter, kinder and less official. Assembly was held in the playground. The girls knew that today was *the* day when they were told to take their gas masks and cases with them, and 'not to leave anything you might want in the classroom'. They were checked, double checked and a roll-call taken. Lines of girls, smart in their green school uniforms, tense and anxious now at having to face the unknown. Some of them had younger brothers and sisters with them. These had been spirited in by parents, after school had opened, so that the hoped-for tenor of the morning was not spoiled.

Jo's eyes had filled with tears when the headmistress told them that they were to be moved to the safety of the south coast that day.

'War is imminent and our young people must be safe. Do all you can to help. Work hard, be sensible and pray that we will all soon be back here, where we belong.'

Her head swam a little as the full import of the head's remarks sank home. The yellow-brick wall of the upper playground seemed to fade and recede, and the poplar trees lining the boundary had shimmered in a strange way.

Jo remembered little of the journey. The day went by slowly and had a dreamlike quality to it, though later she was to comment that the journey was hot, noisy and scaring. On arrival at Bexhill they were gathered in the Park Pavilion, a handsome building set amidst gardens still bright with flowers and as yet untouched by war. The pavilion hall was large and long. Trestle tables had been set up at the far end, on which had been placed a substantial assortment of sandwiches and home-made cakes. There were also large jugs of orange juice, with mugs to one side. At the back of these tables, as if on guard, was a small army of ladies wearing colourful aprons and smiling with sweet concern at the tired, raggle-taggle party of girls, weary after the journey, feeling homesick and strange as events overtook them.

Seats had been placed in double rows round the hall and the girls were encouraged to sit, and 'put your things underneath your own seat ... quietly please girls!' They needed no admonishing for the children had spotted groups of official-looking men and women, all handling sheafs of paper. Jo sat bewildered. Her head throbbed, and she noticed her hands trembling in her lap as she gazed down at them, whilst concentrating on fighting back tears. On the small stage was a group of nurses.

'Are we to have a medical?' one of Jo's classmates asked in a loud incredulous voice ... 'Golly!'

They were guided in groups to the refreshment table and each girl was encouraged to collect an assortment of 'goodies'. Jo's hands continued to shake and she had trouble holding her mug of juice. One of the ladies took it from her, guided her back to her seat and stood for a while, talking to her whilst she drank.

Meanwhile, a large screen had been placed on the stage behind which the nurses vanished, and, every so often, parties of girls were gathered and guided behind this. Jo was curious, but felt too tired to enquire. Were they really going to have a medical? In spite of the noise and movement in the hall she felt dreamy, disembodied somehow. Her turn came to be ushered behind the screen, where two nurses were busy checking through the girls' heads.

'What on earth are they doing?' she asked the girl behind her, who chuckled at Jo's question before replying.

'Seeing if your hair is clean,' was the amused answer. Jo was pushed forward and as the nurse reached for her, she exclaimed loudly: 'Oh, mine is perfectly clean. I washed it this morning!' She then stood mortified, bewildered and troubled as the examination of her head continued firmly. She later learned that they were looking for lice!

As Johanna returned to her seat, feeling heavy in spirit and body, the double doors to the main entrance were flung open to reveal a cluster of waiting people, who now filed slowly into the hall. Immediately the teachers each took up a position in front of their pupils. Miss Hough stood near to Jo.

'Don't worry,' she smiled. 'It will be all right, I'm sure. The people are coming to collect you now. You'll soon be settled and comfortable.' Miss Hough then called out some ten names and continued. 'You ten are in my care. I'll be along to see you tomorrow. We are not deserting you, so try not to worry.'

Every word fell like a hammer blow on Jo's brain. 'Collect-desert-worry!' But she was worried, and she felt as if the whole world had deserted her, and she didn't want to be collected ... no, not at all! She gazed down at her feet for a long time, trying to regain control of these surging emotions of despondency, fear and panic.

The hall was filling up as many more adults arrived, and she noticed that already some of the girls were ready to leave. One of her classmates went by in the company of a young and smiling couple. He was in Royal Air Force uniform, a dark-haired man of about thirty, and he was laughing at Mary as he took her suitcase. His wife was a tall elegant woman, with an oval face and fair hair hanging long onto her shoulders. She was chatting to Mary as if she had known her for years; Jo felt a deep stab of jealousy. 'Mary will be all right,' she thought.

The reality of it was almost too much for her to comprehend. She sat stunned, disembodied somehow, while all the bustle, talk and movement continued around her. She folded her arms across her chest and sat, quiet and still, thinking of her parents, of her home, of anything rather than face this awful reality. She felt her hands trembling again, so she clenched them tightly.

A booming voice startled her. She looked up to see a large face bending down next to hers. It was bearded, a rugged face with a wide forehead and full red lips only partly hidden by the beard. Piercing blue eyes were now regarding her keenly.

'Jean McLeod?' His voice boomed again.

'Oh no ... Jean is over there.' Jo pointed to a small fair-haired girl sitting almost opposite her. The man stood up straight.

'Oh' he said, 'you're not Jean. Well ...' As he turned to go, she marvelled at the size of him. She had never seen anyone so big, and she watched fascinated as he moved over to the line of girls on the other side of the hall. He had broad shoulders, a long wide body and was dressed neatly in flannels and a navy blue blazer. She heard once more his deep throaty voice ... 'Jean McLeod?' and then watched as her classmate smiled shyly and gathered her belongings together to follow him to the wide exit. She waved her arm at Jo, from which dangled her lunch bag and gas mask. Her tall companion had made no attempt to take her case, and when she stumbled, he merely turned round and boomed: 'Hurry girl ... Hurry.' Jo saw Miss Hough watching, a concerned expression on her face.

Another woman approached her. A motherly comfortable lady of indeterminate age, who spoke in a quiet, gentle voice. This time, the child she sought was standing with Miss Hough. She had been crying, and it was comforting to Johanna to see the rapport that quickly developed between the two of them, and to watch as they moved happily together towards the door.

That door! She hated the thought of approaching it herself, of going into the unknown with a stranger. 'Why, Mum won't know where I am this night ... nobody will.' Panic floated up in her once more. She got up swiftly and moved to stand against a pillar, at the back of the seating, almost hidden from view. One of the official ladies came over to her. Jo had noticed her previously searching through her list of names and then making enquiries from various girls, who seemed to point Jo out

'Feeling nervous?' she asked Jo. 'It's all right, really. You are not to worry.' Her eyes were kind and a little moist, as if seeing Jo's fear-filled ones had distressed her. She was a petite person, with neat dark hair, and was dressed in a simple navy suit which Jo recognised as a Red Cross uniform. She asked about her day, about the journey, and again reiterated: 'Try not to worry,' before she left to take up her place once more by the door. She's kind, thought Jo, and wished that she could go with her.

She noticed now so many empty places round the hall. The ladies were busy tidying the trestle tables, and the official-looking people continued to move about with their lists, whilst the teachers still hovered over various pupils, encouraging, explaining and perhaps bullying just a little!

Jo screwed up her eyes. 'We all look like ants,' she thought. 'Ants scurrying here and there; but ants have a purpose, they know what they have to do and where to go, whereas I feel so lost!' She felt sure that she wasn't the only girl to feel this trauma.

Tears welled in her eyes for the first time since the morning in the school playground and threatened to run down her cheeks. She shook her head to chase them away, and then noticed, at the doorway, a fair-haired girl of about her own age talking to the Red Cross lady. They obviously knew one another well. 'A daughter, perhaps,' she thought. 'A lucky daughter who would sleep in her own bed tonight, not in some stranger's house!'

The girl was tall and slender, still in navy school uniform, and with her hat held casually in one hand. She twisted and turned it as she laughed at something her companion said. Suddenly they both looked towards her, and the girl walked swiftly over to where Jo stood. Her eyes were brown, and her smile wide as she asked:

'Johanna Dingle? …. Oh good. I'm Jean Rogers. Would you like to come with me?' Jo said a feeble hello and then scrabbled underneath her chair for her belongings.

'You must be tired,' Jean said. 'Here, I'll take that,' and she reached an arm out for Johanna's suitcase. They made their way towards the now open double doors where Jean introduced her to the nice official lady.

'Mrs Bowen, a family friend.' A nod … A smile, and: 'We've met already and I expect we'll be seeing a lot of one another.' Then they were through the door! Jo lifted her head as they reached the carpark. A light fresh breeze caught her hair, blowing it round her face for a moment. She breathed deeply.

'What a wonderful smell,' she said.

'It's from the sea. Look, just a step away.' Jean replied and pointed between the houses where Jo could see a small section of seafront, and beyond a blue, grey expanse of water lifting towards the horizon.

'We'll go and look later if you like. Come on, Mum has tea ready. You must be starving!' Jo smiled at her new companion and with that smile her spirits lifted. 'Yes, I am,' she replied 'Very hungry indeed.'

Jean's mother afforded Jo a warm welcome when they met a few minutes later in the garden of Park House. It was a blaze of autumnal colour, a long and narrow garden at the end of which was a small orchard whose trees hung heavy with russet apples. Mrs Rogers reminded Jo of aunt Mollie, and she felt immediately at ease with her. She proved to be a wonderful cook and Jo had the healthy appetite of all teenagers. She would later set off for afternoon school with a warm inner glow, after a substantial portion of plum and apple pie, or spotted dick. Rationing hadn't begun to hit home at that time, but later in the war it was impossible to find enough fat or suet to make these wholesome and appetising puddings.

Mr Rogers took the girls on long night walks. Sometimes Jo was reminded of Cornwall, when the stars hung in a deep velvet sky and the breezes from the sea evoked memories of Widegates. It set in her a longing to be back there.

A walk was suggested at one time after snow had fallen for most of the day, soft gentle snow, and then at dusk the sky had cleared. The girls donned rubber 'wellies', spare socks, scarves and even socks on their hands over the hand-knitted gloves … every button of their mackintosh gaberdines was fastened – and they were ready! They went uphill, taking the strange and slippery route over the common, with Mr Rogers talking all the while of storms and winter white-outs remembered from his youth in Yorkshire. At one moment they turned to look seaward and the wonder of the view took Jo's breath away. She had never seen snow like this. London sometimes was white, and Cornwall occasionally, but the depth of this fall was a new and lovely experience. Roofs and trees blended in white mounds, there was nothing angular anywhere! It was just as if the corners had been knocked off all the buildings to leave a series of large crystal 'hedges' as far as one could see. Nearer to them each little twig had its own layer of icing, all of which sparkled and glistened in the moonlight.

It was a circular walk they took that night, and eventually they found themselves at the seafront. A front that looked strangely unreal with the snow right to the waterline. They watched as the incoming tide made inroads on the white perfection, and listened to the swish and slosh of the waves as they met the new smooth barrier! Jo was to tell Bryn of that particular night in her Christmas letter to him: 'It was magical, and I shall remember it forever.'

Her introduction to the new school was made some two days

after arrival when she walked the three miles or so, up behind the lovely little seaside town and over a common, which afforded her a view of the wide bay. She was enthralled. The school was high, situated right at the top of the hill and throughout her eighteen months as an evacuee, Jo would look forward keenly to her walks to and from school, especially if the wind blew and the sky was wild.

'It's a little like being near to Pencarrow Head,' she wrote to Bryn. 'Not as beautiful, but the air is fresh and wonderful; if I close my eyes, then I can feel that I'm back on our headland.'

The sea was her solace and she spent much of her time near to it, running on the wide expanse of sand at low tide, shoes in her hands, racing Jean. Or scrambling on the low rocks that stretched far out into the bay. Sometimes she felt that she could go on and on, with the wind in her face, and her hair blown all ways, and the cry of the gulls around her. At times like this, Jean used to call and call her, worried in case she went too far.

'You don't understand the tide like I do … it's dangerous to go so far out. You might get cut off!' Jo realised that her new friend was right, for although she knew her Cornish coast well, its moods and its dangers, this little seaside town was an unknown quantity. She listened and felt sorry that she had worried her companion.

She joined her classmates some Saturday mornings to chat on the corners near to the front, where they all had fun waylaying a young army captain who was stationed nearby. Captain Clutterbuck was an extremely handsome man, but shy, and the sight of an increasing army of young schoolgirls standing on the corner of the road to wave and cheer as he went by, became a weekly embarrassment for him. He was covered in mortification and often, when the girls became exuberant before he even appeared, having heard the sound of his motorbike, he would positively wobble around the corner … head up and eyes straight ahead, and with such a grim expression on his face that the girls found it even more amusing! He was to suffer this indignity for the whole eighteen months of Jo's stay in Bexhill, though he never actually fell off his bike! Not once did he smile … not once did he wave. Jo knew that had he done so, then his trauma would have been over. It was what the girls wanted. She felt sorry for him, but also a little angry that he let himself be so teased.

The war had changed Jo. Outwardly she was still the fun-loving girl, ready to join in any game or dare, but now she was never the promoter of such fun. She had changed from a carefree youngster and had become a serious dreamer. She loved the lonely walks home, taking in the feel of the common and its wide, open view of the sea, loved the gabled houses she passed, like nothing she'd seen in either London or Cornwall. She loved the Crittal windows which used to look so inviting and welcoming in the early evening light, and she loved particularly the smell of cherry wood burning, the smoke from the fires adding to the mistiness of spring and autumn days. It made the houses part of her dream world … she wanted one … one for her and Bryn, where they could curl up and be safe from all the madness around them. She was not lonely. Jean was always there, and plenty of friends from both her own school and the new one, but she chose solitude at times – to weave her girlish dreams.

She wrote to Bryn and James several times during this period, and had regular letters from them both. They were bright chatty letters, full of the day they'd leave school and be able to get down to some 'war' work!

CHAPTER FOUR

Johanna had joined the British Red Cross Society soon after her return to London. She attended lectures regularly with Mary Baker, a school friend, who lived in the next road, and who had never been evacuated. Mary's parents were rather elderly and had preferred to keep their daughter with them. Consequently, it was Mary who guided Jo through the initially strange routine of Main School, and she was her companion on the three-mile journey, and who, twice a week, walked with her to Dulwich College where the Red Cross meetings were held.

Mary was a tall neat girl, rosy-cheeked and extremely pretty, with even features, button brown eyes, and dark, short straight hair. Jo envied her this, for even on the windiest of days it would keep in shape, the wind-blown strands falling back as if recently brushed. She was a happy person to be with, and she chatted away in a bubbly fashion. Mary would never get into serious conversation when in company, though Jo knew that she cared deeply about many things. Her parents were her world and she theirs, but she had time for compassion and would always be found where help was needed.

Jo passed her first-aid and home nursing courses quite easily, and it was now suggested that she was proficient enough to do some voluntary work. The local nursery were wanting help and she found herself one Saturday morning, on the second floor of the old redbrick building overlooking the park, listening bewildered whilst Sister Morny told her what her duties would be.

'We have a fluctuating number of babies, some of them quite young, whom we care for until a more suitable place can be found for them. Some though have older brothers and sisters already in the play group below. Their mothers are working, so we keep them from 8.30 am until 5 pm … five days a week. We provide good food and generally try and give them as normal a day as possible.' Jo couldn't resist a smile at the word 'normal' for on the way upstairs she had observed a touching scene. Some twenty or so toddlers, all on 'potties', shuffling around the floor, and forming little groups with their heads together ... talking and laughing. 'Potty' time was obviously normal to these little beings!

'Occasionally,' Sister Morny continued, 'occasionally, we have special babies. Those that need nursery care when the parents are no longer here.' She studied her new young helper keenly ... 'Like this little chap who came in last night.' Sister stepped to the corner of the sunny room where a wide-eyed baby of about eight months lay quietly.

'His parents were killed last night. Father was home on leave, which makes it all the more tragic. He was found in his cot unharmed, so we are caring for him until relatives claim him, or another home can be found for him.' Jo leant over the side of the cot and touched the baby's cheek.

'Poor little man – what's his name, does anyone know?'

'I'm afraid not, but we're calling him Thomas, after the policeman who found him.' Just then Jo felt a tug at her finger. She had left her hand in the cot gently touching the side of the baby's face. Thomas now held her with his own chubby hand – held her tightly too. She turned to the cot amazed at the feeling, an overwhelming feeling of love and tenderness that now swept over her. Sister watched her and approved of her gentle handling of the baby. 'Poor little mite, it's just what he needs now,' she thought, but aloud her professional side spoke.

'It doesn't do to get too fond of our charges, Johanna. None of them stay with us long. Come, let's get started with the bathing.'

Jo pried her fingers gently from the plump little fist, stroked Thomas's soft curls, and followed Sister Morny into the next room where a young girl, perhaps a year younger than Jo, was busy filling two baby baths with hot and cold water alternately. The room was warm and slightly steamy, and with that special smell about it that Jo was to associate with babies all her life.

'This is Maureen. She helps here most Saturday mornings, Johanna, and knows where everything is kept, so if ever you find you are needing something, then ask Maureen.' The two girls smiled briefly at one another as Sister continued. 'We've eight babies to bath. Have you handled a small baby before at all? … no … well, just do as I do.'

It was so bewildering, but Jo wasn't given time to get nervous. Maureen returned her questioning look with a shrug of her shoulders and suggested that she sit in front of one of the baby baths. Both were set on stands, half-full now with warm-to-hot water. Maureen placed a white towel over Jo's knees, just as Sister returned from the nursery, a baby held tightly in each arm; she placed one firmly on Jo's lap.

'Hold tight, mind – she's a wriggler. Start undressing her ready for the bath.'

Jo felt helpless, but watching Sister coping with an even smaller baby, she tentatively untied the nightie strings … removed the little flannel vests, and somehow unpinned the cumbersome terry-towelling nappy that seemed to swallow up half the little body. Christine, for that was the baby's name, wriggled and stretched, but Jo watched how Sister handled hers and learnt; she learnt very quickly, feeling only a small twinge of unease when she held the tiny unclothed body in her hands and let it down gently into the water. Christine smiled … she gurgled … she kicked. 'Fun,' thought Jo. 'I'm going to like this.'

At first Maureen was at hand to pass her the various garments, pins and bits necessary to complete the baby's toilet. Jo felt awkward as she moved the little body on her lap into various positions in the struggle to dress her.

'They are not frail, Jo,' it was Sister again. 'Babies are stronger than you think … don't be afraid of them. They like firm handling, it helps to make them feel secure.' At last Christine was done – bathed, changed and fresh for the day ahead … temporarily at least. Jo sat back, but before she'd had time to draw breath Christine was taken from her and another baby, a little boy this time, was placed on her lap, complete with towel.

'Sister likes them all done before ten o'clock,' Maureen whispered… 'So we don't have time for a rest.'

The hour went in a haze of wriggling limbs, lusty cries and fighting nappy pins, but at last the eight little morsels of humanity were clean and settled.

Jo got up and stretched her back, while Maureen began to tidy the things away. Sister Morny moved towards the door. 'Oh Jo, perhaps you'd like to bath Thomas – you could use the bathroom. Maureen will show you.' She was gone!

The next half an hour was a happy one as, with her helper to guide her and little Thomas to charm her, Jo felt really wanted and useful. He was a sturdy little chap, seemed content whilst in the bath, but not active at all. He appeared a little sleepy if anything. 'It's the shock of last night,' thought Jo. 'What an experience for such a tiny mite.' By the time Thomas was dressed, his eyes had closed. Gently she placed him in the cot, where he lay, flush-faced and angelic, one little finger poised just by his mouth as if ready to pop in.

Sister Morny asked her into the office and commended her on her handling of the babies.

'You're a natural, and we'd appreciate your help every Saturday if you can manage that ... more if you can take it!' Jo wisely settled herself for the Saturday visit only. It was voluntary work and she was happy to give her help, but she had her commitments to school and, with matriculation looming in a couple of months, felt she must leave herself time for the necessary swotting.

At the next Red Cross meeting, she compared notes with others who'd 'started out' as they called it. One of the ladies was coping with toddlers and had some laughable tales to report. Another was giving her time in an old people's home and adored it. She was a bubbly person, about thirty-five years old, and Jo couldn't help thinking that she must appear like a ray of bright sunshine to the elderly. Mary was helping to man a first-aid post. 'Not so interesting so far,' she commented to Jo, 'but it has possibilities.'

Every Saturday saw Johanna at the nursery. The babies changed, different faces, different wriggling bodies, but they all charmed her and she loved the work. Young Thomas grew and became more lively as the weeks went by. He still hadn't been traced as far as relatives were concerned and had now been put forward for fostering with a view to adoption. Jo was dreading the day he'd leave, but knew that it would be best for him, and particularly as early summer brought another spate of bombing. It was wrong to keep him here when he might be out of London and safe in some country area.

She had not been well – a flu virus – so two weeks had elapsed before she could get to the nursery. Jo still felt a little tired as she walked through the grounds of the old brick building, but she climbed the stairs happily, longing for the moment when she would see Thomas once more and hear his chuckles.

The nursery room was quiet, but she could hear voices, low voices coming from the room where the cots were set in line against the far wall. Maureen came out. She started on seeing Jo, and with tears in her eyes said … 'Don't go in yet, Jo. The doctor is here. Little Thomas is very ill.' Jo's world seemed to collapse, she felt weak at the knees and sank into the nearest chair at Sister's desk.

'What … why?' she began.

'The doctor thinks it's the flu germ that's going around. He's been ill all week, and should be getting a little better now. Doesn't seem to want to, the doctor said.' Sister appeared. 'Better now, Johanna? Good! Can you cope this morning for a while? There is only one baby to bath and then perhaps you wouldn't mind looking after Thomas. He's very poorly and needs some special attention.' She left the room with the doctor in tow.

Jo stayed at the nursery late that night. The morning had been a busy one after all. Following Sister Morny's instructions she had bathed the one child, but there were two more admissions. Twins, some six months old, who were to stay at the nursery until their mother recovered from an operation to her hand. Beth and Barbara were good babies, with large brown eyes and fair curly hair, the same colouring as Jo, and it was an attractive combination on such little ones.

With Maureen's help she settled them in and did the paperwork necessary, leaving this on the desk for Sister to check. The rest of the time she spent with Thomas, who had become increasingly restless and fretful as the day progressed. He would take no sustenance, though she did manage to spoon a little boiled water into his mouth at intervals, watching carefully that he swallowed the fluid before trying again. At such times he remained fairly passive, fixing his gaze sometimes on the window where the sun shone brightly, far too brightly for his young eyes, Jo thought; then sometimes he stared at the side of the cot to where a cluster of bright woollen balls hung.

Sister popped her head quickly round the door at regular intervals to check that Jo was managing.

'Lift him out, Jo, if he's too fretful. It's what the poor little mite needs.' Jo needed no second urging. She gathered Thomas up, wrapped him warmly in his cot blanket, and sat in the old armchair near to the fireplace. He settled immediately and seemed more comfortable in a slight sitting position. The doctor patted her shoulder, commenting 'good girl', when he made his afternoon call.

Jo watched Thomas. His face was flushed, his breathing difficult, but he looked beautiful. At times she rubbed her hand gently over his head where the soft fair curls lay flat with perspiration. She hummed softly to herself as she gazed round the bright, warm room at the pictures on the walls, mostly hand paintings and done by the toddlers downstairs. Glancing down she saw Thomas gazing up at her with a direct look – an enquiring look, and when she softly said, 'Hello, Thomas ...' his baby mouth grimaced slightly into a tiny smile of recognition. For a long time he kept his eyes on her, and then slowly, as Jo continued to talk softly to him, slowly his eyes closed. He was asleep – in a restful sleep for the first time that day, so that when Sister returned to the nursery at five-thirty, with an apology on her lips for being late, Jo stopped her with a whispered ...

'He's asleep. He seems a whole lot better now.' Together they settled him in his cot. He didn't waken and. Jo stroked his damp head for a minute, pleased to see him peaceful before she left.

'Can I pop in first thing tomorrow?' she asked. Sister nodded her head as she busied herself at the desk, checking on the paperwork for the new admissions.

There was to be no early morning call at the nursery for Jo. Instead the telephone woke her and she heard her mother talking quietly, then after a few moments heard steps on the stairs. Mrs Dingle entered the room after a gentle knock on the door. Her face was sad as she said, 'Baby Thomas is dead, Jo. That was Sister Morny. He died about an hour ago ... in his sleep Sister said. I'm so sorry Johanna, but perhaps his mother called him ... we'll never know, will we?'

Somehow Jo got through the day. She was alternately tearful and restless. She busied herself in the garden, where Bill was making a new rockery. He was glad of her help and in his own way did his best to console her. She cooked for her mother, cleaned all the family shoes, and then, rather than sit, flung herself out of the door to walk the quiet Sunday streets until she tired. She didn't contact Mary, she just didn't want to talk to anyone.

On Monday morning she sat with her peers at school taking matriculation examinations. The invigilator was Miss Hough, the school physics teacher and commonly known to the girls as 'the dragon'. She had returned to Main School soon after Jo and now she watched Jo at work, scribbling away furiously, with her face flushed, and noticed the tears that every so often welled up in her eyes and were brushed away as quickly.

'Johanna, are you well?' she asked.

'I'm all right, thank you. It's just that a baby I knew died yesterday …'

'My dear – I'm so sorry.' If Jo had seen the continued look of concern on Miss Hough's face, she would have wondered just how she had been nicknamed so dreadfully.

That week Jo attended her second funeral within a few months. Mrs Dingle and Bill, who was still on leave, accompanied her. Sister Morny and Mary were there as the tiny white coffin was carried into the church by the policeman who had first rescued Thomas from the ruins of his shattered home. Just as the service was about to start, four of Jo's classmates joined the small party of mourners, and it was their clear voices, lifting high into the church, singing the one hymn chosen by Jo – 'All things bright and beautiful' – that lightened this otherwise sad event and eased the sorrow of Thomas's passing. They had found his real name— and it was Thomas – Thomas Green.

That night they experienced one of the heaviest raids on London. A beautiful spring day had been followed by a wonderful moonlit night. The warning went at eleven pm, just as they were settling for sleep, and the raid lasted until dawn. There were very heavy casualties and many beautiful old buildings, mostly in the West End of London, were destroyed. The firemen and emergency services fought long and hard throughout the night to stem the flames and help the casualties. Finally, the fires burnt themselves out, for the Thames was at a very low tide and water for the pumps was difficult to obtain. Traffic was badly dislocated, and Bill, who had to report to Hornchurch, got badly caught up in the aftermath of the raid. He ended by shouldering his kit-bag and walking right across the devastated streets and out to Essex.

The beautiful May weather had given way to a cold, cloudy June. The skies were dark and forbidding, and an air-raid warning had just sounded as Jo and her mother arrived at Paddington station to catch the train westward. The bus journey through London's streets had been slow, and both had been anxious in case they missed the train. As it was, they had to wait some forty-five minutes for the raid to end before they could depart. They heard and saw nothing, and were happy to settle themselves in the compartment near to the back of the train. Mrs Dingle always like to travel at the back. They journeyed through country areas seemingly untouched by war. It was restful seeing fields of animals; little woodland copses and isolated farms. Jo was bubbling with excitement for she had heard, just a few days ago, that Bryn was to be in Cornwall, staying at Pensilva with James. It was all impossibly lucky that their visits should coincide. Her mother had her notebooks out and seemed busy. This visit was to enable her to set in motion plans for transferring children from Beckenham to Cornwall and safety. She was to stay at Widegates, but didn't expect to have much free time.

'Tom will keep you busy though, Jo, I shouldn't wonder, and Bryn and James won't allow you to be bored either.' her mother said.

'I'll be fine, mum, thanks,' she replied, and was rewarded with a bright smile, as she hugged to herself the plans she was already making for their short break.

They approached Widegates, taking that familiar, well-loved road along the low wooded valley, past the huge rhubarb-like plants that grew in abundance along this lush area, where the trees overhung the roadway, so forming an archway, sheltered as they were from the sea winds. It was a tranquil valley, but now, with a darkening sky, it seemed to have a dream-like quality to it, as the car weaved and turned along the smooth, winding road. Soon they were through and going uphill towards the headland. With no shelter, the stunted trees leaned inward against the prevailing wind, and were lichen-covered, with knots and whorls of strange cankers on each gnarled branch. Jo saw and heard the skylarks against the grey sky, and then, as they drew up at the gate of the farm, the storm that had been threatening for some time burst into life. The wind roared and the trees shook, and the rain lashed down. Both women were relieved to enter the warm kitchen of the farmhouse, where the aunts and uncle Tom awaited them.

Edith had her raincoat on and a small attaché case in her hand. She was just off to spend the weekend with a friend in Penzance and was taking advantage of the taxi to make the return journey to St Austell and the coach there. It seemed strange without grandma, Jo thought, but she was soon caught up in the lively chatter; hearing news of the farm, of the new animals, of the neighbours and finally of Bryn and James, who had called earlier suggesting that she might like to accompany them to Launceston in the morning to collect a new calf for Mollie.

The night had been a wild one, and dawn brought little respite from the tempestuous south-westerly winds. Tom had commented, 'It will be rough for those at sea,' as he puffed his pipe, sitting near to the French windows that overlooked the sweep of lawn, and then beyond to the headland. He could see the wind whipping the row of small conifers at the edge of the vegetable garden, sending them bending back and forth in a wild dance of green fronds. The larger cedars bent dangerously, and the odd dry twig came tumbling down, swinging in wide arks to land on the lawn near to the house. The hedge of honeysuckle that screened the cowsheds and tumbled so prettily over the old stone walls, a cascade of bright green in the early spring, was now in danger of being torn away because a roll had formed, which was getting tighter and larger with each gust of wind.

'If the lads come in before dark,' thought Tom, 'then I must get them to fix that for me.'

By mid-afternoon the sky was becoming darker. It was a wild darkness, almost black, as if the storm were renewing itself and gathering force for the night ahead. Between the folds of the headland the sea was swept with white water … he could see wave upon wave come thundering in, and indeed Tom could hear the roaring thunder of it, whilst safe and secure in his room. 'I'd not like to be at sea now,' he thought.

The door flew open and Jo appeared. Rosy-cheeked from her walk up the lane, her eyes laughing at him and her face registering still the legacy of her pleasure at fighting the elements.

'I came over by the church,' she said. 'Golly, uncle, but it's wild. The wind is fierce here, but through the churchyard it's blowing right across from the estuary to the headland … so wild and strong. I had a job standing, let alone walking! The boys should be here soon.'

Tom looked at her as she stood shaking her soft hair and releasing the buttons on her mackintosh.

'Not the sort of weather for a young gal like you to go walking!' he said gruffly. She was not fooled. Uncle Tom was glad that she was home and safe. As a countryman, and a countryman living near to the sea, and this particular wild part of the coast, he had a healthy respect for the weather and its moods.

'It's to be another bad night. You'd best see that all the outhouses are shut tight, and if the lads get back, mention the honeysuckle, will you?' Tom pointed to the wild mass of fronds which now seemed to have a will of their own and a desire to tear themselves from the wall.

'I will, uncle. Everything is well battened down though, aunt and I did it before we came in. The boys are coming up the roadway and should be here any minute, so the honeysuckle will soon be fixed.' Jo went out into the kitchen to look for twine and scissors to start the job herself. Aunt Mollie came through the door of the dairy as she reached the kitchen, her face red and shiny from her recent exertions in the wind.

'There, lass, that's the cows milked for the evening. I've put them in the yard for now. We'll let them into the field when this little lot subsides, meanwhile it won't do them any harm to have a little cover and some hay to munch instead of grass. One or two are scouring anyway, it's all a bit rich for them in that new pasture as yet. Now where are you off to again … haven't you had enough of wind and rain yet?'

'I could never have enough aunt … I just love it!' Johanna opened the door which nearly blew off its hinges as the wind caught it. She hugged it to her and eased herself round the jamb, pushing it tight shut behind her. She heard her aunt say – 'be careful' and then turned to see Bryn and James trudging across the yard, heads down and moving awkwardly as they led the new young calf between them to the stall which had been prepared for it earlier. The quiet of the stall was in complete contrast to the howling madness outside. All three stamped around on the deep straw, settling hay and feed for the little animal. Jo produced a bucket of milk, recently put there by Mollie, pushed the young head into the bucket towards her fingers, upended in the milk. She felt the rough mouth near her hands; felt the bucking strength of the calf as it tried to resist this unknown person and unknown situation; she felt with joy the mouth close over her fingers, and the first milk being drawn up, sucked up hungrily. She felt the calf relax and then tremble slightly in satisfaction, as it drank steadily. She drew her fingers away slowly. 'Poor little thing – he's had a dreadful journey here,' Bryn remarked. 'The van broke down near to the gully, and we had to manhandle him the rest of the way. Didn't dare leave him in the van, it's almost heeled over.'

'What are you going to do about it?' Jo asked.

'I've phoned home from the corner house,' James said. 'They are sending the tractor out. I'm just off to meet it.' Bryn stayed where he was and raised a farewell hand to his friend.

'No sense two of us going, is there? I'll see if Jo needs any help, all right?'

Four eyes turned to watch James leave the byre. They listened companionably to the little calf sucking the dregs of the milk until, finally gone, it tried to lift its head out of the bucket and became tangled in the handle. They had a job trying to release the strong little fellow, but once free he raced round and round the pen, kicking his hind legs up in the air happily, before settling down to nuzzle at the hay spread for him.

'He's a lively one,' Jo laughed. 'I shall have to find a special name for him.'

'Call him Storm,' said Bryn, and she nodded her head in approval.

'By the way, uncle said would you mind helping with the honeysuckle. It's in danger of pulling right off the wall … you know how he loves it.'

She searched deep in her mackintosh pockets. 'Here, I've got the string and things …' They both pulled their raincoats tight up to their chins, then wrestled with the barn door between them, laughing happily, as one with the elements.

'You love it, don't you, Jo …' Bryn said, 'and so do I!'

Mrs Dingle settled her business at Pendower House three days later and left, happy in the knowledge that a local carpenter was to do certain alterations before her next visit. Sarah Burnett had proved to be a remarkably aware lady. She had a ready knowledge of what was needed for the children, and a heart to go with it. In short Miss Burnett was looking forward to putting her home to some good use, more particularly because young children were involved. She had never married, but had lived in the vast house with her parents since childhood, and it was that childhood she remembered as being the one truly happy time of her life; when Pendower House was full of young cousins and their friends, coming to stay and take advantage of the spacious home, its pleasant surroundings, and the freedom it afforded.

With the promise to return in two months to make final arrangements, Mrs Dingle returned to Widegates to collect a rather quiet Johanna, and so to the station and home again. Jo was loathe to go, but was buoyed up by the thought that Bryn would be in Beckenham before the weekend and had arranged to come over on Sunday.

James and Bryn had been returning from a walk along the cliff path on the afternoon of Jo's departure, when David had met them and they'd gone to his cottage for a cup of tea. The afternoon was breezy, for although the storm of two days ago had blown itself out, it had left in its wake a skittish wind, a cool wind, and a dancing sky of white clouds which looked paintworthy in the sunlight. It was too cold for the patio, so they squeezed into the one little room, cosily watching the sea throw spumes of white spray at the cliff below them. Bryn was always very aware of the isolated life that David lived when he was actually shut in the cottage. Outside there was a friendly air about things ... about the sun on the headland, the sea birds wheeling and turning, and even their plaintive cries were sort of homely. But the cottage with the door closed seemed to gather an isolation about it that disturbed him. He couldn't explain it at all.

'You should live in a huge house on a vast plain,' James had commented on the way back to Pensilva when Bryn had been trying to explain his feelings. The boys mentioned David to Tom when they returned the following day to Widegates for tea. Mentioned the isolation of his life on the cliff, and the spartan existence. Tom explained:

'Mollie has persuaded him to come for the occasional meal now, when it's quiet on the farm ... he doesn't feel he's being a nuisance that way, for he understands the frenetic sessions that we go through as the various seasons progress. We've talked a lot. He's an extremely intelligent man, a wasted intelligence some might say, but the job he is doing gives a lot to the community, and gives him a certain peace of mind. I think that he earned that during the last war. He sustained some nasty wounds, but makes light of them!'

They didn't ask more. If David wanted them to know, then in time he would tell them, but, being young and vital and with the whole of life ahead of them, they could not imagine what his life of quiet must really be like.

'It wouldn't do for me,' Bryn commented seriously. 'I love it here, indeed would like to live and settle in this area, but not alone … not alone at all … !'

David had spoken to them at length that afternoon. A serious talk about London, the bombs, the reality of war over all the country … over Europe … indeed over all the world, and finally finished with these words: 'No matter what the circumstances under which we live, it is our attitude to life that counts. The future happiness of the world depends on how willing we are to forgive our enemies. Everybody's time will come … the result of such a time depends on our attitude to life here.' David puffed his pipe for a while, his eyes distant and dreamy. He coughed a little and then went on : 'What man does today reflects often in years to come!'

Both Bryn and James pondered over these words, listening to the 'puff – puff' as David drew on his pipe. They then talked of their impending 'calling-up'. Bryn already planned to enter the Royal Air Force and James, although he was necessary on the farm and in a reserved occupation, had made enquiries about joining the armed services and was waiting to hear from the army recruitment centre. His father had been more than dismayed when his son announced that he'd like to go and 'do his bit', but he was not totally surprised, and immediately made plans for extra help on the farm to replace James. The war now really impinged on Jane Trevarder's life and she was most upset at the thought of losing her son to the forces. She lived a busy life, but a secluded, sheltered one. The war hadn't touched her in 1918, and of this one she was so far scarcely aware, except perhaps for the clothing coupons and ration books. The rations, of course, could always be supplemented by farm produce. They were not short of food, but clothes she did miss! She was a tall, upright lady, with a mass of fair, fly-away hair that she still kept fairly long, but tied it back neatly during the day. She had an oval face and a marvellously rosy complexion. She loved to dress in vibrant colours ... in fact visitors always referred to her as an artist, because of her flamboyant outfits. Yes, clothes she did and would miss ... Now James had brought the real war near, terribly near, and her peace of mind had been shattered. James was a gentle, kind son and hated to hurt his parents, but he had a strong conviction that he was needed and that was his motivation.

'They will get used to the idea,' he told David. 'I've warned them in plenty of time, for I doubt I'll be called up before next year.'

Back at school Jo was concerned about her exam results. She worried that she had found it difficult to study. Perhaps she should have worked harder. She worried that on the actual day of her examinations she had been grieving so hard for baby Thomas. Thoughts of him still reduced her to tears. Her mother was a tower of strength, continually reassuring her that her results would be fine, but Johanna could not remain calm. She was tense and uncertain about her future, yet now was the time to think seriously about it. Jo had a leaning towards teaching, but this would entail attending training college out of London, and she was loathe to leave her mother during these trying times. Instead, she obtained a place at a secretarial college situated near to the city. It was a year's course and included typewriting, bookkeeping, sociology and business studies generally. She wasn't sure where it would all lead, but it was enough that her immediate future was settled.

In early June Bryn was summoned to Cardington in Bedfordshire, the site of an old balloon station. Here, over the course of two days, he was given written tests on mathematics etc, aptitude tests, physical co-ordination on various devices, and finally an interview with a board of officers, and was later told that he had been accepted as suitable for pilot training.

Bryn was pleased with himself!

He was expecting 'call up' sometime in July, and so, with exams behind her, Jo had time for herself and Bryn! They spent as much time together as they could. Sometimes he would spend the day at her home, from where they'd take long walks, often through deserted, war-torn streets, past shops that had been boarded for over a year now; and to Blackheath, where the barrage balloons still hung in the sky, and where whole sections of the heathlands were fenced off for the anti-aircraft guns. They attended a little church there. Loving it when the wind blew keenly, and when, on dark summer nights, they walked home under heavens bright with stars that sometimes looked as if they could be plucked from the sky. They went to the cinema … sitting in the back row if they could, where they held hands and chatted throughout the intervals, their heads close together. They talked about their war commitment, and Bryn mentioned just how much he hated his firewatch duty night at the local bank. 'It's so airless, Jo. The windows are never opened, the doors are kept mostly shut through the day, and after the staff have left at night, it's all shut up; the air is stale, it is musty, smoke-filled, and I feel I just can't breathe! I envy you your duties as a messenger for at least you are in God's clean air.'

'Not always, Bryn,' she laughed. 'There is the endless dust floating around the bomb sites. I like it best when the weather is wet. The rain seems to settle everything and everywhere, and it all smells so fresh. How is the play going?'

Bryn was happily engaged in putting on a charity show for the Beckenham Home. He had got together a group of interested people to put on a play about a match factory in Yorkshire. It was both touching and humorous and, thanks to the dedicated cast, was coming along well. Johanna had been roped in on various occasions to help with prompting and scenery painting, and now, with just three weeks to go before opening night, he requested more help.

'We need some more costumes, Jo. Do you think your mother would help? The men are all set, but one or two of the factory girls still need long dark skirts and rough aprons.'

'Ask her yourself, silly. You'll see her at teatime! I'm sure she'll be happy to help and I will too!'

'I've a different job lined up for you,' Bryn replied. 'We have to get some leaflets printed and also tickets. Uncle Jim has said we can use his office at weekends for this, and one of his colleagues has supplied us with paper. It's old headed notepaper, but with the top guillotined off, it will be marvellously useful. Then we'll need some posters. Care to take over this side of things for me?'

'I'll help, Bryn, of course, but I'm not at all artistic as you well know, and …'

'It's all right,' he interrupted her. 'We've got an artist. Robert Cready has mapped out ideas for several posters already. No, we need you to type out the tickets and leaflets, and then I thought you could work together over the posters. You provide the words, and let Robert loose on the illustrations.'

The play was finally put on in late June at the local church hall in Beckenham. It was well-attended; enjoyed by both participants and audience, and Jo felt proud of Bryn, as he stood on the stage offering a vote of thanks to all those who had given freely of their time to the production, and support of the show in aid of the children's home.

Once or twice, Jo's mother gave them some complimentary tickets for the opera. They travelled home on the train from town with their ears ringing, both wishing that they were on their headland, where they could have sung as loudly as they wished. As it was, Bryn contented himself with a soft humming, while Jo relived once more the sad poignant ending, until tears formed in her eyes and threatened to spill over.

They played tennis in the 'rec'. Ran over and round the cinder track, up and over the railway bridges, both counting the steps like young children. In short ... they both had a marvellous time. Two young things trying not to let the imminent parting and war affect them.

But it was to end all too soon. Bryn was called up in late July for training and reported to the Aircrew Receiving Centre at St John's Wood, near to Regent's Park and the London Zoo. Here several hotels and blocks of flats had been requisitioned, where he and the other recruits had their meals amidst the noise of the zoo animals.

'It is just as if we are another species needing to be cared for and fed ...' he wrote to Jo.

Immediately on arrival he was kitted out, suffered numerous inoculations and had documents drawn up. Bryn was bored with this mundane introduction into the Royal Air Force, and this lack of interest must have manifested itself, for on one of the first parades, when the sergeant told him to get a hair cut ... he then added:

'I can see we are going to have trouble with you!' Fortunately, for both Bryn and the sergeant, his stay at ACRC was short. Within two weeks he was posted to Torquay and again accommodated in a requisitioned hotel. It had been stripped of all its luxuries of course, but was beautifully situated on the side of a steep hill overlooking Torquay's picturesque bay.

'The weather is marvellous,' he wrote to Jo. 'And with sea breezes to cool us, it is about as perfect a place as I could wish for. There is a small side balcony I've found that is rarely used. I sit there when I can to recharge my batteries and to think of you, Widegates and our headland. Our 'heads' are being worked overtime. We have classroom lessons on all subjects appertaining to flying, for example – the 'principles of flight' – navigation – hydraulics – meteorology and others. We use various classrooms in the town, and frequently have to double-march to different locations between lessons. It's all rush, rush, rush, but I almost look forward to these little breaks, and seeing more of this delightful little town. I will bring you here one day, Jo, when everything is back to normal. From one vantage point you can see across the bay to Berry Head and beyond … I screw up my eyes and imagine our headland unfolding, but of course the glimpse is purely imaginary and consequently momentary. Time for dreaming is nil! How are you dear girl? I anxiously await a letter …'

His absence left such an emptiness in her life, and particularly now that she'd left school, with most of her friends dispersed, and even Mary away staying with her grandparents in Scotland for the summer. Consequently, Jo became a fairly lonely girl in the quiet of wartime London. She helped more in the nursery, sometimes coping with the toddlers and finding it enjoyable, even the 'pottie' sessions! The children loved her and she thought up various games to help keep them amused during the long day.

The local grocer asked if she would help him for a while as his wife was in hospital and he couldn't manage on his own. She welcomed the chance of earning some real money for the very first time and was soon being taught the intricacies of rationing. Most of her time was spent with careful weighing up … first the sugar, into little blue bags. The ration was eight ounces per person, and the sugar was bagged in two sizes, for example half-pound and one-pound bags, and sold dependent upon the size of the families.

Mr Taylor was a tall bespectacled man, thin-faced and almost bald, who always wore a coarse brown apron over his suit. He smiled rarely, but had a caustic wit that at first had bothered Jo. He taught her how to mark the bags with various abbreviations. Dried fruit became dd.ft ... and macaroni ... mcni, etc. When the Christmas delivery of dried fruit arrived at the end of August, she weighed and priced the packets, and put them into the wide-necked biscuit containers at the front of the counter, ready for sale later in the autumn. Jo remembered when these containers had housed all sorts of biscuits ... round, hot ginger ones, plain arrowroot, shortcake, cream ones, and, best of all, those coloured wafers in the most delicate pink, filled with layer upon layer of soft cream. Biscuits were a thing of the past, but the containers were being put to good use! Gone too were the sacks of broken biscuits that used to stand at the corner of the counter, complete with scoop so that customers could help themselves. This, in the past, had been a real treat, and Jo had been allowed to go to the shop as a child and scoop her own bagful. These were carefully sorted and shared out on the kitchen table, so that her brothers had the same mix. Odd ones went to their parents!

As she studied the empty shelves, she remembered too the tins of fruit salad, peaches and apricots that used to make the back of the counters so colourful. Occasionally these luxuries did make an appearance and were quickly snapped up. It was a question of first come, first served, although Mr Taylor did keep certain of these special items for his regular customers.

One end of the shop was given over to household requirements and these days housed only packets of soda for washing-up, and great bars of square washing soap, yellow and hard. There were none of the small tablets of Knights Castille, Lux or Pears that once had made that corner of the shop so attractive and sweet-smelling. When occasionally a small delivery of these did come in, the message got around very quickly ... they were sold almost before they'd been unpacked.

She learnt to handle the butter, wielding the initially ungainly heavy wooden pats to cut, smooth and form butter into various regulated sizes. Her arms ached some days! She tidied the shelves, noting the produce by colours. Dried fruits were always in brown bags, sugar in blue and rice or macaroni usually in strong off-white bags, all clearly marked on the outside, identified and priced as she'd been taught.

Jo carved the bacon. The slicer was a lethal weapon in inexperienced hands, but she was well-taught and always very careful. The thickness of the rashers was all important. Many people preferred to have the thinner slices because the bacon was sold by weight and one extra slice for the man of the house seemed a good idea. The cheese was cut with a wire cutter which had a round wooden handle in multiples of two ounces, again dependent on the size of the family. It was carefully packed into greaseproof paper ready for the weekly allowance.

Such a small portion per person … her mother called it a 'mousetrap portion'.

Johanna enjoyed her summer in the shop and, although the weather was perfect and she often longed for Cornwall, she had fun later spending the money she had earned, and even splashed out on a pair of snakeskin shoes, with the help of her younger brother's coupons. 'Ray doesn't need anything at all,' her mother had said. 'Use them, Jo – it's all right.'

It was a warm September day. Jo sat on the beach, her head resting against the rocks and listened to the thumping of the waves as the incoming tide smacked heavily against the cliffs at the far side of the bay. She heard a dog bark somewhere on the cliff path, then its owner shout … 'Not that way.' Otherwise, she was quite alone. The tide washed, rolled and pushed the pebbles up and down at the water line, grinding and tumbling them continuously. She heard, above the sea sounds, the wild screeching call of the gulls as they wheeled and dipped over the cliffs, catching the shifting currents of air. How graceful they look here, she thought, and smiled to recall their atrociously noisy behaviour yesterday evening at the quay, when she and her two companions had enjoyed a Cornish pasty. They struggled with their cumbersome packages, laughing together at the gulls as they squabbled over the odd titbit they dropped.

She was on her own again now. Bryn had returned to Torquay last night, and James was even now catching the train from St Austell for his long journey to Scotland and his first introduction into the army. It had been marvellous that Bryn had got a short leave to see his friend. With the three of them together, it had been just like the old days.

Jo's own journey back to London was delayed because her mother needed just a little more time to settle things at Pendower House.

There was such a lot to do before she could move the youngsters down to Cornwall. Bryn was due to visit London in two weeks' time, and she was looking forward already to seeing him once more, before he finally moved to heaven knows where …

'Perhaps I'll get some tickets for the opera. *La Bohème* is on now, and that would be marvellous for us both,' Bryn had told her as he left. They had all had such 'singing' fun sitting on the smooth rocks of the bay. Her own rendering of 'Mimi's song' had been a laugh, but both the men took the story line seriously and had good tenor voices. She had loved listening them, their faces distant and wrapt, as they tried hard to reach the notes, and suggest the poignancy at the same time. The gulls at least hadn't minded, but had landed on the rocks near to them, settled and watchful. Just as well really, she thought, for if they'd screeched and cried, then the whole show would have collapsed.

CHAPTER FIVE

Johanna's secretarial course began on 23 September, and it was a bewildered girl who, arriving late, was ushered into a classroom housing some twenty students. There was music playing, each girl was sitting in front of a typewriter, the keyboard covered, and typing in rhythm: dd … ff … gg, and so on. The keyboard was pictured on a wide blackboard at the front of the class. Jo heard the teacher say, 'Heads up, girls … backs straight. A good typist doesn't try to look at her hands … even if she could!'

Some moments later, settled in front of her typewriter, Jo's hands fumbled under the cover as she tried to control the rising panic, the mortification of being late and, worst of all, the realisation that this wasn't what she really wanted to do … no, not at all! Her train had been late arriving at Charing Cross due to an overnight bomb near to the Hungerford Bridge. The journey across the river had been fraught with danger, and part of the repaired span afforded a view of the water far below. The train had crawled across, oh so slowly, and the thought now of returning over that same gap that evening horrified her. The walk to the college had been new to her, and in her anxiety she'd taken the wrong turning, arriving late, flustered, and feeling terribly young and inexperienced. Now this – it was awful! Her hands found the keys, she found the rhythm, and a casual glance at her piece of paper, relaxed her in the knowledge that at least she seemed to be typing sense. Later, the typewriter was to become an extension of herself, a means to communicate, and a source of satisfaction when she did complete a piece of work without any errors. Not so at first though! The teacher had a system for testing speed and accuracy. He would stand at the back of the class, with the girls sitting upright, fingers poised, and then blow a whistle. On each occasion, Jo jumped. However prepared she was, sitting waiting for the shrill call to start

– she jumped! Her fingers hit the wrong keys and she had to take a deep breath and start again. Jo never got the right speeds whilst at college, but she did learn accuracy. The speed came much later.

The other lessons were no bother. She found that she loved bookkeeping and was good at it; shorthand was mind-bending, and sociology a little boring, but she had a seat near to a large window, where the view looked out over the top of old London houses, towards Chinatown. She was fascinated with this, and the cheeky London sparrows who seemed to cope with wartime life, returning time and again to look for titbits on the window sills. Evidence of destruction was there if she chose to search for it, but Jo looked high … up to where the white clouds scudded across an azure-blue sky, or at the dark grey clouds of winter storms, as they bubbled and churned in the heavens. She watched the starlings coming in to roost on the old telegraph wires; the pigeons as they settled on any little ledge, nudging and nestling against one another. She loved it when the snow fell softly from a grey sky … dark flakes against the windowpanes. Then it felt as if she were in a cocoon of quietness. Whatever was going on inside the classroom was shut out somehow, there was a hush about everything, an unreality. Even the traffic below seemed quieter.

It was not always so, for inevitably the air-raid warnings continued to blare their shrill frightening signals. All the girls would then tumble pell-mell down a concrete staircase to shelters in the basement. The noise was deafening from the anti-aircraft guns sited in the local park and the mass of hard shoes pounding on the stone steps. There was an atmosphere of extreme bustle, excitement and fear. Jo would have preferred to step out on the roadway. She hated having to use the shelters, but rules were rules, and she was just a pupil. On occasions they would be high on the flat roof, where a netball pitch had been marked out, and the whole area bordered with high nets, so that the balls would not escape and fall on some unsuspecting person far below. At times like this, the fear was often heightened when they could see in the distance the planes approaching, watch the puffballs of smoke as the ack-ack reached for them, and hear the crunch, crunch of the bombs as they fell, usually to the south-east of them. Once in a while, the terror imbued in the other girls would touch her. On these occasions her breath would come so quickly, she'd feel cold and yet hot, and be quite unable to control the shaking of her hands. In the shelter, the girls would smile at one another sheepishly … sing and talk as loudly as they could, and though often there was bombing near to them, they felt only the upheaval and heard only the crunch. All was well in their college.

Picnics in the park were a joy in early autumn, but as the weather got colder, Jo and a group of friends looked for warmer places to eat. They heard of the British Restaurants run by the Women's Voluntary Service and, with limited pocket money for food, this seemed a good idea to try. The nearest one was in Hatton Gardens, and they would arrive early, before the rush of City folk; join in a small queue of men with plates held out, just like Oliver Twist. On this would be 'plonked' a marvellously tasty and hot portion of stew. Vegetables were added as you went along the line. Jo learned about mushy peas for the first time and found them good. The ladies were wonderful and gave them more than adequate portions, so that the girls returned to college with full, warm tummies. The puddings were a marvel of sweetness; spongy treacle puddings, huge suet roly-polies, with currants like little black flies. Yorkshire puddings, baked on huge platters, with the outside crust curling up, cooked to a light brown, and again, floating in either syrup or smothered with brown sugar. Jo was in her element … the WVS ladies loved them, loved their youth, their brightness and their praise for all the meals. 'Come back for a second helping, dearie …' Jo was told. 'There's plenty for growing girls like you.' Jo thought she had passed that stage, but was always hungry, and so often she did go back for more, spoon in hand, plate held out, just as in Dickens' book!

Hitler very nearly spoiled all that for them with some overnight bombing in the Gardens, but the WVS had determination and ingenuity, and set up a temporary shelter with trestle tables, benches and duckboards for ease of walking. They were in business once more! The food was cooked now in an old dark hut, but was just as delicious, and just as hot. The girls huddled together, legs crossed over one another for protection against draughts and, often, driving rain. They sat with workmen, who were engaged in replacing canvas windows or rubble-clearing; next to bank clerks and office workers in their dark jackets and pin-striped trousers. Occasionally, an older gentleman would appear, grey-haired and bowler-hatted. He used to leave the hat on, but if he sat near to the girls, then he would raise it in a polite fashion and place it square in the middle of the wooden table. That he cared for it was obvious, for he always dusted the brim before replacing it on his head. So, through October, November and half of December, Jo and her friends ate, not elegantly, but well! All good things come to an end! The principal of the college heard of the girls' lunch venue; felt it wasn't seemly for his pupils, and arranged for those who needed a hot meal at lunch-time to eat at the local infant school. Twelve-thirty each weekday would see them climbing the dark concrete stairway of the school. A stairway that somehow always smelled of cabbage and pine disinfectant. With wrinkled noses they waited outside the top door. Each day, a tall, angular and frozen-faced head teacher would appear at the top of the stairs and attempt to quieten her noisy visitors.

Eventually they were ushered into a dining-room and fed. The meals were acceptable, but not like those at the British Restaurant. They cost the same too, but were usually half-cold, and eaten in a quiet restrained manner, with 'frozen face' in attendance. The chairs were small, the tables low and not really suitable for girls, now almost young women. There was much humour from the large members of the group about this. Spring, however, fortunately returned and the park was accessible once more for carefree sandwich fun lunches!

The train was late as it pulled into the little station near to the recreation ground. The day was hot for October, and the journey had been tedious, with each compartment overfull, necessitating some passengers have to 'strap-hang'. Jo had been one of these and her arms now ached with the pulling and swaying of the whole weight of her body, which had been constricted for movement in the packed compartment, as she moved with the motion of the train. It had stopped for long periods. People near to the windows peered out, anxious for explanations or reasons for the delay. Those further in prayed that it didn't mean an imminent air raid. Passengers rarely communicated during the dangerous journeys to and from London. There was the occasional smile or comment on the weather amongst the regular travellers, but on the whole people were withdrawn and quiet. It was as if they were perhaps searching for strength to prepare themselves for another wartime day, or, on the homeward journey, sitting heavy and enervated, but putting what little strength they had left into willing the train forward – forward to safety and home!

Today nobody had spoken when the train stopped, but looking round Jo had met eyes everywhere. Eyes looking startled; anxious eyes in strained faces; sleepy eyes in the heat and, occasionally, twinkling eyes from some person who sensed the edge of panic and did his or her best to relieve it a little. An air-raid warning whilst travelling on the trains made one feel very vulnerable.

Now, walking quietly by the flowing river, Jo twisted her neck, eased her shoulders and relaxed her arms. The peace was there again. The air somnolent and heavy, sweetly scented from the riverside shrubs. She was tired following last night's raids, when they'd been awakened by the sirens on three occasions. Eventually, she had dropped into a deep sleep in the early hours of the morning, only to be jolted awake by the alarm clock. She felt herself heavy somehow ... heavy and depressed. Bryn's last letter had been short and unenlightening. He had mentioned a short weekend leave, but not when. Jo was impatient with the war. 'When will it end? When could they all breathe freely again?' She had quite forgotten what it felt like to be safe, to go to bed and know that you'd not be disturbed; to go to college and not worry all day about her home and her mother. Each evening's walk from the train was spiced with a dread that her house would not be there.

The front door was open wide when she reached the house, and a weary Johanna called to her mother and went straight upstairs to change, just as her young brother, home for a few days from school camp, tumbled down the stairs, a handkerchief over his nose.

'Bryn's here,' he called as he passed her. 'Can't stop – my nose is bleeding.'

'Bryn here,' she said to herself in disbelief. Then the words really registered, she hurried up the two flights of stairs to the second landing. Jo could hear voices, she stopped to catch her breath, and perhaps to still the sudden wild beating of her heart ... 'Bryn's here...' she murmured. A feeling of intense excitement lanced through her. She sat down on the stairs and watched as the dust motes danced in front of the landing window. Small strips of coloured glass, as yet untouched by the war, lent them a new dimension as they floated and whirled lightly in the air. 'Like little coloured gnats,' thought

Jo. More contained, she pulled herself up by the bannisters, and turned the corner of the stairway. She heard her eldest brother laugh …'You see them off, laddie … you!' She did not hear Bryn's reply, but she could see his hand, that large strong hand with beautifully shaped nails was stretched round the jamb of the door. She could see through the doorway, the top of the dresser and the chest of drawers. Watched as her brother took a small flat tin from the top of the chest, opened it and spread a thickness of grease on his hands, then rubbed them together and applied it to his hair. Brylcreme! She saw the tin, lid on once more on top of the chest, its outside rim still greasy, with a film of dust over all, smudged now by her brother's fingers. She watched as he rubbed the grease over his head, watched as he reached for two brushes and smoothed his hair backwards, then sidewards, until, with a final smoothing at the back, he flung the brushes down, reached for his jacket, and she heard him say …

'Come on, Bryn … let's go and see Alan, he's on leave as well!' Only then did Bryn appear from behind the door… a strange Bryn in Royal Air Force uniform. It suited him, suited his tall elegant, and yet strong, figure. He looked casual, as if he had worn air-force blue all his life. She noticed that the rough cloth had marked his neck where the collar was still stiff. He looked good. Bryn glanced up and held her gaze, his face broke into the usual well-loved grin.

'Ray told me that you were working late tonight, otherwise I'd have been at the station to meet you.'

'We had a bomb scare, so the special clinic was cancelled. Hello Bryn – lovely to see you.' Jo leant forward to kiss his cheek as Bryn enclosed her in a tight hug.

'You look bonny, pet.' She felt it too … all tiredness gone, her face flushed and eyes smiling!

Her brother flung himself down the stairs, said a casual 'Hello, Jo', and called to Bryn to follow.

'See you later,' Bryn said. He stood for a while as if loathe to go, then turned and slowly followed her brother down. She leaned against the door jamb – against the very door that had supported his weight just a few minutes before. Her heart was beating, throbbing faster than usual. She caught sight of herself in the mirror of the wardrobe, bright-eyed, happy-featured, a rapt expression, and hugged herself with delight. Bryn was here – Bryn was staying for the evening meal … Bryn had come to see her. She was sure of that … to see her!

Johanna rushed upstairs, the final two flights to her own bedroom, and hastily rummaged through her clothes. Everything looked well-worn and dowdy – 'coupons are an absolute pain,' she thought. Her cloths consisted mostly of mother's alterations, for she was wonderfully clever with her needle and thought nothing of turning outfits to make them fresher, or cutting down coats to make skirts for Jo. Finally she found a brown pleated skirt. Jo wore this regularly to college, it was made of good suiting material, kept its pleats well and always looked smart. The stockings from America, a gift from her cousin, were in the top drawer and under them a brand-new yellow jumper that she'd been knitting for ages and had only just completed. It was a bright canary yellow, covered in holes, airy-fairy holes as depicted by the pattern. She put it on and it suited her, then brushed her hair, changed her stockings and slid her feet into her very best shoes of brown snakeskin. She looked good – certainly better than a moment ago in her black jacket, check skirt and dark red blouse.

Jo tripped downstairs. Her mother smiled at her in appreciation and made no comment on her choice of clothes, but young Raymond was sitting on the back steps, a large wad of cotton plastered to his nose. She could see underneath the white pad, his huge smile and twinkling eyes … 'Got yourself pretty for Bryn, then? I hope that he notices …' The moment was spoilt! She felt a certain loss of confidence, and turned away as her mother came over to stand by the table and show her how to put the finishing touches to an apple pie. 'Where did Mum get the fat for the pastry?' she thought.

'Don't bother about your brother, Jo – you know he's a tease, and the first person Bryn asked about was you. Why, if Bill hadn't been home, he'd have been down at the station waiting for you.'

'Would he really mum – would he really?' and then seeing her mother's indulgent smile, added: 'Yes, of course he would and that would have been nice.'

'Nice', she thought to herself. What an understatement. For Bryn to have met her would have been marvellous, wonderful … She set to, trimming the pastry, and the apple pie was soon ready to put in the oven.

Meanwhile, the three young men were comparing notes. Alan had first met up with Bill at Chagford. He had come down from Scotland to Wickwar in Gloucestershire to join the remnants of the 23rd Royal Artillery back from Dunkirk. He had found life difficult mixing with this hard core of battle-weary veterans, some five to six years his senior. Much army equipment had been lost at Dunkirk, and Alan told Bryn the impossible story of how in Scotland, with the invasion imminent, they had been issued with bayonets welded to metal gas pipes! Their sole means of defence against foreigners on British soil! Bryn, new to the forces, shook his head incredulously, until Alan was to remark: 'As our warrant officer said to the new recruits at Redford, when I first reported for duty… 'You've still got cradle marks on your bottoms and are wet behind the ears!' Bryn almost upset the tenor of the moment by saying: 'They don't treat us like that in the RAF.'

They talked of what the future might hold, of the bombing raids that were increasing in force over Germany. Alan's comment of – 'don't be too anxious to join in, laddie,' which was directed at Bryn's wish to get his training over, and be ready to fight, quietened him as he thought of David Grant and heard again his voice … 'There's no glory in war!'

Bill was pleased with the prospect of being housed properly after a month under canvas. The new billet was to be a cider factory and had been the source of much laughter, and many jokes. He hadn't as yet seen it, but he hoped it wouldn't smell! Since Dunkirk, although their training had continued, the lack of equipment had made it all seem very unreal. Now, in a few short weeks, both he and Alan were to move to Chudleigh for more training on Dartmoor and to complete their gunnery course with real guns and real ammunition for the very first time!

The hour went by swiftly as they talked, but even so Bill noticed Bryn glancing at his watch on several occasions, and he thought of his sister, without a doubt waiting anxiously at home for their return. 'She's really fond of the laddie,' he thought, as he studied Bryn's restless expression. 'No wonder really – they've been pals for so many years.'

'Time to go,' he announced. 'Come over on Sunday, Alan, mum would like to see you.'

For Jo, that same hour seemed interminable. She helped her mother prepare the meal, set the table, helped Ray with his nosebleed by holding on to the bridge of his nose very tightly until the bleeding stopped, as she'd been taught to do during her first-aid courses. She heard her brother and Bryn return, just as she'd finished washing her hands after administering this treatment. They came round the back of the house and straight into the kitchen. 'Dinner ready yet, mum?' Bill sniffed appreciatively, as he poked his head over the stove and into the saucepans bubbling on top. Bryn came right in, took the fork from Jo's hand as she began to mash the potatoes, and proceeded to prod and stir them with energy. Jo sat on the kitchen stool, leant her elbows on the table top, face in her hands, and watched him as he mashed and chatted to her mother.

'How are your plans, Mrs Dingle? Is all going well at Pendower House?'

'Indeed it is, Bryn, but slowly. Just as soon as we think things are finally settled, then another problem comes our way. The council have now approved everything, and we are desperately looking for equipment, suitable furniture, and of course, storage space for Miss Burnett's treasures. I'm longing to get started there.'

'You'll get there,' Bryn encouraged. 'All that work and planning won't be in vain, I'm sure.'

'Yes, of course we will, and the sooner the better.' Mrs Dingle looked steadily at Bryn. 'We had a young boy come to us yesterday. He'd found his house in rubble on returning home from school and both parents taken to hospital. Poor little chap … now he could do with a change of scenery and some good Cornish air!' Mrs Dingle paused for a moment, before adding: 'It was so awful … his father was home on leave for just one hour!'

Jo paled. It was her main dread that one day she'd turn the corner of the road and find her home demolished. They were all quiet for a while, thinking of that sad story, but it wasn't the time to be serious for long. Jo's mum teasingly congratulated Bryn on the consistency of the mashed potatoes.

'That's lovely, not a lump to be seen. Would you carry the dish in please, and, Jo, call the boys!'

Bryn wiped his hands, turned to Johanna and said: 'Will I do?' A blush spread over her face. She had not been aware that he had known she had been studying him for some minutes. His eyes had been on his job, or her mother, but he had felt her intense gaze. He flashed her a friendly smile as he saw the flush.

'You'll do,' she said, thumping his arm as she went by. Yes – he'd do … he looked wonderful, so grown-up somehow in uniform. His face seemed more rugged, and there was a firm line to his mouth that she hadn't noticed before. They reached the dining-room, where Mrs Dingle, Ray and Bill were already seated.

'I've put you there, Bryn,' Jo's mother said, indicating a seat next to her daughter, but Bryn had already gone to the opposite side of the table, given Raymond a nudge as he said: 'Change places, Ray, Jo wants to study me!' Her embarrassment was complete, and particularly so when her young brother looked at her keenly and remarked …

'What are you blushing for Jo?'

The warm days of early October vanished overnight and London was covered in mist and light rain for days. Everything took on a grey appearance, and, with the regular raids opening up new areas of devastation, the journey to college became daily more depressing. The trains ran at odd times, often arriving early, and consequently connections were missed, whilst at other times they'd be late or cancelled. Jo didn't know which was preferable. She always understood the 'leaving early' types, for she felt more and more anxious when travelling on the railway, and only relaxed a little after they'd navigated the central London stations with safety. One felt very vulnerable, stuck immobile on the lines during a warning – like a fly caught in a web, quivering, but not able to get free!

It was unpleasant in the morning to realise that within a few hours the same tensions would have to be coped with, and the same fears subdued for the return journey. She felt cold these days. Cold as she walked through the recreation ground to the local station in the morning, and colder still when she came home at night. During the warmer days and longer evenings, it had been a pleasure to walk through the little park, for it afforded a time of quiet, away from the traffic on the main road, and it was particularly lovely of an early morning. A sweet promise, far away from all thoughts of war. Such a contrast to the hustle and bustle of the roadway, spoiled on both sides with air-raid shelters, the dark-brown earth still spilling everywhere. This was a green oasis where for a few minutes of every day Jo could forget the turmoil, dread and ugliness of these times. After a day at college in central London, it was a haven of peace and offered a welcome, so that most of the day's traumas seemed to evaporate as she walked through. Only the thought of what she might find at home prevented her from being completely relaxed.

Jo used to walk through the 'rec' from church on Sundays, when the early morning smells were varied and compelling. There was the fresh smell of the river, dank smells from near the willow on the bank, queer sharp smells from the huge cinder pitch used by local boys before the war for football matches. There was often the smell of new-mown grass, the dust smells when eddies of fine soil whirled about on a windy morning; smells that wafted over from the nearby hospital … clinical and sharp, sometimes tinged with bacon smells from breakfast being cooked there. Jo would sniff appreciatively, and then hurry home in the hope that her meal would include some … but with rationing, bacon breakfasts were few and far between!

The 'rec' could be spooky at dusk, when the tall poplars cast dark shadows along the path, and when the lights from the hospital, the trains and the nearby offices had been blacked out. There was an alternative route home, but Johanna rarely took it … preferring the little park or a shorter walk through the local churchyard, where she saved some ten minutes of time. All through the train journey home, she would debate with herself.

'It's getting dark … you must go the long way round by the road,' her sensible self said. 'It will be well into dusk by the time you reach the station.' Then, another voice would cajole: 'Take the short way through the churchyard … it will be dark in there, with the low-lying cedar trees, but a quicker walk – you'll be out onto the main road in no time at all.' Again, a wise voice said: 'Go through the 'rec' … you can run easily along the wide paths.'

These were, of course, autumn and winter decisions. Spring and summer days afforded her long light evenings, when it didn't really matter which way Jo went home. During the winter, however, she would invariably choose the churchyard; walking softly on crêpe-soled, flat-heeled shoes, with her torch in her hand, ready to turn on for light or to use as a weapon – against she knew not what! She trod softly – oh so softly, peering into the gloom as the path wound down into the little valley covered by low trees. The gravestones loomed up on either side, white and strange. Jo imagined over and over again that someone, or something, would be hiding there, waiting to pounce on her! She never ran, though every fibre of her being urged her to do so, and she never lit her torch, but somehow felt safer in the total darkness, as she hastened through until the noise of the traffic and the dimmed road lighting, welcomed her to safety! Relaxing, she pondered quite seriously why she walked that way alone each night.

One wonderful evening, Bryn was at the station to meet her. He'd got a twenty-four hour pass before being sent to Scotland for the next part of his training. They walked through the 'rec' in companionable silence. The moon was up and the whole area bathed in silver light.

'It's so beautiful,' Jo breathed, utterly content.

'Hmm.' Bryn's mouth was grim. 'Jo, I hope you don't walk this way on your own at night. Go the long way round, just to please me, will you?' She didn't promise him, for she knew that she wouldn't be able to keep it, but instead asked him about his uncle, who she knew had been ailing in health. The subject was changed, and they were soon relaxed and chatting away.

'He ought to come and live with mum and me. At least he'd not be on his own at night.' Jo remarked.

'He's closing the business temporarily. Perhaps opening up again after the war, and going down to live in the West Country. He has a friend in Taunton, with a grand old house by the river there. James and I used to visit him when we were at school. He's to stay there for now, and I must say I shall be content to know that he's safe and well-cared for. Now there's only you to worry about.' His arm was about her shoulders and he gave her a tight hug.

'I'm all right, silly,' Jo replied as she snuggled close.

'I might have guessed you'd say that, but you will take care, Jo, won't you? Don't go looking for trouble, be sensible.' His face was serious, but seeing her happy smile, her happy, mocking smile, he gave up. 'You –' he said, 'you.'

It was three years into the war and clothes were fast becoming a real problem for Johanna. Whilst she had been a schoolgirl, her needs had been few, and the coupon allowance had seemed adequate. Now, however, she required more adult clothes and in these her wardrobe was sadly lacking. She hadn't grown a lot, in fact had slimmed down, but her present outfits looked young and dated. The coupons, or rather the lack of them, were not the only setback to purchasing decent outfits, for there was a dearth of good clothes to buy. Even basics were hard to come by. Jo's mum continued to sew, and patiently undid, recut and turned various of her skirts for her daughter. They both rummaged through her stock of material. Mrs Dingle had been a compulsive hoarder and had in the past collected agreeable remnants whenever there was a sale. Now, these lengths of material were a miracle for them both! Between them, they made underwear out of dainty floral cotton; checks and stripes became smart blouses, and one dark-blue length of woollen cloth was fashioned into Jo's first adult suit – she loved it!

The local wool shop had ceased to exist, but the frail, grey-haired lady who owned it operated at times from her flat above the premises. Knitting-wool was impossibly difficult to get, but occasionally word would get round that she had a small supply. Jo was always quick to take advantage here, for she loved knitting and had for some time been making balaclavas, mittens and scarves, all in khaki for soldiers. Her godmother had presented her with a large quantity of skeins, so she spent hours knitting furiously, thinking all the time of her brother Bill, of Alan and of James, who was now at officers' training camp somewhere in Scotland. She liked to believe that they would eventually benefit from her industry. Jo often knitted whilst on the train and was amused one dark evening, after they had been shunted into a siding because of an air-raid warning, to hear a fellow passenger remark:

'What I don't understand, miss, is how you can knit in the dark, but you seem to go even faster. Now that really puzzles me!'

'It's the agitation,' replied Jo. 'And I count the stitches as I go along, so that I know I haven't made a mistake.' Mind you, at such times Jo only attempted scarves!

Once, by dilligent searching, she obtained some pale pink wool, enough to make a jumper. Another time her aunts had presented her with skeins of wine and pale blue. She knitted them together to make a cardigan – Aston Villa colours! And, best of all, she obtained from a shop near to the park some cotton crêpe in cream and white, and made from this two short-sleeved tops, complete with a shell edging at the neck. They looked smart over her skirts and kept their neatness all day, unlike the cotton blouses. The white one in particular looked marvellous with her new suit.

Stockings were another worry and were Jo's favourite hate, for those obtained were plain, thick and old-fashioned! The summer sun had browned her legs, so that she had no real need of them at first, but later, the draughty streets of London made her shiver and stockings became a necessity. They were scarce and stocks were sparce. To obtain a pair you just had to be in the right place at the right time. She did have some smart ones from America, sent by her cousin, but these she kept for very special occasions, and they were washed after each wear, dried and put back safely in her drawer. Later, when Bryn was in America, he used to send her small parcels of stockings – beautiful light-tan, silk ones that were the envy of every female around!

It was all such a fight. A daily fight, and Jo was often heard to remark: 'When the war is over I'm going to throw this lot out and start again. I shall have lots and lots of lovely new clothes ...'

The remembrance service was still held at the Cenotaph in early November. It was mostly attended by local people who had sons or daughters away from home. Jo's Red Cross detachment turned out in full force, with the Boy's Brigade, the Guides, the St John's Ambulance representatives, and the Army Cadet Force, who provided the band as they marched some two miles from the Clock Tower.

So many tired and careworn people praying for victory and peace. Jo stood in her uniform this November day; it was mild with a misty sunshine. The air was sweet and fresh with an autumnal dampness still lingering, and their singing was uplifted somehow, with a sweetness and poignancy that affected them all.

Jo was still young and bewildered, both by the impact of the horror of the bombing, and the sadness of their daily lives, which at times seemed intolerable. She watched as a few golden leaves dropped onto the grass at her feet, gazing at their beauty for a while, her thoughts wandering. Perhaps over Germany now, there were other mothers, lovers, and friends, asking God to take care of their loved ones – praying for victory and peace. It was all so very confusing! Jo had found herself of late looking for some 'good' in each day. She had learnt to accept the bad without understanding why, but always said thanks for the 'good' things in life.

'Thank you, God,' she murmured now, as another golden leaf began its descent from above.

Gradually the local nursery where Jo spent each Saturday had begun to close down. Most of the children had been transferred to the country areas, some with their mothers and others for fostering. Only a small nucleus remained, and Jo found herself idle sometimes now and wondered what she'd do with her Saturday mornings when the nursery finally closed at Christmas. Sister Morny, who had enjoyed having her as a helper, suggested that the hospital needed help:

'Why don't you go along and see if they can use you, Johanna?'

Mrs Dingle wasn't sure about that. Jo was rather young still she thought, and although the local hospital had been part of their life for as long as she could remember, it was a strangely forbidding place to look at and housed now, she knew, many casualties from the bombing.

'Why don't you make plans to do something nice with your weekends, Jo? We'll sit down and think up places you could visit, shall we?'

But Jo was adamant, and particularly so, because several days later, at the weekly Red Cross meeting, help was requested for the hospital.

'The nurses are having to cope against very great odds … if you have time and are willing to use what expertise you have, then go and help – please!'

Jo offered them each Saturday … was asked to do each weekend, and willingly accepted this commitment.

CHAPTER SIX

Just before Christmas, Bill arrived home on embarkation leave. Jo's mum was devastated. She had been planning a family Christmas and had arranged for Raymond to come home. She was visibly shaken when Bill told her that he and Alan were now attached to the newly created First Army. They were happy, excited almost, though Bill was often caught watching his mother and sister with a worried, intense look. Jo in some way understood his anxieties, for since their father's death Bill had felt responsible for the family, and although the war had taken him away from home, he had still been able to keep in touch by regular letters and visits when leave permitted. Now though he was leaving the country, and he realised more and more how vulnerable they were, as civilians in war-torn Britain.

The days went by quickly and with leave over, they embarked on 24 December from Gourock, near Glasgow, attached at first to a convoy in local waters, before turning west for Newfoundland, where the accompanying destroyers signalled – 'Goodbye and good luck!' as the converted Dutch liner, with some 2,500 men and a few women on board, set off at full speed and alone. South first to the Azores, and then east to Gibraltar, *en route* for North Africa to help with the worsening situation there. History was to show that the newly created First Army, by attacking Rommel's African Corps from the rear and cutting off supplies, together with our tenacious holding of Malta, prevented the German domination of the Mediterranean.

Christmas was a quiet and worrying time for them all. Jo and Mrs Dingle did their best to liven things up for Raymond. They played monopoly … cooked a special dinner of boiled ham, with whatever vegetables they could find. Jo introduced her mother to roasted apples, when John Kimber, an elderly neighbour, produced some he'd kept in his cellar all the autumn. He joined them for a meal and brought his contribution: half-a-bottle of sherry to have with the pudding. John had arrived at the doorway, clutching his bottle earlier that afternoon, well-wrapped-up against the cold, and he had raised his hat to Jo and wished her the season's greetings as she had ushered him in. It was a gentlemanly greeting, and she'd found it quite endearing. John was a tall man, extremely thin, his clothes seemed to hang off his shoulders, and the fine bone structure of his long face was most pronounced. At some sixty-five years, he still sported a mop of dark hair. He had a wide generous mouth, was clean-shaven and his dark eyes regarded everything and everybody quizzically over half-rimmed glasses.

Jo had made the pudding, using half the Christmas dried fruit ration. She'd cut up dates and figs to add to the taste, commenting drily that, if not flavourful, it would at least be good for them! The Christmas cake had been given to Bill. They all drank his health, and hoped that he would be able to have a 'sort' of Christmas on the ship.

Dusk fell early on that dark winter day, but before Jo pulled the curtains against the night – this was done even though the windows still housed canvas – she noticed, through the skylight, that snow had started falling, gently, softly, and soon all outside noises were muffled and strange. As Jo helped John Kimber down the wide steps of her house, prior to seeing him home, the snow crunched underfoot. There was a bright moon appearing from behind the dark clouds, and both hoped that the Germans would be otherwise occupied, for it was a perfect night for a bombing raid!

Mrs Dingle lay in bed, snug in her feather mattress, and yet shivering inwardly with fear for her first-born; she was comforted only by the thought that she was not the only mother feeling as she did now. The war was wreaking its own particular havoc in tearing families apart. No one was divorced from it!

The raids diminished during the early months of the new year. Occasionally warnings went, but with no sign of an invader, and there was often a tendency to shrug one's shoulders and ignore the wailing, compelling noise, with a 'blow Hitler … I'm busy' attitude.

Jo and her mother, however, learned a healthy respect for the air-raid warnings with a frightening experience in the local high street. They had almost completed their shopping and had only the fishmonger to visit, where they'd heard a new batch of cod had been delivered. The warning sounded as they walked along the wide pavement. People were mostly scurrying for shelter, but others, like Mrs Dingle and Jo, made their way towards the next proposed shop with lengthening strides. They arrived at the open-fronted fish shop, and there, sure enough, was the cod; huge white cutlets, fillets and tail pieces, set out on the sloping marble slabs. Water from hoses, which trickled constantly onto the marble to keep the fish fresh, had made the pavements wet, and so both were loathe to put down their parcels and bags.

'That looks good,' Jo pointed with an elbow to a large fillet … Her mother was about to reply when, suddenly, the air was rent with the most horrific noise. It seemed to erupt above them. Over the shop appeared the dark sinister shape of a plane. It was flying low; they could see the pilot and recognised the awful swastika markings on the wings. The plane banked and spat flames …

'Why, he's firing …' Jo thought, and was instantly alert – brought back to life and awareness by the danger, she moved towards her mother, but as she did so, felt a hand push hard into her back … 'Here lass … down …' and she found herself kneeling on the wet floor, amidst the water drips and large, dead-eyed cod heads at the side of the counter. Huddled over her was the shopkeeper, and to her left she noticed her mother, in the same awkward position, her face pale and eyes startled. The plane moved along the high street, shooting up anything and everything. The noise was fearsome; the memory of it made Jo tremble as she knelt there in the wet. In the quiet, as the plane went further away, she heard the laboured breathing from the fishmonger who was crouched over her.

Somewhere the plane banked and turned, for some minutes later it returned with a crescendo of noise once more. She caught a glimpse of the fearsome dark shape as it turned away, up and over the town hall, and after a few moments heard the crunch of bombs. How long they stayed there in the wet she never knew, but it seemed as if it were forever. The fishmonger and her mother were pale with shock, and Jo imagined that she must be too. A cup of weak tea was made as they gathered their wet bags, and two old kitchen-type chairs were produced from somewhere at the back of the shop for them to sit on.

'Don't hurry away now, miss … madam,' the shopkeeper was concerned. 'Take your time … he'll not be back!'

Later that evening as they shared the fish with John, both laughed at the spectacle they must have made amongst the fish heads, fins and waste that were thrown down under the counter as the fish were prepared for sale. But they never ignored a warning again … at least not for a very long time.

Johanna commenced her weekend duty at the hospital in early February. She'd been unwell with a head cold for about ten days and it had left her feeling tired and jaded.

'What you need, my girl, is a good holiday, not to start working seven days a week …' Mrs Dingle still disapproved of her hospital commitment, feeling that it would be too much for Jo.

She entered the gates of the hospital at eight on Saturday morning. It felt strange going through the gap between the tall pillars where, previous to the war, had hung some fine iron gates. The porter at the entrance greeted her with 'Good morning, miss – have a lovely day.' Her spirits lifted a little at his cheery greeting and smile. She was ushered up four floors by a cleaning lady and along a wide corridor, to stand eventually at the desk of the sister in charge of the female ward. Sister Brown looked up quickly, said a brief 'I'll be with you in a minute', then left the room hurriedly. Jo was left to look about her. The office was small, spotlessly clean and neat. It boasted a large desk, behind which stood a swivel seat, with two low armchairs facing the front of the desk. These were covered in bright floral cotton and made the room look homely somehow. On the wall were various charts about health – a notice-board, which was hung with bits and pieces of paper, and one whole side wall was given over to cupboards. Some had glass fronts and Jo could see bottles and jars inside. One smaller cupboard in the centre was labelled, in large red lettering: 'Drugs' … It had a lock and she knew that Sister had the key to that on her person somewhere.

From the window she could see the high street stretching in either direction far below her. The roadway was fairly busy now on this weekend morning, and the winter sunshine made even the shelters across the road look pleasant, now that a covering of grass had grown over the once mounds of dark-brown earth.

Sister arrived back with a flurry. 'Now, Johanna. It is Johanna, isn't it?'

'I'm usually called Jo … '

Sister interrupted her: 'Good, Jo then. I need you straight away. Would you take Maureen to the theatre please? We are short-staffed today and there is nobody else to do it.' She watched as Jo removed her Red Cross raincoat and fixed her white cap.

'Yes, that will do – now please hurry!' Sister Brown went straight from the office with Johanna almost running at her heels. She stopped abruptly at the entrance of the ward, studied Jo's strained, flushed face for a moment, and then tapped her gently on the arm and smiled apologetically.

'It's all right, my dear. You just take the trolley to the theatre and then wait to bring it back – quite simple.'

Jo was relieved at that, but even so, the responsibility of taking a patient all the way to the theatre in this huge and strange building appalled her. She squared her shoulders, however, and followed Sister into the ward, where a young girl was already settled on the long trolley, looking pale and tired.

'This is Maureen,' Sister said. 'Jo is taking you to the theatre now, my dear, you'll soon be back with us.' She stroked the strained young face with gentle hands.

'Right along the corridor, Jo, turn left, then right and go as far as you can. You'll see the signs … now off you go.'

Jo caught hold of the top end of the trolley and started on her way. It felt heavy, cumbersome and unwieldy. The corridor was polished, and she was thankful for her rubber-soled shoes. She was progressing quite well, taking time off from looking about her to smile occasionally at the young girl in her charge.

'Are you new here?' Maureen asked, and Jo explained that she was a weekend helper.

'I think I know you,' the girl said dreamily … 'you go to Red Cross lectures at Dulwich with my sister Susan. I've seen you there when we've met her.'

'Yes … I remember,' Jo replied. 'And you got hurt when they bombed the school a while ago, didn't you? Susan told me about it. Are you having another operation this morning?'

'I have to go to the theatre to have the dressings changed … It would be too painful otherwise. I don't know whether they'll save my legs or not. The doctors try to cheer me up, but it's such a long painful time and …' Maureen turned her head away, as the tears gathered in her eyes. There was nothing Jo could say, so she squeezed the child's shoulders and hurried on her way.

About an hour later, Sister called her into the office.

'Sorry about rushing you this morning, Jo. Now I want to welcome you. We really do you know, for staffing problems are desperate. You will cover mainly for any of the nurses who go off-duty, for we never know when we'll need another pair of hands. You will never be left on your own; there will always be a qualified nurse in charge, but there are many, many ways that you can help. Let's have some tea and then I'll introduce you to the rest of us, and of course, the patients!'

Jo found she accepted hospital life very quickly. The ward was large and filled with some thirty-two beds, all occupied with mostly elderly or old ladies who'd been injured and some made homeless by the bombing. She was bewildered on the first morning to be asked by one of the patients to scratch her toes, only to find that both legs had been amputated.

'Pretend you're doing it … there's a good girl.' The words were spoken by a patient in the next bed. A tiny wizened face looked at her from over well-stretched bed covers. Two bright button eyes observed her keenly, as she did as suggested and found that the amputee seemed comforted by the 'pretend' ministrations. Mrs White smiled and said, 'Well done.' Jo stopped briefly, tidied an already immaculate bed, and to convey her thanks. She learned that Mrs White had been in hospital for some months now, her body still and useless, but with a mind like quicksilver. From her prone position she watched the ward with interest and had noticed Jo's arrival on that first day. She had also noted the bewildered expression on her face as the weekend progressed … that and the tiredness! She had thought then of her own young days. At eighteen or nineteen years she was having the time of her life … parties … long dresses … boy friends. 'Poor little lass,' she thought. 'We expect far too much of children these days.' Mrs White had a smile for Jo all the time, and would call a high-pitched 'she's back again,' when Jo appeared on the ward early each Saturday morning. When she could, Jo spent time talking to her and found that the old lady had sustained a back injury during a bombing raid, when her house had collapsed around her. She told Jo all this quite matter of factly, until she mentioned her pet yellow canary. 'I loved the bonnie little chap,' she told Jo. 'He used to sing to me all the time, but then I expect he's waiting for me "up there" – don't you?' Mrs White raised her eyes to the ceiling, a hint of tears and mischief in them.

Nearer to the door of the ward were some six patients all suffering from recent bombing injuries. Amongst these was Maureen. Sometimes Jo used to help with turning her, and was horrified to see that both legs were encased in plaster from ankle to thigh … stained plaster, where the wounds beneath were still seeping. Maureen used to cry … 'No, please no …' before the nurses even touched her. It made Jo go cold for the cries increased as they gently moved her body to ease the pressure on any one point; prodding pillows to prop up her back, or underneath her knees. When finally it was over Maureen lay back exhausted, keening soft little cries that, if anything, were more disturbing than her loud protests. Johanna asked Sister about her.

'We don't know quite how she'll do at this stage Jo. She's not strong in herself, but if the infection doesn't start improving soon … well then, we will just have to amputate.' Jo shuddered … on such a young girl this seemed impossibly cruel.

There were humorous times too. Dr Andrews came in one morning elated with the news that he'd just become a father; a fact that was obviously too much for him, for he fell asleep over his coffee in Sister's office. Sister Brown put a white nurses' cap on his head, tied it under the chin and painted both his cheeks with bright blobs of lipstick. Everyone heard about it and came to peek. Matron came too, and if she noticed that she was led by an agitated Sister past her office, both on entering and leaving the ward, she said nothing, and kept the same calm, half-smiling expression and professional manner throughout her visit. Just after she had left, Dr Andrews appeared at the office door, white hat in hand, dishevelled, and with bright-red cheeks where he'd tried, without success, to wipe off the lipstick! It was obvious that Matron had known what had occurred when she met him shortly after in the corridor and congratulated him on being a father … 'and Dr Andrews,' she concluded, 'Plenty of soap and water for … well, you know!'

Sometimes local ladies would come into the ward just to chat to the patients or join in a singsong. At these times the cheery porter would take over, livening things so that all the old ladies were chuckling.

Matron was solely in charge and was held in great respect throughout the hospital. She always had a smile and a kind word for Jo, who thought her a gentle, pleasant person. She couldn't understand, but was amused at the agitation which her visit engendered prior and during the ward rounds. The beds would be tidied, each patient settled firmly with arms under sheets, which were then pulled tight under chins, and the corners of the bedspreads enveloped neatly. Trolleys were cleared or covered; the sluice room thoroughly cleaned, and the lockers placed exactly in the same position throughout the ward. The patients suffered all this, at times even catching some of the nurses' agitation. Matron though was no dragon, as was obvious on the day the hospital secretary arrived in a breathless state and tiptoed onto the ward during her visit. He was clutching a bunch of spring flowers … 'For you sister …' he called, hurrying forward. His smiling face registered shock as he observed Matron; he had intruded on the 'holy of holies' – Matron's ward round. He stopped in his stride, lost his balance and fell flat on his face. The nurses were appalled, but not so Matron. She collapsed on a chair by the desk weak with laughter. 'Well done, John,' she said. 'Sister Brown, you have an admirable suitor!'

Jo came to love her days on the ward. She loved it when, on arrival, she was greeted by the long-term patients; loved it as she went from bed to bed tidying; helping patients with hair-brushing; writing letters for them and being useful in a million other little ways. The old ladies always had a kind word and a smile for her, and she was happy seeing them animated. So many times she observed them, looking so old and half-alive as they slept, and had wondered at their powers of endurance. Johanna enjoyed walking the length of the ward, now quietly efficient in her soft-soled shoes; her uniform starched; apron bright and clean, and her hat, with the red cross embroidered on the front, set well on her soft loose curls, now tied in a bun. She felt good, and knew that she looked good! Helping made her feel special, and each weekend became easier, so that finally Mrs Dingle relaxed over losing her daughter for Saturday and Sunday, and indeed, it made her feel less guilty herself when she spent most of the weekends at the Home with her charges. Jo had one wish at that time ... 'How I wish that Bryn could see me now.'

Meanwhile, Bryn was expecting to go abroad for further training, but while waiting for the boat he was posted to an operation airfield in Yorkshire. It was a Bomber Command airfield, and it was obvious to Bryn that they were taking some severe losses. He wrote to Jo: 'They have put us to work in the bomb dump. Imagine rolling 500-pound bombs down a ramp until they stop with a "clang" against the last one in the row ... The armourers assure us it's quite safe. I do hope so, for I don't want to get "my wings" that way!'

A week before the Easter holidays, Mrs Dingle announced that they'd be able to go to Widegates for a few days. Pendower House was now operating, with some twenty children already installed there. A local nursing sister was in charge of them, with the help of two local ladies who came in from the nearby village daily. Jo's mother wanted to check that all was working well and to arrange schooling for two of the older children. It had been hard for her to relinquish the responsibility of running the new Home, particularly too as she got on so well with Miss Burnett, but at the last moment, it had seemed impossible for her to leave the Beckenham Home, which had been temporarily reprieved from closure. She was still needed there to manage with the placement of the charges she felt so very keenly about.

'I can't go yet, Jo,' she had said. 'There's nobody else willing to take on the task at this end. We can keep going for another year now that funding has been approved – well, I just can't go.' She looked appealingly at her daughter, who was rather stunned by the news, although she knew well the difficulty of making such a decision, for her mother was being pulled in two directions over this. Jo knew just how much her mother had longed for a change; for the quietness of Pendower House; for a chance to watch the children come back to life and new-found happiness in the wonderful gardens and beautiful old house that would welcome them. But, nevertheless, Jo understood her attitude on this. She was rather like that herself when it came to responsibilities. After completing her secretarial course she had planned to look for work in the West Country ... 'But they would manage somehow,' Jo thought. 'I'll wait for mum!'

Perhaps, now that things were improving on the home front, as far as the war and bombing were concerned, perhaps it won't be too bad, they decided together, as they talked over future plans into the night.

Johanna had a letter to say that Bryn was leaving for America just after Easter to complete his training. They arranged to meet at Widegates ... he would leave from there! James was already on leave when Jo and her mother arrived at St Austell, and he met them in the old Bedford truck. He looked wonderful in uniform; it seemed to make him look taller somehow, and he wore the khaki with pride and grace.

'Lovely to see you, Jo,' he said, as he hugged her close. 'Bryn doesn't arrive until this evening. I thought you might like to come and meet him with me.'

'That would be wonderful, James. How long have you got? Where do you go next?'

'Hold hard ...' James laughed down at her. 'I'm not supposed to let out secrets ... but I've got a seven day pass. I'll be able to take Bryn to the station when he leaves on Thursday. I have to go to Wadebridge that day for dad, but will get back in time to meet him off the passenger ferry.'

Jo was quiet. 'Thursday ... so soon.' she thought. 'Just three days and then he'll be gone!'

James continued ... 'Bryn has to visit his uncle at Taunton tomorrow, and we are going to drive down together, then he hopes to "borrow" you for the next two days, or at least I think that's what he has planned.' They lapsed into silence, Jo feeling her tummy churn at the thought of so little time left with Bryn. James watched her, glancing sideways and catching her reflection in the driving mirror.

'Poor Jo,' he thought. 'She and Bryn really do care for each other. I ought to be jealous, but I'm not. I suppose it's because I love them both ... they are both so very dear to me.'

He turned to her for a moment. 'It will be all right, Jo,' he murmured. 'It will be all right.' She started, and then threw him a grateful glance.

'Sorry, James ... all these good-byes lately are not much fun. It's not like the old days, when we all said '"cheerio – see you in the spring" and knew that we would. I hate the uncertainty of wartime life – really hate it!'

Early the next morning Jo had a telephone call from Mr Trevarder, asking if she'd collect a Margaret Wyatt from the station.

'The boys have gone to Taunton ... do you mind?' Jo assured him that it would be all right, then he laughed. 'She'll be recognisable by her curly red hair!'

Margaret Wyatt was to help at Pensilva. She was a land army girl with very little experience of farming, but an interest that would make up for that, a strength that Jim Trevarder needed now, and a lively young person to help in so many ways, now that James was settled in the army. His parents missed him terribly, both as a companion and for the help he had afforded round the farm. He'd always been there to cope with seemingly impossible tasks, or to cushion them when journeys necessitated using the unwieldy Bedford truck. He'd helped and advised the farm-workers, had run the kitchen garden alone and, most of all, had been a happy, cheerful person to have around.

It was James who'd suggested a land girl. He had met some whilst in Scotland and sung their praises to his parents. 'They are so keen, dad, and love the new way of life. Much better than a young boy whom you'd have to train, and then perhaps lose to the war. You need someone to help with the animals; who can drive a tractor and the truck, who's bonny and pleasant and has no problems. Now I think I've got the right person for you!'

James had heard of Margaret Wyatt through a friendly farmer in the north. 'Had to let her go,' he'd said ... 'now that we are running the farm down and getting a smallholding. I've got her address though James, if you want it. I should contact her quickly for I think she's on leave at present and might just be directed to another place. Get in quick, lad ... she's bloody marvellous!'

James had been surprised to hear from her almost by return, and even more surprised to learn that for three years she'd held down a senior secretarial post with the London County Council.

'I just couldn't stand it any more ... the noise ... the mess ... the feeling of futility. So I packed it in, had my training and haven't regretted it a bit. Yes, I'd love to come to Cornwall. Just say when and where!' She had enclosed a photograph. It was black and white, but on the back she mentioned that her hair was 'red'. It was certainly very curly, and her round face looked pleasant and jolly. She'd do for mum and dad, James thought.

Now Jo waited as the train pulled in from London. Out bounced the most lively, colourful girl she'd ever seen. Red hair bobbing, bags and containers strung all round her as she struggled up the platform. She was dressed in bright yellow. 'Just like a daffodil,' thought Jo, who knew her immediately and went to help.

'Hello – I'm Johanna Dingle. Mr Trevarder asked me to meet you. Welcome to Cornwall.'

They liked each other instantly. On the journey to Pensilva Jo told her about the family there. It was reassuring talk, for Margaret had been uncertain as to the situation at her new place of work.

'You'll be happy there. They are marvellous people.' Jo concluded. Margaret then asked about her home, and was surprised to hear that Jo was still coping with life in London.

'I can't help it really,' Jo replied. 'Mum is there, and I'm doing secretarial training in town. Then of course there's the weekend hospital duty.' The girls chatted as they left the station; were still talking as they waited for the car ferry, and even as they drew up at Pensilva. Here Jo had to interrupt Margaret to say: 'here we are …' and then watched her new friend's reaction at her first sight of Pensilva with amusement.

It was a beautiful home, set in about an acre of colourful garden, with the rolling hills and fields of the farm enclosing it, and stretching to the moor. Rhododendrons and azaleas were in bloom now, creating masses of vibrant colours, and covering the several archways formed over the drive hung a soft mauve, the beginnings of wisteria blooms. The smell was exhilarating.

Pensilva House was a black-and-white dwelling, unusual in these parts. It was long and narrow, boasting four gabled windows, whose glass this bright morning caught the sun and reflected it widely. The lower front of the house had been built out into a long sun-room, extending the entire length of the building. The whole sat in a slightly elevated position, and yet, with the shrubs, trees and fields around, it gave the impression of a house 'nestling'.

Margaret sat and looked, eventually making one comment only.

'I don't think I have ever seen anywhere quite as beautiful as this home.'

And now it was time for him to go! He was to take the evening train to London from St Austell. Good-byes had been said to the aunts and uncle Tom … light easy farewells, given to hide the true feelings, and to make the parting easier, though Johanna had been surprised and touched to hear her uncle's gruff voice, break on his … 'good-bye, lad … see that you come back to us now', and then to see the long, sincere and gentle look that he gave to Bryn. Bryn had made no reply, but shook hands firmly, and gave a friendly tap on the older man's shoulder. Then, with a wave to the aunts, he had made his way to the side of the barn where his bicycle lay on a mound of grass, just where he had flung it those three hours before, when they'd met in the yard and, with hand holding hand, had climbed awkwardly over the stile and taken the path to their special place on the headland.

'Now he was to go …' Jo had collected her bicycle from the small covered way attached to the cowshed and was waiting for him whilst he arranged his cycle clips. Sensing her watching, Bryn inclined his head to one side and looked up at her. His eyes sparkled, and his grin was wide and generous, as he announced that he'd beat her down the lane. She had noticed previously that his lips were tight, as if to hide emotion, and realised that the parting with uncle Tom, who'd been his mentor, friend and often surrogate father for so many years, had upset him more than he would like anyone to know.

Bryn bent over once more as he struggled with his clips, one strong hand rested on the bars of the bike to steady it, as he shifted his weight from one leg to the other. His neck was brown with the spring sun and winds. Strong tendrils of hair curled above the line of his collar, and she traced those curls all over his head with her eyes. Dark curls … she longed now to thread her fingers through them; indeed the feeling was so strong that it became a pain which shot through her whole being, and she quickly put her hands behind her, willing them to stay there, as she balanced the bike with her knees. She continued to watch him; his shoulders were hunched, bony shoulder blades showing through the old sweater that he'd worn for this day on the headland.

'Oh Bryn … come back safely,' she thought as she struggled against the feeling of loss that was already assailing her. He looked up at that moment … stopped still, his gaze holding hers in an intense look until she felt that he could read into her very soul. She was bewildered at the expression of appeal and question in his eyes, and dropped her gaze.

'And now it was time for him to go …' The phrase again beat into her mind as she raised her head, seeing the familiar landscape and buildings that comprised part of the farm, seeing them as through an unreal dream. It was as if time itself were standing still. She heard the bees droning in the honeysuckle on the fence and along the barn wall; heard the low chugging of a tractor engine as it moved slowly over the contours of the hill two fields away … heard the call of the skylark – seasonal bird, as it dipped and swerved, flying low near to the dry-stone walls of the farm, and the distant cry of the gulls as they weaved and turned in the eddies of wind over the headland. She felt the warm spring sun on her shoulders and neck, and for a moment recalled how they had both sat, shoulder to shoulder and facing out to sea – watching, as they had done for years, the wheeling of the seabirds, the wonder of the spindrift, as the wind whipped up the white foam, the currents and eddies, and the odd brown mass of weed that had of late been spoiling their otherwise perfect sealine. They had watched as two sailing boats came out from the shelter of the harbour, and as they had raced round the point; they had made playful bets with one another as to the one most likely to win. Watched as a large freighter, heavily loaded, made its way across the bay, leaving the pilot boat to return to the calm of the estuary. All this they had done together many times over the years, but today, she thought … today somehow was different. They weren't just watching, there had been an awareness of each other … an awareness that had hastened her heartbeat, and at one time, as Bryn leaned nearer to point out the direction of a flying cormorant, skimming the waves far below them … she had felt a blush come, and had turned away from him quickly, pretending not to understand.

Now she looked down again as he struggled with his clips. Her lips began to tremble. 'I'll cry in a minute, and then he'll think I'm stupid,' she thought. Jo gave a great sigh, and then slapped his hands as they steadied his handlebars, and shouted … 'Race you to the crossroads then!' She gave a huge push to her bike which sent it careering across the yard, through the gate and over the field path, scattering the bantams, geese and ducks as she went. Her breathing was heavy, her chest hurt and the tears that had threatened now overspilled. 'But at least Bryn can't see them,' she thought … 'and by the time we get to the crossroads I will hopefully have regained my composure!'

It wasn't really a race. Bryn was too torn with doubts and fears at his imminent departure. He took the field slowly, marvelling at the look he'd seen in Johanna's eyes. She did care, just as he did … he was sure! Why on earth hadn't he said something positive to her on their headland walk. He'd heard his pals say time and time again: 'We always ask the girls to wait for us … matter of principle … don't always expect them to, mind.' But that was it! He wanted Jo to wait, indeed hoped and prayed that she would. Hadn't it been his dream, their dream, since they were children, that one day they'd start a farm together, here, near to the headland that was so much part of them. He looked ahead to where she waited at the crossroads. 'I'll ask her … I must, before I go,' he thought.

Johanna was now in control of her emotions and greeted him with a bright smile. 'Slow coach – I won that easily!' If Bryn noticed that the smile was too bright and that the previous tears in her eyes still made them shine more than usual, he said nothing. He stood studying the highway.

'We will have to take care here,' he observed. 'The road is narrow and with all those bends, but let's try to ride side by side if we can.' However, it just wasn't to be. Vehicles came repeatedly from each direction. Jo had never seen this road so busy. Heavy army lorries on the way to the camp near to the moor pushed them into the hedge at the side of the road, and at one time, a tractor and trailer passing on a narrow bend necessitated them scrambling half-way up the bank for safety. Bryn held on to both bikes as it trundled slowly by. Even when they stopped at the stile to take one last look at Pencarrow Head, they had to share this moment with a small group of tired walkers, who'd decided to use that spot to rest and regroup. Bryn was desperate as they found themselves at the top of the hill with now only the steep, steep descent to the foot ferry before the parting.

'I wonder if James is there now,' commented Jo, her thoughts already flying ahead to the moment, not far off now, when she'd watch James's light-blue car, show itself as a speck fleetingly on the hill opposite, before plunging into the trees and away, away to St Austell and taking Bryn with it! They were both quiet as they walked their bikes down the hill. Bryn put an arm around her waist pulling her close, manipulating his bicycle with one strong brown hand.

'You'll write me often, tell me about everything won't you?' His voice was soft as he leaned over her.

'Of course I will … and …' she stopped as a huge painful tightness constricted her throat and threatened to choke her. She lost her breath for a moment …

'Hello, son … going now are you?' It was Ben from the shipyard, an old friend of Jim Trevarder's, who looked after Bryn's boat and who had helped teach him all he knew about sailing and the different moods and dangers of the sea. Ben was a stocky, thick-set man, with a well-used face, a broken nose and beetling brows over piercing blue eyes. An old fisherman's hat crowned his head, resting lightly on a mass of coarse greying curls. He wore thick navy trousers, a polo sweater and a large oilskin was flung over one shoulder, anchored there by the straps of a chunky fisherman's bag. He carried his rod over the same shoulder. Now he looked keenly at Bryn.

'I hoped to catch you to wish you luck. I'm just off for the afternoon fishing. The sea is running high today and should be good for pollack. The yard is closed, lad, but leave your bike in the back shed and I'll see that it gets back to the farm safely in the morning. All the best … you just show 'em what's what, eh?' After a long, strong grip of Bryn's hand, he plodded up the hills, whistling to himself with, as always, a blade of grass between his teeth.

'You'll be careful how you ride back, Jo, won't you?'

'Of course I will – don't worry about me, just you take care of yourself.' Jo had recovered her voice once more and gave him a quick smile as she reached in her saddlebag and produced a small rectangular parcel which she passed to him.

'You might like this to remind you of me sometimes,' she said, and ducked her head again to hide the blush that was fast spreading over her neck, face and head. The gift was a photograph of her taken on the headland during her last visit.

'I'll open it in the car … all right?' Bryn said, observing her keenly. 'And Jo – I'll never forget you … never!' Their eyes locked. His expression stern almost, and hers full of appeal and with pupils misted with unshed tears. There was so much to say, but now no time at all to say any of it. A feeling of peace came over Bryn as they continued to face each other … Johanna looked down, but he touched her gently under the chin and brought her face up to his once more. 'I never will, Jo … you know that don't you?' Johanna nodded her head, too overcome to speak, and they turned downhill once more, totally overcome with emotions that were bubbling, turning and churning within them.

Bryn was swept away at the quay by a small group of local friends who'd gathered to wish him well. His bike was tucked away in the back shed, and he was hustled to the waiting ferry, where Walter the ferryman had festooned the whole boat with bunting. Jo never really managed a 'good-bye'. Bryn was able to whisper a quick 'bless you Jo', as he hugged her tightly for a moment, before being clutched by friendly hands and hustled to the ferry. She stood alone on the quay … a little distance between her and the group, who were standing on the steps calling out happy, silly little messages. She looked over the water and saw a light-blue car; saw its lights flash … once, twice, and she knew that James would be there for his friend.

Bryn stood in the boat, one hand raised in farewell, and she thought her heart would break. She couldn't smile … His face was stern, his jaw tight, and as the boat turned to make its way over the river, the sunlight on the water, that had seemed to twinkle so merrily when they'd seen it from the top of the hill, blurred and fused as the quiet tears fell down her cheeks. She waited on the quay until the ferry-boat landed on the far side and she saw Bryn as he went up the ramp, and so onto the road towards the car. Waited, sad and lonely, for the fleeting last glimpse of light blue, as James's car rounded the bend and plunged into the wooded valley to St Austell, and then waited again until she could control her tears; only then did she turn to join the small group of friends, sitting quietly now on the quayside.

'All right, Jo?' Margaret said. 'I'll ride back with you.'

Exams were over in late June, and although the girls still attended college, rules were more lenient and free. Several of them, and Johanna was one of these, asked permission to visit places of interest in London so that they could familiarise themselves with various areas. It was depressing some days, when they found an area of complete desolation, where whole streets and landmarks had been wipe out by the bombing. They visited St Paul's Cathedral and marvelled at its beauty, standing brave and lonely amidst the rubble and ruin. Jo did fairly well with her exams and her marks were high in most subjects, but she had a lower typing speed than most.

She had been applying for various jobs since early May, and finally was accepted as in-patient secretary in a central London hospital. She thought with dismay of the continued travelling to town that this would necessitate, but she liked the thought of hospital work. Now she would learn about it from a completely new angle!

There was just time to squeeze in a short visit to Widegates in late July, before commencing work on 4 August. 'No more long summer holidays now,' she thought. 'Not ever!' Her journey to Cornwall, on her own this time, proved extremely difficult and long. The main line between London and Reading had been damaged, so the journey was slow from the start. Overnight bombing at Exeter caused more delay and a change of train; a long-drawn-out process. The day was wet, with gales blowing from the south, and at times the gusts of wind seemed to rock the carriages. As they travelled through Dawlish, the train slowed to a stop, then crawled along, for the seas were unusually high and had flooded the line. It felt strange creeping along on rails you couldn't see, and with tidal water on both sides of the train. Jo was glad when they finally arrived at St Austell. Margaret was there to meet her. Aunt Mollie had been to the station earlier, but couldn't wait because of the milking. Jo was pleased to see her friend, and doubly pleased that she'd brought some sandwiches.

'I knew you'd be hungry, Jo. It's taken you hours to get here today.'

Jo devoured them all. She had left her lunch at home on the kitchen table, realising its absence only when other passengers had begun to unwrap their food parcels. She had felt near to tears over it and, as the journey progressed, had felt sick with hunger.

She heard from Margaret that all was well at Pensilva, that James was due for embarkation leave shortly and that Mr Trevarder had employed another land girl – Jean Darley – and they got along splendidly.

'We share the cottage now,' Margaret said, by way of explanation. Jo knew it well, situated at the back of Pensilva, just where the fields gave way to the moor – a beautiful spot.

'It's like a dream,' Margaret continued. 'I don't ever want to go back to town living!'

'You'll have to find yourself a nice farmer and settle down here then,' Jo laughed. Margaret looked at her keenly, wondering at the innocence of the remark. Jo couldn't mean James, surely she knew how James felt about her ... everybody did!

During the week they went together to the headland. They approached it from South Down, looking over the sweep and curve of Lantic Bay and the little coves that can be reached only by boat from the sea. The headland looked majestic from this side with its wide grass paths that separated near to the edge of the cliff, one curving round and down, to finally end with a scrambling stone path to the beach and rocky foreshore, whilst the other led eastwards, towards Lantivet, past David's cottage, and on to another rocky headland, jutting southwards. Here the tiny village of Lansallos stands high, the church tower being a landmark for miles around.

Margaret loved it all. She was an energetic walker and they covered the distance quickly and with ease, talking all the while. As they stood on the cliff at Pencarrow Head and heard the sea surging over the rocks far below, rumbling and roaring a little, Johanna told her friend about Bryn. A gentle smile softened her lips as she spoke of how they'd both loved to come to this headland on storm-ridden days – when heavy swells gathered speed, forming lines of huge rollers which broke in foaming white at the base of the cliff and roared on until the shoreline broke their power.

Today the sea was bubbly and showing little puffs of foamy white, caught from the top of each wave and blown by the wind. Margaret listened, watching her friend's face as she spoke of Bryn. 'Poor James,' she thought. 'Poor old lad – he doesn't have a chance!'

David was in his cottage when they called. He made them welcome, and seemed pleased to meet a new face. He and Margaret hit it off straight away. Jo told him her news; what news she had of Bryn, and Margaret was able to get James 'up to date'. They spent a pleasant hour drinking tea and listening to the sea rushing and rumbling on the rocks below them.

'Come again both,' David said as they made to go. Then he turned to Margaret. 'Call in, won't you, any time you are passing!' Jo felt a certain relief, relief and pleasure that David might have some new company now that most of the old were scattered far and wide.

Veronica called at Widegates. She'd heard that Jo was there and so drove the long way round after dusk. They talked about the 'boys', compared news of Bryn from his letters, and then recalled some of the happy times they'd had together in the past.

'It's awful, this getting older,' Veronica's mouth turned down a little bitterly. 'This beastly war is taking our youth away – no fun, no dances, just boring work, day after day, after day …!'

'I know,' Jo sympathised. 'There seems to have been a war forever. The news is good though, and things will improve soon, I'm sure – don't let it get you down now!'

Johanna told Aunt Mollie about Veronica and was answered with a sniff and shake of the head.

'She always was a sulky girl – has things too much her own way at home. Do you know, Jo, she's the only young girl in Fowey who does nothing for the war effort. I asked her to collect for the Pendower House Fund last month, but she turned her pretty nose up disdainfully. I'll not ask her again!'

Jo wondered at this, for her aunt never spoke ill of anyone. Veronica must have really offended her by her manner. But there was more to it than that. Vee was continually asking about Bryn. She was persistent in her questioning … 'Did Jo and Bryn meet much in London? Is Bryn coming here when he comes back from America? Do you think he'll go to live in Beckenham with his uncle once more after the war?' Mollie and Tom had both discussed her.

'She's wanting Bryn for herself,' Tom had said. 'He's Johanna's though – thank goodness, and that is that!'

CHAPTER SEVEN

The London train seemed to drag on Monday morning, 4th August, when Johanna started her first day at work. The hospital, a solid Victorian building, stood in the middle of a wide pavement, near to the town hall. It had an imposing frontage, though the stonework was grey with dirt and each window sill was marked white where pigeons rested overnight. The bombing had been slight in this part of town, so all the windows were sound, but they looked dark and dull on this misty morning, dark and somehow solid. Jo stood for a moment looking up at her new place of work. She felt strangely apprehensive and would have given anything to be back at school or college, in familiar surroundings and with familiar people around her. However, she squared her shoulders, went up the three wide steps to the main entrance, pushed the door and entered. As the door clicked shut behind her, she became aware of her surroundings.

The entrance hall was large and square, sparsely furnished with two leather-covered easy chairs, and a wide table stood against one wall. The huge notice-board that hung above it was covered with pamphlets, and similar leaflets were stacked on one side of the table. Straight ahead was the iron cage of a lift. She could hear it trundling up out of sight somewhere, and two nurses were waiting by the lift gates, looking up through the cage to ascertain its progress. To her left was the office, where she'd been told to report, and looking over the highly polished wooden floor she saw a double door with a large notice above, on which she read 'Out-patients' Department'.

A tall woman came down the stone stairs at the side of the lift. She moved gracefully, with a slight swing to the hips that went strangely with her austere brown outfit and severe short haircut. She smiled.

'You must be Johanna Dingle. I'm Enid Bray. Come along in, we are expecting you.' Jo was then ushered into the office. It was a wide, almost grand room, with a huge centre table on which were the largest ledgers she'd ever seen; these were open as if being worked on. The windows, those that had looked drear from the outside of the building, afforded the room plenty of light. It was a bright room; walls washed in pale green, white paintwork and a beautifully carved fireplace. There were two desks both housing typewriters, and Johanna was directed to the one nearest the telephone switchboard. So began the most muddling day of her young life!

Having been given a quick résumé of what would be expected of her that day, which included a short, sharp lesson on the various wiles of the switchboard, Jo now sat at the typewriter with trembling knees and proceeded to type appeal letters. These were special letters comprising differing types: those that were sent to firms and factories, who either had an interest in the hospital or who regularly sent employees to the casualty department for treatment, or to people who had donated in the past and, it was hoped, would do so again. She typed slowly and with care, marking each card afterwards as she'd been shown. Soon a little pile of neat letters and envelopes grew on her desk. Jo was sure that the day would be easy and settled into a nice rhythm. She was content and felt safe behind her typewriter. But then the switchboard started playing tricks. Up to now she had answered only single calls, which had been immediately put through to the required person or department. Now all three incoming lines started to 'buzz'. She selected various holding keys and asked people to wait. Jo even managed to answer one or two enquiries about in-patients at this time. The list of patients was on the wall near to the switchboard, and general comments about 'making good progress' or 'quite comfortable' were indicated by the abbreviations 'mgp' or 'qc' by each name. It was the rule, and in most cases quite acceptable.

Jo's first mistake was with an incoming call for Matron. She had it 'on hold', contacted Matron in her office on the first floor and, with a polite, 'you're through now', inadvertently selected the wrong key and cut Matron's caller off! An irate call came through on the internal line, three outside calls came together, and Jo floundered badly. The whole board became a mass of buzzing keys, and she didn't know where to begin to get things right. Miss Bray fortunately came to the rescue. Her hands moved swiftly over the board, her soft voice apologetic to outside callers and to Matron, who had again rung down demanding better things of 'whoever is making such a mess of the switchboard'. Jo's humiliation was complete, and though she continued to answer the telephone, outwardly giving the appearance of being in command, inwardly her whole being was in a state of nervous tension in case the situation repeated itself. 'Why … oh why didn't the secretarial course include learning to operate a switchboard?' The phone became a frightening instrument, an instrument of terror. She jumped every time it rang, and coped nervously with each key she had to manipulate, so that by lunch-time she was an absolute wreck. Added to that, her appeal letters were suffering as her hands hit the wrong keys every time the switchboard buzzed, just as they'd done at the beginning of typing tests at college! The typewriter erasers in those days were harsh solid rubbers that had to be handled carefully, but that morning Jo rubbed holes in several sheets of notepaper! Miss Bray commented drily, 'This is a voluntary hospital, Johanna. We can't afford to waste notepaper like that …'

Lunch-time did arrive though, and after a quick wash and tidy, all the clerical staff trooped down the stone staircase to the basement for lunch in the nurses' dining-room. It was a cheerless room, and the route to it even more so, down around the lift-shaft from the hall, along a narrow stone passage that housed the stationery and store cupboards, and finally into this cold, bare basement room. Clean, clinical walls and several white-covered tables, where groups of nurses sat chatting quietly. Matron appeared, and immediately a hush came over the room … Jo was back at school!

She enjoyed the meals provided, however, and found that the puddings satisfied her longing for sweet things completely. The windows were set high in the walls and afforded a narrow view of the pavement outside. Jo spent lunch-time after lunch-time, watching feet pass by the window. Big ones, dainty ones, flat shoes, high heels, heavy plodding feet and light stepping ones. Policeman's feet and often the dust-smothered boots of workmen … she used to imagine what the rest of the body looked like … it became a game!

Her feet passed the same window each day as she walked off the hot, steamy puddings. Most of the roads were untouched by war in this area, and she spent a nosey half-hour peering into wide windows level with the pavements. Each road was different, high graceful houses gave way to tiny terraced dwellings; closely packed and with gardens that really could be described as 'backyards'. Some of the larger buildings housed offices below ground, and in these the lights would be blazing, enabling Jo to see in clearly, opening, for her, other dimensions of people at work.

There were always people about; people rushing to catch the underground trains; people with shopping bags, hoping to get something special for tea, men with briefcases, bowler-hatted and dark-suited. She was continually reminded of the gentleman at Hatton Gardens eating lunch with her college friends. Jo was content and smiled readily at anyone. It was natural to her to be friendly. Nobody had warned her that in London it was better to remain singular and aloof. Her smile was very nearly her undoing, for one bright summer day, soon after she'd started work, she walked on light happy feet to Edgware Road. She was thinking of Bryn and smiling at her own thoughts, when she caught and returned a smile from a dark-haired man. He was of average height, nicely suited and about 45 years of age. A father figure, she thought. He walked towards her, commented on the beauty of the day and then walked with her. Jo was a little flattered at first, and then peeved at his presence; she had been content on her own, with her dreams of Bryn.

'How much further?' the man said suddenly.

'Oh, I work just round the corner,' and Johanna mentioned the name of the hospital. The man reached out – grabbed her arms tightly, his face suffused and with eyes like steel. Jo tried to back off …

'I don't like a tease,' he growled. 'Don't dare do that again!' and with a last push of her arms that almost overbalanced her, he set off, back in the direction from which they'd come.

Jo felt slighted, troubled and didn't understand, but she mentioned it to Miss Bray later in the afternoon. She then had her first real lesson on sex: the seamier side of sex. Jo scarcely believed what she heard, but was sufficiently chastened and scared. On her return journey home that evening, she kept her eyes down, resisting even the ticket collector's cheery 'goodnight miss, take care' as she went through the barrier at Charing Cross station. For a while every male was suspect, the usual friendly smile was severely controlled, so that anyone making an innocent overture was instantly rebuffed by the cold stare he collected in return. She had a lot to be thankful for to Miss Bray, as Jo realised later in life, but it was a rude awakening, and the thought of the narrow escape played on her mind for weeks. Later she accepted and coped with even the seamiest street in town, learning how to walk with deliberate purpose, never to dawdle and, most of all, 'never to smile at strangers'!

It was some weeks later that she learned about VD. Whilst making lists of various clinics, and the number of patients attending them, she came across 'Special Clinic'. On enquiry, she was told by Miss Bray … 'Oh that's the VD clinic.' Jo was bewildered once again about this and anxious to pursue from so forthright a colleague the meaning of something that had troubled her for years. VD headed all the red notices in the public toilets. It was a warning to all who read it: 'VD is catching …' She recalled with what care she selected a toilet cubicle to use; with what diligence she checked on the toilet seat … it worried her! Once she had ignored her body's warning cries, choosing to pass the public lavatories and head for the train, a decision she regretted and never did repeat. Air-raids meant delayed trains, and sitting in agony in a packed railway carriage, all because of a fastidiousness about public lavatories, was absolute folly. But how did one get VD?

Johanna had never discussed this with anyone. At one time a friend of her mother's had been talking about some young person they'd both known who'd contracted VD. Her mother, Jo noticed, was solicitous and a little embarrassed, casting anxious glances at her daughter. Not so the friend … 'Of course she knew about it – everyone knows about VD, don't they, Jo?' She had nodded her head in acquiescence, not wishing to lose face, and intending to ask her mother later. But the right moment never came. Girls of Jo's time led a very sheltered existence, that and the fact that Jo never sought out companionship of groups of girls of her own age; indeed at one time London was not the place to find young people at all. Her dreamy nature meant that she often preferred to be on her own. All this, had left her with an innocence which is perhaps unnatural in these modern times. 'Life' was not discussed, not even with her special companions Mary, Margaret and even Selina; it was not necessary – they had too much else to interest them and talk about.

After a few days, Jo was well settled at the hospital and found that she loved the work. Most afternoons were spent in the out-patients' department, either making notes on new patients and interviewing them or finding records for those who had attended previously. It was a friendly, busy department, and she noticed from the very first that the same gentle, conscientious attention was afforded to each and every patient, without regard to status or background. The clinics were large and often ran late, necessitating that she travel home later in the evenings, when the stations were quieter, and without the usual crush of people in the carriages, swinging back and forth as they strap-hung when seats were scarce. Occasionally Jo had a complete carriage to herself, and at such times she would settle, head back against the cushioned rest, listening to the rhythm of the train, and imagine she was going westwards, to Widegates, her headland and Bryn!

All her days at the hospital were interesting and full. She learned to cope with people; some thankful for the attention and care they'd received, others nervous and full of apprehension at an operation ahead of them. She visited the private wards, writing letters for patients committed to days on their backs with bandaged eyes. So many people to help!

The office work never eased because of the continual need to get the appeal letters out. These were typed whenever there was a quiet moment. Johanna found after a few weeks, that she could do them automatically, and so, to relieve the boredom, she would select a song, or a piece of music to hum … typing then within the rhythm of the tune! The pile of letters grew very quickly. Miss Bray did check these very carefully though. Jo caught her going through her work looking for errors. She never could understand how her young colleague could type correctly to music, changing the tempo as the tune changed.

Weekends were still spent at the local hospital as a Red Cross nurse. The men's ward was short-staffed for a while, and she was directed there to help. Initially Jo was shy and nervous, but the patients teased her quite naturally, and she soon got used to their banter and learnt to find sharp answers for them. The men were mostly very young or middle-aged, and suffering from minor injuries sustained whilst helping with fire-watch duty, or helping victims out from dangerous buildings, or a casualty of bombing themselves. One lad of almost 19 years had actually fallen through a hole in the floor, some 20 feet up, when he'd been going for water to douse a small fire from an incendiary bomb. He had fractured both his feet and sustained a back injury that gave him a lot of pain. Nevertheless, he rarely complained. He had a keen and wicked sense of humour, which he used on everyone – even Matron. She made a special fuss of him and called him her 'dear boy'. With Johanna he was brotherly, asking about her life, her family, her interests, and she loved to watch his eyes light up when she spoke of Bryn, and then of Bill, now in the midst of fighting in North Africa.

'I'm going to join up as soon as I'm fit, Jo. Navy for me though … I'll follow the sea, just like dad.' She learned then that his father was first officer on one of the merchant ships that continually, and in great danger, ran the gauntlet of German submarines to bring food, ammunition and other things necessary to our isolated island's war effort.

James managed to get to see her in London at the end of his embarkation leave. He was waiting outside the hospital one warm sunny evening, looking spendidly fit, and they walked to Regent's Park from there. The park was welcoming after the dusty streets, and they found a central seat which afforded them a long view of shrubs, trees, flower-beds and the immaculate grass areas. Some air-raid shelters had been positioned here, but to the side of the park, so that much of its original beauty remained for people to enjoy.

James told her of his training in Scotland, of the beauty of the mountains, the midges and the mists.

'I always felt at home on those misty days, Jo. Even the damp smell on the heather was just like our moor!'

She studied him as he spoke. How much older he looked, and he was leaner, harder after his training. Jo told him of her life at both hospitals, of her trauma on the first day at real work with the switchboard, and he laughed aloud at her discomfort. She mentioned her visit to Widegates and of Margaret and David.

'You've been down since, James. Have they met – properly, I mean?'

'Oh yes, and it's good to see David content. He walks over the high moor to the girls' cottage some evenings for musical sessions. Mum says she can hear it at Pensilva. I joined them just a day or two ago, but somehow it wasn't the same without you and Bryn.' James was quiet for a short while, then asked:

'Have you heard from him recently?'

'Oh yes. He writes regularly, James, and seems very content. Funny to think that he's been gone for such a short while … it seems like forever. What will I do with both of you so far away?' Her tone was pensive as she watched the ducks come waddling over from the nearby lake, intent on searching out titbits.

'Write lots of letters to me Jo … I shall expect it!' James drew her close for a moment. 'Look after yourself, keep happy. I'll fix the war for you, you'll see.' She smiled up at him, grateful for his ability to change her sombre mood.

'Of course I will, James … and you write often too.'

Bryn wrote nice cheery letters to Johanna. He had made several comments about the crossing being grim, but did not, or perhaps could not elaborate on this. However, he did mention the strange feeling he had as the miles gathered between them, and of the time spent on 'lookout duty' for enemy planes, mines and U-boats. 'I did my turns of duty on the four-hourly watch … a strange, lonely feeling at night, and particularly when I had to walk a "cat-walk" which went right out over the water with nothing but swirling blackness below me. I often thought that nobody would know if I slipped in – or something awful reached out to swallow me up. I'm so thankful now to be on solid ground.'

He was settled now in Canada and training quite seriously for his wings. That he was happy with life was obvious by the several remarks he made, and that he was loving flying was revealed by the comments he made about the gulls over the headland. 'Now I almost know what they feel like … so free!' He wrote of the country, of people he met, and he wrote again and again of his longing to settle somewhere in the West Country, and to start a farm. 'It would be good, Jo, wouldn't it?' She knew somehow that she was included in his future, but sometimes, when she reread his letters, Jo looked for more from him – more commitment with words. She would have been so happy with three 'special ones', but they didn't come, and so her letters to him remained bright and breezy and non-committal too! She told him of various happenings at the hospital; of London and the bombing, which was thankfully much less now. She spoke of the drabness of their lives in London and of the bravery of people – but all this only fleetingly. Mostly she wrote of Widegates and her longing to be there. As her pen filled the pages, she saw the future, her dream of the future, with Bryn. It was so clear that it made her restless and impatient.

'Why does the war go on and on?' she thought. At times like this she would go walking, covering the ground quickly, but this didn't always give her the peace she sought, because each local road and park had been walked with Bryn in the past ... they were full of memories! Jo was erratic in her moods towards her mother, who did all she could to cushion her path.

'Jo, be patient. Things will get better. Why, they are improving all the time ... just be patient!'

One evening Johanna jumped up from the easy chair near to the fireplace, stalked out of the room, slamming the door shut. 'You don't understand at all – you just don't understand,' she shouted as she rushed upstairs to the seclusion of her own room. Her mother sat stunned for a while, and then whispered to herself, 'Oh, but I do, Jo ... indeed I do.'

Mrs Dingle asked her to attend the autumn show at Raymond's school. It was a bright bawdy affair, with her saucy-faced brother dressed as a pirate. She envied the boys their way of life at the camp. Everywhere was green and fresh in its woodland setting; a complete village, where the war could not impinge. They ate dainty buns cooked by the boys, cups of tea were handed round by the boys, and groups of these same bright-eyed, well-scrubbed youngsters showed them round the farm and workshops. It was the clear eyes that her mother noted too.

'Look, Jo, these children are never awakened, their sleep is never disturbed as in London, just look at their bright eyes!'

Raymond was longing to come home and was promised a weekend before the Christmas break. It was cancelled though, as half the school had come down with a virus, and it was thought wise to contain the infection. Ray remained fit, however, and his letters showed he'd had a marvellously funny two weeks helping on the farm, and even doing a stint in the kitchen, when the staff there began to succumb. He wrote of the pigs getting loose and playing havoc with the kitchen garden; of the boys who'd collected the eggs safely, and then decided to take a short cut back to the main house. They had been chased by several heifers and fallen into a pit of slurry, breaking all the eggs and getting themselves into an awful, smelly mess. He wrote of the silage cutting and the smell that stayed in the mouth for hours afterwards, then finally he described how he and a friend watched a Beaufighter doing stunts from Holmby Hill. A plane for fun, thought, Jo ... 'now that has to be a promise for the future.' She realised though that the pilot of that plane had probably been dipping and weaving in real combat with an unseen enemy.

Selina Williams, the pilot's daughter, married her sailor at St Lowell church in early autumn, and both Jo and her mother visited Widegates for a weekend to attend this. Selina had known Bob for some years: she was older than Jo and had worked in an accountant's office in Fowey since leaving school some five years previously. Bob was in the navy, so they'd decided that it was pointless to look for a home of their own at this time. Mr Williams had converted the top of the old barn attached to his house on the Polruan headland and had made a small flat for them there. They could come and go as they pleased, but Selina would not be totally alone for the long spells when Bob was away at sea.

It was a beautiful wedding. Perfect weather for October, with a misty cool morning that had developed into a bright sunlit afternoon. A colourful marquee had been set up in one of Widegate's fields, almost opposite the church, and for two or three days the kitchen at the farm had been overflowing with helpers, all preparing special food for the occasion. Aunt Mollie had made and iced the cake, the fruit having been saved over many months by them all for this special event. The inside of the huge tent was hung with garlands of greenery, with tall flowers set around each support pillar. Jo arrived in time to help with the flower decorations for the tables and the church. She chose to do the latter herself, loving the quiet peace of the old grey building, after the hustle and bustle that was taking place at Widegates. She had made garlands for the end of each pew, choosing flowers from the garden and hedgerows. After setting them in place, she stood back to admire the effect. The little church looked quite beautiful, and the smell of the blooms hung sweetly in the air.

'Lovely isn't it, Jo, and thank you.' It was Richard Williams who had come to see that everything was ship shape for his daughter's big day. 'How's young Bryn?' he added. Jo told him all she knew and, as he left, she sat herself down in a front pew for a while. Talk of Bryn always unsettled her. 'If only it were us getting married, Bryn … if only.'

Mollie found her niece there, sitting as if in a dream. She didn't disturb her, and later Johanna wandered back to Widegates to join in the last flurry of preparation: that of getting the food to the marquee. The farm had offered the use of their kitchen for the wedding preparations, being the nearest home to the church. Mollie was thinking it would be a good practice run for when Jo and Bryn had their special day, for she never doubted that this would happen. 'It is meant to be,' she murmured to herself, watching Jo fondly as she put delicate parcels of cakes and sandwiches into baskets, in readiness to transport them up the lane.

The sun shone on the bride that day. Selina, a slight, almost frail girl, with straight dark hair and blue eyes, looked very lovely in her dress and veil. It had been her mother's and had needed very little alteration. Mr Williams had been startled to see his daughter when she first came downstairs … 'She looks like you, my dear,' he smiled at his wife, now a plump, pretty 50 year-old.

Bob, tall and handsome in his officer's uniform, made his vows in a clear strong voice. Three rousing hymns were sung and then, as the day permitted, the whole congregation followed the bride and groom, to walk along the lane to the entrance of the field and the marquee. It was a delightful village wedding.

Everyone enjoyed it, and almost everyone had helped in some way or another. The food was enjoyed, the cake cut, the speeches made, and finally the happy couple were waved on their way for a short honeymoon in St Ives. Only Veronica felt it 'not quite right'.

'I intend to have a proper reception in a hotel when I get married,' she told Jo as she left for home, leaving a contented, chatty group of women, men and girls, still in wedding finery, to clear away and tidy Widegates' huge kitchen for Mollie and Edith.

Since hearing news that a Sicily landing had been achieved by the British forces, 'on the soft underbelly of Europe', Churchill's quote, Jo wondered often how James was faring. Some of her concerns for Bryn and Bill had now transferred themselves to him as well, for she knew he was involved in fighting somewhere in the Mediterranean.

A letter came, and she learned that he had landed in Sicily on the third day. His letter was chatty, but he complained a little about the arid land and the heat which was particularly searing in the south of the island; the contrast in temperature for cold-blooded northern people was appalling. Food was scarce and amenities most unpleasant, but he sounded overall quite buoyant. He had been fascinated by the oval tomatoes that grew wild in the sand and the prickly pears that lined every road.

Johanna wrote back telling him of the state of things in London and of the rush, rush, rush of her life there. 'Mum used to say – all work and no play makes Jack a dull boy! Does that apply to females as well, James? If it does, then it's all wrong, for my life seems all work, all direction, but it is far from dull. I spent two long hours in the records room at the hospital yesterday, trying to find notes for one of the consultants. The patient concerned hadn't attended the clinic for some six years, and his notes were stacked away in a basement room. It was dark, cold and very spooky, and I jumped at every little noise; even when the hot water pipes creaked! Strange how quiet and isolated I felt down there, when I knew of all the activity going on above me. I almost hoped for a warning to give me an excuse to go upstairs. I found the notes and fortunately made my escape, rushing up the stone stairs as if a thousand ghosts were after me!! Remember when Tom used to tell us 'spooky' stories to frighten us? I've no doubt if I told him of this little episode he'd make much of it and I'd be scared to venture into the basement again.

'Tom doesn't ride any more, James. Such a shame, for it gave him a certain amount of freedom round the farm. He gave me "Horse" for my birthday and I'm thrilled that he is mine. We get along famously. He's such a gentle old thing and we look after each other well. Uncle Tom is happy that Horse can now stay on the farm. Sallie has had to go. She was always too nervous for him, but is happily settled on a farm near Bodmin. I can still remember Tom's first schooling of her, way back during our last long summer holiday together. I can't believe that four years have gone by, and all "devoted" to the war!

'It is Monday morning, bright sunshine outside, softened by a light autumnal mist. The trees are colourful, but the leaves now sadly disappearing! I'm hoping to get an earlier train this morning and will walk through the "rec" now to enjoy it's cool sweetness and think of you both.

'My love, and take care …'

CHAPTER EIGHT

October and November passed slowly in a mist of greyness. It was a hazy time, with only the occasional glimpse of a weak autumn sun to lend a little light to the odd hour and to brighten the changing leaves. They fell softly from the trees; no winds to tear them off and scatter them, but they collected round the boles of the trees in deep carpets of yellow, tan and dark brown; lying damp and heavy in the moist autumnal air. Jo loved to brush through them with her shoes stamping a little, and then sniff the dank, earthy smell that emanated from them when she walked through the recreation ground to her train.

The garden shelter became very damp and the bedding musty. Mrs Dingle brought it all in to air by the warm kitchen stove and the house smelled strangely of mildew – an unpleasant smell, Jo thought.

Raymond wrote that he had hurt his leg, having slipped whilst clambering over a stile during a cross-country run. He had cut his knee deeply on barbed wire. The wound had bled freely, but he finished the course, coming in second. As an afterthought he mentioned that the local hospital had put in several stitches and that he'd had a tetanus injection, so they weren't to worry. A letter arrived from the school to confirm this on the following day. Mrs Dingle asked Jo to accompany her to the camp the coming weekend, but an air-raid in the early hours of Thursday morning stretched an already overworked staff at the local hospital with the resulting new intake of casualties, and Jo was needed there. The staff were indeed weary and tired-eyed when she reported for duty early on Saturday morning, after seeing her mother off on the bus for her visit to Surrey and Raymond.

'Good, Jo – you're here,' Sister greeted her. 'Will you take Denise to the theatre and stay with her, please?' A trolley was thrust at her and on it a wide-eyed little girl of about two years stared up at her seriously.

'Hello, Denise. I'm Johanna,' she said as her hands guided the trolley round huge card boxes of equipment left stacked near to the lift. Tears welled from the child's eyes, but she managed a wan smile. Jo began to recite: 'Oh dear ... oh dear sighed the poor little mole. A fairy has tumbled right into my hole ...'

At the theatre door the trolley was whisked from her hands and she was told to don a gown and mask and then come in. It was Jo's first time actually inside the operating theatre. The light struck her first, the cleanliness and then the quiet. Theatre staff wore soft-soled slippers which, with their masks, headgear and long gowns, created a dream-like quality about the room as they moved, or rather, seemed to float about. To Jo their movements were slow, but of course first impressions are often strange, and it was the deliberate movements she was noting. Little Denise was already anaesthetised. Jo was asked to hold her shoulders firmly.

'She won't feel a thing, but both arms are broken and need to be manipulated before we can plaster them. Hold firm please, nurse.' Two brown eyes looked steadily at her. 'Have you been in the theatre before?' Johanna shook her head. 'You'll be all right. Just hold firm and remember, even though this little one might cry out – she won't feel it, or remember anything about it.' The surgeon was kind. Jo did as she was told and some minutes later watched in the plaster room, while Denise's little arms were encased in white from shoulder to wrist. She opened her eyes for a moment, smiled at Jo and went straight back to sleep.

When told about this later on Sunday evening, Mrs Dingle felt proud of her daughter. Jo seemed to be able to cope with so many things these days. 'Yes, I'm really proud of her,' she thought. Another side though wished that Jo could have a happy, lively life. One that she felt every young person deserved ... time for mixing with groups of young people her own age; time for dancing, for dressing up; eating out, and most of all she wished that her daughter had time for laughing. Jo was becoming far too serious, and at times, sad almost. It worried her!

It was true, for Jo coped with her days with an outward patience, but inwardly there was a seething impatience for the war to end. For Bryn to come back ... for life to be settled and happy, and that every day would not be fraught with weary war news. She hated each morning, looking at the tired faces of fellow travellers; some were withdrawn, with a look of utter weariness about them; each looked troubled in some personal way and with eyes that caught your glance, only to turn swiftly away, seeming to prefer to be isolated in their own thoughts and fears. The constant talk of bombs and bombing from those at work who had not experienced them grated on her, and always there was the overriding fear, that one day she might arrive home and find her house not there! Oh yes, she was weary!

Her mother never commented when Jo decided to turn the house upside down in a cleaning foray. Sometimes piling all the furniture in the middle of the rooms, to wash and then polish the dust away, until she was tired and dropped into bed exhausted; not to rest though, but to toss and turn fretfully, even on nights when no warning sounded, allowing most to sleep in peace. Mrs Dingle worried about her. She had lost weight, her hair lacked lustre and she had developed a nervous habit of rubbing her hands across her mouth.

'You ought to have a short spell in Cornwall, Jo. Why don't you come down with me when I check up on things at Pendower House? I shall have two young boys to take with me and you'd be a help on the train. Try and get some time off, there's a good girl.' And so it was that the first week in December saw her striding across Pencarrow Head with David Grant. She had run into him the day before, when he'd found her sitting on the jutting rocks; a smile on her face, but her eyes wet with tears. He'd said nothing – just enfolded her in his strong arms, whilst she cried, cried hard and long for the first time in months, and felt better for it.

'What would we do without you, David?' she murmured as she blew her nose and wiped her eyes.

'What would I do without all of you,' he chided. 'Come, Jo, … enough of this. Come and see what I've got to show you.' They had made their way along the cliff path to his cottage. The day was calm; the sea like slate, looking dark and cold on this December morning. The air had a tangy smell from the seaweed washed up during the gales of the last weeks and left to dry, high up on the rocks, out of reach of the tides, until the wind got up once more; the water heaved and washed it back to sea. Jo sniffed appreciatively. Oh, it was nice to be home …

David had a young otter in the little shed at the back of the cottage. It had been found down at the Pill in a very poor state, coated with mud and some oil from a passing freighter. The young lad who had found it had heard about David and his love of wild creatures, and he had walked up over the fields, crossed the heather hills and so out to the headland during a force five gale, with the little otter snuggled warmly under his jacket against his chest. David was very impressed with the boy, and John and he were now firm friends. The otter answered to the name of Pen. It was thriving, though it had taken David all his time and expertise to remove the oil and calm the little creature, but now he was charming, friendly and mischievous.

'Will you keep him?' Jo asked.

'Through the winter maybe, then he'll have to go back to the wild. John and I thought we'd take him further inland to one of the moorland streams. He'll stand more chance there.'

David then told her of Margaret, of the time they spent together, and how she was fast becoming as knowledgeable on wildlife as he was himself.

'She's visiting her family right now, and I miss her; miss her more than I can say.' He puffed at his pipe for a while, his gaze fixed fondly on Pen, who had scrambled into his lap and now lay curled up and quiet for a while. There was nothing to say, but Jo reached out her hand and squeezed his shoulder. She understood all about missing someone!

Jo met Veronica at the village hall in Fowey, where they were holding a special evening to raise money for the Pendower House Christmas party. Mr and Mrs Prouse had arranged this, and Johanna's mother had been delighted about it. Aunt Mollie secretly thought that they were making up for their daughter's deficiencies in this direction. The evening was well-attended. Various stalls sold local produce, and the first prize in the raffle was a real banana, brought back from abroad by Selina's husband. Mr Prouse was responsible for a 'bonny' punch, and with chairs pushed back, the tables folded and a local violinist to provide the music, almost everyone had a lively time, whirling, stamping and dancing to reels so well-known and practised locally. Jo won the banana and took it to Pendower House to share, where each child had a tiny ring of the fruit, and had to be encouraged to eat what for them was very strange food indeed!

The four days she spent in Cornwall were as good as a month's holiday to Jo. She was spoiled by the aunts, teased into eating mountains of food by uncle Tom, had the headland for peaceful walking and David's company daily. She rode Horse regularly over the wide moor and slept through each night for some ten hours. Her mother was delighted at the change in her.

'Why don't you stay, Jo, and get work down here? I'll be all right on my own. I could stay over at Beckenham during the week,' but as she saw Jo shake her head slowly ... she enforced: 'Well, think about it. There are ways to help here in Cornwall as well you know!'

Jo felt that she just couldn't leave her mother to cope with the London way of life on her own. She felt too that she'd be letting the war effort down if she forsook her weekend hospital duty. Oh ... but it was a tempting thought, and she would think about it, but not just yet!

About this time, our little island became an arsenal for weapons and men. Everywhere there were soldiers and masses of machinery, and Cornwall was no exception. Road markings and signposts were removed and huge camouflaged camps grew up. Large properties were requisitioned and many of the local farmers found fields and outhouses being used to store a variety of vehicles in readiness for the forthcoming invasion of Europe ... or D-day as it was later called.

Suddenly Fowey was alive. Veronica blossomed as she joined in the various activities engendered by this influx of men. Men from all nationalities. The Americans, casual, laconic and friendly, held dances. Not sedate foxtrot occasions, but lively jiving sessions, for it was the beginning of the 'jitterbug' era. They were bright young men, anxious to be friendly, who introduced us to peanut butter and tea served with 'hot' milk! They were also ebullient and noisy and their ranks lacked the 'stiff upper lip' and respect for position that the British army stood for.

A meeting was held in Polruan village hall to discuss the arrival of these men from across the Atlantic. It was well-attended. Mollie manoeuvred Tom's wheelchair down the steep incline of the village, and it required all her strength to hold it back in spite of the brake being half-fixed. She had been glad of the strong hands of the pilot when he reached out to help. Tom had not felt at all insecure, but had rather enjoyed the experience. His smile was teasing as he told Richard Williams:

'I would have thought she'd have been happy to let me go, considering the nuisance I've become, but she didn't, did she? Not after my money quite yet!'

At the meeting ways were discussed of helping with this influx of strangers into their quiet lives, and most undertook to ask groups of them for meals, and so to help introduce them to the local way of life.

Edith had gone to visit her friend in Penzance when Mollie found herself entertaining three young Americans for Sunday lunch. They arrived laden with parcels: tins of chicken, peaches and candy, but best of all, she was handed two pairs of real silk stockings, which she whisked upstairs and into her drawer with speed. Edith didn't find out until several days later, when Tom told her.

'Your sister's got some silk stockings … pity you missed out on that.' Mollie stared hard at her brother, stalked out of the room, only to return some few minutes later to pass one pair to Edith. Nothing was said, but Tom kept the 'niggle' going by saying pointedly each Sunday …

'Your legs look nice, girls. Both of you!'

With all the activity of war preparation around them the local people felt real involvement at last. For some time they'd been aware of the difference between life in the rural areas of England and that in the larger cities. They heard news of the bombing, but had not experienced it. Plymouth was about the nearest the Germans had got in the West Country. They had coped with rationing,and indeed for people actually in the villages the shortages were as acute as in the larger town areas, but those who farmed were cushioned somewhat, for apart from vegetables, there was always the extra egg; some butter from an excess of cream, and at times … illegally … the odd side of bacon.

Raymond arrived home for a peaceful Christmas. The Royal Air Force had now virtually established air superiority over the United Kingdom, so that the scattered 'hit and run' raids were few and far between. The war news on the whole was good. No more talk of a possible invasion. There was optimism everywhere. Comments such as 'the tide has turned …' or 'when the war is over …' were heard regularly in conversation. Jo's mood was buoyant too as the holiday season approached. It was only late at night, in bed, that she pondered on the length of time the war might still need to pursue its course. Often then she drifted off to sleep in an anguish of impatience, but awoke the next morning full of bright optimism once more.

Mrs Dingle roped them both in to help with a party at the Beckenham Home. Some local children, the few that were not evacuated, had been invited too, until finally some 25 or so happy youngsters sat down to a splendid tea, with food donated by friends of the Home. The police and home guard for that area had got together to raise money for gifts, and large paper bags had been set aside for each child, and filled with whatever 'goodies' they could find, together with notebooks, pencils, rubbers and colouring crayons; some old stock donated by a stationery shop in the high street.

Games were played. The usual musical chairs, where Johanna and Raymond both worked hard, and with much laughter, to see fair play. A local conjuror put in an appearance. A strange tall figure, dressed entirely in white, who commanded attention by his very mannerisms. He had long slender hands and fingers and used them to good effect. Rabbits were found in his top hat, broken coal turned into cakes, bright scarves, a never ending line of them, were produced somehow from the toe of his long flat shoes. He didn't speak, but used his expressive hands, encased in white gloves to indicate his wishes and to maintain order. A remarkable feat with so many excited youngsters.

Ray organised the boys who took part in a special ball game, whilst Jo and her mother took the girls into the wide hallway, where they danced to piano music played by one of the local policemen. Finally, the children were led in a long line up the back stairs of the beautiful old house, along a dark corridor with hands clutching waists, to emerge at the main stairway in giggles and squeals of laughter, to collect their presents. It was a good, happy party and by the time every child had either been put to bed, or seen home, everyone was dog-tired. An army of local ladies helped with the clearing up, so that everything was shipshape; clean and tidy for the special service the next morning. Then Mrs Dingle had two days with her own family!

Food was always a consideration at Christmas and plans were started early. They had made the usual cake with the dried fruit allocation, and sent it out to Bill, who was now in Italy. Jo's mouth watered as she sniffed repeatedly at its richness, before it was finally wrapped in greaseproof paper, then put into a tin, sewn into a linen bag, and finally labelled and posted. Aunt Edith somehow procured more dried fruit and made them another cake, which she'd given to her sister when Jo's mother called on them once again, about ten days before Christmas, to attend the special party at Pendower House.

It had been a pleasurable evening at Widegates. A gay one too, for the aunts had invited their three American soldiers for a meal. They had arrived breathless, having walked from the camp high above the river. Once again, all were laden with gifts: peaches, two tinned chickens, ham, cigarettes for Tom, and finally Mollie's eyes watered a little when she saw bars of chocolate, all put down casually on the kitchen table. Such bounty!

There was a good deal of hilarity as to how the chicken got into the tin. 'The boys', as Mollie called them, were bright, carefree young men, keenly interested to learn our ways. They enticed Tom to talk about his life on the farm, and as the evening wore on, old tales that his sisters had heard so many times before, improved with the new telling, so that they too joined in the laughter and comments at the end.

Mrs Dingle had been given some ham, a tinned chicken, peaches and some of the chocolate. These were produced as her Christmas surprise. The bird was divested of its metal casing without too much difficulty. It emerged elongated and squashed; not suitable for carving, but the meat was succulent and tasty and nobody cared what it looked like on the plate. John Kimber joined them. His contribution towards the meal was the vegetables taken from his fast depleting store. They had roast potatoes, carrots, parsnip and a generous bowl of 'out-of-season' spinach that John had nurtured in his greenhouse. The tinned peaches provided a very special sweet, and afterwards they drank everyone's health with John's next to last bottle of elderberry wine. 'The last one I'm keeping for the day the war ends, and it's down in the cellar for safety,' he commented as they sipped slowly at their glasses.

Later they huddled round the small table near to the wood fire and played monopoly, which Raymond won! He had plenty of practice with his friends at school, and took the most appalling risks with 'buying up' the houses and hotels. It was a tired, but happy boy who finally took himself to bed.

'A lovely day, mum,' he said as he kissed her. 'But I wish Bill had been here as well.'

Their thoughts had been with him all day. They hoped that he was having a happy Christmas, but most of all they hoped that he was safe.

'Perhaps 1944 will bring peace for us all,' John Kimber said as he left for home. 'Thank you for a lovely day. The nicest Christmas I've had since my Mary died.' Jo saw him safely up his steps and then sat on the low wall at the front of her house for a while. It was a clear, starlit night; the narrow strips of sky visible between the row of houses was in sharp contrast to the spacious heavens seen from Widegates. It was beautiful though, so still and quiet. No noise from the Bofors tonight, no planes droning their terror as they came nearer, no warning to evoke the chill of fear – a lovely night! 'Just like last year,' thought Jo. She tried to imagine Bryn's Christmas; to see him with his air force pals enjoying himself, but she couldn't. The only picture of Bryn she could recall was a tousled head and long arms reaching up to tame the honeysuckle, years ago during the wild storm over Widegates. A young Bryn … a smiling Bryn … her very special friend!

One of the things that had made this time so pleasant for Jo was the carols at the hospital on Christmas Eve. She had been asked to join in a choir of off-duty doctors and nurses to tour the wards and sing. It had been a magical evening. The hospital had sought out what decorations they had, so that everywhere was festive. The carol-singers carried bright tinsel stars, which caught the dimmed ward lights, making them shine and sparkle. The children's ward was especially gay; the young patients had eyes filled with wonder as the procession made its way through the ward, with some of the children joining in the 'Sleigh bell carol'. It was a touching evening, filled with beauty and hope. Jo felt mature somehow, as she smiled happily at the old ladies in her special ward, and remembered David's words of a few weeks back when she'd mentioned how much older people seemed in London compared to those she met in Cornwall. 'Lack of future and the denial of it make people older, more mature.'

Was she suffering from a 'lack of future'? Jo certainly felt frustrated and impatient for the war to end, and certainly, at times, she was unsure of the future – all Londoners were. Tonight, though, she didn't ponder too long on David's words. Soon it would be 1944 – a few months more and Bryn would be back in England. 'Please let it be a good year for us all,' she prayed.

In early February she spent a few days at Widegates. She had developed a heavy cold that she just couldn't shake off.

'Cornwall will clear that up for you,' her mother had said. 'Take some time owing to you and just go!' So she had!

'Don't go far, love,' her aunt said as she watched her niece struggle into her wellie-boots at the dairy door. 'We are off to bed. Leave the door on the latch and lock up when you come back, won't you?'

'I'll not go far. Just to the byre to check all is well. One little lamb would be a treat before I go back to London.' She kissed her aunt, both hands on her shoulders and looked straight into her worried eyes. 'I'll not go far – promise,' she reassured her, then smiled briefly, turned and waved a gloved hand as she went through the door to the yard.

Jo hated the thought of missing the lambing. Just another week and they'd be busy on the farm, morning, noon and night. How she'd love to be there amidst all the sorting of the sheep, the dabbing-on of the dye to both mother and babe; the lifting and pushing of the hay-bales to form little rooms for the newly born and, most of all, the gentle nursing often needed for a weakly or orphaned lamb. Right now she was distressed at the thought of going back – back to a grey, war-torn London. Back to the dust, the noise, the fear; and most of all, back to the weariness of life in a city worn down by years of constant bombing. People here in Cornwall were so full of energy and life, and she wanted to be part of that life, not with the careworn people in town. These thoughts instantly filled her with remorse. How could she feel like this? Of course people here were smiling, fit and happy. They had no real cares. Life for them was much the same, and even rationing was conditioned by the extras to be gleaned from local farms. Londoners though were war weary – weary of lining up for extras for the cook pot; weary of seeing each day the mounds of rubble where houses used to be. Weary of hearing that friends or neighbours had been killed or wounded; weary of having to rush for shelter … of having to sleep in damp, dark Andersons each night, and then often to be awakened to the sirens blaring and the distant clumping sounds of bombs landing … and the noise of the local ack-ack fire. Weary too at having to experience the rising fear as the bombs got nearer, until the raids diminished at dawn, when they caught a few short hours of peace in a troubled sleep, that was ended all too soon by the onset of another day. Another tedious day … another weary day!

'How awful of me,' Jo thought again. 'How awful of me not to wish to be a part of it all, part of the help – part of the civilian war.' She hugged her arms across her chest as she stomped across the yard and said aloud … 'But I still wish that I could be here, just to see one little lamb – so there!'

The snow wasn't deep, just about three inches, and it had fallen straight and softly all afternoon. No blizzard and high winds to send it piling into impassable deep drifts. It was just as if a huge sieve had spread icing sugar over the land, a gentle covering, shining so beautifully now in the moonlight.

She crunched her way to the stable, where the old door creaked as she tugged it hard against the wedge of snow. Horse whinnied at her appearance, his eyes soft and gentle regarded her almost questioningly. 'I'm going back in the morning,' she whispered against his throat, as she stroked the white band between his eyes, one arm thrown gently over his neck. Horse ducked his head and searched for her pocket.

'You old rascal – you know, don't you?' Jo produced two rings of carrot from her glove. It was a pattern and he had grown to expect this titbit.

The stable was warm, the smells familiar and pleasant, of trampled hay, of damp bran, and then the wild horse smell that she loved so much.

'I'll miss you.' She leaned against him and sighed heavily as Horse turned his head to seek her friendly pat again. Jo looked up to the roof of the stable … 'Oh, I'll miss you … you and all of this.' Tears started in her eyes. She felt her chest tighten and a lump form in her throat – a painful tightness as she fought for control. 'This won't do, old fella,' her hands rubbed his ears as he nuzzled her neck. 'See you at Easter and that's not so far away now, is it?' She left, closing the gate to his stall as Horse quietly watched her. The air outside was crisp and cold and at first hurt her nostrils after the warm dustiness of the stable. She trudged over the yard towards the lower field, where the ewes huddled together against the cold night. The open shed was empty, but she heard movements from within the byre and imagined them all, close and warm and waiting. They were quiet and settled.

'No lambs tonight,' she thought, with disappointment, but Jo did peer into the several straw-baled units that she'd helped her aunts to set up that afternoon. Units that next week would house mothers and newly born lambs for those first caring days after birth. None now though!

She raised her eyes as she left the shelter of the huts. The long field stretched before her, wide always, but now it was like a vast sea, unrestrained by hedgerows and fences that had somehow vanished in their covering of white. All was shimmering, glistening, and only by screwing up her eyes could she make out the form of the hedges on either side. The snow was virgin, smooth, untouched. Ahead across the field lay the headland. She felt the 'pull' – it was as if some force had taken her over. It must look wonderful now, she thought, and started up the field, but then she remembered her promise to Mollie, and knew with certainty that she would be in bed, but wakeful until she heard her niece return and the key turn safely in the lock. 'Never mind – I'll go to the gate at least. It's clear and I should be able to see the marker from there and the sea beyond … I'll say my good-byes from the gate.'

She walked heavily on, over and up the field, turning every so often to examine her footprints in the smooth snow and to glance at the farm and church, nestling now in the folds of the hill.

Jo sat perched on the top rung of the gate. To her right she could see the gentle curve of the land, stretching out towards the headland. The deep dry-stone walls were shadowed with their covering of white and appeared like huge mounds. The monument looked foreshortened, snow-capped and somewhat squat in appearance. The sky was clear, a dark velvet sky twinkling with stars. A three-quarter moon afforded a silver light as she turned her gaze back to the land, the twinkling was apparent there too, in the fields of snow. It was alive with little specks of sparkling light. Jo looked towards the farm. The view was breathtakingly beautiful. Below her the field dropped steeply and she could see her footprints marching clearly from the lambing enclosure. The bleakness of the silage container and outbuildings was softened now by the covering of white. Widegates, always low-lying in the curve of the valley, seemed to have nestled in even further. The church tower in the distance stood stark and impressive against the sky. The trees at Pill Pont were heavy with snow, the hedges and walls scarcely definable even in the valley, and she could see, in the distance, the dark, dark sheen of water, where the river flowed seawards.

The sky hung above her, dappled with a myriad diamond stars, and over all there was a peace that brought tears to her eyes again and a lump in her throat.

'If only you were here, Bryn … if only you were here!' Jo thought of the many times the three of them had enjoyed the snow together at the farm. The rough-and-tumble of tobogganing in this very field. Racing each other towards the haystack in the corner and to land in a hopeless, helpless mass, laughing and tumbled! 'What fun we had when we were young,' she thought. 'Growing up is pretty awful right now.' She pondered for a while on the thoughts of a peacetime youth. Parties, carefree meetings, clothes, nice things to eat, and a Widegates that would welcome her whenever she wished. That at least was true, not half true, for Jo's life was not free, but conditioned by her duties towards the war effort, her job in London and her need to be a comfort to her mother. She's been a real brick since dad died, she thought. I've no right to be miserable – no right at all. Spring will soon be here – Bryn will soon be back. With that happy thought, she jumped from the gate and ran scrambling through the snow back to the farm, stopping only at the yard gate to open it and then make it secure once more. She glanced up at her marks of progress through the field; no clear footmarks now, but a wide swathe had been cut into the virgin white as she'd rushed and tumbled down. Mollie had watched her from her bedroom window … 'She'll do,' she thought as she hurried back to bed where she was found by Jo, sitting comfortably reading, when she popped her rosy-cheeked, tousled head, round the door to say goodnight!

CHAPTER NINE

It was Easter time and Johanna had returned to Cornwall. The day was beautiful, with fresh sweet air blown on a soft wind straight from the sea. The sunlight dappled through the trees as she made her way down the leafy lane towards Lantivet Bay. Beneath her feet the ground was soft, where layer upon layer of leaves had mulched to form a cushion over the bedrock. Her feet stirred the leaves, sending up that musty dank smell that was special to this gully walk. She took a deep breath, it was cloying and sweet, a smell of Cornwall! Jo felt so happy to be back; happy to be treading the familiar track to the sea and, most of all, happy that in just a few weeks' time Bryn would be sharing it with her.

The post had arrived early that morning. She had heard the gate shut as she finished the milking, and had met the postman in the yard.

'Hello, lass – nice to see you back. I've a surprise for you!' He handed her a letter. She glanced at the familiar handwriting and her heart lurched sickeningly.

'My lass, but you're looking peaky. That town life bayn't good for 'ee – no, not at all. Best get out to the headland and blow some colour into your cheeks.' His smile was wide, kind and concerned as he gathered his bag onto his shoulder and went through the farm gate.

'I'm all right, Bill,' she called after him. 'Really I am. It's just that we've been overworked at the hospital; there are so many people down with flu.' For a short moment she recalled her life in London, the drabness and bleakness of it all, and felt guilty at being at the farm, with all the peace and beauty around her. I can think of so many people who could do with a holiday here, she thought.

'Well, see that you enjoy yourself now, lass,' His eyes twinkled as he leant on the gate, having shut it firmly. 'Can't think that you won't, for Mollie and Edith will be spoiling you I shouldn't wonder. Mollie told me that Bryn is expected home in a month or two …' He poked his finger at the letter in her hand … 'S'pect that's from him, so I'll leave you in peace to read it. Stay happy, lass.' Bill turned to tread slowly up the lane, whistling as he went.

Jo waited until she got to the heath above the bay to read her letter. She sat on a rocky outcrop, warmed by the spring sunshine, the papers blowing in the breeze, so that she had to hold each page and read it in sections.

Bryn's words were subdued. He was looking forward to his return, but seemed weighted down somehow with the thought of his final weeks of training and examinations. He had developed a cold that he hadn't been able to shake off, despite his move to the warm climes of California. 'It's all so unreal here, Jo – no sign of war. Large ornate modern houses; shops bursting with produce, and people have an energy that folks at home haven't known for some time. Oh, I know that you all do wonders, but it's the spirit that drives you all. Here it's sheer strength and well-being that comes with good food, plenty of peaceful rest and a certainty that any plans made for tomorrow will be fulfilled. People here have a boundless, driving energy. A desire for progress. I don't seem to belong here, Jo – I'll be glad to get back!'

She sat for a long while after reading all of the letter. It was so unlike Bryn to be anything other than buoyant. Perhaps though the frustrations of war and not being able to work for or plan for the future was affecting him too, for Johanna felt daily an impatience that the war should end. Four long years – it was enough!

She pondered on this as she sat there, enjoying the soft breeze that stirred the long, lush grass, setting it waving like the sea. She listened to the soft lap of the water far below, and watched for a while as a flock of sheep made their way across the field to settle in a corner where the deep hedgerow framed the edge of the cliff.

Bryn would soon be home and her heart soared. But a different Bryn; she sensed his maturity in his letters. He had grown up; but then, so had she. How could anyone cope with this way of life and not change. She hoped that Bryn wouldn't mind too much this serious Jo. The carefree, laughing and perhaps selfish youngsters had gone for good, and in their place were two hardworking, caring people. Jo longed to be with Bryn now to comfort and help him through whatever was troubling him. 'Oh, why did there have to be a war – why?'

Jo's thoughts now dwelt on commitment. Was that what she wanted? Marriage, yes … undoubtedly. To be settled and raise a family; that was her dream – she and Bryn and a farm! What bliss it would be to have a chance to settle here in the West Country. For a moment, she forgot the war and envisaged a farm, a little like Widegates, settled and nestling in its own land – but she shook her head. Enough of that … enough of dreaming … dreams were for children and those days were past. Now it was the real life she had to consider!

She was sure that Bryn cared for her and that his plans were for them to share a life together. In reality though, what commitment could he make? Neither of them had any money. Bryn's love of farming would not buy him a farm. No, he would have to return to Beckenham, to accountancy, to work and save for his dreams!

Jo's plans for moving to Widegates had progressed no further. She was hoping to take a teacher training course, but until the war ended, everything had to remain status quo as far as her work was concerned. Now just wasn't the time for a change and, in any case, what would be the point of her moving west, with Bryn working and living in Beckenham? Oh – it would take years for them to save. Wasted war years, she thought. We will never catch up with them, never recoup the time. We can never take back the years. Jo stared ahead with unseeing eyes, remembering her talk with Selina on her last visit. They had walked west of the estuary to check on Selina's aunt who lived in splendid isolation at Guslake. Selina had talked proudly of her husband and of how she worried about him.

'Each time I hear the news and learn about the losses at sea, my heart turns over, but I wouldn't have it any different, Jo. It was right that we married. Bob says that he takes extra care now that he has someone – something to live for. He's always planning for the future and intends staying in the navy, and I …' Selina stopped for a moment and looked through the trees to where the estuary flowed seawards on a lowering tide. 'I think of him every moment of every day and pray that all will be well with him.'

Jo understood. She felt the same about Bryn, but Selina's quiet life here in Fowey made the waiting that much harder to bear. 'Much better to be busy,' thought Jo. 'Less time to think!'

Selina had asked about their commitment to each other and then laughed as Jo floundered, not being able to explain.

'Yes, of course I love him, Selina. I always have!'

'But have you told him so?'

'No, but I'm sure he knows. Yes, of course he knows – we both do.'

'Jo … Jo, you should tell him; tell him when you next write. Men need to be told. Why Bob didn't know how he felt about me until I said 'I love you' to him. Get it out into the open – you'll feel better for it.'

They had walked on in silence for a while – then …

'Has he kissed you, Jo?' Selina's voice was quietly questioning. Jo stared at her friend and felt a blush rise from her neck. She ducked her head and nodded … 'Of course …'

But had Bryn kissed her … really kissed her? Yes, they had hugged often, and he had planted kisses on her nose, in her hair and sometimes on her lips. Gentle, friendly kisses, with his eyes wary and watching. How many times had she longed to fling her arms round his neck … to reach for him, and how many times, that quiet watchful gaze had prevented her. What was his question … what did Bryn want from her?

She recalled an incident that had happened on her train journey down several days before. The stop at Taunton was longer than usual and Jo was gazing out of the window wondering why. A young couple stood close by, totally absorbed in one another. He was in army uniform, his kit-bag leant against a pillar, and they were saying a farewell. The girl's face was alight, aglow with love as she flung her arms round his neck, her hands stroking and pulling on the short curls at the nape of his neck. They kissed long and slowly, seeming to blend and fuse together. Jo had watched in wonder. All that feeling …! Her heart flowed out to them, wishing them both well as she sensed the sadness of their parting. They drew apart. He held her face in his hands and gazed down at her. The guard blew his whistle. Only then did Jo look away; she couldn't intrude on their good-bye any longer. She had seen clearly the young man's face, and in it such unutterable anguish she thought her heart would break for them both. The soldier drew away swiftly, gathering his kit-bag, and flung himself at the open carriage door. As the train drew out of the station, Jo glanced at the girl who was smiling bravely, but with tears falling down her cheeks. 'Love you' … her mouth formed the words.

'I love you, Barbara,' his voice carried clearly over the increasing noise of the engine as it gathered speed and left the station … 'I love you.'

Tears welled in her eyes as she recalled the incident and fell softly on the letter still clutched in her hand. No, Bryn had never said 'I love you, Jo'… if only …

A hawk flew high overhead shrilling its haunting cry as it wheeled away over the cliff. Jo squared her shoulders. This won't do, she thought. It won't do at all. Of course Bryn and I have a future together, and he'll soon be back. With that thought in mind she set off along the path to the cottage and David. He was waiting for news of Bryn and James, and she'd heard from them both!

The country was now moving towards thoughts of an invasion of Europe. There were endless rumours and speculations. Notices were still prominent everywhere, on hoardings and in trains and buses. 'Careless talk costs lives' – 'Be like Dad – keep Mum!' But in the confines of people's homes, behind the safety of blackout curtains, families discussed this possibility until it became a probability – but when? Uncle Tom commented that 'Our little island will sink if another American soldier or tank has to be housed on it …' The West Country was certainly a 'buzz' of activity, though for Johanna, life in London remained more or less the same. Veronica wrote to Jo of the lively dances and gatherings she attended now that the Americans were there in force. These newcomers to the war front brought a brash confidence with them that served to increase the buoyancy of the mood about them. 'The war will soon be over' was the thought in every person's mind. Vee was certainly more light-hearted. Jo had been troubled about her of late and a little impatient with her too. Her letters had been full of woes and moans since Christmas.

'She's spoilt,' Mollie had said. 'It would do her good to think of someone else other than Veronica!' Jo did wonder at her mood swings, for she felt that Vee was in a very enviable position. Jo would have swopped lives any day. 'A boring job,' to quote Vee, 'A boring job in a bank in Fowey' would be well worth the joy that actually living in Cornwall would be for Johanna.

Her daily hospital work became at once more difficult and demanding, and yet more rewarding. Miss Bray was hospitalised for an operation and would be away for some three weeks. Jo was in charge and she loved it. She found all the staff helpful; the minor difficulties she had with formulating operation lists and sending for patients were resolved with the help of the registrar and she enjoyed the personal contact with the wards and patients. The days went by quickly and quietly with no raids to disturb the peace. Jo even found it possible to read on the train journey to and from London. She began to visit the local cinema with her mother, where both of them were transported to another world for a while by such films as *It Happened One Night*. They left the cinema feeling relaxed and rested to enjoy the walk together through late evenings, when everywhere smelled fresh and clean.

Mrs Dingle obtained several dress lengths from a friend in Beckenham and these were made into simple day dresses. Jo loved a navy and white cotton print, the skirt was full enough to swing a little as she walked and the top, neatly tailored in a shirtwaister style, was very suitable for work. How lovely to have new clothes. she thought, and was sure that Bryn would like them. Jo stood in front of the long hall mirror at the hospital and studied her reflection. She looked good and a little thinner. Her hair had been cut fairly short, just below her ears, and soft curls now framed her face. The mirror showed a poised, slim and confident young lady. 'Bryn will be surprised,' Jo thought, before running up the stairway with a message for matron.

Her mother attended a meeting at Oxford in the hope of setting up a new home for orphans near to Abingdon. Raymond was due home, so for the first time Jo excused herself from the weekend hospital duty and helped to make her brother's short break a happy one. They packed sandwiches, took the bus to Keston Ponds and spent the day wandering in that lovely part of Kent. It was like being in another world, so quiet and peaceful, though both were aware that in these skies had been fought some of the bitterest aerial conflicts during the Battle of Britain.

The two huge lakes were bright with water lilies, and they watched as ducks, swans and little black coots swam, dabbled and searched along the water's edge for food. A squirrel shared their lunch, and also the bravest of the ducks! Ray spoke of his longing to be home. His mood was happy, teasing at times. Jo had never seen him look fitter; his young face was tanned with the early sun; eyes brown and vibrant and almost hidden by the long, fair eyelashes that matched the crop of hair that sprang from his head in all directions, thick and straight. A dimple teased the side of his mouth as he poked fun at the ducks, likening them to some of his friends at the camp. He asked Jo quite seriously what she thought he should do about his future. Somehow, she had never thought of her youngest brother as grown-up. He was always 'young' Raymond, but of course he was almost seventeen years now, time indeed to think about his future.

'What do you want to do, Ray?' she questioned him.

'Horticulture. I'd love to go to college, but will mum be able to manage, do you think? I suppose, realistically, I should get a job as soon as I leave school.'

'Bill and I are the workers, Ray. You go ahead and make your plans. Sounds a good idea to me.'

He spoke then of the growing excitement in the camp as they noticed all around them the continuing build-up of men and armaments. Every available space was fast filling with war transport. Miles of tanks, lorries etc lined the roads, heavily camouflaged with netting and sheltered by the trees now coming into leaf. New tented camps had sprung up and huts were built in the most odd places.

'It's exciting, isn't it, Jo? After all this time we are at last going to "do" for Hitler.'

On the way home they were both amused at a notice on the bus … it read:

'Face the driver, raise your hand,
You'll find that he will understand …'
Underneath had been written:
'Of course he'll understand, the cuss …
But will he stop the ruddy bus!?'

Later that week Mrs Dingle smiled when Jo told her about Raymond's hopes to take up horticulture.

'I've spoken to his personal tutor already, Jo. Provided he gets his School Certificate fully, he'll be able to start college in September of next year.'

With thoughts of a forthcoming invasion of Europe, most Londoners were lulled into a sense of security. For them, they felt the war was over! This proved a false premise as events overtook them. For Jo and her mother it was disaster when their house was bombed by a chance hit-and-run raider in mid-May. Both settled things as best they could and made for Cornwall … Widegates for Jo and her mother to Pendower House. Mrs Dingle left a few days before Johanna, who had to arrange leave with the hospital. Mr Kimber made up a bed for her in his spare room, and gradually, between them, they filled it with bits and pieces that could be salvaged from the ruins.

Mollie watched as her niece vanished over the top field. She saw her small figure turn and wave, as if in recognition of her watchfulness, and nearly dropped her basket of fruit in her anxiety to return the acknowledgement. She stood now, stretching her back in relief. She felt stiff from bending over the low-growing blackcurrant bushes – watching Jo as she trod the wide grassy path to her favourite place, the headland. Her figure got smaller and smaller. It disappeared from sight only to give her aunt a fleeting glimpse once more through the gate, midway along the field. Jo was striding along, head up, and Mollie knew that on this incredibly lovely early summer day the air would be like nectar, the sea breezes cool, strong and tangy with seaweed from the little bay. The hawks would be flying; the gulls wheeling high, and over all the slushing, roaring sound of the sea as it reached further and further up the wide expanse of beach, to beat with ever-increasing force against the rocks of the headland cliffs.

'She'll find peace there,' thought Mollie. For something was wrong … very wrong. Poor lass, she's lonely, but it's a loneliness of the soul. Why do youngsters have to feel things so deeply? She turned her thoughts back, way back. She used to feel that way about Donald, and the headland had had the same spell for both of them. When, during the last months of the first world war, she'd had that awful telegram – 'Killed in action' – she too had fled to the same headland for comfort. The thought still hurt her, for it wasn't comfort she'd found that day – just a wild, mad hurting that even now, after so many years, was only lightly buried, half-alive still, and waiting to take her over in waves of memory and anguish. She stretched once more, pushing her hands hard into the middle of her back, and stood looking round at the farm as it nestled into the folds of this beautiful valley; she saw the estuary water gleaming in the sunshine and, from high overhead, heard the lark, the wild skylark, trilling away as if in joy at such a lovely day.

'I coped,' thought Mollie. 'She'll cope too with whatever it is, and I'm sure she'll tell me when she's ready.' She bent once more over the bushes, reaching out for the soft ripe fruit, parting the stems to find hidden clusters of berries deep inside the plants. Blackcurrant pie for tea!

Mollie welcomed the peace of everyday things, the surroundings of the farm, and her quiet life looking after her brother and sister. Welcomed the seasons here and the village life. On the whole, the years had been good … but, if only …! No use though, thinking back. Nothing on earth will change things now, and she was far too old for fanciful dreaming. Just so long as Jo was all right. 'Please God, don't let her lose Bryn, they are meant for each other …' she murmured softly into the sweet air.

Jo had arrived just the evening before, seemingly for a short holiday spell from London, and had told them that she'd applied for a job at the local village school as an unqualified teacher. She had an interview at the beginning of the week. Both aunts and Tom were thrilled that she might settle locally for a while.

'But what of your mother?' Edith had asked.

'Hasn't she been in touch? Hasn't she told you?' Jo seemed shocked. The aunts shook their heads.

'Told us what? What is it, Johanna?'

'The house was bombed! Half of it's gone and mum came down to Pendower House. She's been planning to for ages and wanted to keep it as a surprise. But then last week – Jo's voice faltered … 'It was awful really – we are lucky that we are still here,' and she bent her head for a minute, shook it back and forth as if to get rid of something unpleasant.

'Don't tell us if you don't want to,' Mollie's voice was gentle. 'We will hear about it later.'

Jo jerked her head up. 'No – I'm sorry. I should have taken my time, not blurted it out like that … but it's all such a muddle, a nasty, hurtful scary muddle.' She took a sip of water from a glass that Edith had passed her, before continuing.

'We were having lunch on Saturday. Mum had made some fish cakes from our last tin of pilchards and the one egg allowance for that week. She'd managed to get some carrots from John Kimber. He still has some in his garage laid down in sand from last autumn, and he also gave mum the first picking of his peas, so we asked him to lunch to share our fish cakes. It was like a party really. Anyway, the warning went. We'd not heard it for ages and, well, nothing seemed to be happening, so we stayed at the table. Suddenly, without warning, we heard the first 'crump' of a bomb. It was so loud, a roaring somehow, and then we heard falling debris and felt the ground shaking. We all left the table and ran to the shelter as another landed. I think this was at the bottom of the road. Then we heard a swooshing noise and it was as if the whole world exploded. Mum and John were inside the shelter as another blast shook us. I was thrown inside ... we were enveloped in dust ... there was a roaring again, and then the dreadful noise of cracking and falling beams, of bricks falling heavily and occasionally the tinkle of some small fragment as it pinged against the metal of the shelter door. We hugged one another.

"I think it's the house," Mum said. We were all trembling and frightened and stayed like that until it was quiet again, until the falling noises had stopped. Then we heard the sound of fire engines, and the explosive noise of the Bofors as they fired futile shells into the sky. I looked up out of the shelter door to the bluest of heavens, and down to the mess of rubble and dust ... bits of blanket, scraps of clothing and glass, that was our home. The house was a broken mess with all the top two floors open to the sky. It was awful – so awful!' Jo looked at them in turn, smiled wanly.

'We were lucky though because we were all right. A whole family at the bottom of the road were killed, and old Mrs Simon at number 11, was blown across her kitchen as the bomb fell on us. She suffered a black eye, but otherwise was unhurt. She was in a real rage when I saw her. "I'd just cleaned the kitchen, Jo," she said. "Just got the fire laid and was about to settle for my afternoon nap ... and now look at all this mess!" Then she raised her clenched fist to the skies, as if the bomber could see her. It wasn't much good doing anything to the house. It's all such a mess! Mum and I worked all night salvaging odd little things: a few tablecloths; one or two glasses that miraculously hadn't broken in the sideboard; the photos, which fortunately we kept in the cupboard under the stairs, but basically, clothes, bedding, treasures ... all gone. So mum just came down as she'd planned to do. John Kimber put me up and helped with the salvage. Mum looked awful and we both felt so scared – so here we are!'

Mollie stretched over the table to enclose her niece's hand in a warm clasp.

'And how glad we are to have you, Jo. This has always been your second home, you know, and now we'd love you to make it your first.'

'We'll go out tomorrow and shop,' said Edith. 'I've lots of coupons and we'll soon have you kitted out again.'

'Thanks aunt,' smiled Jo. 'But I can claim coupons as we've been bombed out. Lend me some, please, and I'll pay you back. I would like to have a decent dress for the school interview next week. I lost all of Bryn's letters, you know …' Jo added, as she left the kitchen to wander round the farmyard for her evening talk to Horse.

Mollie stretched herself up again to ease her back and thought of today. The morning had begun well. Jo had eaten a good breakfast and had said that she would probably take Horse for a ride later.

'That is if you can spare me,' she asked them all.

'Take it as read,' replied uncle Tom, 'But don't go too near the edge on the headland path. There's been some erosion and it might be dangerous after all the rain.'

'I thought I'd take the Hall walk round the estuary. The sun is right there this morning and I'll call and see Veronica. Mother might be coming over from Pendower House this evening, so I'll be back early.'

Jo had wandered round the yard. Had told Horse that he would soon be out on a treat, checked that the goats would still answer to the names she'd chosen for them, and then she had sat on the gate waiting for the postman. A few weeks back she'd written to Bryn and told him to address her letters to the farm. She'd mentioned her plans to move back to Cornwall, and was confident that she'd get the job at the local school. 'But even if I don't, Bryn … I shall go back anyway and find something to do. London is so lonely without you. It's such a miserable, sad place to be. All the young people have been sent off to work in munition factories or into the armed forces, but my job at the hospital has prevented me from doing just that, for they won't release me! It's a sad city, and very brave, but I've had enough. I want to get back to fresh air … to the sea and our headland, where I know you'll be there in spirit, and I shall feel easier about waiting for your return.'

But there was no letter, and she had set out for the headland in a wave of disappointment. Mollie looked up again bewildered.

'I thought she was going to see Veronica and taking Horse!' she murmured.

The job at the school didn't materialise. A local girl who had her name down for teacher training the following year was employed to fill the post. Jo enjoyed her visit there, however. She loved the atmosphere of the village school; the cheeky smiling faces of the children, and appreciated the advice given to her by the headmistress. She now made up her mind to apply for teacher training, and would set those wheels in motion as soon as she was back in London – for back she must go now! The idea of a new career cheered her spirits, and the thought of returning to the city, a thought that had seemed impossibly fearful just a few days ago, was accepted and almost looked forward to so that she could make plans for her future.

CHAPTER TEN

Jo's return to London was arranged. The aunts and Mrs Dingle had argued, cajoled and even pleaded with her to stay in Cornwall, and to make her life there, but she felt it would be wrong. It was difficult to get employment, and she knew farm life would not suit her as a full-time occupation … too much time to think. She fell back on her main reason for returning.

'But the hospital work is so important, they really need helpers like me and especially now!'

Her mother arranged things for her. Their damaged house was empty of all furniture now. What was worth keeping was being housed by friends locally. Amongst these was Mrs Jackson, a long-term family friend and someone who had watched Johanna grow from childhood. She lived in a double-fronted bungalow near to the air-raid warden's post; she had no family of her own and had lived there alone since Christmas 1940, when Mr Jackson had suffered a heart attack and died suddenly. She would be happy to have Jo.

'Give her space,' Mrs Dingle had said to her friend, loathe to leave her daughter still with the hazards of war to cope with.

'Jo will be all right with me,' Mrs Jackson had assured her, and it was so. They got along extremely well. Jo welcomed the meal that was usually waiting for her each evening; enjoyed chatting about her day with Mrs Jackson, whose gentle manner was a calming one, so that she found often at bedtime her mind was peaceful – she was in a 'looking-forward-to' mood!

They worked in the garden during early summer evenings and weekends. Tidied the paved pathways, cut back shrubs that had already flowered in spring, tied up a huge trailing honeysuckle, its perfume strong now and evoking memories of past happy days for Jo. Mrs Jackson was content to have someone to care for once more. It gave her a purpose to each day. She was an elegant lady, petite, but with an upright carriage that gave the impression of height. Her clothes were always dark and hung freely. They seemed to emphasise the ageing beauty of her rounded face and perfect complexion. Her white hair, cut short and softly curling, framed a face of surpassing sweetness and her low lilting voice completed the picture. Often her slight figure could be seen walking in a brisk, short-stepped way to the shops, seeking out something different for supper. Food remained a problem, but she would return occasionally with some almost forgotten luxury to make a plain meal more appetising. A packet of sage and onion stuffing could do wonders for a vegetable pie, whilst a tin of dried egg powder was a treasure to be guarded. The allotments near to Jo's bombed home were still producing vegetables for those who cared for them, and it was usual for Mrs Jackson to call with her basket and request early peas, salads and young spinach to add spice to their meals. She would usually barter, for Mrs Jackson was a great bottler of fruit. Her garden housed a huge mulberry tree and cordons of soft fruits hung along the wall. These were gathered and bottled each year and her stock cupboard was well-known for its colourful and fruity contents! John Kimber struck up a friendship with her and was often asked to a meal. Jo loved these evenings, it gave her a sense of 'home'. She knew that John had hated the thought of her mother leaving for the West Country, and felt happy that now he'd found another friend.

The damage to the Dingle home had proved to be not as extensive as originally thought. The top floors were gutted certainly, but structurally it was still sound. Mrs Dingle had arranged with a local builder to have the roof sealed and it now looked strange, covered in an enormous tarpaulin sheet, which hung well down on all sides, as if it wore a hood! Jo wandered through the unhinged back door one evening. The house smelled strangely dusty and sour. Her room was reasonably untouched however, with one wide crack over the doorway and various blow-outs on the plaster walls, but the flooring and window areas were still firm. The canvas had been replaced and, with the evening sun shining faintly through, the room had a golden glow. It looked welcoming and familiar. Jo almost wished she could move back again, but her mother had been aghast at the idea, and Mollie had also remonstrated with her.

'Your mother's had enough troubles and worries, Jo. Isn't it enough that she's conceded to your return to town? Stay with Mrs

Jackson for now, there's a good girl.' Johanna, now almost twenty years, didn't feel at all girlish but she respected her mother's wishes, buoyed up as the days progressed by the thought that Bryn would soon return home.

At this time everyone knew that D-day must be imminent. The wireless news was listened to avidly. In the waiting room at Charing Cross station Jo often joined a group of businessmen and young office girls, huddled together over a radio, listening carefully, but always with a watchful eye for their trains, which were pretty erratic as far as departure times were concerned. There was an expectancy in the air. 'The war is nearly over …' People hurried about their days with a lighter heart and firmer step.

The D-day landings were announced on the morning of the sixth of June and it was a great relief to everyone Jo knew. She sat in the back kitchen with Mrs Jackson looking at a darkening sky. The weather had been atrocious for early June and even now the skies were lowering and forbidding. She said a prayer secretly for those involved, and another thanking God that Bryn was not yet back from his training. The next few days were celebratory – everyone smiled broadly – everyone had a happy word to say. The weather cleared and an old gentleman on the morning train patted Jo's hand.

'There, my lass … it's nearly over and then you must get on with your life. Make it a good one!' Jo smiled her thanks. He had been a frequent travelling companion, and their eyes had met many times during the worrying bombing sessions. He raised his hat to her as he left the station. She never saw him again!

The peaceful lull did not last long, for about a week after the invasion commenced a new menace appeared from the heavens. Jo later learned that it was Hitler's first secret weapon – the V-1's, or 'doodlebugs' as they became universally known. She saw her first one through the open bathroom window, on a day when low grey clouds were scudding across the sky. The warning had sounded, but all was quiet, no local gun barrage and she experienced a disbelief that anything serious could happen at all, now that we were 'after' Hitler.

She heard the droning noise and saw a dark shape against the clouds. Flames were pouring from it, and excitedly she called:

'We've got one. It's coming down.' Everything went strangely quiet and then the air was rent by a terrific explosion. 'The bombs were still on,' thought Jo. 'How awful!' Some five minutes later, just as she'd completed her toilet, the same thing happened again. Another plane on fire – another explosion and in about the same area. She found it strange, but was elated by the thought that she'd seen two enemy aircraft in flames. The 'all-clear' sounded and she made her way to work, where later that morning the secretary arrived in the office, agitated and pale, to announce that flying bombs were falling on London. The warnings were continuous, and to begin with they all huddled under the huge office table. Later it was realised that these bombs had a limited range, and the hospital lay beyond that. Jo worried all day about Mrs Jackson and other friends living in her home area.

Within a few days barrage balloons were flying, stretched across an area in the south-east, and making a wall of differing heights to make it hard for the bombs to get through to London. They came, however, thick and fast, day and night, usually in pairs. During this time those that did get through the curtain of guns, fighter planes and barrage balloons fell in Jo's area, the south-east of London, and it became known as 'doodlebug alley'. The daily anguish Jo had always felt on leaving home for central London was heightened with this new awful menace. People moved out of London, children were evacuated once more from the danger areas. Mrs Dingle wished over and over again that she had refused to let Jo return to town, or that she could be there with her, but she couldn't leave Cornwall. Her work with the children mostly orphaned through war committed her to staying. Meanwhile, her workload increased as more and more youngsters came under her care. The new home was opened at Abingdon by a colleague, and another wing was made ready at Pendower House, with further staff taken on to cope with some 20 more children.

Now, late on this summer evening, Jo sat up in bed in her narrow half-basement bedroom. She missed her spacious, high-ceilinged room, but felt somehow secure, safe in this small space. 'My own little shelter,' she thought.

The day had been hot and Jo welcomed the cooling breeze that came through the open canvas-covered window. She could see the trees at the end of the garden, tall graceful poplars. A half-moon floated low in the sky behind them, its silver rays spreading mystery and magic all around, so that she longed to be outside with it all.

'Strange,' she thought, 'strange how natural it would be for me now, were I at Widegates, to dress, go outside and sit on the back steps to enjoy the beauty of the night. Not so here in London ... and particularly now.' She smiled at the thought that Mrs Jackson would think her mad, baying at the moon like the wolves!

The canvas on one of the windows was torn at the bottom. Jo had bent it back, holding the fold with two large pins, which now looked like silver brooches in the moonlight. This afforded her some air when the weather necessitated the window being closed. Now though, she had all the air she needed from the open window. A slight breeze came again and wafted a fragrance into her room from the rose arbour. She inhaled and felt a deep pleasure and somewhere a memory – a memory of what?

'Time for sleep,' thought Jo as she stretched her body, her head still turned towards the window. Her eyes caught sight of the letter propped against a photograph frame on the chest by her bed. Aunt Mollie had written: 'Bryn is here, Jo, he's not at all well, but recovering. Come when you can, dear girl – meanwhile we are looking after him.' Jo telephoned her mother at Pendower House and learned that Bryn had arrived at Widegates in a collapsed state with pneumonia, that he was much better and longing to see her.

'I'll ask for time off in the morning, mum,' Jo had said. 'Give him my best love, won't you?'

Now she sighed deeply. A happy relaxed sigh. Bryn was back in England and soon she would see him again. Not once did she wonder why he'd made for Widegates instead of London. It just seemed right that he should be there. 'I'll pack a bag in the morning and take it with me to work. Perhaps I'll be able to get the evening train,' she thought as she settled for sleep.

The familiar drone reached down into her sub-conscious mind – fixed itself there, throbbing her into wakefulness, and then instant alertness. Her eyes searched the heavens from where she lay, neck straining as the awful droning sound got nearer and louder.

'Let it go over – please God, let it go over ...'

She saw the dark sinister shape join the moon behind the poplars, a jarring note to the beauty of the night; she held her breath at the sudden silence; heard the swishing rushing sound as it dived earthward, and then the roaring crunch of the explosion, followed after a while by a silence so complete that her ears strained and strained to hear just one little recognisable sound. The breeze stirred the loose canvas at the window, the moonlight, the poplars, the garden were all back to normal once more. She gave a fleeting thought for those people suffering from the bomb and then closed her eyes to drift into sleep before the next 'chug-chug' awoke her.

It was a bad night. The bombs came over frequently, falling all around them. Jo was awakened repeatedly – fretful and tense – listening to the drone, then the silence and finally the explosion, relaxing with relief each time that they were unharmed. She found herself drifting near to sleep when the whole procedure would start again. 'Oh Bryn, Bryn – I wish I were at Widegates now …'

Mrs Jackson called her.

'Come and have a cup of tea, Jo. We'll not get any sleep tonight.'

It was a tense, tired eyed girl and a watchful brave old lady who shared the terror of that night. In between bombs they talked. Mrs Jackson asked about Widegates, about Bryn and her aunts. Jo relaxed as she spoke of the people and of the place that meant so much to her.

'It's so very lovely. A happy place to be. The smell of the farm, the heather and the sea. Oh – it's everything – everything!'

'I wonder you don't go back, Jo,' Mrs Jackson said quietly, 'I'd miss you, child, but it's obvious where your heart lies.'

'Perhaps I will,' Jo replied. 'Perhaps I will.' But she knew deep inside her that whilst there was the slightest chance of Bryn coming back to work in Beckenham when the war was over, she'd stay … just to be near to him.

They went to bed as dawn broke. Jo fell into an uneasy sleep, a sleep that was shattered by an explosion so loud it seemed to fill the air around her. the noise reverberated through her head, bringing her tired mind back to consciousness, back to its alert, watchful waiting. Her legs felt weak as she got out of bed and her body trembled. That one was close – real close! The garden was pale in the dust mist, the sweet air now polluted. She leant from the window as a huge pall of smoke rose skywards from near to the high street.

'The Hospital – they've got the hospital,' she whispered, her stomach sick and taut with fear and horror.

She flung on her clothes, thankful that she had planned what to wear to-day, and had set a clean blouse and skirt aside last night.

Mrs Jackson appeared at her door, white-faced and wide-eyed, and Jo felt a moment of compassion for her elderly friend. Compassion a little tinged with guilt that she hadn't sought her out first to see that all was well.

'I've made some tea. You must have some before you go.' Jo sighed thankfully. She had half-expected Mrs Jackson to attempt to stop her.

'You knew I'd go to the hospital. Will you be all right? Shall I ask John to come up?'

'No, my dear. I'm all right. It's thinking of those poor souls out there that makes me feel bad. Do what you can, dear girl, but take care. No risks, mind, I promised your mother.' She sipped her tea, paused to look at Jo. It was a direct look, her chin was determined as she squared her shoulders.

'For two pins I'd come as well.'

'Best not,' Jo breathed quietly, 'best not,' and she touched Mrs Jackson's shoulder briefly as she left. It was five am.

She was late for work of course! The day that had begun so badly now followed the same pattern throughout. The scene that had met her as she turned the corner of the road was worse than even she had imagined. The hospital main building was gutted and still on fire. The explosion seemed to have been centred on the administrative wing, which was fortunate, but above were wards, and Jo could see the figures of nurses, porters and helpers silhouetted against the flames from the inner building as they carried and helped patients to safety.

She had run the last few yards, stumbling over the firemen's hoses and the rubble that spread out across the wide pavements The morning light was eerie and still heavily dust-laden. A slight rain was falling, the air was warm, but Jo shivered, bewildered, uncertain what to do and where to help. A voice called … 'Can you help here, lass? Some of these folks need a bit of cheer. See what you can do.'

Jo was directed to the wide grass verge outside the hospital, where patients, having been rescued from the wards, were set down, blanket-covered and frightened, to await removal elsewhere. Jo gave what help she could. Making some more comfortable on the damp ground, reassuring others, and finally handing out copious mugs of the warm sweet tea provided so efficiently by the local Women's Voluntary Service.

Ambulances began to arrive to ferry those injured patients to various other hospitals. The rain eased, the morning brightened, but, if anything, the scene appeared more devastating. Little groups of nurses, some still in nightwear, had stood and drunk thankfully at mugs of hot tea, before scurrying along the lines of patients offering help here, a smile and kind word there. Jo had guided the walking patients to the ambulances. The air-raid 'all-clear' had sounded and a little cheer went up. One old man started to sing, and a few feeble voices joined in. Smiles formed on faces; hands reached out to Jo and, as she clasped them in hers, she felt such a feeling of happiness that she was there, able to help just a little.

'Well done, lass.' It was the policeman who'd first guided her. 'Well done, lass and thank you!'

She had watched as the last patient was taken to safety; watched then as the fires were slowly extinguished, leaving stark gaps in the buildings. The path lab and dispensary were totally gutted, a white pall of smoke hung over the area and Jo gagged as the smell from this reached her. It jolted her into awareness and she had turned wearily away.

The train had been slow on her journey to work. 'Perhaps the line has been bombed,' Jo thought. The carriage was half-empty, a fact that had worried her until she realised that this was a much later train than the one she usually caught. She smiled at a young girl sitting opposite, and then got a little flustered as she noticed for the first time since leaving the scene of the bombing just how messy she was. Light dust had settled in patches on her dark skirt where she had knelt in the damp to help. Her arms were covered with it and her hands were grubby. She put up her hands to her hair, then dropped them wearily in her lap. What did it matter. What did anything matter. She had done her best, and Bryn was back in England! She rested her head against the frame of the carriage window, relaxing to the rhythmic movement of the train. Then she remembered Widegates – her suitcase! Oh, she should have gone back to the bungalow. She'd forgotten her suitcase. Distressed she looked up and caught the young girl's enquiring gaze.

'Was it bad?' she whispered to Jo.

'Bad enough,' Jo answered. 'But it's all right really.'

Their gaze held for a while, then, as the train stopped at Waterloo station, she watched through the criss-cross-taped windows, as the people hurried up the platform, and saw the sun was now shining brightly. 'It's all right … really all right …' she thought. 'I'm safe, I'm here and tonight I'll be at Widegates.'

But it was not to be. Her late arrival at the hospital did not go unnoticed. Both Matron and the secretary were standing in the office doorway as Jo made her way across the hall towards the stairs and the staff cloakroom. She would just have to get clean and tidy before starting work.

'Have you a moment, Miss Dingle?' It was Matron's voice and Jo was compelled to return. Both adults eyed her up and down, noting the state of her clothes, hair and dirty arms; there was no understanding or compassion in the look from Matron's dark eyes, and her mouth moved slightly to show distaste.

'It was a bomb …' Jo began, but was interrupted immediately by the secretary, who announced that Miss Bray had been slightly injured coming to work. Her train had shunted into the station barrier and passengers had been thrown about.

'She will be off for at least one week. Will you take over, Jo, please?'

During her lunch hour Jo wrote to Bryn explaining the difficult situation. She compared the two worlds she lived in: the comparative peace of central London, compared to the day-by-day terror of 'doodlebug alley'. She wrote at length. It was a letter full of hope and anticipation of her visit soon to come. She told him of her life here in London, of how the new terror from the skies affected all their lives, of her weariness through sleepless nights, of the bravery around, of the local bombing of the hospital that morning and still so very much with her. She asked gently about his health. 'And Bryn, if I can't be there to care for you, then I'm glad you are at Widegates with the aunts. Rest well, breathe in that healing Cornish air, and I will come just as soon as I can.'

She posted the letter in central London, not trusting the post locally with so much destruction going on there. Bryn read her words some four days later. He had been concerned at not hearing from her and disturbed by her non-appearance. The letter was received well initially. He had read it over and over again, but as the days went by, with still no word of her impending arrival, he wondered about her continued absence. Veronica was visiting regularly and one morning, when Bryn was talking about, and worrying over Jo, wondering why, even now, she still didn't come, Veronica had made a tart comment.

'Work or not, nothing would keep me away!'

His illness had left him pale and weakened, fractious at times. Nothing seemed to please him now that Johanna wasn't coming. Veronica had sown a seed of discontent. He asked Mollie what she knew about the situation as far as Jo's job was concerned. It was explained readily, for Jo confided in her mother, who passed the news on to her sister.

'She'd come if she could, Bryn,' ended Mollie quietly.

'Perhaps she doesn't really want to,' was his morose reply, to which Mollie made no answer, but left his room shaking her head.

When eventually Jo did get down to Widegates it was mid-July. Bryn had been back for four weeks and was well on the road to recovery from his pneumonia. He met her at St Austell. Tom had insisted that he take the little Model T Ford.

'Go over the ferry, lad, it's a shorter journey for your first time out.' And so it was that Jo travelled back to the farm in some comfort. They stopped above Boddinick. Bryn eased the car to the side of the road, drew her into his arms and kissed her gently.

'Long time no see, Jo …' again his eyes held that questioning look.

'Oh Bryn, it's so good to be back here … so very good to see you.'

'I wondered really whether you had some other pull in London, Jo. I've so longed for your visit, and when you didn't come … well, stupid really, I suppose!'

Jo laughed up at him. Why, he was jealous, and for no reason. The thought somehow made her happy.

'Silly old boy,' her voice was husky as she pulled him to her. 'I've waited a whole year and three weeks for this moment.' Later they sat for a while in companionable silence, watching the white cumulus clouds race across the sky, row upon row of them, moving towards the headland where the sun shone. There they dispersed into the blue sky over the sea.

'Are you fit now?' she asked, her head resting on his shoulder.

'Fine really. Good enough for a walk tomorrow at any rate. I have another medical next Wednesday and expect then to be pronounced fit for active duty!' He spoke with pride, but the words and all their implications only served to make Jo shudder. So it had come at last. Bryn was ready to do 'his bit!'

'I'll be all right, Jo.' Bryn's voice was gentle as he sensed her alarm. 'My training was the best ever and it will be good to put it all to some use.'

The evening meal at the farm was a jolly occasion. Veronica had arrived whilst Bryn had been out meeting Jo. Both were a little dismayed to see her holding forth to Edith about the situation on the 'new front', as she swung her legs back and forth, so that the rocking chair positively bounced along the floor. She threw herself at Bryn and hugged him.

'So my favourite man is better, is he? We will have to find ways of entertaining him now.' Veronica turned to Jo: 'London let you go at last?' It wasn't a question that needed an answer; just a statement really and Mollie thought how clever of her … a statement with implications!

Jo answered all their queries about the new menace, the flying bombs, and was careful to make light of it all. Bryn watched her, hanging on every word, but shaking his head at times, when he seemed, or maybe knew, she was not giving them the true picture. Veronica was talkative, recounting various aspects of Bryn's training that she'd gleaned from him during his illness. It somehow gave her a proprietorial air and Mollie bristled whenever she spoke, her lips tight and her eyes strangely watchful. She relaxed only when she noticed Bryn reach out his hand under the table and clasp Jo's. 'They'll do,' she thought!

Mr Prouse arrived to take his daughter home. Tom and the aunts went to bed after clearing away the dishes, and finally the young people were on their own. The evening was chilly so Mollie had restoked the fire. They pulled the old settee round in front of the blazing logs and toasted their knees. The firelight glowed on Jo's face in the half-light, and she was happy … so happy that she thought she'd burst. Her eyes studied Bryn's face; it was leaner now, probably due to his illness, older-looking too, more serious somehow. She was completely absorbed and started when she heard his old teasing voice say:

'Yes, it's still me,' and she saw the same well-known, well-loved smile lighten his face.

'That's what I've been looking for, Bryn,' she said softly. 'That smile – now I know you really are back!'

'How long have you got, Jo, how many days?'

'A whole week,' she said. It felt like forever. 'What shall we do with it?'

'I've thought, no dreamed about it for months … headland, headland, headland and so on … all right?'

Jo threw back her head and laughed, a clear, pure happy sound that carried through the house. Mollie smiled to herself when she heard it and nodded at Edith's comment of

'I haven't heard her laugh like that for ages.'

Jo turned to Bryn happily, and met a direct look from those grey-blue eyes. His smile was teasing and watchful. Bryn drew her closer to him and gazed at her for a long timeless while, earnestly and with longing.

'Jo, I …'

Her eyes shone excitedly. 'He does love me – he does love me,' she thought, and a smile of sheer joy softened her lips. Bryn said no more, but bent his head to kiss her; their lips met, softly at first until a feeling exploded inside Jo and she reached up her arms, twined her fingers in the short curls at the nape of his neck, and gave herself up to the magic of the moment; she seemed to float away, lost to everything except the reality of Bryn – Bryn kissing her as he'd never done before. Bryn calling her name over and over again.

They broke away, too full of emotion to speak and leant back against the settee. Bryn reached an arm up and round her shoulders, pulling her close once more, so that her head rested in the hollow of his arm and against his chest. She could feel him trembling, could hear his heart thudding as if trying to escape. 'Oh Bryn … Bryn …' she said quietly to herself.

'Jo,' he whispered, 'Jo. I've waited so many months for this moment. I've waited one whole year and three weeks as well, to walk out there with you. Veronica has been offering to accompany me, but it's our place, Jo, yours and mine. Will you walk out to see Mr Pencarrow tomorrow with me, and ask him to keep me safe for you please?' She could only nod her head, too full for words. They sat cosily together until the last logs turned from flames to glow; from glow to embers; only then did they creep quietly to bed. The little room welcomed her as always. The night seemed to fill the room with country summer smells. She breathed them in deeply, safely. She was at Widegates – away from the war and Bryn was sleeping just two doors away. Jo felt a deep peaceful contentment as she drifted into a long undisturbed sleep.

Mollie noticed a change in them both the next morning as she fussed over their breakfast, and was happy for them.

'If you're going to the headland this morning, lad,' she began, stopping as both of them burst into laughter, happy carefree laughter.

'Care to share it?' and as Jo shook her head she went on. 'No … oh well! But, Bryn, make sure you wrap up. It's a lovely day, but the breeze has a chill to it. I've had enough of nursing a great chap like you, so take care!' Her hands rested for a while on Bryn's shoulders as she gazed over across the table to wink at her niece.

'Yes, ma'am. I will – indeed I will.'

Later that day as they walked slowly to their favourite place, Bryn asked Jo about the reality of the new bombs that Londoners were having to cope with.

'It's pretty grim, Jo, isn't it?'

They were sitting now on a grassy bank, facing out to sea, within the shelter of the high rocks that formed Mr P's noble forehead, when she told him. The sun was warm, the sea sparkled and the gulls, strong and graceful in flight, uttered their sad, haunting, mewling cries as they flew in huge arcs over the cliffs, before striking out to fly low over the water. The incoming sea thundered against the cliff below them, the breeze whispered through the gorse and set the colourful stems of montbretia waving. A small fishing-boat was returning to the harbour accompanied by a cloud of white, gnat-like gulls, too far away to be heard.

'Such peace – I've dreamed of it so often,' Bryn remarked as he settled further into the rocky crevasse, his face relaxed and sunkissed. Jo told him of the flying bombs. Of the terror they imbued as they came in from the distance, nearer and nearer with the recognisable chug-chug-chug … drumming on all her senses. Of the fearsome time when they cut out, and then swished swiftly to earth.

'The most awful thing, Bryn, is that we can do nothing about it. Oh I know that the barrage balloons prevent hundreds from reaching us, and the air force shoot down many, but we are in the

direct line of fire. One good thing though, I don't have to worry
about mum any more. It's such a relief that she's at Pendower House
and safe.'

She smiled up at him a little coyly.

'I slept like a log last night, partly because I knew I was safe and
because I knew you were there! I think it's the lack of sleep that
bothers me most. Somehow I seem able to cope with the fear, the
sights and the noise, but there are times when my head screams for
sleep.' Bryn pulled her head onto his shoulder.

'Give it all up, Jo, and come down here. I worry so about you!'
But she shook her head against his shoulder.

'I just feel I'm needed, Bryn. The hospital is so short-staffed and
now with more and more casualties, and most of these women and
children ... well, I just can't leave. I really can't!'

They were quiet for a while. 'All right, dear girl. I won't press that
point further, but promise me you'll take good care.' Jo nodded,
her smile radiant.

'Now, Bryn, let's have a wonderful seven days.' And they did,
that is until the evening before Jo was due to leave once more
for London. As hoped they spent a good deal of time on the
headland, and walking the coastal path. Bryn was stronger as each
day progressed; the fine weather held and the wind dropped, so
enabling them to take many rests in the warm sun without the
risk of getting chilled. They talked of their plans. Jo mentioned the
possibility of teacher training and Bryn told her that his uncle was
back in Beckenham preparing to open the business once more.

'I wish I didn't have to return there, Jo, but we've no future
unless I work and save.'

'We'll manage somehow,' she replied. 'At least you will be near,
just a short bus ride away and we'll be able to meet often!'

They discussed the aunts and how they were managing Widegates
now that Tom was relinquishing the responsibility of it more and
more.

'He's often in a lot of pain, Jo. Did you know? But he'll never let
on.'

'Poor uncle Tom. He's so proud. Mollie and Edith would be
pleased to care for him, but he pushes them off. Any kind word said
to him now gets rebuffed with sarcasm. He's not easy you know,
Bryn.'

'Oh, I know. I've been staying haven't I? He still insists on doing some tractor work. An impossible task with his disability, but he manages somehow. He has a good heart and lots of determination.'

'And cussedness,' Jo added. 'And we love him!'

They clambered down to the cottage just to sit on the patio nearer to the sea, though they knew David would not be there. He and Margaret had become engaged in April and they were now visiting her parents, and hopefully discussing wedding plans.

'Will you be able to get down for it, Bryn?' Jo asked.

'I doubt things will be easy in that direction once I'm back in the swing of things, but I'll try. What makes you think the wedding will be here? Margaret's parents live in London, don't they?'

'Margaret and David have a "feel" for the area, as we do, Bryn. It's to be held at St Lowell church. They are buying the little white bungalow at the top of Polruan. You know, the one with window boxes and the clematis over the roof. Margaret wrote that she's thrilled with it. We always thought it small. Not much bigger than this cliff cottage, but there is an extension at the back which houses a large kitchen. A 'family room', Margaret calls it. From there they have a view of the mouth of the river, St Catherine's Castle opposite and Gribbin Head – it's quite spectacular.'

'Wonderful the way things happen,' she continued. 'Four or five years ago, David was about the loneliest man I've ever met – and now …' They were both silent for a while; Jo happy for Margaret and David, but wishing that she and Bryn were able to think of serious commitment. As if he read her thoughts, Bryn said quietly:

'They are older than us, Jo.' The comment didn't need an answer. She knew what he was trying to say, but her heart was heavy for a while, and the old restlessness was there, waiting to take over again. Why, she wondered, why should I feel like this when Bryn is back and we are here together. But it was the war that still controlled their lives, they were conditioned by it, day by day. They could dream, but they couldn't plan and it wasn't enough.

'When, oh when will the war end, Bryn?' she whispered. He didn't reply, but tightened his arm about her shoulder, kissed her cheek and peered over her head to watch where several shags struggled to maintain their balance on a rock, caught now in the swirling incoming tide.

They were happiest on their own that week. It seemed that both had so much to catch up on, so many things they'd not been able to share, and were now learning about.

There was a strange awareness of each other too, a tension that hadn't been noticed before. Bryn's expression was often serious, sad almost at times, and she caught him watching her with that same questioning look.

Veronica called at the farm twice and found them out. Jo thought that Mollie revelled in this fact.

'Sorry, Veronica – they went for a walk. Took lunch too. I've no idea where they went, no idea at all.'

Two days before Jo was due to leave, Bryn heard that his medical had been put forward. He was to go to Plymouth to keep an appointment the following day. Mr Prouse, who had a business commitment there, offered him a lift. Veronica mentioned *The Mikado* was showing at St Austell; a local amateur society production and she knew several people involved. She asked them to join her there. So it was arranged, a meal with the Prouse family and then the theatre. Jo would go over on the foot ferry later in the afternoon to join them, and Richard Williams, Selina's dad, would give them a lift back over the water and drive them back to Widegates.

Jo waved Bryn off in the morning with a swift kiss and a light 'good luck'. She went straight to the stable to saddle Horse who had been somewhat neglected so far on this visit. He was restless and anxious to be out. She had saddled him and was almost prepared to move off, when Edith called her: 'Telephone, Jo – Veronica.' She hurried across the yard wondering what, or if, anything was wrong. Vee's voice was breathless, as if she'd been running.

'Jo, such a shame. I can only get two tickets for this evening. Bryn said he'll come with me and will stay the night. Do you mind very much if we cancel the other plans? I know Bryn was looking forward to Gilbert and Sullivan – it's a shame to disappoint him as well.'

Jo was quiet for a while. She heard Veronica's tentative enquiry. 'Jo, are you there?'

'Yes, I'm here.'

'Would you mind awfully, Jo?' Vee sounded young; her voice pleading. We haven't been too kind to her all these days, she thought. Strange, though, that Bryn had agreed to a change of plans that excluded her.

'It's OK, Vee – I understand.' she answered.

'Thanks, Jo – thanks from both of us,' and Veronica rang off. Jo's initial surprise at the request turned now into a deep disappointment. She'd miss Bryn, and it was her last night here. Mollie's comment on the change of plans was as succinct as ever.

'You should watch Veronica – she's a trouble-making madam.'

Jo immediately sprang to her defence.

'It's all right, aunt. Vee really thought she could get three tickets. Bryn finds it difficult to say no to her – she's like a kid sister to him. After all we've had five days on our own and we have been avoiding her. I'll enjoy a day on the farm.'

She took Horse across the wide moor, high up near to the cairns, where the views of the sea and moorland met to form a wide expanse of beauty. The morning air was fresh and heather honey-scented. Horse was lively, sensing her mood and she galloped with him to the boundaries of Pensilva land. Her heart was happy. Bryn, her Bryn was back and they'd got closer over the past five days. She now trotted home sedately, still thinking of Bryn – yes, her heart was happy, but why then did she feel unsettled about this evening … why?

'You want him all to yourself, my girl,' she admonished herself, 'And that won't do at all.'

Aunt Mollie greeted her as she coaxed Horse through the wide farm gates.

'Selina telephoned. Bob is home and with a friend of his. She wondered whether you'd care to join them this afternoon as your plans have changed.'

'What a lovely idea, Mollie,' Jo replied. 'I haven't seen Selina for ages. I could just do with a lazy afternoon looking out over their marvellous view of the river.'

'You can help me in with the things for the jumble sale then. There's almost a shed full of bits and pieces I've been collecting for ages. We can go into Polruan together,' Mollie said with some satisfaction.

They busied themselves before lunch filling the boot and back seat of Tom's little car with bags, packages and boxes. Mollie explained that her shed had been used as a collecting point.

'Old Mr Hughes from Pennybont wanted me to house an old carpet, but I refused. How on earth he expected me to get that into the village I don't know,' she bristled indignantly. Jo had time to change and wash her hair before lunch. The breeze from the open car window now tossed her soft curls about and fluttered the collar of her dress against her chin, as Mollie manoeuvred the car along the winding lane towards Polruan. She wore her navy and white dress, her legs were bare and tanned and she had flung a bright red cardigan of Edith's round her shoulders against any possible chill.

The afternoon was pleasantly quiet, as Jo had envisaged. Both Bob and his friend Gareth, a stocky, dark-haired young man from Wales, with the bluest of blue eyes, were entertaining; regaling the girls with stories of sea adventures, all very light-hearted and harmless. Selina sat close to Bob, touching him every so often as if to make sure he was really there. Jo felt an intruder somehow, and suggested to Gareth that he might like a walk to the coastguard station, a short way along the cliff. The sea was smooth below them here, sheltered from the onshore wind by the high jutting rocks at the mouth of the estuary. The narrow path meant that they had to walk in single file, but Gareth's voice was clear and confident, and he had plenty to say to keep Jo amused. She glanced at her watch ... four o'clock. About the time I should be catching the ferry across to Fowey, she thought, with a sharp feeling of disappointment. The dress she now wore had been saved all week for this, her last night at Widegates. If only Veronica had managed that other ticket! If only Bryn hadn't accepted his so readily ... Gareth was gazing out across the river.

'It's a bit like the Gower y'ere,' he announced. There was a longing and pride in his voice. Jo questioned him, and he spoke for some time of his home on the beautiful Welsh peninsula in South Wales.

'Makes me feel homesick being y'ere. The sea smells the same, and the cry of the gulls – just like home.' Gareth then explained that this was not a real shore leave.

'We have to be back in Plymouth tomorrow morning by eleven o'clock. Nice of Bob to bring me and to put me up for the night. I feel a bit of an intruder, but,' he turned to her with a teasing glance ... 'but I'm the transport, see. We came on my motorbike!' As they wandered slowly back along the path Jo told him of Bryn, and her voice was proud when she mentioned that he had just got his wings.

'Will he be sent to the Far East, do you think?'

'Gosh – I hope not.' Jo tried to be light-hearted to hide her sinking feeling of dismay at this thought. 'He's only just returned from America, and has a further spell of training to cope with the different weather conditions here. Out there it was all blue skies and sunshine, you see.'

They arrived back for tea, where the four of them kept up a continual banter that left Selina's parents bewildered. It was late when Jo left, Gareth offering a bike ride as Mr Williams went to get the car. She ran after him, a little breathless.

'Gareth has offered to take me back, and I can't resist a bike ride in the moonlight ... so thank you, but please don't bother to get the car out.'

The road to Widegates was bright with a full moon in a cloudless sky. She rode pillion, her arms tight round Gareth's waist, and her head resting a little on his shoulder for security. It seemed to 'earth' her somehow and made her first bike ride feel safer. She caught glimpses of a sea that was fanned with silver beams, as they followed the high road, and St Lowell church was a feast of moonlit grey. As they rode towards it the tower seemed to float away. Jo puzzled over this until she noticed a light mist was forming over the land and settling in the hollows.

Gareth was singing in Welsh a song he had been teaching them all evening, and Jo joined in, forming the difficult words as best she could. They arrived at Widegates in a flurry of wheels and laughter. Jo bade him a friendly 'goodnight and good luck' as he planted a brotherly kiss on her cheek.

She watched him go up the lane, the engine noises fading as he turned up past the church, and then she leaned for a while on the farmyard gate, drinking in the silvery silent magic of the night. She heard a step behind her, and turned to see Bryn standing still and tall in the moonlight. Her heart turned over as she reached for him, but Bryn stepped back. She caught sight of his face – it was angry!

'You've obviously had a gay old time. Where have you been? I thought we'd arranged to meet!'

'But ...' Jo hesitated, she was hurt and a little cross at his tone. She took a deep breath and replied clearly.

'I thought we had too, Bryn, until Veronica telephoned.' Then she added wistfully. 'It's my last night and I'd hoped we could spend it together ...'

'That's quite obvious! I've been back for ages. Jo, where ... why?' He was livid. A new Bryn as he questioned her angrily as to her whereabouts, who 'that man' was who'd brought her home. A bewildered, upset and angry Jo tried to explain, but Bryn wouldn't listen, and eventually stormed off into the house and to his room.

A tired-looking aunt was waiting for her as she went into the kitchen. She said nothing, just hugged her niece, shook her head at the folly of the young ... and with a quiet, 'don't stay up love. It will all be right in the morning', she went to bed.

Jo stayed up very, very late wondering what to do. Should she knock on his door and make Bryn talk this over. Why doesn't he come down – he must know how upset I am. Her family never went to bed without settling arguments; it was a rule that her father had made years ago. 'Always say you're sorry.' ... Well, she was sorry; sorry that Bryn was so mad, sorry that there was this discord between them. Veronica had been so certain. Veronica – had she been telling the truth? Had she perhaps been making trouble as Mollie said? Had she wanted Bryn to herself, for they'd certainly seen a whole lot of one another since his return and illness. No – it's ridiculous to think this way. Vee was a good friend. Jo had been happy that she'd given Bryn the company he needed when she'd been stuck in London. It had all been a ghastly misunderstanding ... and yet some little twinge of disbelief remained, but she put it away from her. She was so very upset that Bryn had behaved that way, he had been so strange that she had hardly recognised him. Whatever was the matter ... where was her kind, loving man? The one she'd grown so close to this week! Jo sighed and shrugged her shoulders, a move that belied the torment inside her. The clock chimed three. She heard a step on the stair. He was coming to apologise – everything would be all right after all; Bryn stood just in the doorway, gazing at her earnestly. She felt shy, awkward as she held his gaze. He appeared haggard, unshaven, and a nerve at the side of his temple throbbed visibly. An aura of power emanated from him – he was a stranger to her in his anger.

'You must have known, Jo, that I wouldn't go without you – you must have known!' His voice was rough, hurt. She glanced towards the fireplace, unnerved by his expression. What could she say? Veronica had seemed so sincere!

She took a step forward, but Bryn had already turned as with a curt 'goodnight ...' he climbed the stairs, and she heard his door shut. Jo sat in the kitchen for an interminable time, until sad, hurt and sorry she finally turned out the lights and took her feelings to bed. As she passed Bryn's door, it was only the moonlight that shed its rays under the wide space at the threshold. He was probably asleep. Well, she would try to do that too, otherwise she'd be a boring companion to her mother on their shopping expedition tomorrow.

The early afternoon sunlight was caught, trapped and dispersed by the huge leaves of the old chestnut tree. A light breeze stirred them and the sun reflected on the water of the lake like a moving shadow. As she sat, Jo could imagine that the lake was full of silver fish, darting first this way and then that, as they did in the sea off the headland. It was a peaceful corner of Pendower House grounds, out of bounds for the younger children because of the deep lake. Jo had walked from the house a short while before, calling to her mother.

'I'll be by the lake, mum. Call when you're ready.' She had passed the long, high windows of the house that looked to the east, and had taken the path through the sunken garden, where pots of begonias glowed colourfully against the low curved wall. Then she had gone past the conservatory, where Miss Burnett sat in her lounger, asleep in the afternoon sun; then on beyond the heather beds and into the parkland that spread down to the lake.

The grass, newly mown, was springy under her feet, sweet-smelling too, mixing its fragrance with the honeysuckle that clambered and clung over the old rose arbour to her right.

She had walked round the lake; stood for a while and watched the waterfall that trickled its way to the stream on the boundary of Pendower land, and listened to its light tinkling music as the water fell almost lazily over and around the slabs. She had watched as a beautiful green dragonfly darted over the water – its whirring wings forming a mauve and green arc around it. The golden fish ... hiding now under the raised rim of the lake, were secure in their haven, for while she was there no heron or kingfisher would venture near. The huge chestnut-tree had afforded her shade on the far side, and there her feet had crunched on tree debris ... great conker shells, opened and empty where either the badgers or perhaps a small deer had eaten their fill. Small twigs and brown, dry leaves had crackled under her feet as she enjoyed the cool shade, before continuing on round the lake, past the wide blue border, to where the path led to a small arbour with a rustic garden seat placed to face the lake. Here she sat. Her heart was heavy, for Bryn hadn't shown for breakfast, and he was not back to say 'good-bye'. She felt restless and unsure of herself, unsure of life and afraid of what might lie ahead. Bryn's outburst last night had unnerved her. He had been an unknown Bryn, and it had frightened her. She remembered now as she sat in the peaceful garden, the anguish she'd felt at his absence and the longing always for his return, but somehow things were not the same, and certainly they were not how she imagined they would be! Perhaps it would have been better if she'd been able to see him before this, perhaps he felt uncared for. But oh … how she'd wanted to come. How she'd begged the hospital to release her for just two days, and had indeed almost got her wish until Hitler and more bombing had intervened. She had been needed in London, but she had been needed here as well – she knew that.

No! Things were not the same. She felt almost that they never would be again, but then, how could they be? All of them had been affected by this cruel war. The carefree youngsters were gone forever. Their feelings towards each other had changed too. She sensed an awareness, an awkwardness at times that had not been there before, and Jo didn't know how to cope with this. 'I want – oh, what do I want?' she thought.

Did she want to return to the way they were four years ago? Two relatively light-hearted young people, taking each day's pleasures as they came. No – they were older now, and wiser she hoped. The war had taken their youth, taken the light-hearted young girl and left behind a serious woman. 'Bryn might not like this new me …' she thought. 'But I can still be fun, still be happy, still be gay at the small things, and our headland still sends me in raptures with its everlasting beauty.' Right now though, Jo felt weighed down with life … with longings, and with a strange disappointment that Bryn's homecoming that she'd looked forward to, longed for and dreamed of for so long had somehow turned sour. It wasn't joy she felt now, but a strange loss. She had mentioned it to Aunt Mollie that morning, when she'd taken in her early morning tea.

'I know, love, I remember,' Mollie had said. 'Take time, Jo. It's because you both care so deeply that you hurt one another. Take time – it will sort itself out.' She hoped that her aunt was right. Bryn was older now too. The war had taken the bright, smiling youth away, and left a serious-faced man. His once mobile mouth seemed more often to be set in a firm, unsmiling line, and his hands, always so still and relaxed before, were often clenched and tight, whether thrust into his trouser pockets, or resting on the arm of some chair.

'What was wrong?' Jo wondered. She was committed to Bryn. Indeed had been nearly all her life, for so very, very long, but now that they were old enough to voice that commitment totally, something, or someone, seemed always to be in the way. They were both tense at times. Maybe it was a good thing she was returning to London this afternoon. Bryn still hadn't been cleared by the forces doctor and would remain here with Veronica for company for at least another two weeks. Aunt Mollie's ministrations would help him, and perhaps they'd find time to talk quietly. Mollie always helped when she was in trouble, and she knew that Bryn was almost as special to her. Jo was amazed and scared at the sense of relief she now felt at leaving. Was she escaping – escaping from Bryn or her own feelings? Was the reality better than the dream? She sat for a while, drinking in the beauty of this quiet garden, then heard a soft tread on the grass behind her, and felt two hands rest lightly on her shoulders as Bryn bent down and whispered:

'No, don't move. I've come to apologise. Jo, I'm so sorry, so very sorry. My darling girl, I wouldn't hurt you for the world.' His voice was soft and charged with feeling. She rose swiftly, turned and felt his arms enclose her in a hug so tight that she could scarcely draw breath. Tears, the tears she had held back since last night fell down her cheeks, a sob tore at her throat ...' 'Bryn, oh Bryn, I thought ... I don't know what I thought ...' Her words were muffled as Bryn stroked her hair gently. 'Sh ... sh ...' She felt and heard the strong thudding of his heart as he pulled her head close, to rest in the curve of his shoulder. He turned her face for his lips to meet hers in a long deep kiss.

Mrs Dingle watched them for a moment or two as she came over the grass to collect Jo for the shopping expedition they were to share before her daughter's return to London. She turned and went back to the house where Mollie was putting the finishing touches to a birthday cake for one of the boys. It was a carrot cake and she was decorating it with her last few crystallised fruits. Mollie always made the cakes for the home. She loved to visit the grand old house, and to potter about in the huge, cool kitchen, with its wide central wooden table, marble slabs and the long working surface set just under the window. She too had seen Bryn go down the garden and hoped that he and Jo would be able to sort themselves out. 'Poor young things,' she said to her sister, but the latter put her fingers to her lips, then crossed them and said:

'I think they'll be all right. I've left them for a bit – they need to be on their own right now.'

After a while Mollie left for Widegates and Mrs Dingle called her daughter and watched contentedly as they both sauntered up from the lake, arms entwined and glowing with happiness.

'Ready, Jo?' she asked. 'We've a whole lot of shopping to do before you catch that evening train.'

'Coming, mum,' Jo returned, and Mrs Dingle left them to say goodbye, whilst she busied herself with sorting out Jo's luggage, an assortment of small bags that she found easier to cope with on the often crowded train. The rest of the afternoon was fun. Jo spent all of her latest allocation of clothing coupons and was now relatively well set up for an autumn and winter in town and at work. She had talked to her mother about plans for taking up teacher training.

'There's a year course I might be able to do … it's a special course, but I'd qualify, I think. It would be lovely to come down here and start at a local school. What do you think, mum?' Mrs Dingle was pleased for her daughter. The course would mean that she had company. Young company probably, and would not be so isolated as in London. The hospital job was demanding and the extra time she spent in the local hospital wards at weekends was wearing her down. She noticed the dark rings under Jo's eyes – eyes that now had a glint of real happiness once more, and at times a dreamy, fulfilled quality. 'I wonder if he's proposed,' she thought.

Later, on the train back to London, Jo fell into a fitful sleep. She was so tired, but excited and happy as well. He did love her … she knew that he loved her, and Jo felt she'd scream at the intervening weeks before she would see Bryn again.

CHAPTER ELEVEN

Bryn stayed at Widegates for a further two weeks and then was pronounced fit and told to report to an advanced flying unit at Shawbury. He made an early start, because the day before he was due to leave Mr Wilks the vet called to look at one of the calves.

'I'm going to St Austell, lad, early mind, about five, but you're welcome to a lift.' Bryn accepted, knowing that it would save the aunts the trouble of getting him to the train, and it would mean too that he could catch an earlier connection, and so be at his destination in daylight.

Mollie was in the kitchen preparing dinner, when Veronica rushed in.

'Where is he please ... I've really hurried to get here before he goes,' and she threw herself into the rocking-chair.

'Well, lass – you have missed him after all. Bryn got a lift in at daybreak with Mr Wilks – he's been gone some time.' Veronica gasped. Her mouth dropped open and she stared at Mollie and Tom in turn.

'But he couldn't ... he couldn't ... no, he couldn't go without saying good-bye.'

'He did that, Veronica. I heard him last night when he phoned you.' Mollie's tone was firm.

'But it's not the same ... he shouldn't have gone, just like that!'

Tom had been watching, his blue eyes keen and wary. Mollie touched Vee's shoulder.

'Never mind lass. You had a lovely time with Bryn whilst he was here, and he'll be writing just as soon as he can, I'm sure. Now, how about a cup of tea?' Veronica didn't acknowledge the kind words. She sat staring out of the window, rocking the chair back and forth, back and forth. Her mouth was sulky, and her eyes a little wild. Tom was disturbed about her. What a childish way for her to behave, and so immature. Veronica wasn't a child any longer … why, she was as old as Jo, and just look at the difference in their behaviour. He thought of his niece and then of the proprietary manner Vee had with regard to Bryn.

'He's not yours, lass,' he said quietly. 'He's not yours. Bryn and Jo belong together – didn't you know?'

Veronica's lips formed a stiff line and the rocking stopped abruptly. She now sat bolt upright in the chair. Mollie watched her as she drank her tea. It was hot, but Vee didn't seem to notice. She made to talk to her, but Tom shook his head, and very soon Veronica put her cup down heavily on the table and jumped up.

'I'm off then …'

'Wait a moment, Veronica,' Mollie said. 'I'm going into Polruan and can give you a lift to the ferry. We can put your bike on the back of the car …' she stopped in mid-flow, for Vee had moved swiftly to the door, with a loud 'no thanks', and hurried across the yard to where her bicycle had been left leaning against the yard gate. In no time at all, she was pedalling down the lane, past the church, and going as if something, or someone was chasing her.

'What a strange girl she is at times,' Mollie remarked to her brother.

'Oh aye … that she is,' was Tom's laconic reply, as he continued to puff and pull on his pipe.

Veronica pedalled her way along the top road to Polruan, looking neither to right or left. Her face was set and angry as she finally reached the top of the village and wheeled her bicycle down the steep hill. She went straight to the boat-yard, where Ben was sitting on an upturned barrel surveying a small vessel that had come in for a re-fit.

'Have my bike please, Ben. I'm going sailing!' and she was gone before he could answer.

The boat was moored off the Polruan quay. It belonged to Vee's father, but Mr Prouse seldom took it out and gradually she had claimed it as her own. She was in the process of untying the mooring ropes when she heard her name called.

'Vee … Vee … can I come with you?' It was William, eight years old and her neighbour's son. He'd often had trips out with her on the river and was now hopping from one foot to the other in gleeful anticipation. His mother waved from the far side of the quay and called to her son.

'Not now William, we have to visit aunt Maude.' 'Please ,Vee …' the boy's eyes were pleading.

'Oh, all right. Hop in,' Vee said, and then called out. 'I'll not take him far – don't worry.'

The boat left the quay with William's mother standing exasperated and bothered as she watched them for a while tacking back and forth near to the little beach.

'Go across … please, Vee,' William said. His dark eyes were alight with boyish excitement as the slight breeze tossed the light brown curls over his forehead. His face was full of mischief and challenge – just like Bryn, thought Vee, and her mood suddenly lifted, she felt light-hearted, reckless almost, as she prepared to move across the water.

'Hold on then, and mind the boom,' she admonished as the light craft lifted and turned towards the centre of the channel. They tacked back and forth across this wide part of the river, playing a game of missing the larger boats. William loved it and Veronica's handling of her craft became more and more skilful and reckless, so that, for a moment, she was caught off her guard when a large vessel loomed alongside. William too was distracted. His face showed shock and fear as he watched the boom move towards him in seeming slow-motion … 'Down, William … ,' Veronica shrieked … but the bar knocked the side of his head, sending him tumbling overboard. His young body was sucked under the larger vessel, the propeller caught him, taking off half his shoulder and the side of his face. Veronica had seen what had happened. She sat still and stunned as the ship bumped alongside her small craft, and then proceeded up the river, unaware of the tragedy.

William wasn't found straight away. His mother had been fetched and when they finally brought his small body ashore, she rushed over. Selina's father held her back, his arms cruelly tight around her, but his voice was gentle as he murmured, over and over … 'Best not, love … best not … best not …'

'But I must. He's my baby!' and she tore at the restraining hands, but after struggling for a moment or two, her eyes on the little bundle even now being carried to a waiting police car, she collapsed onto the quay wall, crying and pleading.

'He's my baby. I want to hold him … I need to hold him, he's my baby … my baby.' Richard Williams was almost out of his depth and was relieved when several women from the village appeared to comfort and lead away the distraught mother.

Meanwhile Vee had vanished. The assistant pilot remembered seeing her tie the little red sailing vessel up, and then saw her wheel her bike away up the steep hill towards the top road. She never reached the highway, but vanished when his eyes had strayed to the sad scene being enacted on the quay.

Mrs Prouse was told of the accident and her husband came back from Plymouth that afternoon. Veronica hadn't shown up at all, and now her parents were getting concerned for her safety. They couldn't believe that she'd been downright irresponsible about taking the boy out on the boat with her.

'It was a fun thing to do! That's all it was …' Mrs Prouse said, when the police questioned her. 'She is always lively … just a fun thing that turned sadly wrong!'

It was four days before she was found. Some thought she'd cycled away and left the area, perhaps sought refuge from one of many friends who lived on outlying farms, whilst others thought Mrs Prouse was secretly hiding her until all the sad fuss about the accident died down; but those people close to the family knew the concern, fear and worry that her parents were going through. Veronica had vanished off the face of the earth!

She was finally found in the old warehouse: the derelict, dark and damp building opposite the clay-loading station, where the squat, ugly dredgers that worked to clear the river channels were moored. An old gentleman had been walking his dog, who had set up a frantic barking and wouldn't return when called. He had scrambled down the neglected, bramble-strewn path and found Veronica lying in the damp, her face white, eyes open and out of focus, but alive! The ambulance was called, her parents notified, and soon she was being cared for in hospital at St Austell. She remained in deep shock for some two weeks, waking quietly the day after young William's funeral. She didn't ask about him; didn't mention the accident or ask why or how long she'd been in hospital. Just looked about her for a long while … then softly asked her mother …'Can we go away somewhere, please?'

They went to friends at Taunton, Mr Prouse taking them that very afternoon in the car. Neither Jo or Bryn were told about the accident, and when they heard later it seemed wrong to mention it to Veronica, but it did explain to them her aversion now towards the river, and her new, quiet, almost subdued self. The old ebullient and bubbly Vee had vanished, gone for good.

Jo didn't see Bryn with his wings until some weeks later when he stopped over at Mrs Jackson's for a short 48 hours' leave. He was now a sergeant pilot, looking splendid in his uniform and posted to an advanced flying unit. She learned that he was attached to a Bomber Command conversion unit on Wellington bombers. Her heart turned over at the thought that soon, very soon, he would be flying over Germany, releasing 'murder and mayhem' on women and children over there. Jo never got used to the fact that men made the wars, and the women suffered them. She didn't feel hatred for the German people as a whole, just Hitler, and she felt also an overriding sadness, that one man had sucked so many others into this maelstrom of madness, cruelty and death.

The weekend was warm but damp, with a hazy sunshine giving way to soft rain at times, but it didn't deter them from enjoying themselves. They borrowed two bikes and cycled to Keston to sit near the lakes where everything was still, warm and unchanged. The tree canopy afforded them shelter from the soft showers; ducks and swans demanded a share of the sandwiches so lovingly prepared by Mrs Jackson, and the war seemed miles sway. Only the occasional glimpse of a silver barrage balloon through the trees and, once, the familiar throb of a flying bomb going past them, to the east and towards London, spoiled the peace of the day.

The heather was in full bloom, a tiny patch of mauve whose fragrance sharpened their senses and reminded them of the wide moor near to Widegates.

They watched a green lizard taking the sun on a sandy path, laughing together as it darted quickly away when Bryn's hand moved too near. They drank the clear pure water from the well and finally made their way home as the evening turned misty, cycling slowly, side by side, happy and content at being together. As they propped their bikes against the wall of the bungalow, Bryn reached out and drew Jo to him. His lips were in her hair – whispering his longings, her arms reached up in joy at his nearness and their lips met, softly at first and then fusing in a wild longing that left them both breathless and startled. Johanna loved him ... oh, how she loved him! She had never imagined feelings so deep. It seemed that Bryn was more and more dear to her as the days progressed; more and more dear, but as out of reach as ever, for now the war had really caught up with him, and she wanted to hold him close and safe forever.

She went with him to the station the next morning in a haze of misery, but trying hard not to show it. Breakfast had been a quiet meal; Mrs Jackson had grilled some tomatoes, sprinkling their wrinkled skins with a little sugar. Bryn had eaten well, but he had been watchful, his eyes bright and never leaving Jo's face for long. The precious moments ticked away swiftly, and she felt again a surging longing to hold him close. She walked behind his chair and ran her hands through the tight curls, cut short now and feeling strangely strong and wiry.

'I'll be all right, Jo,' he said, trapping her hands round his neck. She rested her chin on his head for a moment.

'Of course you will, Bryn. We've plans for the future, haven't we?'

The recreation ground was deserted. Several flying bombs had landed there during the week and the vast craters, with the mass of mud and stones on the once wide expanse of clean grass, depressed her suddenly. She said so to Bryn.

'You're funny, Jo,' he replied. 'We've passed damaged houses, gaps where houses should be, mounds of bricks and rubble, and yet, only now, here where a bomb crater can't matter, can't do any real harm, only here does it depress you!

She wanted to tell him then just how precious this small area of green peacefulness was to her. It was somewhere that had remained the same, up to now; where the trees and shrubs came into leaf in the spring, flourished in the summer and turned golden in the autumn. Where the seasons did what was expected of them; where birds still sang; where the little river still trickled cleanly over smooth-washed pebbles; where there had been no mud, no rubble, no dust … a green haven of peace, until now! But there hadn't been time to tell Bryn. The train came in early and they had had to run to catch it. She'd waved him off, laughing for his sake, but with tears in her eyes. A sense of loss, desolation and loneliness descended on her as the train drew out of sight. She walked swiftly, stumbling a little on the old wooden steps of the footbridge. Her heart longed for her headland and the solace she might find there, as she hurried, with restless steps, through the churchyard, taking the main road back home, avoiding the 'rec', now spoiled by this dismal, long and dreary war.

Jo went to bed early that evening, excusing herself to Mrs Jackson and John Kimber who had shared their evening meal. The flying bombs arrived just before dawn, disturbing their rest, so that she overslept and had to rush to the station to catch her London train. She sped by the mounds of earth in the recreation ground, giving them just a casual glance. It was a new day now, Bryn had gone, she had her own war work to do, the park would recover! As she ran down the steps of the bridge, a cheeky little robin flew from his perch on the archway, and Johanna was smiling as she reached for the door of the train.

CHAPTER TWELVE

The flying bombs continued to fall on south-east London during August and early September. Some of the raids produced an appalling death-toll, mostly of women and children. Early on Jo's twentieth birthday she went to help at the scene of an attack. The devastation was near to home and she arrived almost before the dust had settled. Jo was horrified to see the hand of a young child, almost a baby, sticking out of the wreckage. It was just a hand – beautiful, white like alabaster, and conveyed in one moment all the appalling sadness, futility and cruelty of war.

The new bombs were still a continual source of conversation and excitement at work, for very few of them reached central London, so her colleagues had no real experience of them. Jo remained quiet all that day – remote almost, whilst an inward terror built up as the day progressed and stayed with her on the dangerous journey home. She was comforted only by her mother, who had come up for a few days to check on the progress of the house repairs. Mrs Dingle welcomed Jo on her arrival at the bungalow ... a birthday surprise, and just what she needed.

'Come on, love, you've been so brave up to now,' Jo's mother said on hearing of the sad event that had so upset her sobbing, trembling daughter. 'The war will soon be over ... you'll see.' She held her close for a while, and then murmured ... 'Not the right moment to say "happy birthday" though, is it? Happy year instead, darling girl,' and Mrs Dingle was rewarded with a tremulous smile.

Later the following week, Jo had another unexpected experience with the 'doodlebugs'. The raids were still heavy with even more bombs raining down on the south-east. She had been made late for work over several days, and it was suggested that she might like to stay at the hospital in one of the nurses' rooms, for a complete rest from the trauma, and for a good night's sleep! However, Jo's mother was still in London, so she declined the offer and left the hospital at the usual time.

Her bus was late and she arrived at Charing Cross station just as an announcement was made that all trains were cancelled! There was extensive damage further down the line, and passengers were advised to make their way home by road, or stay overnight in the station restroom, where some spartan facilities for their comfort would be provided.

It was all hustle and bustle as people milled about here and there, undecided what to do. Jo wondered whether to go back to the hospital for a moment, but quickly dismissed the thought, and set off with a couple of girls for the footbridge over the Thames. It was almost dusk by now, and the last rays of a dying sun limned the dark, creeping clouds of night as they approached the bridge. It was eerie there, with no lights to show the way, and the river, dark and oily somewhere far below them. They held arms and sang to keep up their spirits, and soon found themselves safely over and walking strongly along the main bus route to Jo's part of London. The buses that did come by were all full, so the girls decided to walk further, and eventually, after some three miles, were able to scramble onto the top of a bus going right to the bottom of Jo's road. What a relief it was for them all. The V-1 raid seemed to have eased, although there was evidence of recent damage as they crawled along; past groups of firemen, policemen and wardens, with often mounds of dust and debris in the road, forcing the bus to make difficult detours. People were scrabbling in the rubble for special treasures. 'Poor things,' thought Jo, remembering her horror when her home had been bombed!

Her two companions had left the bus, and she was gazing out of the tape-banded windows, leaning her head against the back of the seat wearily, when she heard a loud spluttering noise. She had been aware of the strange sound for some little time, but couldn't recognise it for anything she knew. The elderly conductor came up the steps and said to her.

'I should come down here, girlie. Those "things" are coming over again and it will be safer below.' As he spoke a sudden silence developed, broken only by a whooshing sound which got louder and louder, until it seemed to fill the whole world around them. They both looked to the back of the bus, and there, following them

along the road, was one of Hitler's secret weapons! A fearful sight
– so near – so dark – so long, and gushing fire from its tail. Time
seemed to stand still. Everything appeared to be in slow motion.
Jo saw the 'monster', registered her fear, but couldn't move. On it
came – nearer and nearer. 'Christ,' said the conductor, and grabbed
Jo's hand intending to pull her away, the only way they could go, to
the front of the bus; for it seemed as if the rocket was going to slice
right through the top of the vehicle, just where they were standing.
As they both watched, petrified, it went over, but only just over!
The dark shape blotted out the last of the evening light ... the tail
flames seemed to envelope them, and a huge swishing, screaming
noise filled their ears. Then it was gone. The bus came to a screeching
halt as the driver became aware of the danger, and he flung himself
to one side of his small cabin. The bomb was now in front of them
and losing height rapidly. 'Down,' the conductor shouted, and they
both threw themselves on the floor as an enormous explosion rent
the air, and rocked the vehicle. Jo felt her clothes being pulled, and
her hair standing out from her head, whilst all the time there was a
continuous roaring, with dust and debris falling all around them.
The 'pinging' from the shrapnel landing on the roof of the bus,
the screams and cries from all around, brought them both back to
the realisation that they were safe, and they struggled to their feet
with vast relief. The elderly conductor, his face pale and strained,
hugged Jo.

'That was a close shave,' he said, 'Now let's see what we can do
for the others.' They made their way down the stairs, checked on
all the passengers, who were frightened, but otherwise unhurt,
and then rushed along the road to where clouds of dust were still
rising from the buildings that had collapsed. The main blast had
gone the other way, fortunately. It was an old factory that had been
hit, and although houses opposite were damaged, it appeared that
nobody was really hurt. In typical London fashion, people stood in
little groups, chatting and offering help, so Johanna slipped away
to walk another mile or so home. She was crying by the time she
reached her house – crying because it was still there, and because
her mother and Mrs Jackson were waiting for her at the gate, in the
dark – worried, and now so relieved that she was safe.

'You'll never believe ...' Jo gasped. 'You'll never believe the
escape I've had. I was chased by a buzzbomb!'

Mrs Dingle stayed on in town for a further two weeks, and experienced some of the reality of life in the south-east. The pilotless planes were unnerving; they came at all hours of the day and night, and nothing could be planned. Even her daily trip on the bus to Beckenham proved impossible at times. She learned to be patient about this, to take each day, or rather each moment, as it came, and not to fret if plans didn't work out as expected. Her respect for the local people grew by leaps and bounds. She admired the way they coped with days and nights fraught with danger; admired the way they helped one another, and most of all, admired their optimism and spirit. 'Not much longer,' was like a password, or 'we'll soon fix Hitler!'

As the Allied armies advanced into France, the launching sites were evacuated and the raids eased. Then, in early September, the first of the guided rockets fell from the sky. This new menace was a greater danger than the flying bomb, though less alarming psychologically. They fell without warning and caused more destruction, and there was no defence against them!

Jo thought she had seen devastation with the 'buzz' bombs, but this new weapon produced unbelievable havoc; whole streets were razed to the ground and the casualties were enormous. Mrs Dingle quite expected her daughter to collapse under this new onslaught, for she had appeared tense and weary during most of her visit, but it was as if Jo was suddenly injected with a new source of courage – a new vitality. She was helpful wherever she was needed, often spending long evening hours as well as weekends at the hospital. Old wards had been reopened and several temporary buildings put up in the spacious grounds bordering on the 'rec'. The hospital was fully operational again and help was a valued commodity.

About this time she heard from Bryn that he was to train pilots in North Wales. Her relief at this news, and the thought that he would be relatively safe based in the home country, helped to contain her buoyant mood.

'It can't last long now, mum,' she said when Mrs Dingle finally prepared for her journey back to the West Country. 'I'll be down for the wedding – perhaps it will be over then,' she said, with doubtful optimism! Mrs Dingle didn't suggest that her daughter return with her. She knew Jo would refuse, and as she waved her good-bye from the train, she felt a deep sadness and concern for this young and vulnerable girl. A pride too – pride at the way Johanna was coping once again. She reiterated her sister's comment as she sat in the almost empty carriage. 'She'll do!'

Bill was now in Italy and sent fairly frequent letters home. When he couldn't write, he got Alan to do so. They had, fortunately, been posted together throughout their campaigns and Jo felt somehow that they looked after each other. She wrote them both long, newsy letters, saying little of the raid situation, just a light-hearted reference to the 'doodlebugs'. She told Bill of Bryn, and how thankful she was that he was training future pilots; of Margaret and David and their forthcoming wedding, of her visit to the cinema with John Kimber – 'We saw the most beautiful film, Bill, *The Warsaw Concerto*, it was poignant, and so sad, and the theme music quite lovely. I walked home with it ringing in my ears!' … and … 'We are experiencing the most wonderful autumn. The mornings are cool and hazy and the evenings misty. I feel quite melancholy walking home through the 'rec', for the beauty is tinged with sadness now at the thought of these lovely, yellow, brown and orange leaves falling. I'm 20 now – over five years of war. It's enough! Fix it for me, brother dear!'

Bryn did make the wedding after all, although he arrived too late for the church service, having been held up for several hours at Exeter. The wedding was over, and bride, groom and guests had converged in Fowey. David had hired a room overlooking the river for a small reception, and it was here that Bryn joined them in a toast to the happy couple.

It had been Jo's responsibility to see to the flowers in St Lowell church for the wedding. She had arrived late the night before and had found the dairy sink full of autumn colour, where Mollie and Edith had picked flowers and shrubs for the displays.

'We'll all get up early and lend a hand, Jo. Margaret has already put ivy on the pillars, and we'll wire some chrysanthemums into that. She requested garden flowers, so they are all from here and Pensilva.' Jo nodded her head, grateful for the help. She was tired after a trying journey down and still felt tense about leaving Mrs Jackson on her own.

'I phoned her,' Mollie said, when Jo mentioned this. 'She's fine – John is staying the night and she says you are to enjoy yourself.'

'Has mum been over?' Johanna queried.

'No, she's quite wrapped up in her charges and says she'll see us at the wedding. Now you go to bed lass … you look tired out.'

Jo settled in her little room and was pleased to find a hot-water bottle in her bed as the evening was chilly. She slept well and was up early to do the flowers. Some two hours later, she stood back to admire her handiwork. The church was transformed. White flowers on the columns stood out clear and pure against a background of green. Over the end of each pew she had hung a small garland of mixed shrubs. The yellow leaves caught the sun as it streamed through the windows, and the berries from the cotoneaster plants glowed with warmth. At the altar she had set a more formal arrangement, and the pulpit was now covered with sprays of autumn leaves, bright shrubs and bronze chrysanthemums. Jo felt sure that Margaret would be pleased with the result and was happy.

Outside the sun was warm for October, and she stood for a while looking up at the sundial over the porch. The gravelled path, which led to the steep slate steps up to the tower, had been swept clean and raked. Jo gazed up at the tower as it stood, grey against an almost clear blue sky. Fluffy white clouds were folding onto one another overhead, giving a feeling of movement, of spinning. She reached out to touch an old tombstone to steady herself, looking now at the steep fields rising towards the headland, and then to where the ground fell away sharply, to the wooded river valley below.

'What a wonderful day for a wedding,' she thought, as she wandered back to the farmhouse, where Mollie and Edith had already changed into their wedding attire.

'Come along, Johanna,' Tom said, as he wheeled himself into the kitchen. 'Come along, the girls have been ready to go for at least an hour!'

She looked at him fondly. How smart he looked in his dark suit. Tom's blue eyes caught and held hers. There was amusement in their depths.

'Surprised to see your old uncle look tidy then, lass? Oh aye …' he added, as she made to remonstrate. 'Aye, I expect you were at that. I'm not too careful how I look these days, am I? Will I do now though?'

Bryn's words, thought Jo. 'Yes, uncle, you look marvellous, and I shall be glad to have you escort me.'

The wedding was to be held at noon. Bryn had phoned that he hoped to make it, but his plans weren't definite.

The church was surprisingly full. Mollie was glad of that, for it made the singing so much nicer, and Margaret had hoped her wedding would be well-attended. She had settled well into the community and was an energetic member of several village clubs. David, though, was not a 'joiner' but he was respected and well-liked by all who met him. It seemed right now that they should have such a send-off.

Margaret was radiant in a forest-green dress. The service was simple and sincere, and David looked so very proud and happy as they walked from the church into the now misty autumnal sun. As she left, Jo looked up again at the tower and the beautiful castellated corners, clear against the sky. Then her glance wandered to the distant clay hills near to the moor, blue-grey now in the afternoon light. It was a perfect October day!

Bryn arrived just as toasts were being made to the happy couple. His eyes sought Jo's, and he moved swiftly across the room towards her. Veronica was quicker though, as she flung herself at him.

'Look who's here – Bryn's here, how wonderful!'

He managed to disengage himself after a moment or two, and made Jo's side as Mollie took Vee firmly by the hand.

'Come and help me with glasses, there's a good lass.' Veronica's expression was explicit, but for once she didn't protest, but threw a backward, wide smile at Bryn as she was led from the room.

Later, when Margaret and David had left for St Austell and the train that would take them further west to Penzance for a brief honeymoon, Jo and Bryn sat at the wide bay window and watched as the little boats bobbed up and down at their moorings; watched as the pilot boat left, seeing Selina's dad quite clearly in the late afternoon sun. They watched the orange and white car ferry operating back and forth from Boddinick; watched as the water sloshed up the steep slipway, scattering the gulls as they strutted noisily about – quarrelsome birds, with fierce eyes and cruel beaks, until they flew up and away, suddenly beautiful, their sad plaintive calls sounding like lost souls in the wilderness.

They admired the house opposite, on the far bank of the river and settled in the side of the cliff. It was ivy-covered and mysterious, with a female figurehead set onto a beam at the front and facing seawards; her proud face gazing towards the estuary as if longing to be back on the prow of the ship where she had once belonged. They sat and talked until Mollie came to fetch them just before dusk for the last ferry crossing. As they reached Widegates they could see heavy storm clouds rolling in from the west, the wind had risen and was tearing through the copse at the back of the farm, sounding like an express train.

'A good night to be in,' commented Bryn, as he shut the kitchen door and looked around the familiar, well-loved room.

There was lots of fog during November and the early part of December. Thick, evil-smelling 'pea-soupers', caused by the continual burning of coal fires and the persistent, damp, heavy weather, with little or no wind, which forced the smoke down and prevented any dispersal. Consequently, it became thicker and thicker. It was yellow and obnoxious and was known as 'smog'.

Johanna walked to the station each day with a torch pointed towards her feet, and her body forcing its way through a wet impenetrable 'blanket'. It hurt her eyes, gagged her and made her feel sick, so that she tied a silk scarf across her mouth for protection. Some relief was afforded in the railway carriages, when there was much divesting of scarves and home-made masks; much coughing and nose-blowing, before one finally settled for the journey, sitting quietly and breathing shallowly.

At times the fog was so thick that people passed within a few feet of one another without being seen by either party, and Jo was constantly reminded of the early war saying – 'Look out in the blackout!' She hated it when she heard footsteps, and would slow down to a shuffle, cough and then listen to the other 'body' do the same, as they manoeuvred around each other … stalking like cats prior to a feline fight. Buses crawled through the streets at a snail's pace, but even so, crossing the wide main road was a hazard she dreaded; the initial searching for the kerb stone with one's foot, and then teetering on this, scared of taking the plunge into the abyss, for so it seemed to Jo at times, when her imagination ran riot and she considered … 'Suppose the roadway isn't there … suppose there's a void and I fall, and fall …'

The actual crossing stretched her nerves and senses to the maximum, as with head turning to listen, eyes peering into the gloom in the hope of seeing something … a light perhaps, anything other than this yellow, hanging, musty-smelling 'smog'!

'The fog is bad,' she wrote to Bryn. 'How I long for the clear air of North Wales or Cornwall. Mrs J is scared to venture out, so dear old John does most of our shopping, such as it is, for food is scarce in the shops, and even now, coming towards Christmas, there is a dearth of those "special" buys we have come to expect. Mrs Jackson continues to make marvellously tasty meals with what little we get. John has taken to eating with us and it's surprising what a difference those few extra ounces of meat ration makes to a small family such as ours has become.

'All is well at Widegates. They send their love and hope you'll be able to spend Christmas there. If you do, Bryn, then I will! Mum is happy with her charges and getting more and more involved with education now that some of them have reached school age. She is talking of returning permanently to London in the new year, now that repairs to the house are progressing, and of opening a nursery school locally, though where she'll find the accommodation for this I've no idea! So many places wrecked by the bombing. Mum feels that there will be a need for nursery schools when people start returning, and I imagine women will still be fully employed for a while, or at least until you men get back … so the children will need caring for. Do you ever wonder, Bryn, what it will be like for us females? Having held the fort for so long, worked in munitions, on farms, on buses etc, and then to have to revert back to the old ways, to the confines of home and to bringing up the children? I think for some this will be a very daunting task.

'Bill is in Italy now and separated from Alan, who has been slightly wounded, an arm injury I believe, and he is at rest camp for a while. Brother dear managed to get bitten by a dog, and was given anti-rabies injections. He described it fully in his letter, but with humour – I hope the antidote is foolproof! We have stray dogs round here quite often. Mrs J puts out scraps for them, but John reports them to the police and they are nearly always taken away. Sad really, probably pampered pets at one time too!

'I have a friendly robin who's decided to take over the garden. He reports each morning on my windowsill, looks at me with bright button eyes and waits for a few breadcrumbs I keep by for him. I'm hoping to train the little chap to take food from my hand. Mollie said she often gets them tame at the farm, and indeed when we were down for the wedding, one saucy little bird hopped in through the kitchen door when we were breakfasting.

'Remember the Christmas cards with robins on them? We've been making ours this year. I'll not let you into my secret – you must wait and see. We've also been making tree decorations for the hospital – silver wrappings from cigarette packets tied into shapes with odd bits of ribbon and tinsel, really look quite pretty. Some of the nurses are collecting eggshells, washing them and painting them bright colours. Such industry, but well worth the effort.

'I've a feeling that this will be our last "war" Christmas. Just think how lovely it will be to hear the church bells ringing once more, and to see lights flooding from doorways, shops and windows … and the street lights too … imagine the luxury of those! How we took all these things for granted, Bryn, back in the old days.

'For my part, I'm pleased that you have been posted as an instructor, and can imagine you training the bombing crews, though I know how keen you are to "have a go" at Hitler yourself. Mollie said her prayers were answered, so you see it's not just luck, or the fact that you are obviously superbly capable!

'I had a long letter from James. He recalled his sailing to join the Sicily landing and wrote of the dolphins diving and leaping ahead of the ship. Remember how we used to look and hope for a sight of them off our headland when we were young? His letter was a little serious, plaintive almost I thought, and I hope that he is all right. He has been in a lot of fighting, I hate to think of that. James seems somehow to be so much a part of Pensilva and the land, and should really be at home farming and producing food for Britain.

'Mum has asked for a song for Bill on *Forces Favourites*, so we listen avidly to the Sunday programme hoping that it will come up. Tom apparently likes Vera Lynn, and makes the most disparaging remarks to the aunts about their "caterwauling". I think they both have sweet voices, but Tom appears to be his usual irascible self concerning this.

'Darling – I have to go … miss you …'

Jo spent Christmas in North Wales with Bryn. He only had two clear days and was not able to leave the area. However, he found a Welsh farm on the peninsula that took in guests; obtained a sleeping-out pass and they had a quiet but special time together in a little annexe attached to the main building.

The farm nestled in the hills east of Harlech, with wide views of the sea to the west and mountain ranges eastwards: a perfect setting. They wandered along the wide expanse of beach on Christmas morning, with the wind blowing the soft sand in their faces and whipping the water to a white foam. They explored Harlech Castle and later climbed the hills at the back to look down on the magnificent grey turrets as they stood solid against a dark tumbling sky.

Bryn told Jo that he'd been promoted and was now a flight lieutenant. She wished that he had worn his new uniform and could imagine how dashing he must look in it. 'I'll get a photograph,' he promised her.

The annexe to the farm was delightfully cosy, and Mrs Jones, a dainty, dark-haired lady of about 50 years, fed them well, particularly setting out to tempt Bryn's appetite.

'I like to look after the brave lads if I can,' she said, when Jo had helped to clear the table and followed her into a vast kitchen, so like that at Widegates. Mrs Jones took a photograph down from the high mantel-piece. It was of a young, dark-haired man in RAF, uniform. He was smiling widely, his look direct and vital. 'Who …?' began Johanna.

'My boy,' Mrs Jones replied softly as she gazed longingly at the picture. 'He was one of "the few" – died the second year of the war. That's why I always look after our pilots … it helps, you see!'

Both nights they sat in their own little sitting-room, close to a sweet-smelling log fire, and watched as the resin bubbled, popped and sizzled from the wood. At times like this, when Bryn held her close, Jo was once more overwhelmed by the depth of her feeling for him. With her head resting against his chest, thrilling to the strong beat of his heart, she would whisper in her head … 'I love you … oh, I love you, Bryn.' They were so close in thought with plans they shared, that Johanna felt at times Bryn would hear her. That he loved her too couldn't be doubted, but still there nagged the one wish, one thought – 'Why can't he say so?' She remembered Selina's advice – 'Tell him, Jo – if you love him!' But somehow she couldn't. She wanted Bryn to say those words to her first, and so, in spite of their closeness, the happy hours they spent together, there remained a slight barrier of strangeness between them.

Bryn watched her closely, hanging on her every word and gesture. She was his whole world, and yet still he hung back, for how could he ask Jo to marry him when his future was so uncertain? How could they manage on RAF pay? No, he wanted things to be right for them, peace, security and a home of their own. Jo deserved the best and he would get it for her!

A tense uneasiness settled on them both when they parted, Jo to return to London and Bryn to his base to the north of the farm. The same questioning look was there in his eyes as he said farewell – a look that stayed with Jo through the journey home, not as a pleasure and source of comfort, but rather it gave her a feeling of insecurity. All the blissful closeness of their few days together had vanished. 'What did Bryn want from her?' It never once occurred to Jo that he too was waiting, longing for that full commitment, those words – 'I love you, Bryn.'

Work and responsibilities set her back squarely on her feet once more, and within a few days she was writing happily to him.

'The rockets aren't so frequent now, Bryn, and sometimes we have clear nights without the flying bombs as well. How wonderful to wake in the mornings feeling fit and bright. I've so much energy now, with the war situation improving all the time in Europe, I can really plan to put that energy to good use. Next week I'm to spend a whole day at the local church school. I've taken a day from my holiday for this. My application for teacher training has to be in soon and I'm anxious to see just what I'm letting myself in for. It should be fun!

'Day after day we wonder how Bill and Alan are, and where dear James is now. Have you heard from him? How very thankful I am, Bryn, that you are safe in North Wales. I picture you often with your trainees, or wandering the hills when off-duty, and long to be there with you. Be careful darling, if you walk alone … I understand the weather can be treacherous at this time of the year, and the mountain tracks dangerous in bad weather.

'The "rec" has returned to real beauty in the snow, with those horrid holes not ugly any more. John Kimber has been ill and, just like Tom, makes caring for him very difficult. Mrs J wanted to have him here, but he resisted the idea firmly, so every evening we've popped down the road to see that he has everything he needs for the night. It has been pleasant walking on these frosty nights, even that short distance, for in spite of the devilry that comes from the sky, the magic is still there. Tonight the stars are bright and a three-quarter moon has spread its brilliance over the snowy street. The road and pavements are sparkling, and each step brought that remembered crunchiness we used to love so much as children. I found it hard to contain myself, but in deference to Mrs J I didn't dance along on all the untrodden patches, but walked sedately with her, arm-in-arm with my memories!

'Our house has been reroofed. It looks more like home now that the awful tarpaulin has gone. Sometime this week, I must find time to investigate the repairs because mum is making noises from Pendower House about returning soon. I must say that it would be more than nice, for in spite of the comfort here it's not my home!

'John touched me deeply this evening when he handed me part of one of your letters. I quite thought I'd lost them all in the blast from the bomb, but he came across this amongst a whole lot of papers he bagged when clearing up for us. So, dear boy – I have a little bit of our past back again and will treasure it. It's now in safe-keeping under my bed, in an old biscuit tin – amongst your more recent letters!

'You will know we are safely through another night when you receive this. Take good care of yourself, and teach the lads well. I miss you all the time.'

CHAPTER THIRTEEN

January and February brought increasing good news from Europe. There was a feeling of hope everywhere. It showed on people's faces as they discussed the news in the streets, on the trains and in shopping queues. Careworn faces smiled more and more, and even the harsh winter weather could not suppress the excitement – this expectancy of war's end that pervaded everywhere. Blackout became a dim-out, and shaded headlights were now allowed on vehicles once more, replacing the slits. Jo found this strange to adjust to at first. The traffic on the main road at night took on a totally different appearance, and the headlights made it difficult to gauge distance.

The optimistic mood faded, however, for by early March a weariness seemed to settle over everyone in London. People were despondent at the news, that against all odds, the German forces had managed to break out of our encircling armies and push forward once more. An unhappy lethargy took the people over. All desperately wanted the war to end now … they had had enough!

Raymond left the safety of his school at Christmas and went to live with his mother at Pendower House. His application for college in the south east had been a disappointment, and Tom thought he might stand more chance in Plymouth, but unfortunately no place could be found for him until September 1946. He had more than a year to wait!

He was useful at Pendower House, and Mrs Dingle found him a comfort. The children responded well to his teasing manner and he often helped by taking small groups out into the extensive grounds and organised games and races for them. His young strength was used in so many ways, including helping in the kitchen garden. Ray, always an early riser, could be seen before breakfast gathering the vegetables in for the day ahead. He liked to imagine the walled garden was his, and made up his mind to own a similar one when he was older … perhaps with a little lodge in the corner that he could make his home!

Home conditions had worsened with food supplies shorter than ever. Raymond, perhaps for the first time, was made aware of the struggles that went on in the real world, away from the school camp.

Britain had to help feed Europe as whole areas were liberated. The radio put out special programmes of advice with regard to saving fuel because coal production was down. Mrs Dingle learned to shred cabbage and cook it in a cupful of water! She also used an old heavy steamer that Mrs Jackson had found in her cellar to cook complete meals, the vegetables being tied in 'rag' bags and cooked underneath. The lack of nourishing food was very depressing at this stage, and bread rationing only increased the burden. It was a special day when they all sat down to a rabbit supper. These, when obtainable, were off-ration, and one shilling would provide a rabbit large enough for four people. Mollie gave Raymond lessons on how to skin them, a job that neither Jo nor her mother could face. Time was needed for all this preparation of food and Mrs Dingle often became cross.

'Is this what we are fighting for, Ray?' she would complain. 'Your dad wouldn't like this way of living at all. It's a good thing he's not here to see it!'

At such times Raymond would remain silent and help all he could. The work for the homes was sapping a good deal of his mother's strength. The years of deprivation, sorrow and loss were telling on her. He was amazed to see grey hairs framing her face, and tired lines appearing round her lips and eyes.

John Kimber visited Cornwall for a few days. He was delighted with everything he saw and spent a good deal of time with Raymond. It was fortunate that John was there when Ray was called up for work in the mines. Jo's younger brother was devastated at the thought of his plans for the future being shelved, and for a while his usual happy-go-lucky nature changed. He became silent, morose, and frequently flung himself out of the house in a fury of agitation. John Kimber finally spoke to him – firmly but kindly.

'What about your mother, Ray? How do you think she feels at losing you again? It won't be forever you know, and every experience is worthwhile if you tackle it correctly. What of your sister too – think about her war!'

Raymond was suitably chastened and apologetic, so that when the day came for him to leave, he was almost cheerful about, as he termed it, 'his real and first adventure'.

They missed him. Mrs Dingle hadn't realised just how much they'd relied on his youth and strength for the harsher chores around the big house.

Two rather scrappy letters from Bill came. One had been completed by Alan, which set Mrs Dingle worrying, until John calmed her down with a sensible comment.

'No, don't go on like that. You'd have heard from the authorities if anything were wrong. He's just extra busy chasing the Germans out of Italy!'

Of course John was right, but neither Jo nor her mother were settled in their minds about Bill, until some ten days later and they heard from him once more. He was away from the front having had a tooth removed.

An abcess had developed causing such pain that he'd passed out. 'It's OK, mum,' he wrote. 'Don't worry. I'm at base for another week at least and must say, apart from missing Alan, it's a wonderful life. Hot showers – a real bed, and time to sit and read. Johanna's latest letter arrived and right now I'm thankful for the Argos she enclosed. Love to her and "the sprat"; I shouldn't call him that I suppose, now that he's a "Bevin boy" and working in the coalmines. Poor old Ray – it must be pretty rotten. Still, he'll soon sort out the coal production.'

Jo had an acceptance letter for teacher training and was hoping for a place in September. Apart from her family, she kept these plans to herself. Time enough to tell the secretary of the hospital when everything was more definite.

Bryn wrote that he was now attached to the Pathfinder Force. Jo worried about this, but was reassured by John Kimber when he commented. 'Don't fret, lass. The war is nearly over. There won't be time to send the lad out on foreign duty.' Jo was to remember these words a few weeks later.

The rockets continued to fall, though not so frequently, but they still caused a good deal of death and destruction. Jo was finding her work at the local hospital still very necessary. She found now that it was almost enjoyable, for as a well-known and accepted part-time member of the staff, she was asked to join in many activities, and found herself most Tuesday evenings sharing an 'appreciation of music' session with two nursing sisters and several ward nurses. Records were difficult to come by, so Jo was delighted when Mrs Jackson offered her collection. She selected several symphonies and favourite operatic arias, and these were much appreciated. The latter brought back many happy memories of earlier days with Bryn and James.

Towards the end of March, news came through that the German army was crumbling. The last rocket fell on 27 March, and the war in Europe ended in early May.

Initially people were stunned – it was unbelievable – a dream surely, not reality at all … but once convinced that the war was really over, then everyone went a little wild. Family after family came out of their homes and mingled together in the road to dance and cheer, to sing and chatter. The war was really over! Shop lights went on, windows blazed once more. Blackout curtains were torn down, and houses, without their dark shrouds, became homes once more to the outside observer. Nobody bothered to pull curtains at night. It was as if they'd been shut in for so long, that now they needed the communication with every passer-by. Many houses still had some canvas windows, but every home had had glass replacements in the main rooms.

There were street parties for the children. Food was gleaned, prepared and shared. Paper hats were made from old newspapers and painted with bright blobs of colour. Trestle tables and chairs were borrowed from schools, and gramophones set up for music.

A wireless blared from every house, the voices strident and buoyant, and groups of young people appeared magically on street corners.

Bryn came home. He arrived rather dishevelled having got a lift with a despatch rider. It was his first experience of pillion travel and he appeared strained, but so alive and alert.

'Half the war is over now, Jo. It won't be long before we're free to start our own lives again.' He held her close, his eyes bright with excitement. 'Let's go to the Palace.'

The train to town was packed and they found themselves wedged in tight in the guard's compartment. People laughed and talked together, Christian names were banded from one to the other, and hands were stretched out amongst the bodies and shaken over and over again. A violent rainstorm held them up, but when they finally reached the city, celebrations were going along hysterically. Everywhere there were people – a mass of cheering, stamping, singing people, who pushed and shoved their way towards Buckingham Palace. It was bright sunshine now and Bryn kept close to Jo. He hugged her to him at every opportunity, murmured her name over and over, and she loved it! She welcomed the crowd that engendered the closeness, it was as if they were part of the mass and yet not. They were swept along with them all, but it was just them, just the two of them celebrating, together and privately in this very public place. The mass ringing of the church bells added to the magic.

Outside the Palace, crowds stood and sang, all hoping that the Royal family would appear. Bodies were clinging to the Victoria Memorial, and somehow, from somewhere, people had found flags and rattles. The whole Royal family came out onto the balcony of the Palace, including the two Princesses, Elizabeth wearing her ATS uniform.

The crown cheered and cheered and sang 'God Save the King', and 'Land of Hope and Glory'... They sang madly, joyously, lustily and the air was electric with excitement!

Bryn and Jo didn't remember just how they got home, but it was almost dawn when they trudged, weary and happy across the 'rec'. The morning air was fresh and delicious after the dustiness of London and the stuffy train. They stood for a while on the bridge, watching as the water whirled round the rocks, and Jo leaned against Bryn as she recalled the many lonely times she had stood on this very spot, wishing the war would end.

They heard the early morning news on the radio, and smiled happily at each other when Big Ben sounded the hours once more: then sat quietly listening to snatches of Winston Churchill's VE Day speech.

In late June Mrs Dingle moved back home. Jo joined her and was thrilled to have her spacious, airy bedroom once more. The repairs were far from complete, however, for most walls had needed replastering and took ages to dry out, so decorating them would have to wait. The walls in Jo's bedroom had been patched, the windows reglazed, the ceiling cracks repaired, and several 'wonky' floorboards nailed down. It was as good as new, if a little strange as far as decor went.

By early July Jo's mother had set up her nursery school in the two back rooms of the old corner dress shop. The proprietor still lived above the premises, but the shop had closed two years into the war. With stocks exhausted, little hope of replenishing them, and an ailing wife, he had finally given up. Mr Cook, a short, balding, pale-faced man of some fifty years, was pleased with the new arrangement, because it afforded him a little extra income. It also gave him a new interest, for day after day he would plan and work for the little school. He reshelved the walls for books and equipment, built and painted small tables and stools for the children. He found he had artistic talents, and set to painting large posters for the drab walls. He even visited local offices and shops, begging for pencils, paper, paints and crayons, so that Mrs Dingle came to rely on his ability to get 'things'.

'Leave it to Mr Cook,' she used to say when something was needed. 'He'll sort that out for us.' He put a notice on the school door asking for paper, packages, boxes, string and in fact anything at all that might be useful in the schoolroom. Parents and neighbours who had become 'squirrels' during the war years searched their cupboards. Nothing had been thrown away that might be recycled, and Mrs Dingle soon found her school shelves well-stocked with useful 'junk'. The local newsagent produced some old colouring books. They were a little damp, having been stored in the cellar, but Mr Cook dried them out carefully, and the children really enjoyed the treat … they were pre-war and a little out of date, but that didn't matter at all!

Jo became more and more involved herself. She loved the evening preparations with her mother, and they both spent many happy hours planning events for the day ahead. She kept the books, tidied and swept the classroom in the evenings, and helped to make shoe bags from odd remnants of material that her mother had gleaned from neighbours. Finally, she took two days of her annual holiday to spend in the nursery school 'to see what it is really like'. She loved it! So different from Polruan School where she was a regular visitor; lighter somehow, more fun and she readily learnt new simple songs, poems and movements that she could do with the children. She found that stories conjured from her 'head' were popular with the little ones, and she began to compile a small book of these for her mother's use.

'I need more help, Jo,' Mrs Dingle had said early one warm July evening. 'If the numbers continue to grow now that people are returning home, then I could open another class. Mr Cook has said that I can use the shop front. How about joining me?'

Johanna had been reading a letter from James who was now somewhere in Greece and not on his way home as she'd hoped. She answered her mother in a half-hearted fashion ...

'Maybe, mum ... maybe.'

She was thinking too of Bryn's last letter, written when he'd returned to his unit two weeks after the magic and joy of VE night. He hadn't mentioned the headland once – it was a significant omission, for this they had arranged, would be a special sign that he was going abroad – leaving England's fair shores for who knew where? She sat dreaming of her memories ... the days and weeks she'd had with both Bryn and James as children as young adults.

Now they had both gone to war ... A surging restlessness overcame her. She jumped up from her chair.

'I'm going walking Mum ... won't be long,' Jo called as she fled for the door.

Johanna heard that the teacher training course would have to be deferred for another year. She was disappointed, but understood that the course was popular and priority was given to young people leaving the forces. A place for her in 1947 was definite, and so she decided to leave her hospital secretarial work in September to join with her mother. It would be good not to have to make the long train journey every day, and working with the children really appealed to her. Any doubts she had about this decision vanished immediately when a letter came from the headmistress of the infant school in Polruan, who requested her help as an unqualified teacher for one month near the beginning of the autumn term. 'Widegates, for a whole month!'

Mrs Dingle was happy for Jo, though she'd miss her. Raymond was home now, so she wouldn't be on her own. He had been involved in a minor accident in the mine; a rock fall that had damaged his left hand. It was healing well, though he had lost the nails from two fingers. All of them secretly hoped that the coal shortage would improve so that he would not be needed in the mine again. Ray had developed into a quiet conscientious young man, serious about his future, solicitous of his mother's welfare, and interested in the nursery school. He promised Jo that he would help all he could whilst she was away. Nevertheless, she was concerned for her mother. The evening clearing and cleaning became impossibly difficult. Jo was often late home when the clinics at the hospital ran late or trains were delayed.

'You ought to get someone in, mum, permanently I mean,' Jo remarked one evening after studying her mother's tired features. 'We can afford it now.'

So they employed Nancy Grant, a middle-aged widow, to help clean and tidy every day. She always arrived at school just before the children left for home, and helped them with their coats and hats, her face aglow as she chatted quietly to each child she handled. She had rosy cheeks, in a happy smiling face with deep laughter lines round her dark eyes, and greying fly-away hair that she was forever pushing off her forehead. Her sturdy, but compact figure, in its dark-blue apron became a special part of school life. Nancy Grant had no family of her own and gave extra time freely. She was a 'gem'. The school work became the nub of her day and both she and the children benefited from this new arrangement. 'My children,' she called them all. 'My good children.'

Jo left the hospital the same week that she reached her 21st birthday. Her colleagues took her out for a meal in a smart restaurant off Marylebone Road, where they sat down to an unheard-of four courses. It was a quiet, sedate evening and, for Jo, tinged with a little sadness at the thought of leaving a job she had always loved.

Her birthday was celebrated at home. Mrs Dingle had asked several friends, mostly neighbours who'd known her daughter since childhood; John Kimber produced a carrot cake sparsely filled with a few sultanas, and lightly covered with sugar frosting. It proudly displayed 21 assorted candles, all of which had been stuck straight into the cake and now leaned over slightly. He also embarrassed Jo by making a speech. She realised that his intentions were good, nevertheless hated every minute of it. The cake had been cut and the meal cleared away when Jo left the room for a while to check on something that had been worrying her for some time. That afternoon, she had noticed that the wall in the long passage that led to the bathroom and toilet was warm to the touch. She had slipped on the floor earlier and, on putting out a hand for balance, noticed the heat. Mrs Dingle had laughed at Jo's concern.

'It's only the boiler dear. I've stoked it with wood as well as coke, and it flared up the chimney a little.' Jo was not convinced, particularly when she noticed the the wall seemed warmer each time she checked.

Now she was alarmed. The area of heat had spread, and putting an ear to the wall she heard a slight roaring sound. Raymond went to phone for the fire brigade, whilst she told her mother. The firemen arrived very quickly, took one look at the wall, touched it, listened by it, and then proceeded to smash it in with their pickaxes. Mrs Dingle was distraught, for her house had only just been repaired. Jo peered into the widening hole over the firemen's shoulders and saw that several great beams were ablaze – indeed as she watched the fire became fiercer, heat and flames reached out from the hole. She had been right to be concerned!

Later the firemen told them that they had had a lucky escape for the fire would have taken hold completely had they left it for much longer. It appeared that some of the chimney brickwork had become dislodged with the bombing, and this had allowed the flames to reach through to the wooden beams. Johanna always remembered her 21st birthday, for she spent the rest of it clearing up the wet, muddy mess left by the firemen.

'As if I hadn't seen enough rubble and mess with the war,' she had commented to John.

Jo was overwhelmed to hear a few days later that the war in the Far East was now over. The final stages, she knew, must have been horrific for the Japanese nation, with the dropping of the atomic bombs on Hiroshoma and Nagasaki. Her mind reeled at its consequences, but under all that, and in spite of the horror, there rose within her a feeling of such joy at the thought that Bryn would now be back – safely back, and everyone would be able to get on with their own lives. No more directions because of the war – no more longing, wishing time to pass, and best of all – no more waiting!

Another letter from Bryn explained that, having been posted to 617 Squadron and despatched to fight the Japanese, the bombing of Hiroshoma had forced a rapid end to the war in the Far East, and he had been redirected. He was now in Egypt and sounded unsettled and frustrated. Jo was happy to hear that he was not 'so far away' and quite expected he would be home before too long.

VJ night in London, on 2 September, was as gay, as mad, as noisy and as crowded as VE night had been. Jo didn't join in the fun in London, but helped at a party at the local hospital. All of the walking patients assembled in one ward, where staff put on an impromptu cabaret for them. There were many rude impersonations of Hitler, comical references to Churchill, and much singing of 'Roll out the barrel,' and 'We've hung out the washing on the Siegfried Line'. The evening ended with an emotional rendering of 'When the Lights go on again', sung by a tiny dark-haired Welsh nurse; there were few dry eyes as she finished the last note.

Jo accompanied her mother to Beckenham where the children's home was being closed. Mrs Dingle felt that some of the equipment might be useful to her in the nursery school. After helping to collate various books and toys, and then boxing them for transporting later, she walked to the shopping precinct to call on Bryn's uncle.

Jim was looking tanned and rested after a short break in Taunton, and he welcomed her with open arms.

'Come along in, Johanna. How good to see you. Heard from Bryn? Yes … well so have I. Wonderful that the war is over and we can all pick up the pieces now, eh?'

He peered at her over his glasses. A tall, neat and chubby-faced man, with greying dark hair and eyes so brown that they were unfathomable. Jo noticed that he stooped slightly now, and that his movements were a little ponderous as he collected a chair from the outer office and placed it near to his desk. He must be getting old, she thought, and made up her mind to ask Bryn his age when next she wrote.

'We are open for business now, Jo, and things are going quite well. Lots of people seem to need us to sort out their finances. I think by the time Bryn returns we'll be well-established once more.'

'When do you think that will be, uncle Jim?' she said quietly. His large hand reached out across the desk to pat her shoulder.

'There, Johanna – don't fret. Bryn will be back just as soon as the air force allow it. Can I make you tea, my dear?'

'I'll do it … you sit there and rest for a while.' Jim studied her. What a lovely young lady Bryn's little tomboy friend had become, but how serious, and, right now, how sad! Well, the war had been pretty awful for the young, and he knew and was proud of the fact that Johanna had coped with more than most, living in London all the time. For his part Taunton had been a dream and he'd not wanted to leave. His wish now was to get the firm operational, Bryn installed, and then go back to the peace of North Devon, where he had so many good friends. The gentle way of life suited him.

'Everything has changed here, Johanna. I seem to recognise so very few people, and there is a hustle and bustle of newness in this area.' Jim's voice was pensive.

Jo understood, for she felt the same in her part of London. Each day boarded shop fronts were removed, and new ventures started. Many of them seemed a little brash compared with the long-established businesses of pre-war days. The whole structure of her home area was changing.

'I know just what you mean, uncle Jim. We can never go back, people and places will never be the same; the war was too long, much too long for that. Tea all right?' she said as she sat down companionably near to him.

'What does Bryn think of returning here Jo? He is reticent with me, agrees with everything I say and plan, and yet I feel, deep down somewhere, that his heart is not in the business.'

'Oh it is uncle ...' Jo was anxious to reassure him. 'But you see we have a dream – a dream of farming in the West Country, but we know it's almost impossible really, Bryn would have to learn about agriculture, and then we'd have to save for many years.' Her voice grew wistful, and she looked down at her hands clasped tightly now in her lap.

'Does it mean that much to you both, my dear?' Jim said gently as he watched her.

'Well,' Jo began, and then flashed him a happy smile. 'Well, you see we've always talked about it, ever since we were children, but Bryn has never committed himself to replanning his future. I know he expects and hopes to come back here and work with you ... our dreams are for later!'

'You do have to work on dreams, young lady – to make them come true,' and as she nodded her head, he continued. 'But I'll have a chat with Bryn and see how the land lies. I don't want him to think that he has to return to accountancy, although I have reopened the firm for him. Wouldn't have bothered for myself. I loved my life in Taunton too much!' Jim was rewarded when Johanna leant over and kissed him softly on the cheek.

'We know, uncle Jim, and we are both very grateful. It will give us a really good start.'

'Hmmph …' Jim was embarrassed and delighted. 'Hmmph … we'll sort it all out somehow, when the lad gets home.'

Sitting with her mother as the bus moved carefully through well-lit streets alive with people, Jo told her what Jim had said. '… and mum, I really must go to see him regularly when I return from Widegates. He seems lonely somehow, and so much older!'

At Polruan Infant School the staff and children were in assembly when Jo arrived towards the end of September. She stood near the hall listening to the piping, happy voices of the children singing 'Daisies are our silver', and wished that she were in there with them. She had been given a class of some 29 six-year-olds, some of whom she recognised. There were roughly equal numbers of boys and girls, and they had already formed their own special little groups or gangs. One group of three boys she nicknamed 'The Three Musketeers'. They were always together, three bright eyed, cheeky little rascals.

James arrived home on leave from Greece; he'd been posted there after VE-Day. Hearing from his mother that Johanna was down, he made for Widegates without letting them know, arriving at the kitchen door just as they'd finished breakfast. He looked well, tanned from the Mediterranean sun, and thinner. He greeted the aunts warmly before looking towards Jo.

'How's my best girl then?' He reached out his arms and hugged her tightly, then stood back and looked at her – a warm, long look, and his face softened as he whispered …

'Hello, schoolmarm. May I meet you later after you've dismissed the little rascals?'

It was a difficult but happy month for Johanna. She settled in well to school life, feeling strange and a little uncertain only when it was her turn for dinner duty. The lively, chattering children overawed her en bloc, until she found that by raising her voice slightly she could be heard clearly. There were always one or two youngsters who seemed to ignore authority; these she managed to quell into silence when necessary, with a long direct look. As she became more sure of herself, these moments ceased to be threatening, and instead became amusing to her.

The classroom situation was different. Here it was her domain; she was in total charge. Jo made her lessons interesting, and her innate sense of fun saved many difficult situations with her 'musketeers'. She worked hard each night on preparations, with Tom offering alternate advice or condemnation at the hours she was expected to work.

'I don't have to, Tom, I want to. It's good to go into class prepared; it makes things easier for a new girl like me. I'm lucky, you know, to have this opportunity to try teaching, and you never know, if I do well, they might just ask me back!'

'Would you like that, lass – to live and work here?'

'Oh yes, Tom. I couldn't think of anything I'd like better. Bryn wants to return and farm here somewhere, when we can afford it. It's a dream he has!'

'I thought so,' answered her uncle. 'I thought so,' and he wheeled himself slowly back to his room. 'Goodnight girl – God bless.'

What a dear man he is, thought Johanna. A real softie underneath all that gruffness. He misses Bryn a whole lot, I know. They've always got along so well. Work forgotten, Jo sat dreaming – a little voice at the back of her head repeating Bryn's name, over and over again, as if she could will his presence… 'Bryn … Bryn … Bryn!'

James had two weeks' leave and they met as often as possible. He took her to Plymouth for a performance of *Giselle*, her first experience of ballet. Main theatres in Plymouth had suffered almost to extinction from the bombing in 1941, so the production company from the Midlands performed in a fairly small cinema to the west of the town. The stage at times appeared overcrowded with dancers, but nevertheless it was a magical musical evening.

They returned to Widegates on a silver moonlit night with their ears ringing and hearts lifted.

'What a lot of good things we've missed through the war, James,' Jo said sadly as they sat high on the top bar of the farm gate, loathe to let go of a perfect evening.

'Yes,' James peered closely at her and his eyes were teasing. 'And what a lot of fun we'll have catching up on them, Jo!'

Early one morning they fished from the rocks at the bottom of Pencarrow Head – scrambling down the steep, often frightening path like teenagers, to sit perched on a small platform of rocks, just out of reach of the sea spray. Laughing, some two hours later, they presented Mollie with a two pound pollack which was filleted and grilled for tea. James heard about Mollie's sweet tooth and of her longing for 'something nice', so he took a minor, but active part in the local black market, bargaining with one or two mementoes he'd brought back from Italy and Greece for sweet coupons. They searched the whole of St Austell before locating Mollie's very favourite dark chocolate, and delighted in her happy, bewildered pleasure when they gave it to her.

Veronica asked them both over for the evening. It proved to be a jolly occasion as she'd included several other friends from the area. Vee was in sparkling form. She talked about Bryn a good deal and brought out a large old atlas to pinpoint his exact whereabouts in Egypt. Her new job with the Health Department at St Austell excited her. She was attached to a large department, and had met many of the young people working there. It was a lively, friendly office after the stuffy bank, and even the slightly involved bus journey to and fro did nothing to deter her happiness with the change. She spoke of the trauma of her interview in May.

'Just imagine, Jo, ten senior members of the department, sitting safely behind a huge boardroom table and all looking severe! I was ushered in to stand in the middle of the floor. I felt so lonely and scared. Then I remembered Bryn had said … "We are all people … just people." The sun came out, blinding my eyes for a moment and I relaxed. It was just as if he'd flown into the room to help me!'

James and Johanna exchanged glances when one of their friends commented… 'You and your Bryn, Vee …' Jo shivered visibly, feeling lost, adrift and scared for a moment, until James squeezed her hand under the table, his eyes warm and friendly. 'She was always like this … remember, Jo?'

They went for a meal in the newly-opened steak house at St Austell. A bright, brash-looking place, with dark-red decor, tables with pink tablecloths and red wooden candlesticks set in little alcoves round the room. The meat was rather tough and strong-smelling … 'Whale meat probably,' Jo commented quietly. 'It's supposed to be like beef.' Once James had got over the shock and slight aversion to the steak, they talked about the worsening food situation in town.

'People swop clothing coupons for food, James. We eat rabbit if we are lucky and Mum makes the most of what vegetables we can find by adding pulses. The aunts did quite well with haricot beans in the kitchen garden, and we always take back a supply, but it's so very, very boring. We eat to live, not because we enjoy it. When things improve I think I'll open a fish-and-chip shop. Remember those meals we used to have sitting on the wall at Fowey ... with the seagulls?'

James had a faraway expression in his eyes.

'Yes, I remember, Bryn used to name the gulls according to temperament, didn't he? Funny that he learnt to fly. He always said he wouldn't mind being a seagull when he watched them soar freely over the estuary.'

Jo missed James sadly when he left. Her daytime was filled with schoolwork, children and people, but in the evenings the quiet peacefulness of the farm made her restless. She took to walking back from school along the cliff path to South Down. There was one particular spot that always drew her, where a small grassy patch afforded her rest, and where a tree was struck some years ago by lightning; its silvery, black branches reaching starkly to the sky fascinated her. It was a dramatic spot, prominent and offering views of the wide bay in both directions. The tree dominated the skyline, gentle, green with lichen, and sad-looking when seen against a soft, blue sky, but grim and forbidding when dark storm clouds rode across the heavens and presented for it a wild backcloth.

David was away in Scotland during her stay at Widegates, but Margaret asked her to share a meal, and they spent the entire evening talking about food. Food they would love to have, and then when that subject was finally exhausted – about clothes! Neither of them bothered too much about the sensible, plain, and well-worn attire they were forced to wear, unlike Vee, but both longed for new, young-looking 'undies'. 'Silky ones,' dreamed Jo, 'and with lashings of coffee lace everywhere.' Margaret mentioned her cousin who was visiting Ireland.

'She's hoping to bring a dress-length or two back for me. Material is no problem over there.' She looked down at her dark-brown skirt and sighed ... 'Do you know, Jo. I was the smartest of girls in the office. Nobody back there would recognise me now!'

'Everyone in town is drab, Margaret. Most of us have had a go at dyeing things, just to make them look different. It works as far as colour goes, but leaves the cloth limp and even more old looking. Anyway – your casual wear suits your happy face!'

Margaret flashed her friend a candid look. 'Yes … yes Jo … that I am – very happy!'

It was late in December, and the nursery school main room was fast filling with adults, whom Mr Cook and Nancy Grant were ushering to seats, which had been set out in a semi-circle. The lights glowed on the walls which were brightly covered with pictures completed by the children in readiness for Christmas. Mrs Dingle and Johanna were putting the final touches to costumes … it was the night of the nativity play and the excitement was intense. The little group of children waiting to perform were bubbly and talkative, but followed directions readily, with one or two of the little girls taking the lead and actually pushing the more hesitant boys into their places. The kings looked splendid in velvet cloaks made from some of Mrs Jackson's old curtains. She had spent a whole week making them, sewing on glass beads and sequins to resemble jewels. Jo had made the crowns, with help from the children, and was fitting them now, but having a little bother with Henry's, which was overlarge and balanced precariously on his ears in a most unroyal way!

As the piano music began, the whole school filed in singing 'Away in a Manger', followed by the nativity procession. It all went well, and almost without a hitch. Nancy was found shedding tears of happiness, and Jo thought she had never heard the children sing so sweetly. Her thoughts had also been with Bryn and the boys momentarily, for she wondered what they would be doing during this first peaceful Christmas.

Since returning from Widegates in late October, the weeks had flown by. The nursery school was now well-established, and had a full complement of young pupils. In consequence, both Jo and her mother had been rushed off their feet, organising, planning and teaching. Christmas preparations had almost been the last straw, but Nancy had helped a good deal, and both had enjoyed the commitment and now felt proud of their charges and of their own achievements.

A letter came from Bryn a week before Christmas when he wrote of a meeting with James, Bill and Alan in Greece. He had flown over with a group of VIPs who were attending a conference and found himself with some 36 hours to spare, so he looked them all up. 'It was wonderful, Jo. James looks so fit and was able to tell me all about your weeks at Widegates. I was quite jealous about the ballet, for I had hoped to be the one to take you to your first … but so glad that you enjoyed it. Bill looks older somehow, more like your father, and is longing to get back home. He mentioned that he is due home-leave, so you might have him arriving on your doorstep fairly soon. Wish that I could join him!

'Have a happy Christmas, my darling. I will be thinking of you. Next year I intend sharing it with you once more, but in safer and happier circumstances. My love as always … Bryn.'

Jo was delighted with the letter and read it over many times. Small gifts had been wrapped, a rabbit pie prepared and John Kimber had presented them with another apple and carrot cake. Jo sang carols in the wards of her local hospital on Christmas Eve, feeling a little dizzy, headachy and strange. During the night she developed a bad throat and temperature; by Christmas morning she was unable to move, suffering from a severe bout of flu. For two days little imp-like creatures drummed their heels on the footboard of her bed and her whole body was awash with pain. Ray and her mother came in and out of her room, but she scarcely noticed. On the 28 December, Bill arrived home without warning, and it was a pale, wan sister who greeted him, looking small and lost, swathed in blankets by a roaring wood fire. Mrs Dingle had asked Ray to cut up her husband's treasured wood collection. Things had finally come to that!

Bill was shocked by his sister's lethargy. Where had his bright lively Johanna gone? 'It will pass,' his mother assured him. 'Influenza usually leaves people depressed. Jo was already at a low ebb healthwise, and so it's affecting her badly. You're like a tonic to her, Bill, right now.' He set out to entertain, regaling her with fun stories of Christmas spent on a train from Italy; of his work in Greece; of lighter war experiences in Sicily and Italy, and finally of the meeting he'd had with Bryn and James. She came to life a little at that and listened with increasing interest, and humour, at the evening they had spent in a cavern renowned for its belly-dancers.

'Bryn got up and joined them, Jo … he was really good!'

Bill told them that a recommendation for the Military Medal had been approved. His mother's face glowed with pride and love.

'What did you do, Bill?' Ray's eyes were fixed on his brother with admiration and interest, as Bill related how he had swum across a fast-running river to take the field telephone lines to a small bridgehead on the other side, which was surrounded by Germans. He was fired on repeatedly by the enemy on his return journey and only escaped possible injury or death by diving under the water and letting the current take him out of danger. Further downstream, he swam his way back in an exhausted state, helped finally by overhanging tree branches that afforded him shelter, and to which he clung tiredly until his mates were able to pull him out.

Mrs Dingle sat for a while gazing at her eldest son.

'All this, Bill and we never really knew …'

'But you did, mum. It was about the time that my tooth flared up. John wrote that you'd both been worried. I reckon you and Jo kept me safe …'

'What's the MM like, Bill?'

'Haven't a clue, sprat, but we'll soon find out. Now, how about Monopoly, everyone? I'd like to see if I can make myself a millionnaire whilst I'm home.'

By the time Bill's leave was over, Johanna appeared stronger in both body and mind. Bill hugged her close and said with unusual emotion, 'Take care, little sister, you are precious to us all. Write soon, won't you?'

The early months of the new year went by in a fury of fierce winds and lashing rain. The bright, frosty weather of before Christmas never returned, though in mid-February some three inches of snow fell to create, for a day or two, a winter wonderland of the local streets. The wind howled through the house and they suffered from draughts they'd never experienced before. Only the schoolroom was free of them, for Mr Cook worked carefully, plugging each little crack and cavity to conserve heat.

The war had been over for ten months now, but life was still hard, food scarce, clothes even more so, and fuel at a premium, in spite of the young army of lads sent to help in the mines. Raymond had not returned there. His hand still troubled him, but he was happily placed at a local college doing a part-time botany course, prior to commencing his horticulture training later in the year.

Only the nights were different now, in that they were peaceful. No more shattering of the quiet dark hours by the piercing shrill of warning sirens, nor the crumping explosions of bombs; yet Johanna found it difficult to sleep!

Spring did come, its presence heralded by bursting buds on the trees and shrubs, bright bulbs springing to life, and the soft sweet birdsong.

It was about this time that Johanna was continually overcome by a state of extreme restlessness. The start of each day became a torment, and she wondered how she'd ever get through it. In the same way, the end of the day and the forthcoming hours of darkness gave her no rest, so that she often spent time downstairs at night, quietly working, lest she disturb her mother. She spent hours setting out plans for the nursery school and writing long letters to Bryn, pursuing her interests until tiredness overcame her, often until well after three in the morning. Her sleeping hours became less and less, and yet she always woke readily at her usual seven o'clock. Jo found that she could cope with each day physically, but always with this restless need to get on to the next job, just as if she were waiting for something, or racing towards something.

This was when the dreaming began. She had walked from the house early one evening. The birds were still singing their exciting spring songs, the blackbirds' piercing and shrill, and the plaintive, wild call of the mistle-thrush as it sat, high up on top of the spruce tree surveying the scene around and calling … calling!

'I wish I could call to you, Bryn, and that you would hear me,' Jo thought.

Her walk took her up the tree-lined hill. It was a lovely evening, the sun's rays still strong, and shining on the windows of the houses, creating a golden glow that spread out, and seemed to encircle the whole of the road with an orange light. The flowering cherry tree at the top of the hill was in full bloom now. Jo stood for a while gazing upwards through the full, pink blossoms to the blue sky beyond. It was so very beautiful – heartachingly so and, somehow, full of promise too.

'Promise of what?' she thought … 'Promise of summer to come, of blue skies and cloudless days, promise of warmth, of life … of love!' Johanna stopped her thoughts in this direction, for there was no promise now. Only days to get through, weeks to get through, months to get through in this haze of longing and loneliness. 'Come back … oh, come back soon,' her heart cried.

Johanna's steps led her to the left, where a tree-lined close gave way at one far corner to a little fenced lane. There were bollards across the entrance and she noticed the honeysuckle that fell and tumbled down one high fence, reminding her of the one that scrambled all over the barn and fences at Widegates. It was almost in bloom, and held a faint perfume in the evening sun, which only reduced her to an even sadder longing – a longing now for her beloved Cornwall. The feeling was so great that it became like a pain, a pain creeping all over her, tightening her chest and throat. A sob was forced from her … 'Something nice just has to happen soon,' she thought. 'I honestly can't stand much more of this waiting – waiting, always waiting!'

She followed the narrow path round between the fences, watching the sunlight phasing between the tall trees and making flashes of brightness across her vision. An old man passed her, leaning heavily on his stick with gnarled hands.

'Good evening,' Jo's greeting was involuntary, and the product of years of closeness with country living, where everyone was friendly and, it seemed, everyone was a friend.

'Hello young lady,' the old man replied. 'Didn't I see you admiring the cherry tree just now?' They chatted for a while, initially about the glory of the tree, then about spring and of course, as always, about the war.

'My grandson is still out there. Greece, you know.' The old man's voice was proud, but he added wistfully. 'Haven't heard for a while, but there I expect he's all right and will be home soon.'

'I'm sure he will be,' replied Johanna. 'You'll find a letter on your mat in the morning I shouldn't wonder!' She turned to go and it was then that she saw the tree …

The path led to an open park at the back of her house. The same park that had housed the noisy Bofors during the war, and the grotesque, ugly shelters. These had all gone now, and new gardens had been formed around the area. The tree, covered now in bright-green leaf, was the one she saw from her bedroom window. The same one that last autumn, when she'd arrived back in London, had greeted her with its fall colours. The same tree that had shed its leaves in late November, and then splendidly shown its trunk, branches and filigree twig shapes to the winter skies. It had been beautiful, even without its foliage, and Jo remembered waking one morning in February, after a fall of snow, to find the same tree etched out in white against a grey, grey sky. The rays from the morning winter sun had caught it fleetingly, and each little twig had been traced in a sparkling brightness. She'd not forgotten that sight.

Now the tree was green – springtime green, bright and clean. The leaves were curled at the edges and still not full, but in the evening sunlight it was splendid. She walked towards it … sought its shade and leant her back against the huge bole, spreading her hands out to feel the bark, which was warm to her touch. She experienced a sense of elation, her hands touching the rough bark of the tree anchored her to reality, and yet she had the feeling that she was not of this world. Her heightened perceptions made everything around her unbearably beautiful. She felt light-headed and strange, as if she were floating!

For a while she stood there as slowly a feeling of peace crept through her, and she felt the restlessness ease. A light breeze had got up and stirred the leaves above her so that they seemed to sing softly. The birds were flying now, looking for roosting places. There was a rustling near to her feet, where old brambles had grown and rotted over the years, and again she heard, in the distance, the thrush calling. A sound so sweet, so sad, and yet so full of promise and joy that she could scarcely breathe. She located her house from the row of those which looked over the park. Her window, high and almost opposite where she stood, was ablaze with the evening sun. Jo could picture what it would be like inside her room, for with her mirror placed opposite the window the reflection would be glowing and rosy.

'You splendid tree,' she said quietly, as she pushed herself away from her leaning position and continued on a path that she knew would lead her to the main road and the corner shops. Her steps were slow, and her mind peaceful, as she made her way back home with the restlessness all gone.

Johanna wondered whether the tree could have some special healing properties, but then decided against it. More than likely, the old gentleman had made her realise that she wasn't the only one with worries and troubles. It seemed that at this time everyone had someone or something to be concerned about.

On arrival home she greeted her mother cheerfully, picked up her knitting and settled down to listen to an evening concert on the radio. Lost in her dreams, she started as her mother got up and said 'goodnight'.

In the morning the feeling was back again though. The same restless nervous energy. That same feeling of seeking – and for what? At odd moments during the day she thought of her tree. 'I'll go there again this evening,' she thought … and she did! The tree became for her a reason for living, or embodiment of all her dreams, hopes and aspirations for the future. It became intertwined with Bryn's life in some undefinable way. If she visited the tree, he would be all right.

The dreaming then began in earnest! If she visited the tree he might be there… Hadn't they often met under the great oak on the small green at Pensilva. Perhaps he knew about this tree and one day, one happy day, she would find him there. So, most evenings, some late afternoons, and occasionally in the early morning, she would take the same walk. Up the hill, through the bollards and into the little narrow fenced lane, then out to the spread of grass and the tree!

Some days she'd leave home and imagine he was there, waiting. She would hurry up the hill fearful of meeting anyone or anything that might delay her journey. Her steps would race through the cut and then slow down, in eager anticipation, as she neared the end of the fenced lane. The tree was always there, and if Bryn wasn't, well then, she hadn't really expected it. Perhaps tomorrow! She would lean her back against the bole – spread her hands wide as the first time, and feel the rough bark. Always she experienced a sense of peace, just as if he were there with her; just as they used to be on the headland, in quiet companionship, so very many times, and so very many months ago …

Sometimes she'd feel sad on leaving home. Her walk would increase that feeling, until, as she neared her special place, she feared that the tree wouldn't be there, that it would have disappeared. Sometimes her longing for Bryn became more real … wilder and impatient. Then she convinced herself totally that he would be waiting by the tree … that they really had an assignation. Her disappointment then was immense. At the end of the lane she would stand and imagine she saw his tall, lean figure resting against the trunk; saw his hand wave and his body move forward … move forward and fade. The deep sense of loss she felt was so great, and her heart so lonely, that she would fling herself at the bole of the tree and weep as if her heart was breaking.

One day, the old man saw her crying there … He stopped, wondering whether to intrude, but then, after a while, when he noticed she was quieter, he walked slowly on, muttering to himself – 'poor little lass!'

When, some two days later, he met her coming through the close, with shining eyes and a radiant, happy face, he called to her:

'All right, girlie?'

'Oh yes,' Johanna replied. 'Oh yes …' as she screwed her fist tightly over a letter she'd had that morning from Bryn. The first words thrilled her … 'I'm due for demob in early June, so it's only a question of weeks before we meet again. Book me some warm summer rain please Jo. I'm sick of the dust, heat and flies. The thought of seeing green fields and lanes sends me into a frenzy of impatience. Even the winds off the sea here are warm. My lungs are pining to be filled with cool, sweet, fresh air.

'I'll come to London just as soon as I can and then we can start those plans of our own – dearest girl, I just can't wait!'

CHAPTER FOURTEEN

Bryn arrived at the nursery school one warm afternoon in early June, just as the children were leaving. Johanna hardly recognised him in his 'demob' suit. It was brown with a thin red stripe woven in the material; it suited his colouring, but made him look older than his years. On seeing her reaction, his face adopted the old quizzical expression, and his mouth spoke the same words … 'Will I do then, Jo?'

Her greeting was strained in front of her mother and Nancy Grant, but her eyes welled with tears of happiness. Having hugged Bryn warmly, Mrs Dingle pushed them both towards the door.

'Off you go now, both of you. I'm sure you've lots to talk about.' Jo threw her mother a grateful glance as they left, hand-in-hand and unbelievably happy.

'Well, here we are, Jo … both of us … free at last!' Bryn stopped to give her a brief hug, they smiled at each other shyly, and then hurried past the shops, making straight for home, running the last few steps to the front door. Jo's hand trembled as she tried to put the key in the lock. Laughing softly, Bryn took it from her and they tumbled into the main hallway. The sun shone through the landing window: plain glass now, the beautiful coloured panes smashed long ago during the bombing. The hall smelt warm and slightly dusty, and everything had adopted a dreamlike quality. Jo felt Bryn reach out for her, pull her close and as their lips met she was lost, drowning in such a well of feeling. Her head swam, stars exploded behind her closed eyelids. She felt a roaring in her ears; a complete bubble of happiness welled up within her, as for the very first time Bryn really kissed her. Now she knew what Selina had meant!

Finally they broke apart, shaken by the depth of their feelings.

'All right, my love?' Bryn's voice was deep with emotion. She nodded, her head against his chest. They stood close for a while and she could hear his heart pounding, feel his strong arms trembling as they held her.

'Yes my darling – I'm all right,' she whispered.

How long they stood like that neither knew, but it was time enough to quell the trembling of Bryn's arms, and the ringing in her ears. She opened her eyes, watching the dust motes dancing in the shaft of sunlight from the landing window. Gay little things, she thought, as the bubble of happiness finally burst within her. She looked up at him, laughing … 'Would you like some tea?' He lifted her high, twisting round in the hallway, his face alight with joy!

'Come on then love – I'll race you to the kitchen.' She heard his feet tumbling down the stairs to the basement, and then along the lower passageway, before she followed.

Jo went with him to Beckenham later that evening. Uncle Jim was overjoyed to see his nephew, and teased Bryn about his 'demob' suit.

'You look like a door-to-door salesman in that outfit. Is that the best the country can do for a war hero? Look at him, Johanna, he looks about forty, doesn't he?'

Bryn took the teasing in good part, but she could see that deep down he was concerned, really concerned about his uncle's appearance. Jim seemed to have aged so much since reopening the firm, and had lost the healthy tan that was always evident when he lived in Taunton.

His uncle caught the expression and said seriously: 'So pleased to see you lad. Ready for work? We are snowed under with jobs right now.'

'I'll start tomorrow,' Bryn replied earnestly, but Jim stopped him, with a light slap on his back.

'No lad … not so fast. There's a little lady who deserves a bit of attention from you first. Today's Thursday … have the weekend and start on Monday.'

Later Bryn quietly voiced his concern and Jo told him how Jim had come back specially to start the business again for him.

'He's hoping to go back to the West Country, Bryn, just as soon as you are settled.'

'Then I'll have to get settled quickly, won't I, Jo? He will be ill again if he continues here.'

'I can't reach you, Jo. Are you all right?' Bryn's voice was harsh and tense with worry. 'Are you all right?' he repeated. 'Stay absolutely still – I'm coming down.'

She heard a scrambling above her, and as small stones became dislodged Jo pushed her face against the shelter of the rock that was cushioning her fall.

'Here, darling,' Bryn's voice was reassuringly close … 'Can you reach up now?' She looked above her, stretched out her arm and with relief clasped the strong brown hand reaching for her. A steady pull – some scrambling over the steep scree slope, and she was safe once more, on the footpath. She sat down quickly, her knees suddenly weak and she felt a little nauseous as she looked down to the valley, where the river ressembled a shiny piece of string. Such a long way down – even the village was miniature.

'Lilliput Land,' she murmured, which raised a hard chuckle from Bryn as he pulled her close.

'You silly goose …' his voice was harsh but contained, and she knew that, like her, he had been badly frightened by what might have been disaster. 'Silly of me,' she whispered, 'but I was so full of joy … so happy, and the path looked …'

Bryn interrupted her. 'It's like with the bike Jo. You just don't think!' She felt the injustice of that remark. She was not a child now, not that tomboy companion, and he was so wrong. She had had years in which to think before she acted, years of considering others – of doing her duty … but nevertheless it had been silly of her, and she would have to take more care in future … to control her lighthearted carelessness!

Just a short while ago, they were happily scrambling along a well-defined knife-edge path. The ground sloped steeply away on either side, with the pathway along the top of the ridge that reached up and up. The way was blocked suddenly by some rocks, and unthinkingly Jo had scrambled up and over. Her feet had slipped and she had gone skidding down the scree slope, until another large rock, jutting out from the side of the mountain, had broken her fall. She had been so scared there … so frightened to move and again recalled Bryn's anxious calling.

Gradually, she relaxed against him, taking in the splendid view. They were high; some 2000 feet, and stretching away into the distance was ridge after ridge of mountains. To her left, through the valley, she could make out the sea, sparkling, but a little heavy-looking for such a lovely summer day. It was patched with white as the heaving rollers crashed over, line after line of them, as far as she could see!

'Oh Bryn, look – the sea. Do you think if we get to the top we'll see all the bay?'

'I should think so, darling … better now?' His eyes sought hers and the message they relayed reassured him. 'North Wales at Christmas, Jo, was wonderful, but this … this with all the warmth and colour. Well it's like heaven!'

It was mid-August, and for the past two months Bryn had been rather forcibly introduced into the constraints and harshness of civilian business life. The firm had gone from strength to strength, with Bryn taking most of the workload on board to ease his uncle's path. They worked well together and were both disciplined, tidy and methodical, so that even sharing an office proved to be no problem. Jim felt comforted by having Bryn around, and when he saw how well he was managing, began making plans for returning to Taunton. Since late July, when the nursery school closed for the summer break, Johanna had taken over the secretarial duties for them. They had been surprised and pleased when she offered her services, and had appreciated the speedy and efficient way she got organised. Her base was the wide entrance hall. She had installed the filing cabinets there, also the telephone, and Jim had found a small desk from his own study for her use. She produced several large poster photographs of the Cornish coast for the walls and, twice a week, filled a bowl with fresh flowers, from either her mother's garden or Jim's.

The short break in Wales had been organised by Jim as a 'farewell' present. He had booked for them at the same farm they had stayed at before, and how different it all was in the summer. Mrs Jones was delighted to have them back. She prepared the most succulent evening meals, gave them a more than adequate breakfast and sent them off each day with packages of sandwiches and Welsh cakes … 'To stoke up your fires for the day,' she would comment each morning.

Jim was returning to Taunton at the end of the month, leaving Bryn solely responsible for the firm. He had employed an old colleague on a part-time basis to help his nephew cope with the workload, and had approached Johanna about her staying on permanently as secretary.

Jo wanted to stay; it was good, their working together, and she found it rewarding and interesting, organising the diary, arranging meetings, and typing all the correspondence. Jim had soon realised what a 'treasure' they had and so left the main responsibility in her capable hands. But she felt she couldn't let her mother down ... she was needed at the school.

The need to talk about this fretted Jo. Her mother was enjoying the summer break from the nursery, and the right time never seemed to occur.

Bill had finally been demobbed and was working for the Inland Revenue in the City. At odd times, he and his mother were busy fulfilling a dream and getting the garden back into shape, for it had suffered considerably from neglect since Mr Dingle had died. He had been a keen gardener, and his eldest son had a natural aptitude in this direction.

Now Johanna was in the invidious position of being torn between loyalty to her mother over the school and the help so obviously needed by both Bryn and his uncle. It worried her constantly, and as Jim put presssure on her to make a decision, she found a certain resentment building up ... Why did her mother have to run a school and need her help? Why couldn't she be free to make her own choice of what she wanted to do without emotions coming into it?'

She would be irrationally short-tempered and storm out of the house at the least provocation. This usually came from Ray, who, not realising the pressure she was under, teased her relentlessly about Bryn.

'When's the great day, Jo?' – or – 'I expect he'll get a super long legged, blonde secretary when you come back to school ... fall in love and marry her!' It was all nonsense and she should have ridden the joking, but Jo was tense, lost and strangely resentful of her mother.

Mrs Dingle knew of her daughter's predicament. She wasn't sure, though, whether Jo was committed to working at Beckenham full-time because she enjoyed it or because she wanted to help and be with Bryn. It was Bill who put her right.

'Jo's loving the job, mum. Have you been to see how organised it all is now? Can you let her go? She will have to leave eventually, so why not now and give them both a chance to get things going their way?' Mrs Dingle was thankful ... plans she'd been making could be put into action.

'Thanks, Bill. I ought to have gone to see, but I just wasn't sure. Jo's entitled to some plans of her own. I'll talk to her later.'

It was unfortunate, therefore, that when Jo's mother decided to approach her daughter she chose her words without care.

'Jo, I need to talk to you about your commitment to the school ...'

They were having breakfast. Jo looked up from her plate startled, pushed back her chair and exploded verbally.

'Don't you put pressure on me as well, mum ... I'm sick, yes, sick of people trying to organise me and sort out my life ... let me alone ... I'll not let you down, don't you know that?'

She stormed from the room, appearing a few minutes later in the garden, where she could be seen gazing into the fishpond and wiping her eyes occasionally with the back of her hand.

'Give her a minute,' Bill said. 'I'll talk to her.' It was a sheepish but defensive Jo who sat down with her mother some minutes later.

'All right, I'm listening,' she said somewhat aggressively, and totally out of character. Her mother smiled gently.

'I'd have told you my plans sooner, Jo, if I'd known how you felt. We've both been a little too careful not to hurt one another, haven't we?' Mrs Dingle was rewarded with a weak smile from her daughter and continued quickly.

'Nancy Grant has just completed a six-week course that will enable her to become my assistant at the school. I knew you'd be leaving sometime soon, Jo, and it seemed a good idea for me to get organised so that you wouldn't have to worry ...'

'Oh, Mum – but I'd never have let you down, not until I knew things were all right, not until ...'

Mrs Dingle interrupted her daughter. 'It's fine, Jo, really. The change will suit us both, and it makes Nancy the happiest person ever. We work well together, we'll be good for each other.'

Jo knew that she could freely make her plans without worrying about her mother and the nursery school, and was thankful.

'Thanks, Mum,' she whispered, as she left for work ... 'and sorry!'

Christmas found Jo and Bryn at Widegates. They had decided on this break from town on the spur of the moment. The weather had been bad for some weeks and they'd hoped to escape the bitterly cold situation in London for warmer climes in the south-west. But Britain was blanketed with snow, and they spent some four days helping the aunts cope with jobs around the farm. As ever, they enjoyed the challenge and even found time and energy for walking as well. In the evenings they did justice to some splendid meals that Mollie had prepared, and later they all sat comfortably round a large log fire to chat. Edith had a whole lot to say about the new farm helper John Ellery, whilst Mollie was busy training the latest edition to the household, a puppy for the farm. Uncle Tom's dogs had finally gone, both had been ill and died within a few days of each other. Tom missed them dreadfully. They hadn't been working dogs for some years, but he'd valued them as companions. Now most of the driving of the sheep was done by the new helper who used the small tractor to enable him to keep up with the scurrying animals. James's mother had presented the puppy to Tom, but he showed no interest in it, or its training, and pushed the little thing away with his good leg …

'Garn … bugger off!' He had become increasingly irascible, but still insisted on helping on the farm. The girls worried about him, but he hated fussing and, if anything, it made him more determined to do things he shouldn't. He still managed the small tractor. It was obviously very difficult for him to get up on the machine, but Tom had worked it out with the help of various pulleys and a rope attached to the roof of the tractor shed. He was a familiar figure most mornings, trundling slowly up and down the fields of the farm, or even taking the tractor along the coastal road to Polruan to visit David and Margaret, for whom he had a real attachment.

The girls just shrugged their shoulders when people asked about him. Edith was as strong as ever and worked on the farm happily. Mollie had developed some arthritis and found some of her jobs a little difficult to accomplish. On cold days she was happy to stay in the warm kitchen and cook, just as her mother had made it her domain, so now Mollie was in supreme charge.

The break was short for Johanna and Bryn, and they got back to Beckenham just before the weather tightened its grip on the country. Transport was paralysed.

Industry ground to a halt through the shortage of electricity and, by the first week in February, some one million men were out of work. The firm, however, continued to thrive. Jo noticed that Bryn was fast becoming attached to the idea of the business. He talked less and less of his dreams of the farm in the west. She still imagined a different life, but at the moment was reasonably content to spend each day helping them both towards a future together. Marriage wasn't mentioned at all. They went to shows in London, mixed with several friends for parties and the latest fashionable musical evenings. Bryn talked of taking up golf, but somehow that never got off the ground because the work was always first priority. They went from week to week trying to catch up on themselves.

In early February, Jo spent two more snowy days at Widegates and then stopped over at Taunton for Jim to sign some papers which were needed urgently. She was entranced to see his little thatched cottage for the first time, and although Bryn had always said it was like a fairy tale in its compactness and situation, nevertheless she found it far more lovely than she had imagined. Jim welcomed her with open arms, and once she had settled herself in her room – a delightfully cosy one, overlooking a view across the valley and decorated entirely in white and the palest of greens – she joined him in his study, where Jim's housekeeper had prepared tea before she left. Soon they were sitting in front of a huge coal fire, catching up on news from each end.

'How's that boy of yours doing, Jo? I know that the firm is busy, but is he enjoying it?'

She sipped her tea, staring into the flames of the fire for a while before answering:

'That's the strange thing, uncle Jim. He is busy, very busy, and he is enjoying it, thriving on all the work I should say. He seems different somehow … more vital, and never seems to relax.'

'Yes, I'd heard he was working hard. No more dreams of farms, eh!' Jim's voice was teasing and she looked away quickly.

'No more dreams of farms Jim … none at all!'

Jim noticed the sadness in her voice and was quick to add … 'Let him enjoy this, my dear. He's got power for perhaps the first time in his life, power and responsibility, and he's loving the challenge. The fact that he is obviously very competent makes it even more enjoyable … let him enjoy his achievements. You are young yet, don't be in too much of a hurry for your dreams.'

'Oh, I'm not – it isn't the dreams that worry me, it's … oh, it doesn't matter.' Johanna took a biscuit and began to nibble round the edges, just as she'd done as a child. Jim watched her carefully.

'It's the lack of commitment, isn't it, Jo? You want to settle and Bryn is busy working.'

'I suppose so. Well, yes, actually. There's the flat above the shop; we work together, see each other every day; we've got enough money, but why …?' Her voice faltered, and she sat staring out of the window as the evening winter sun faded and the hills opposite became first hazed, then darkened until their shape and form vanished in an early winter night.

'He has talked about these things to me recently, Johanna,' Jim began. 'I would like to know that his heart lies with the firm before I give advice, and I've asked him down for a talk. He'll be here in a week or two, Jo. Shall we see what he thinks then? Meanwhile, take things day by day and have fun. You are so young still, it should be a really happy time for you both.'

Jo felt that she'd had her knuckles rapped a little, but then Jim had spoken the truth. Bryn was enjoying his achievements and the power. Maybe he doesn't want to commit himself, or me, until he's really sure about the future; whatever it's to be, either planning for the farm or staying in Beckenham. I'm so silly to want to hurry things; it's not as if we don't see one another. She smiled at her thoughts, remembering suddenly how just last year she would have thought it a complete and wonderful happiness to have had Bryn here in Beckenham, and that she should have been working with him would have been a dream beyond her imagination.

'Now, uncle Jim. Tell me about what you do here in the village. I promised Bryn I'd find out all about you.'

Bryn did talk to his uncle some weeks later. He re-assured him about working in Beckenham, said that he'd got his 'dreams' on hold at the moment, and finally asked Jim how he'd feel if he and Johanna got married and took over the little flat. Jim smiled widely.

'Best thing you could do, old lad … she's a lovely girl and won't wait forever, you know. I wonder some chap hasn't snatched her up before this … go ahead and with my blessing.'

Bryn sat on the train on the way back to London making forward plans for the first time for ages. His thoughts were entirely with Jo. He'd ask her tomorrow. Book somewhere for a meal and then 'pop' the question. He hoped she'd not mind waiting for their dream farm, and was sure she wouldn't. They'd plan an autumn wedding at St Lowell ... yes, that would be nice; they'd honeymoon on the south coast somewhere. Jo had always wanted to re-trace her steps as far as evacuation was concerned. He'd share it with her, for it was one phase of Jo's life that he knew very little about.

He arrived back late, collected the post from the hall table and took it to bed with him. One letter stood out; addressed to him from a firm of solicitors in Africa. 'Your Uncle Mark died suddenly and your aunt is now on her own,' he read. 'I understand that your uncle arranged for you to come out to Africa should this happen, to help with her plans and sort out anything as far as the family are concerned. If you contact our London office by phone just as soon as you can, we will be able to make arrangements for your journey here. Your aunt has written separately ...'

Bryn sat stunned for a while. His uncle dead: Jim's lively, fun-loving brother; his father's brother ... dead! No, he couldn't take it in. After a while he searched hurriedly through the pile of letters and found a small, self-contained little envelope. His aunt's message was brief ... Uncle Mark had died quite suddenly of a heart attack. She was devastated and needed him ... 'would her dear nephew come as quickly as he could ...?'

There is nothing for it, I'll have to go, he thought, remembering his promise to his uncle some two years ago, when he'd just recovered from his first heart attack.

'The farm will be yours, Bryn, to do with whatever you wish. I think your aunt will want to leave and return to her family in England, but don't force her, will you? It's her home too, for as long as she lives, but she'd not manage it on her own. I look to you now, for Jim is too old to help.'

It had been easy to say 'of course uncle' at that time. Why, he was scarcely in the RAF; young and untried, and the thought of his uncle dying was just not real. For it to happen now though. Now, when he'd just got so near to his dreams with Johanna. Of marrying and starting their life together ... why now!

He sat for a long while, feeling unhappy and dejected, then phoned Taunton. Jim had also received the news in a letter from his sister-in-law. He understood how disappointed Bryn must be at having to shelve his plans, even for a day … and so offered to go to Africa in his stead.

'I can't let you do that, uncle, you'd never survive. No, I'll go. Jo will be all right coping with the office for a month or two, and I'll put in a manager on a temporary basis. There are lots of young men wanting this sort of opportunity to work right now. I'll be back soon, just as soon as I sort out my aunt and sell the farm!'

'You'll sell then?' Jim's voice was quick and sharp.

'Why yes, of course, uncle. Then I can buy a farm in the West Country, and we can really work on our dream …' Jim's voice was loud …'And the business lad?'

'Oh Jim, I'm sorry. I'd quite forgotten. I'm rushing things a bit aren't I? But I will sell. I will come back and then we'll make plans to suit us both, all right?'

Jim knew now exactly where things stood. The firm would be winding up before the year was out – he was sure!

Arrangements for Bryn's visit to Africa went at breakneck speed, and within eight days he had settled everything, except a visit to Jim in Taunton, to tie up some odd ends of the business arrangements. Three days before he was due to fly out, Jo heard from Mollie that Edith was ill, and could she come down for a short spell. She packed an overnight bag; Bryn saw her off on the evening train to Penzance.

'I'll come down to Widegates after seeing Jim,' he promised. 'We'll spend a whole day on our headland, Jo; make it a day to remember,' he reassured her again and again, as they hugged farewell on Paddington station. Jo felt desolate. It was bad enough Bryn going to Africa, but now, to lose even a little time with him … Would he get down to Widegates? She felt fearful that he might not manage it, and wept silently in the dark corner of the railway carriage, seeing once more his tall figure vanish in the night as she waved good-bye.

CHAPTER FIFTEEN

Margaret had met Jo at the station and she quickly relieved her anxiety about Edith.

'She developed a swelling at the back of her ear and was in a great deal of pain. It was an abcess. She's had an operation and is now resting in hospital for a few days. You should see her, Jo, she's loving every minute of it now that she's feeling a little better. There are flowers and cards everywhere. I don't think she's ever had such a fuss made of her.'

'Good for Edith,' returned Jo, laughing at the thought of her 'tomboy' aunt surrounded by flowers.

Mollie looked tired, but she too spoke lovingly and with humour of Edith.

'Do you know, I don't think she's ever been ill before. Even as children she was the last to catch anything and then succumbed only mildly. She works so hard and deserves a rest. I'm glad she's enjoying it now. John Ellery has gone to see her this morning. He left just now clutching a huge bunch of flowers and wearing his best suit! I'd like to be there to see what sort of reception he gets.'

It was common knowledge that John was sweet on Edith. She bossed him around dreadfully, but they seemed happy in each other's company. Mollie enquired about Bryn and seemed troubled that he was off to Africa.

'Oh I shouldn't have asked you to come … oh my dear, I'm so sorry.'

Jo interrupted her. 'It's all right, aunt. He's coming down here to see me before he flies.'

'Isn't there anyone else who can go? What's a young man like Bryn going to do with a sorrowing aunt. Oh dear, I do wish he didn't have to go.'

'Don't fret, Mollie.' Jo was bemused at her aunt's concern. 'Bryn knows what he has to do and the solicitors are helping with all the official stuff. Uncle Jim can't go, though he did offer. He's not well now, and in any case Bryn promised Uncle Mark that he'd step in to help should the need arise. Not that anyone expected it to. It's all so sad really.'

'Well dear, when Bryn comes you are to take him off to that special place of yours … no hanging around the farm and helping. Tom and I will manage for a few hours, I'm sure.'

Jo smiled her thanks and set out for the barn to relieve Mollie of various tasks around the farm. In the afternoon they visited Edith, who looked flushed and content in her 'bower' of flowers.

Later Jo took Horse out for a canter around the headland, stopping every so often to watch the seabirds and to listen to the roaring of the incoming tide. The next morning Jo sat on the gate at the top of the home field, looking down on the farm. The day was bright and clear, already warm for early May. Widegates looked comfortable and settled in its hollow. The blue-grey stone had a glow of its own in the sunlight, and the barns, green-covered in honeysuckle, seemed low-lying, almost as if they had collapsed and fallen into the grass of the meadow. Lambs were gambolling around the field in little groups of ten or so. Sturdy little animals now, thoroughly enjoying the bright warm day. A far cry from those weeks of their arrival, when the farm had suffered under a blizzard. Edith and Mollie had had to work hard to keep the lambs and ewes safe from the weather. Only three months ago, it just didn't seem possible that this was the same place.

Jo had made a fleeting visit and had almost been snowed in. She remembered wryly how John Ellery had got her out to the main road on the tractor. James then had taken her to St Austell, and the train from there. She had sat perched high up next to John, almost willing him not to make it, but he had! Later, huddled in a corner seat on the train, as it moved slowly towards Exeter, she wondered at the beauty of a changed, white and unrecognisable landscape. The snow had reached no further than Exeter, and so by the time she'd left the train at Taunton, Jo felt almost that she had dreamed it all.

She stretched her legs out to ease the pressure of the bars from the back of her knees. They felt sun-warmed, as did the side of her face as she gazed downwards. The church clock chimed ten. Her heart seemed to miss a beat. and she felt an inward tremor of excitement. She had been restless all the morning. Mollie had studied her several times as she scurried around the farm, completing one daily chore after another at breakneck speed and without complaint.

'You've got spring fever,' aunt had commented at one time as they passed each other in the yard, now occupied mainly by geese, goslings and hens, for the lambs were out in the sunshine of the home field. Jo was carrying two buckets of warm milk for the pig swill, and her aunt was wheeling the sack barrow on which perched precariously a bale of shiny clean straw for the byres.

'I just feel good today,' she had smiled at her aunt. 'When I've finished here I think I'll wander to the headland. Can you manage without me for a while?' Mollie grunted. 'And what do I do every day of the year but manage without you? Off you go, lass, and take care.'

Jo had finished feeding the pigs and with a wave to her aunt set off for the lower gate, when she heard Tom call.

'Bryn just phoned. He'll be over this morning. I told him that he'd find you at the headland, all right?'

Jo's heart turned over. So he was to make it here as promised, and earlier than they had thought too. This then was the reason for her inner excitement, her feeling from first thing this morning that something nice would happen. Bryn was coming earlier than she had hoped and they'd be able to have the whole day together! She called her thanks to her uncle as Mollie joined her.

'I'd make a day of it, Jo … it'll be lovely near the sea. Take a picnic with you. This little lot will be all right until this evening.' Mollie swept her arm in a half-circle to encompass the yard animals.

'Are you sure, is everything important done then?'

'Off you go, lass, and have a special day.' Jo hugged her aunt fleetingly.

'Thanks, Mollie. I'd better change. The pigs have made me a bit messy.'

When she appeared in the yard some fifteen minutes later she wore a dark skirt and pale-blue sweater. She looked almost too neat for a day's scrambling over the headland. Her aunt called her over to where she was feeding the hens.

'Be sure you bring Bryn back for a meal this evening, won't you?' Again Jo nodded her thanks. Her excitement was obvious, she glowed, her eyes were wide and clear, and there was a tremulous expectancy about her sweet mouth.

'You care for him deeply, don't you, lass?' It was more of a statement than a question and before Jo could do more than send her aunt a startled expression, she followed with:

'Does he know? Let him know … I would!'

Jo felt her heart thump inside her chest; felt a tightness and pain in her throat. It ached with longing as she thought of the words her aunt had just said … If only she could tell him … if only!

'We're good pals, Mollie – we understand each other.' Jo turned away before her feelings gave her away. She pulled at the lower gate and forced herself through, closing it forcefully with her eyes lowered. Mollie watched her go – saw her wave her hand behind her – heard her say 'headland, here I come …' before she turned back to her hens. She was troubled about Jo and Bryn. All the family had expected that by now their commitment to each other would have been made public; an engagement perhaps or wedding plans. There seemed to be nothing in their way, except perhaps themselves. Maybe they are not ready for commitment, thought Mollie. Maybe they've both changed too much. She looked up towards the gate, where she could see Jo sitting gazing down at the farm.

'I know one thing … I could bang their heads together. Jo's done too much waiting. Bryn might just expect her to wait that bit too long. Damn Africa … poor kids …!' All these thoughts were tumbling round Mollie's head as the hens clucked and scrabbled at her feet, and her hands automatically continued throwing the grain.

'Giving them a month's supply, Mollie,' Tom called as he went slowly and awkwardly past her on his way to the tractor shed. She started. Well, there was nothing she could do about it. Best get on with the day and prepare a nice meal for them this evening.

Now, as Jo sat on the gate in the warm sunshine, she felt settled and secure once more. Bryn was coming, that was enough. Her heartbeat and the throbbing ache in her throat had subsided as she thought of the day ahead. 'Be happy, girl,' she said to herself, 'Be happy … Bryn is coming and that is enough.'

But was it enough? True, he was coming, and in an hour or so they'd be together on their special headland. A whole day with Bryn shone ahead like a golden glow, for although they worked together and met daily whilst socialising, she realised that for the past nine months they'd had very, very little time to themselves. It had been mostly work. She recalled his first kiss, when they'd arrived back at her home after he was demobbed. They had kissed many, many times since then, but nothing like that ... It was often as though Bryn held himself back, and then broke away for fear of offending her, though he still looked at her with that odd expression in his eyes, that questioning look! She had noticed it particularly a few weeks back when James had visited. Bryn had come across them laughing and joking together. He hadn't joined in, just stood there watching them both. It was an awkward moment for them all. Bryn's attitude almost made her feel she had done something wrong, and Jo wondered for a moment whether James felt the same. It was a momentary hiccup, for that evening had been one of the happiest for a long time, when the three of them had toured as many local pubs as they could walk to ... laughing and fooling like teenagers!

Bryn's plane was leaving from London tomorrow evening. Jo had asked if she could see him off, but, noticing his hesitation, didn't push it any further. Now he was coming. He was coming to say good-bye and this was to be their special day. The sun was warm and she was free. Why then this underlying apprehension? Jo shrugged her shoulders and jumped from the gate, landing softly on the grass verge. The road twisted a little before turning off towards Polruan, but Jo was taking the wide grassy path that led up and over to the sea, where the breeze would lift her hair from her neck, sending it blowing back across her shoulders. It should lift her spirits too, the headland and the wind always did this. It would be a good day, she was sure of it.

As she walked the path, the skylarks were flying high and trilling their spring song over the adjoining fields. The wind, stronger now than she'd thought, was blowing over her head, scraping and tossing her hair back and forth and roaring in her ears. She felt now a wild elation. In about an hour Bryn would walk the same path to her; would hear the same skylarks and the wind would toss his dark curls from his forehead and make the same rushing noises in his ears! She wished that he was already here, then, just as quickly, she pushed the thought away. She longed to see him, but the closer that time came, so also would be the time to say good-bye.

Jo spotted, far below on the edge of the golden beach, a small boat bobbing towards the shore. It was blue and yellow, Bryn's boat! He'd come round from the estuary for speed, and was even now clambering out into the surf, waving his friend off, as the little vessel chugged away into the wide bay once more. 'If I hurry we can meet on the wide rock,' thought Jo. She increased her pace, down over the rocky path that led out onto the wide peninsula, where she could see both sun-kissed bays, and the white water bubbling like lace all around the shoreline. Her heart sang. Bryn would be coming up the steps from the beach now, and would soon be onto the grass sward that started the long path to the headland. I'll get there first – I know I will! She stood still for a moment, drinking in the smells from the sea; the blossom, sweetly spilling from the blackthorn sweeping the cliff, and the thyme, gently sending its special fragrance upwards as she trod on its soft cushioning.

She reached the rock ahead of Bryn and was sitting there, knees up, her arms folded lightly round them, watching the path from the golden beach, when he appeared over the hill. First his dark head, then shoulders and tall lithe body. She felt safe and secure and unbelievably happy as she watched his approach. He'd seen her and waved one long arm. Bryn was wearing casual clothes and the dark fisherman's jumper that seemed to have been so much part of him. Her Aunt Edith had made one for both boys some four years ago, and it had become headland uniform for them. Bryn's was a dark grey, and was now well-worn, hanging on his slim, but strong frame rather loosely. It must have swallowed him when aunt first made it, she thought. He strode towards her, smiling and happy to clasp her in his arms, and kissed her long and tenderly.

They stood gazing out to sea where the sailing-boats from the harbour were already gathering for the spring races. With their varied coloured sails waving gently, they resembled hovering butterflies. The scene was picturesque, each bobbing wavelet being capped in white spindrift. One small fishing smack below them, gathering in the baskets for crabs and lobsters, was overhung with a cloud of seagulls watching to see what they could take from the nets strung lightly between each pot. It was a captivating picture.

'I shall miss this,' Bryn said, as he tugged at his rucksack, producing a long beach mat and spreading it on the flat rocks which crowned 'Mr P's' noble forehead. 'Not necessary, I know, the rocks are already warm in the sun, but a little more comfortable.' He threw his long length down, making room for her.

'Well, how goes it, darling?' His smile was warm, 'Did you bring some lunch and how's Edith?'

Jo laughed up at him. 'Trust you to get the questions in that order. "It" goes OK, and aunt Edith is doing fine, and, yes, I did bring food. Coconut cake, yummy and fresh, sandwiches too. Want some now?'

'Please. I left Taunton really early, it was still almost dark. Ben was waiting for me at the station, and it was his suggestion that we came round the bay. It would have taken so long by the ferry, and I'd have been really frustrated. As it was, he had the boat ready, and so here I am. Have you been here long?'

'Just a minute or two. I saw you get off the boat, though I wasn't sure for a minute whether it was yours, it looked so new and shiny.'

'Ben did it for me. He thought we might need it for the summer.' His voice was wistful. 'It would have been lovely, Jo, wouldn't it? If only Africa hadn't intervened!'

She shuddered. 'Cold?' he asked.

'No – just thinking.'

'Better not to think,' he replied, as if he'd read her thoughts. 'Let's make this a good day, a happy day. It's got to last me for a very long time.'

'How long, Bryn? How long do you think you'll be out there. Will your aunt come back with you?'

He thought for a moment, his eyes sweeping over the bay and coming to rest finally on her face. Her hair had been blowing over her mouth, and he reached out gently, tucking it carefully behind her ears.

'You need a hat or something. With all that wild hair you resemble a siren … Remember when we used to say we heard them singing on those wild cliff walks at night?' Jo nodded her head. His look and gentle touch had unnerved her. Bryn continued:

'She hasn't told me her plans yet, Jo. I don't really want to go, but Uncle Mark has left the farm to me, and I did promise that I'd take care of my aunt if ever she was left on her own. I never thought it would happen so soon, though. The truth is, I shan't really know what the future holds until I've seen it all. Mark showed me lots of photographs when he was over here, but it's not the same really as seeing it for yourself, is it?'

'But I thought you'd been there years ago when you were a child with your parents?'

'Oh yes … but that was years ago as you said. I have some lovely memories of my holidays on the farm, but it was all childish excitement. I don't remember the important things. Lots of space I suppose, a large bungalow; miles and miles of view and a dusty wildness. It was fun with all the farm boys, and we used to get up to all sorts of mischief. Then, of course, there were the wild animals and trips into the bush. I was goggle-eyed, but as for the serious part – the actual running of the farm – well, I've no idea at all.'

'What a good thing you've spent so much of your time with James at Pensilva. Perhaps it was ordained.' She laughed up at him, with her heart torn at the thought of the responsibilities ahead of him. Suppose he liked it? Would he send for her? Would she like Africa? Jo realised then what a stupid thought that was, because she'd like anywhere, anywhere at all, so long as Bryn was there with her.

'Do you have cattle? I can make cheese and milk the cows. I'm even good at bedding down animals … Mollie would give me a testimonial, I'm sure …. want to employ me?'

Her tone was light and bantering.

'Love to,' he said, but with that same old questioning look in his eyes again. 'Love to – we'll discuss it seriously later, shall we?'

They were both quiet for a while, each following their separate train of thought. Jo's were on a dream of Africa. Of a huge rambling bungalow, with a verandah facing the hills, and where they could sit at dusk and on into the warm night – listening to the wild African noises. There would be soft music …

His thoughts were different as he gazed down at the water dazzling now in the midday sun. I wonder if I'll ever sit here again … why do I feel as if this is a final good-bye? How could he say good-bye to a place so special to him, special to both of them. He was aware of Jo's slender body leaning against him. His mind was in a turmoil, and he now wondered what she was thinking. I'll have to tell her today. I mustn't leave without letting her now how much I care. I'll ask her to marry me – to wait for me. Perhaps she'll be brave enough to leave her family and this lovely part of England if she really cared, and I think she does. Bryn reached out a hand and touched hers.

'Hey, dreamer, where is the food you promised?' The quiet spell was broken and several minutes were now taken up with unwrapping the cake and pouring the coffee. By that time, Jo had been able to control her emotions. She had been completely absorbed in her dream of Africa, and indeed had made it so real that tears sprang to her eyes at losing the loveliness of it all! Bryn noticed that she was quiet and sat watching her as she folded napkins and filled coffee cups yet again.

'Penny for them?'

She flashed her eyes at him quickly and, seeing their brilliance, he guessed that she'd been crying. The thought hurt him. He wanted to enfold her in his arms and never, ever let her go.

'I'm staying the night,' he said quietly, and was rewarded with a flashing smile and a very direct look that both held. 'James is taking me straight to London tomorrow. He thought it would be nice for us to be together today, just on our own!'

She hung her head, feeling again the familiar tightness in her throat, the forerunner of tears.

'Hey, come here.' Bryn moved towards her, put an arm over her shoulder and cradled her head against his chest. 'You know how I feel, don't you, Jo? There's no need of words between us. We've been such pals always, haven't we? I'll keep in touch and let you know what's what as soon as I know myself. Keep happy, darling girl – for how can I handle all this if you are sad!' He bent his head and touched her lips softly with his own. She was reaching up with both arms to pull him down to her, when they heard a dog bark nearby and a golden labrador was soon slobbering all over them. The owner appeared over the hill as they drew apart. Jo felt embarrassed, Bryn annoyed … but he had lots more time!

'There's this evening,' he thought. 'We can come out here then … I'll tell her then!'

When the man and his dog had finally disappeared along the cliff path, they hastily packed away the debris of their lunch and rolled the mat back into Bryn's rucksack.

'What now?' Her smile was winsome.

'Let's go to the cottage,' Bryn replied. 'David is working there today and I'd like to see him before my adventure … Come, I'll race you round the headland!'

Jo immediately set off down the steep path towards the edge of the cliff. She didn't seem to pace herself, and looked in danger of going right over, but veered suddenly to the left along the edge, just as Bryn called.

'Be careful. The path is slippery after the rain.' She waited for him on the furthest point. Jo could hear now, the rumble of the water as it surged over the rocks far below and sought out the wide cavern almost underneath where they stood. Even on the calmest days it roared here on an incoming tide, and today, with the wind off the sea, the waves were extra powerful. It was a magical sound, which she and Bryn always loved.

He stood behind her, both hands on her shoulders and deposited a gentle kiss on the side of her cheek.

'Look, Jo. Have you ever seen so much white water on such a lovely day?' Both were quiet for some time, drinking in the view, then, holding hands, they proceeded along the winding rugged path to the cottage, all racing forgotten!

From the plane Bryn was watching the coastline of his beloved England get smaller and smaller. He felt insecure, desperately unhappy, and very, very angry with himself and fate. On the journey to the airport he'd resisted James's friendly chatter. He knew that his behaviour was rude, morose almost, and James, sensing he needed to be quiet, stayed silent for long periods. Bryn knew that his friend was presuming it was because he had to leave, but it wasn't only that, for overriding his deep sense of loss and emptiness was an anger that he'd not been able to tell Jo he loved her, or to ask her to wait for him. A moment hadn't come in all those hours they had together that he could claim for them alone. No time when the words, so carefully practised, could have been said. He had wanted to – but fate had intervened!

Yesterday, they had found David in the cottage putting the finishing touches to an article he was writing about this particular part of Cornwall. He had been overjoyed at seeing them and they sat for a while on the patio, talking about old times, and then left to wander towards Lantivet and the seat overlooking the bay. From here they watched as a party of children struggled up the slope from the each. They were chatting noisily and looking back continually, marvelling that just a few minutes ago they'd been playing on the sandy pockets between rocks that were now almost covered as the tide came thundering in. They were a bright happy bunch and Jo thought again of her teacher training course.

What a good thing she hadn't cancelled it, for if Jim closed the firm, she would have no job to go to.

'I think I'll enjoy teaching you know, Bryn … just look at those bright young faces.' He stared at the youngsters as they struggled, pushed and pulled each other up the steep gradient, and saw again two boys and a girl, laughing into the wind, and racing one another up and along to the headland.

'In a perfect world, Jo,' he said quietly. 'In a perfect world, I'd get a farm somewhere near, and you'd teach at the village school. What a dream! Let's try and make it come true …'

Several walkers passed them as they sat. The sun moved westward. Jo suddenly looked at her watch and made to move.

'I promised Mollie that I'd ask you to dinner. Hope that's all right!'

'I'd banked on it,' Bryn replied. 'They aren't expecting me at Pensilva until about midnight, so we've the whole evening together.'

Her eyes lit with joy.

'That's wonderful … but … Bryn, can I come with James in the morning and wave you off – please?!' He looked directly at her – his chin firm, but his eyes were warm and loving.

'I'd much rather you didn't. I just want to remember you here; here in the place that I love; here with all those memories we have together. Do you mind too much, my darling?'

She ducked her head so that he wouldn't see the disappointment in her eyes and said quietly.

'Just as well really. I don't think I could bear to wave you goodbye and watch the plane take you away. So far away,' she whispered almost to herself.

They walked in silence through the leafy lane, both a little out of breath as the going had been slippery over the field. The lane tunnelled rivers of water through from the fields above and was particularly difficult to negotiate after storms. They slithered and frequently lost their balance, and laughingly Bryn put his arm round her to help her along. She felt at peace. Several more hours before she need think about 'good-bye'. They'd make each moment a treasure.

Aunt Mollie met them at the farm gate. Her face was pale and her eyes rimmed pink with crying.

'Thank goodness you've come. Tom has had an accident. The tractor overturned on him in the top field. His legs are crushed. We didn't find him until about an hour after it had happened …'

She thrust out the bad news in short staccato sentences, and then…

'They've taken him to St Austell.'

Jo went to her with outstretched arms. 'Oh Mollie, how awful. Poor Tom. Will he be all right?'

'We don't know yet. I want to go to the hospital. Can you drive the Bedford for me please, Bryn? I don't think I could manage it the way I feel. I've telephoned a message for Edith. It will be a dreadful shock for her.'

Mollie knew that Edith would blame herself for not being there on the farm, but Tom was so difficult. Earlier she had got the small new tractor out intending to take feed to the cattle in the top field. Tom had stopped her.

'Leave it, girl … I can throw a few mangolds to the heifers … leave it, I say!' How she wished now that she hadn't given in … but Tom was forceful. What an awful thing to happen whilst Edith was away.

Bryn jumped into the driving seat of the old van. Jo dashed into the farmhouse for her purse and a warm jacket. Mollie was quite ready. She had on her weekend 'go to church' outfit, and clutched a small case which she had filled with things she thought Tom might need.

'Oh auntie,' Jo said again, as she climbed next to her in the back seat of the van. 'What a pity we weren't here.' She hugged her aunt, who was sitting stiff and upright, her face like stone and hands clasped together so tightly that the knuckles were quite white. 'He'll be all right – I'm sure he will,' Jo concluded.

'Let's hope so,' returned Mollie in a strained, dull voice.

They progressed swiftly along the road. The car ferry fortunately was not crowded, and with no queues on the other side of the river, there was no delay. Bryn drove carefully through the little town, choosing to take the shortest route in spite of the difficulty he had in manoeuvring his large vehicle round the narrow twisting lanes. They were soon out on top of the hill, with the whole estuary laid out behind them. Jo glanced back just in time to see the sun pouring over the headland, before the road turned off to the left and they were on the main highway to St Austell.

The hospital visit was prolonged. Uncle Tom was in the operating theatre for nearly two hours, so they had to wait before they could learn the full extent of damage done to his legs. One was quite shattered, and was removed below the knee. The other, they hoped to save, though the surgeon was not too optimistic.

'How is he? Mollie asked the doctor who had come to tell them about Tom's injuries.

'Fine, really. He's just come to in the recovery room. We'll check him, and then you can see him for a while. The recovery room is empty except for Mr Varcoe and we will probably keep him there for the night. Don't worry too much. He seems a tough gentleman. He'll recover.'

'Does he know?' asked Bryn.

'Yes – he knows. Took it well and is quite convinced that he'll have a wonderful time telling the new generation about how he became "peg-leg" Tom.'

Jo turned her face to the window in distress.

'Poor uncle Tom, first polio and now this. He'll have to do so much adjusting again – it just didn't seem fair!'

The next week passed in a haze of anxiety. Tom developed a chest infection due to the shock and long exposure. He looked so very ill that the girls scarcely expected him to live. However, his fighting spirit showed through once more, so that some eight days after the accident he was ready to ask Johanna about Bryn.

'Has the lad gone, then?'

Jo's heart lurched. She had tried to put Bryn from her mind repeatedly during this worrying time. When thoughts of him wouldn't go, she forced them away; so to hear Tom talk so openly was a shock to her, but she answered:

'James saw him off safely. He is well and truly there by now.' She stared out of the hospital window, her face a mask of sadness and with that same weariness of expression she'd worn so many times during the war years. Tom's heart went out to her.

'It will be all right, lass. It will all come right, you know.' She reached over the bed to pat his hands, which were clasped together on the counterpane.

'Yes, uncle Tom – I'm sure it will. But all the waiting again, just as he was back and we were getting to know one another again after so long. We've both changed an awful lot, you know.'

'Of course you haven't. You've grown up that's all!' Jo looked at her uncle, her lips trembling.

'I don't know how to cope with waiting again. I really don't.'

'Keep busy, Jo.' Her uncle's voice was firm. 'Keep busy, it's the only way. I know only too well. Keep busy and in no time at all he'll be back.'

Her hands set about tidying the cards and flowers on his bedside locker and adding a few oranges to the fruit bowl. She bent to kiss him as the aunts appeared at the door of his room.

'We met James outside. He's waiting for you, Jo. Get him to help move the sheep to the top meadow, would you, please? He said the day was ours, but everything else is shipshape.' Edith turned to Tom.

'Now how's that cantankerous old brother of mine?' Edith at least was better!

Mrs Dingle welcomed her daughter back home on a beautiful morning at the end of May. Jo had travelled overnight, arriving at Paddington station at about six in the morning. London was fresh, with the street dust laid by a passing overnight shower. She was glad to be back. Happy that Tom was doing so well, and that the aunts were coping quite adequately with the help of John Ellery. He was showing himself as not only an extremely knowledgeable farm-worker, but also a good friend.

'They'll be all right, mum,' she answered her mother's concerned questions. 'Tom will take care of the farm as far as the paperwork goes. Mollie helps him now, but he'll take over things again when he's fit. John will manage the rest with Edith's help and advice. They are getting along famously and it's good to see them together.

'How was Bryn?' Mrs Dingle asked gently.

'All right, mum. Tom's accident came in the way of farewells, but maybe that was a good thing!' Jo looked down, and her mother's next question remained unasked when Bill gave her a tap on the shoulder and shook his head.

'The office will be glad to see you at any rate,' he said. 'I was over there yesterday and looked in. Your desk is piled high with papers. A nice young man who seems to be in charge now has the funniest of faces, and took a great delight in saying that the work was "waiting" for you. I'll give you a lift over in the morning if you like.'

Bill was now the proud owner of a super motor-bike, and any excuse to use it was taken up. Saturday morning saw them both speeding along the main road to Beckenham. Jo found it fun, though she felt scared at first. It was a strange sensation, moving along on a contraption over which she had no control.

'I'd feel better if I had some handles to hold,' she commented when they arrived at the office wind-blown and laughing.

Work was good for her and she tackled it with a certain amount of satisfaction. On the first day she sorted out the post, answered urgent letters, reorganised the diary, and in general made significant impressions on what was obviously a neglected muddle. Both men were impressed and pleased to have her back and in charge again.

She heard from Bryn. Two letters arrived by the same post. One had been written at the airport …

'Jo, my darling girl. I'm so sorry that our special day didn't materialise as we'd hoped. I had so much I wanted to say, so much I wanted to ask, and there just wasn't the moment. Poor Tom – do hope that he recovers well and doesn't have any set backs. I can imagine that you are still at the farm as it's eighteen hours since I left.

'I have been thinking about your teacher training. Don't let this opportunity go by if you really want to do it. I can't see Jim keeping the firm going for much longer, and particularly while things are uncertain as to my future. What I would like to do is sell up in Africa get my aunt to come home, and then settle in the West Country as we had planned, but until I get there and see how things are, meet the solicitors etc I can't plan … only dream. It's all so frustrating! I suppose then, the ideal thing would be for me to spend a year learning how to farm in England. As you said on the headland, I have learnt a good deal from James and his dad, but it's only on the surface. I shall have to go a lot deeper if I'm to start on my own and make a go of it!

'So much to think of, my darling … and so much time to do so. How I wish that you were here with me.

'Our flight was called and I am now winging my way towards Africa. A strange sensation not to be in the pilot's seat. I long for the plane to turn right round so that I can come back to you. Pray that things will work out for us quickly – my love as always …'

The other letter was written at the farm:

'The view from the bungalow changes character many times as the sea was always changing for us, remember? Sometimes the surrounding hills look quite close and then at other times far, far away. The land is vast, Jo, stretching away for miles and miles – sweeping and wide. I feel strange here and long for the patchwork comfort of our English farmlands. Sometimes I ride out early, it's the best time of the day. This morning I was out before sunrise. It was quite lovely, the sky clear and the last stars withdrew whilst I rode. The air is so chill at this time, just like the autumnal weather back home. The grass was wet with dew, and I longed for Cornwall. At such times it's hard to realise that the bliss of the cool morning will give way in a couple of hours to a glaring sun, that I personally find so hard to bear.'

Mollie wrote to her sister in London that her invalid was doing well. Edith was quite better and her old strong self again, pushing aside any suggestion from John Ellery or her sister that she take things easy. Tom was undergoing a session of rehabilitation at a special centre in Plymouth, but was due home from there in about ten days.

'He isn't minding too much. Has lots of young company there, soldiers from the war, and is enjoying hearing first-hand all about what happened. He's made some nice friends and I'm hoping that he'll keep in touch with them when he comes home. Tom says that some of the lads have terrible injuries and why should an old chap like himself bother about such a small inconvenience like losing half a leg! It's the right attitude, and we are both very proud of him. Just hope he remains as buoyant …

'Veronica has been in touch. Will you tell Jo to expect a phone call from her, and not to worry too much if she goes on. She rang here in a most distraught state, just after Jo left, asking where Bryn was – why he'd gone to Africa and, most of all, why he hadn't been to say good-bye. She was tearful and strange and I did my best to console her. Her attraction to Bryn still worries me, Lillian … it's as if Jo doesn't exist in her eyes, and Bryn is hers entirely. I can't help thinking that she's trouble. I know that's not a nice thing to say about a young girl, but Tom and I feel the same.'

The next day Jo had a frantic phone call from Vee. 'I'm in London … can I come and see you? I can get a bus, but I don't know where or how …' Jo thought quickly, gave Vee instructions about buses, and told her to get a ticket for the Clock Tower, and she'd meet her there. It was difficult to time things right, and Jo found she was waiting a good half an hour or so on draughty pavements, before Veronica finally emerged from a half-empty bus.

'What's wrong, Vee?' she asked. 'You sounded so strange.'

Veronica stared at Jo.

'What's wrong … what's wrong? It's Bryn. Why didn't he say goodbye to me?' … and she collapsed into tears right there in the street. Jo had a job to hold both her and the overnight suitcase Vee had passed to her on alighting from the bus. They arrived home eventually. Mrs Dingle summed up the situation quickly and took Vee upstairs to the little boxroom which had been prepared for her.

'Come on Veronica. It isn't the end of the world. Bryn has just gone over to help his aunt.' Mrs Dingle's voice was loud and firm.

'B … but he didn't say goodbye …'

'Nor to me either, or to lots of his friends … come along, I've prepared a nice meal downstairs for you and Jo.'

'But I'm not just a friend. I'm special!' Vee was quite out of control and sitting on the edge of the bed, crouched over, rocking herself back and forth.

'Yes, of course you are … a special friend, but Jo is more than that, Vee – and you know it. That's why he said good-bye to her!' Mrs Dingle's voice was just as firm, but the change in tone must have filtered through to the hysterical girl, for she quietened suddenly, cast Jo's mother a sidelong glance, sniffed into her handkerchief once or twice and then nodded her head.

'Yes, I know. I'll just tidy up and be down. I'm really hungry you know.'

As Mrs Dingle watched, Vee seemed to change character and was now almost bright as she held the door open for her hostess. 'Mollie's right,' she thought as she descended the stairs slowly. 'That girl is strange … we'll have to watch out for Jo and Bryn – all of us!'

Jim wrote that he was winding down the business before Christmas. He advised Jo to follow her heart and take advantage of the teacher training. Mid-September therefore saw her at Exeter, happily settled in a bed-sit, surrounded with books and looking forward to the start of her course on the 19th.

She made a flying visit to Widegates to see Veronica who had suffered a nervous breakdown and was only now managing to cope with the odd visitor. Jo found her thin, but tanned by the summer sun. She looked very lovely, but distant somehow, and this disturbed Jo. She made up her mind to write often, and perhaps to ask her up during the holidays.

Tom was fine, though he'd lost a lot of weight and had developed a persistent cough. 'Too much mollycoddling,' he complained to Jo. 'All I need is some fresh air and I'd be better.' He listened avidly for news of Bryn and was happy to see his niece looking lively and laughing once more.

It wasn't always so, for Jo did miss Bryn dreadfully, and she felt, if anything, more cut off from him than ever before. The weeks had grown into months and there was still no news of his returning, though he was writing very regularly about new scenery and new faces. Friendly letters that she was always thrilled to receive, and if, after many readings, they didn't contain what she was searching for, words that showed he felt as she did … well wasn't Bryn always careful with words? Wasn't he more like a brother or close friend in his writings? He showed that he cared deeply when they were together in every gentle look and gesture. No – she was being fanciful once more. Of course Bryn loved her … of course he was hers!

Bryn's aunt could not be persuaded to sell up and move to England. He spent hours talking to her of his dreams of owning land in the West Country.

'But this is your farm, Bryn, when I go. We thought you'd settle here. It's a good life, we were very happy here.' His aunt's tone was wistful, after they'd had another long talk about England and his love of the area near to Widegates. She didn't look well. The loss of her husband had aged her, and she had a slightly haunted look about her. Bryn wrote to Mollie that she appeared 'vague and strange'. He searched for her at meal times in the large garden surrounding the bungalow, and often found her feverishly digging at the flower-beds, beautiful beds in full bloom! She would be muttering to herself and watched by the gardener, who was dismayed and bewildered at the havoc this little old lady could wreak.

'Come in, aunt,' Bryn would cajole. 'Let Simon finish that.' She would look up at her nephew with glazed eyes and follow him into the house. Bryn felt he was putting too much pressure on her, and so the weeks and months went by, with nothing being settled. He clung to his dreams, but could see no way of resolving them. Fortunately the farm kept him busy. Management was new to him, but he learned quickly and sought help and advice from his uncle's friends when he deemed it necessary. His confidence grew daily. He enjoyed the progress he made, the improvements, but always, at the back of his mind, was his special dream – a dream of Jo and a farm in England.

For Johanna, the course was time-consuming, fairly hard and extremely interesting. She found the essays difficult at first, but loved the practical work, and particularly so when they visited various schools, and she was drawn into work with the children. She now led a fairly lonely life, often burning the midnight oil working in her cosy little room. The many opportunities for socialising were turned down. Jo was waiting once more, but this time there were no spare moments for dreaming. She was waiting and working to a purpose. Always towards the dream and the future to be shared with Bryn.

James spent the half-term week at Taunton with an old school-friend and he came over several times to take her out and about. The weather fortunately was good, so they walked a good deal and discovered the beauty of the city of Exeter and the surrounding countryside together. He took her out for a meal; they went to the theatre where they sat close, laughing at a light-hearted comedy. Jo cooked scrappy meals in her room, almost having a disaster with her gas ring as she heated some rice. It boiled up and over, leaving a decidedly awful smell that clung to the furnishings for days.

Veronica came down for the weekend and joined in their happy partnership.

'Two girls and a boy ...' James said, 'Instead of two boys and a girl!' Later Vee wrote to Bryn about her short stay in Exeter, and how much fun Jo and James were having together!

Mollie urged Jo repeatedly to go to Africa for Christmas. 'We'll pay your fare. If you went by air you could have about a week with Bryn. It would be good for you both.' But Jo didn't make any plans. Whether her excuse about work for the college was truthful, or whether Jo was waiting and hoping that Bryn would invite her first, Mollie could never fathom.

Veronica went, though! She had been putting pressure on her parents to let her visit some friends of theirs, who owned a farm some hundred or so miles to the south of Bryn's. Vee determined that somehow she would see him. She begged, she cajoled and finally stopped eating, and became so thin and ill-looking once more that her parents relented and arranged the trip for her. She left by boat at the end of November. When Jo heard, she was devastated.

'But Mollie, why didn't she tell me? We could have flown out together.'

'Could you, Jo? I think not. Vee doesn't want you around, not when she's got Bryn,' her aunt said. It was a cruel comment and not worthy of this kind, sweet lady, but Mollie was cross with Vee over this new venture of hers.

Johanna spent Christmas at Widegates and, for the first time for years, her mother and both brothers joined her there. She was impatient and a little aggressive during the break. Cross with herself for not going to Africa to Bryn and cross with Veronica for being there. Tom watched his niece sadly, until four days after Christmas he suggested that she join him for a drink to the new year. They had almost a full bottle of port between them, as Tom talked of his childhood on the farm, of his marriage, and finally of grandma. The drink, far from cheering, served only to make Jo more maudlin, so that when finally she crawled into bed it was to spend a night of great discomfort, for the bed dipped, tossed and turned as if she were at sea in rough weather. When she opened her eyes for a moment, the room spun round and round, and the moon, shining so brightly through the window, alternated between being a full dinner-plate size to just a speck of silver, as it withdrew across the sky. She supposed she must be drunk, and this was enforced when the next morning she couldn't lift her head off the pillow. Bill came to investigate when she didn't turn up for breakfast; he vanished below chuckling a little about his little sister having 'hit' the bottle, and reappeared with Alka Seltzer, which he made her drink whilst he watched. Some two hours later she was able to put in an appearance, pale and headachy, but sober! Tom kept to his room all day refusing food!

Veronica got in touch with Bryn within a few days of her arrival in Africa, and he asked her over for a visit. She arrived one afternoon, when the sun was blazing in the clear blue sky and the surrounding parched brown land was like a dustbowl. A day when Bryn's thoughts had been of home. She arrived like a breath of fresh air, looking lovely in cool green linen with her red hair caught up at the back with a white chiffon scarf. He was more than pleased to see her. 'You look like England,' he commented as he hugged her tight.

Bryn showed her the farm, the bungalow, and took her to see the little schoolhouse and village. She was reserved with the women, who babbled and giggled when introduced, and she seemed a little awkward with the children, who took an interest in everything she wore. Little black hands stroked the linen of her dress, little black fingers reached for the silver bangles she wore on her arms, and little black ears were pressed at her wrist to listen to the quiet tick-tick of her tiny watch. She bore it all with patience, but secretly thought that never again would she allow them so close.

Bryn was delighted to have a companion other than his aunt, and when Veronica seemed bored he took her on visits to neighbouring farms, where she charmed everyone she met. Aunt thought that she was Johanna. She never coped with the idea that Bryn had another friend. It was Jo who had come; Jo who had come to stay, and Jo who one day would care for the bungalow and love it as she had always done. She made Veronica welcome, so her stay lengthened into first weeks and then months.

Bryn mentioned her when writing home. 'Vee is here, Jo, and it's truly lovely to see her. She's brought a breath of Cornwall with her. My plans are still uncertain. I long to show you all this, but my heart is still in England. I have no doubt that I will eventually find the dream farm at home, but meanwhile Veronica has eased my homesickness and I'm grateful to her.'

Aunt Mollie poured scorn on Veronica's reasons for visiting. 'I knew she wouldn't stay long with her mother's friends … she went to see Bryn. You ought to go, Jo.'

But Johanna, settled once more and working on her teaching course, laughed at her aunt. 'She'll tell me all the news when she returns.' But Vee didn't return. Her parents died whilst she was in

Africa. It was a shocking, wasteful death. Fumes from an old boiler had seeped back into the house and killed them whilst they slept. Veronica was sent for, but she felt she couldn't come. Instead she turned to Bryn for comfort and support. He became totally necessary to her and was content to let matters ride – after all, poor Vee had lost her parents. She hadn't a soul in the world and he was happy to fulfill any role she decided he ought to play if it eased the pain of her loss. She joined Bryn in early morning treks on horseback round the farms, always giving the impression of great interest.

One tragedy often follows another, and it was on one of these early morning excursions that the two young people found Bryn's aunt lying face down in the lake at the corner of the paddock. She had taken more and more to wandering at night in her lonely searchings and, poor lady, must have tripped, knocked herself unconscious and drowned in the quiet of the night – quite alone. Bryn was shocked at the way of it. He felt guilty that perhaps he and Veronica had been too happy, too contented. 'I should have had more time for her,' he thought, but it was a comment by an elderly friend who put things back into perspective for him.

'Don't be sad now Bryn, she's found what she was searching for. Your aunt is all right now!'

The funeral was well-attended, some friends coming from outlying farms, and the bungalow was filled with sedate, quietly-spoken people. All asked Bryn about his future in Africa. One old gentleman, his aunt's lawyer, went as far as to comment amongst a group of friends. 'He'll stay, you know. The farm is his and with that lovely girl at his elbow … he'll be an asset here. We need some new young blood.'

But Bryn was certain that he'd go, just as soon as the farm could be sold. He voiced these plans to Vee as they sat on the verandah in the black velvet of early evening.

'I'll sell up, Vee – sell up and then find that dream farm in Cornwall. You can come back with me. Take up your life again in Fowey. You'll have Jo, James and all at Widegates to help. I know things won't be the same, my dear, with your parents gone, but we'll all be there to give you support.'

Tears streamed down Veronica's face. 'I can't, Bryn. I can't go back. And, in any case, things are not the same. Jo and James …' her voice grew quiet.

'They love you as I do,' Bryn interrupted her.

His voice was gentle. 'We all want things right for you. Come on, try it.'

She shot a sidelong and desperate glance at him.

'But you don't see. Jo and James – they've been seeing an awful lot of each other whilst you've been in Africa. It's been a long time, Bryn, and things change. That's why I came out – to comfort you …'

Bryn made to get up from the wide rocking chair that had been gently tap-tapping on the planked wooden floor. Then he sat down again heavily. He stared at Veronica, but she had turned her head and was peering into the black African night. He shivered – 'James and Jo – Johanna and James … no, it wasn't possible, and yet …' Veronica's words pierced his heart. 'It's been a long time Bryn, things change!' He got up suddenly, knocking the chair against the wall of the bungalow, sending it rocking fiercely now freed of his weight.

'I'm going riding. Don't wait up!!'

'But Bryn …' Veronica's eyes were wide. 'It's not safe at night.' He brushed past her outstretched hand and she heard him call the stable boy. Heard his voice:

'Hurry, boy, hurry …' It was harsh and loud from Bryn, always so patient and kind to his lads. She heard then the horse's hooves cross the pebbled yard and then thud away into the paddock and beyond, fading into nothing … What had she done?

The spring term at college was very demanding. Apart from six weeks of teaching practice, where Jo had in her charge 25 or so six-year-olds, there were essays to do, speeches to make in front of other students, art projects to complete and books to read in order to complete the year's course. She worked hard. Mollie had taken her to task after Christmas, saying:

'You are like me, Jo, but don't be. You just sit back and let things happen. Don't wait for Bryn to ask you. You miss him, you love him – then go to Africa and seek him out! It's been long enough!' Jo's mind and heart had been in turmoil for days after this, but finally she made her plans; she would go for the Easter break in April. The letter was written to Bryn and was waiting to be posted when she heard from him once more. Jo paled as she read, her hands shaking.

'Veronica has told me how you feel about James. I never knew – never realised, but then we were all so close. I always hoped – you know, Jo, but then, no point in dwelling on that. You and James have all my love. Be happy …' Jo stopped reading. Her heart seemed to have stopped beating, her hands shook more forcibly and her mouth trembled. She would telephone Bryn – he just couldn't think this – he couldn't! She would telephone today … But there was more –

'Vee and I got married this week. After losing her parents she felt she just couldn't return, so I offered her a home here. Life is never what you plan or what you dream, but we are good friends and I'm sure we'll be happy here. She seems content to settle on the farm, so now I must make sure that I put all my energies into making it work.'

Jo telephoned the college secretary, explaining that she was ill, and then bolted straight to Widegates, like a rabbit to its burrow, there to work long and hard hours on the farm whilst she burnt out the first deep pain of her heartbreak, rejection and the burying of all her dreams. Sometimes she sat on the outer steps near to the barn as she had when a girl, then at one with the beauty of the starlit skies and to weave her own special dreams. Now the sky, though just as beautiful, afforded her no comfort, rather its splendour reduced her. Her hurt became a physical pain, a burning restless sickness that she hugged to herself in the darkness, her eyes dry and aching with unshed tears. Memories of happier times assailed her daily, here where everything reminded her of him, of them both, and she went through each day in a haze of weary emptiness and loss.

She spoke to Mollie one morning when the house was quiet.

'How can a little piece of paper call a lie to all we've been to each other all these years? Bryn was my friend, Mollie – if he can't be my love, then why do I have to forsake his friendship as well. I can't cut him out of my head and my heart. He is always there, so how can I cope?' She shook her head wildly. 'How will I ever manage … how? Even the headland holds little solace now without him. All the joy of the wind, the rain, the smells have gone somehow, and I just hurt all the time.' She leant her head against the window pane and gazed out on a sun kissed farmyard with unseeing eyes.

Mollie looked long and hard at her niece, always so very dear to her and even more so now. She understood her loss; had experienced the same desolate feelings herself, but Jo's was worse, much worse in that Bryn was not dead – just dead to her!

'I don't know, dear,' she said inadequately. 'I really don't know, but what I do know is that everything passes and time really does heal. It won't take the pain away, not completely, but you'll learn to live again.' To love, probably, she thought, but wisely knew that now was not the time to say that.

James was her quiet companion through hours of hard walking on the headland and moors. David and Margaret called frequently to include her in little outings they'd arranged, but she refused them all. They were so happy together and although Jo was pleased for them both, it only made her own loss the harder to bear.

So it was to James that she turned finally for comfort and release. He had come across her in the stable one evening talking quietly to Horse.

'He's gone, boy,' she was whispering, her face half-buried in his flank. 'He's gone … and he's taken all our dreams with him. I hurt so much – so very, very much. How can I go on, old fella, like this, with nothing to live for – nothing.' James called her name softly, and if she recognised the loving anguish in his voice, she was not aware of it. He held out his arms, enfolded her with a tender care, while, for the first time since she heard of Bryn's marriage to Veronica, she cried, cried out the hurt and the pain, cried until she felt an empty weariness engulf her.

James's voice was deep and rough. 'I could kill Bryn for hurting you so.' Her head was up in an instant and she moved out of the circling arms and stared up at him, her face tear stained, pale and ravaged.

'Don't, James, please don't. He will need you more than ever now. Don't you see, he's lost to me, but not to you. Bryn will need you as much as I do and you mustn't let him down.' She squared her shoulders, reached out a hand to his, murmured a 'thank you' and left the stable. James watched her go, thankful that he'd been there for her, to afford some comfort from a pain that he knew one crying fit would not mend.

'She'll get over it in time, though,' he thought, and remembered one of his mother's favourite sayings – 'Time is a great healer and life has to move on'. He left the farm by the back gate, turning to wave at the lithe, small figure standing gazing up at the wall of honeysuckle, now showing a haze of green. His heart bled for her, bled for them all!

For Jo it was the beginning of a sort of healing. Her pain, like a wound when the edges begin to knit together, raw and burning sometimes, then often just a dull ache, but always there, like skin, newly healed, but threatening to break open into a searing, tearing pain once more. Jo mostly managed to control it, spending her days working; hard physical work on the farm! She affected a false jollity to match Edith that hurt her aunts more than the old silence had done as they watched over her.

She walked for long hours, James often a quiet companion, keeping pace with her restless strides and breaking the silence only when he sensed talking would help. They rediscovered the beauty of the headland together, until slowly, slowly, shared memories were brought to light again.

The healing really began one afternoon when Jo and James had helped with a group of children from the village school, who were on a farm visit. Horse had been saddled and the youngsters, one after the other, were taken for a ride round the home field and out through the orchard, with adults holding the bridle for safety. One little lad … bright-eyed and fearless, had requested that he hold the reins and take full charge.

'Let him,' announced his teacher. 'He actually rides quite well.' They stood and watched as he took Horse, gentle careful Horse, in a slow trot over the field, and then they turned to one another in the joy of a shared memory, as the boy slapped Horse on the rump and galloped him back, his face alight with devilment.

'Like Bryn,' James said. 'Just like Bryn.' She smiled up at him through tear-misted eyes.

'Yes James, isn't he just!'

Johanna wrote to Bryn and Veronica. It was a neat concise letter wishing them well in their new life together. She told them of her plans when the teacher training course was finished. Sent messages from the aunts, and then, finally, sent a special message for Bryn, because in spite of everything, she knew that it was love for her, and his foolish generous, gullible nature, and the enforced absences after their closeness as children, that had been at the root of his mistake … his marriage to Veronica.

'James has always been dear to me, we've known one another for so very many years. He has been my constant companion of late, and has guided and helped me through many indecisive moments. Yes, Bryn, I love him, as you've always loved him. He's a good friend – but we've no dreams to share!'

Of the marriage she refused to speak. Only to say that she wished them well and hoped that the farm would prosper under Bryn's management. She pondered often on Veronica's position in it all, but refused to talk about it, refused really to let herself think too deeply. It was all such a sad, ghastly, silly mistake. Jo could blame nobody but herself. Like Veronica, she should have gone to see Bryn; told him how much she missed him … yes … even told him that she loved him, as Selina and Mollie had advised. It had happened – there was nothing anyone could do now and the pain was hers … hers and Bryn's too, for their dreams had been shared, always.

Bryn read the letter a few weeks later on a bright sun-kissed African morning. He groaned aloud and felt a deep despair at her words. If she had meant to hurt, she couldn't have dealt him a more deadly blow. It had been wrong, all wrong about Jo and James. He should have known when Veronica had told him!

CHAPTER SIXTEEN

She returned to college after eight days and welcomed the waiting workload as a friend. Jim came to take her out to lunch. He was appalled by her appearance; always so neat and glowing, she was now wan, pale and listless, pushing her food from one side of the plate to the other. It's as if a light has gone out in her, he thought, as he watched, and took on board some of the blame for what had happened to these two young people he cared so much for. After all, it was his brother who had died, and he should have gone out to Africa and sorted things, not Bryn. Jim couldn't but doubt that it all had been a mistake and hoped that Jo would explain, but now, wisely, he knew that he shouldn't, and couldn't, talk to her about reasons. It was obvious that the hurt was far greater than he imagined, far greater than he, a contented bachelor could understand!

'I don't want to talk about it, Jim, but if you want to talk about Bryn, then that's perfectly all right. You don't stop loving someone just because you lose them, and Bryn and I have been pals forever.' Yes, there it was again – that neat little word that had always, quite wrongly, explained their relationship.

Jim reached his hands across the table to enfold one of hers.

'It's all right, Johanna. I haven't come to pry, but to see how you are. Dear girl, please remember that I'm just a little way down the road. Come any time, bring your books; the room is always ready, use it for weekends, anything!'

Jo nodded her head and whispered a quiet 'Thanks,' Jim coughed, sat back and searched for some papers in his pocket.

'Now, Johanna. I don't know Exeter and I'm expecting a grand tour. Let us see this jewel that the Germans say they destroyed. Can we begin with the cathedral?'

She flashed him a rare smile, the first he'd had that day; bright sunshine greeted them as they set off towards the city centre.

Jo took to walking by the river, missing the sights and sounds of her beloved sea. The garden attached to the large Victorian house that contained her bed-sit backed onto the river, and a gate there afforded access to a footpath. Sometimes she found time to walk before leaving for college, but mostly she ventured out in the early evening. The clear air enabled her to think; she found words in her head flowed freely, and it was at such times that she sorted out 'sticking' points in her essays.

Mostly Jo's head was full of ideas and plans for her classroom future. She took a notebook with her, jotting down ideas as they came for future use. Often she just needed to walk. She was scared of restlessness, remembering her 'dreaming' days with the tree at home, but it wasn't restlessness she felt now, rather a weariness, and this was when the peace of the river seemed to call her. She would stand and gaze into the dark, flowing water as if mesmerised, with her mind totally empty of all constructive thought. Its movement and depth gave her peace somehow. Occasionally, when the sun shone, she would see a reflection of the overhanging trees, but mostly the river was dark; a dark and peaceful blackness, and it drew her. She would gaze into the slow-moving, slate-sheen water, seeing nothing … hearing nothing, her mind a blank.

It was here that James found her one dull, overcast evening. He had called on his way through to Bristol after speaking at length to Jim on the telephone.

'I'm worried about Jo,' Jim had said. 'Call and see her if you can.'

James decided to stay overnight and had booked a room in a small guest-house a few doors from Jo's place. Finding her out he had taken the river walk himself, as he had done several times before, whilst waiting for her to get back from college. He spotted her small figure some few minutes after, on the bend of the river. The evening mist was rising over the water, and everywhere looked lonely and desolate. It was here that the banks widened, and the water formed a deep pool, with the current flowing mostly on the far side, leaving an almost still area of dark water by the nearside bank. As he watched, Jo took a step nearer to the edge; she looked so small and vulnerable in this lonely place, for the footpath was devoid of other walkers. He hurried towards her, disturbed by her stillness.

'Jo', he said quietly, following her name with a gasping whispered … 'Oh no – my dear girl – not this!' He caught both her arms and held her stiff body close to him; for Jo's eyes, at that moment as she looked up at him, had been blank, blank and unseeing, and he was frightened for her as never before. She stirred in his hold and turned.

'James, where did you come from? How nice that you are here.' She was back again – complete once more, and he adopted a light-hearted reply.

'Just passing through, Jo. I thought you'd be kind enough to keep a lonely man company for a few hours …' As they walked back along the towpath, he put an arm casually round her shoulders and drew her close.

'I've to go to Scotland just before Easter, Jo. Would you come with me, or have you made other plans for the holiday?'

'Scotland … why I'd love to … Bryn always said …' She stopped and looked away.

'I know,' James finished for her. 'Bryn always said that, after Cornwall, it was the most wonderful place in the whole wide world. I imagine the hilly area he is living in now is a little like Scotland, but not as green and colourful. Will you really come then, Jo?'

'Of course. Yes, I'm looking forward to it already.'

And as Jo's mind explored the idea, the more she liked it … yes, indeed, she was looking forward to it. She had been bothered a whole lot at the thought of going back to Widegates right now. The West Country held so many memories of Bryn … and London meant she had to face Ray's efforts at sympathy, and her mother's concern. It would be good to find pastures new, and especially with James for company. Dear, kind, always-there James!

They sat in her cosy, cluttered room until late, making plans, pouring over James' car maps to plan the route they would take, until he called a halt.

'I have got to get to Bristol by ten in the morning, so will not see you before I go. I'll contact you on the way back if I can … otherwise, Jo, you'll be ready and waiting, with bag packed for Scotland. Ten days' time, OK?' She acquiesced with a smile, suddenly happy that she had something special to look forward to. She had never met James's Scottish relations, but had heard so much about them from both boys that she felt she knew them a little already. Happily, she stood at her window and waved him off, then went straight to bed, having her first night of complete sleep since hearing from Bryn.

Meanwhile, in spite of the late hour, James put through an urgent call to Scotland and one to his home. In the first instance to ask if a visit with Jo would be all right in ten days' time, and in the second, to check that his father could spare him. His decision to go north had been made on the spur of the moment on the river footpath. James received ready agreement in both cases and felt now that he could relax in the knowledge that Jo had something definite to plan for. He would make it as happy a time as he possibly could for her.

During the course of the evening he had suggested that she didn't walk the footpath by the river on her own.

'It's a lonely and desolate place, Jo, unlike our neck of the woods, not really safe for a young woman to be on her own. You've had a whole lot of freedom at Widegates, but here on the edge of the city is another matter. Promise me you won't go walking there on your own again.' She had promised, with a small smile on her lips. James was becoming assertive and it rather amused her.

Jo's mother was pleased to hear about her daughter's impending visit to Scotland.

'It will be good for her, Bill, a total change of scenery and people. James will take care of her, I know.'

'He loves her mum, has done for years, but for Jo it was always Bryn. We had a good heart-to-heart when we met together in Greece. It must be pretty awful for him seeing Jo so unhappy. What they should do now is get together!' His mother was amused at the simplicity of the proffered arrangement. Just like Bill, she thought. He always needed a happy ending where his sister was concerned, but life just wasn't like that.

'Too easy,' she answered. 'And proof that you've never been in love …'

His reply was serious. 'I'm not sure that I want to be, mum, if it causes so much pain.'

'Not for everybody, Bill – some of us have years of happiness.' He knew that she was thinking of his father.

At Widegates, too, they were happy about the visit to Scotland. James called round with a list of things Jo had left in her room there, and would Mollie mind packing them for him to take? She vanished upstairs with the list, whilst Edith and Tom entertained James with the antics of the geese, who had taken an instant dislike to the new young postman and were making his delivery of letters a nightmare. He had come from Plymouth and didn't understand country ways at all. Edith's face was alight with mischief ...

'He left a note pinned to the gate yesterday, saying he wouldn't deliver any more post unless we shot 'those vicious hens'! We are half-inclined to shut in the hens and leave the geese out, just to see what happens!

Mollie entered the warm kitchen. The fire leant a rosy glow to the inside of the room; outside, the sun was going down in a ball of red, fringing the clouds with bright edges of orange and the far horizon in warm, rich colour.

'A Bryn evening,' Mollie said quietly. 'He always loved the sunsets.'

'They have marvellous ones out there,' said James. 'Bryn says that the area of sky, like the land, seems vast, and a sunset seen from the bungalow makes him feel really small and insignificant. I'd love to see them.'

'Why don't you go out, James? It would be good for Bryn .'

'Not yet ... not while Jo ...' the unsaid words hung on the air. Mollie passed him a small scrap of paper. 'I found this upstairs,'

'What is it?' James peered closely at the paper. 'Oh another jingle..' He went to the window to read.

'You never knew I loved you. I didn't get to say,
But I told the trees, the sky, the stars – each and every day.
They all kept my secret. Kept it safe and still.
So, you never knew I loved you – And I suppose you never will.
I told the cheeky robin, whilst walking through the snow,
But to you I never mentioned it ... so how were you to know?'

The room was quiet for a while, with the three adults watching him. As he turned from the window, Mollie's voice broke the stillness and the quiet.

'Jo must have written it recently. It's about the sweetest saddest poem I've heard. Poor lass.'

James was visibly moved. He touched Mollie gently on the shoulder, placed the paper carefully on the table, his large hand smoothing it out flat, took hold of Jo's suitcase, and, with a quiet 'thanks', he left, leaving Mollie near to tears and Edith and Tom exchanging bewildered glances.

The car was speeding north. Jo felt glued to her seat, as if she'd been sitting there forever. Despite this, she felt somehow settled, relaxed and able to enjoy the changing scenery, which was particularly colourful at this time, with spring blossom and bright bulbs everywhere.

'Tired?' James asked gently.

'A little. Thirsty too, and I expect that you are both. How far are we going tonight, James?'

'Another ten miles or so, that's all. We are staying overnight at our usual stopping place. You'll like it there.'

'Dear James,' she thought. How very nice right now to have her life organised, to just sit back and let things happen. She continued to gaze out of the window. It was almost 4.30, and they'd been travelling since nine that morning. The roads had been clear, the weather perfect, and only now were the evening shadows beginning to appear as a cloud layer built up in the south.

'So long as there's food, a bath and a warm bed, I'll be happy,' she returned, squeezing his arm gently.

'All that, madam … and more!' he replied with a smile.

They pulled off the road after turning to the right some 20 miles south of Glasgow. The land was softly curving, an area of rolling farmland interspersed here and there with little hamlets. The drive to Old Loake Farm, their destination, was tree-lined and rather forbidding, but then opened out suddenly to reveal a charming, low-lying building of grey stone, rather like Widegates. The drive led directly to some imposing front steps, bright with pots filled with bulbs on either side. The owner, Mrs Muirhead, was there to welcome them.

'Eh lad, but you are all grown up now. Left "my boy" in the army then, did you?'

She was a bonny, dark-haired lady, square of face and body, with thick eyebrows, generous lips, and a strong fruity voice.

Her arm reached out to take Jo's case, but James took it from her.

'Masterful too now, eh, James? Well, I like that … I like that a lot!'

She was dressed in a blue-grey check skirt, a blue jumper of much the same shade, and wore a two-strand pearl necklace. On her feet she sported heavy, serviceable brogue shoes. She looks solid and dependable, thought Jo. Solid and dependable, just like the house …

Mrs Muirhead turned to Johanna.

'I'm pleased to meet you. I've heard so much about you from the lads. You must be tired, come along in …' She stood aside for Jo to enter the house. It was cool inside and smelled of polish and fragrance from a wide arrangement of spring flowers, which occupied the centre of an oval table set against the wall. The hallway was square, with three passages leading off. One of these led directly to a flight of wide but shallow stone steps, curving gracefully upwards. At the top Jo was shown into her room. She held her breath; it was beautiful, large, light and airy with a high ceiling. A four-poster bed dominated one side. The walls were decorated in shades of apricot and cream, warm inviting colours, and from the wide bay windows she could see across the gentle landscape to distant hills.

'Oh how lovely,' she turned to her hostess, but only James was there.

'Like it?' He put an affectionate arm across her shoulders and drew her nearer to the window.

'I'm next door – shouting distance, and the bathroom is just beyond my room. Mrs Muirhead's a dear. She's known me since I was four. I expect that I have changed lately, but she never seems to. Why, I think she even wore that skirt, jumper and the pearls when I first met her!'

A substantial meal was served in a downstairs dining-room that overlooked the garden. A fire had been lit in the wide stone fireplace and glowed on the copper pots hanging from the ceiling. Johanna did justice to roast lamb with all the trimmings. This was followed by Mrs Muirhead's special rhubarb jelly with lashings of thick cream. They sat for a while into the evening in the large, elegant lounge, before saying 'goodnight'.

'I'll call you, Jo. We've about the same distance to go tomorrow, so an early start is important.' Jo kissed his cheek, gave him a fleeting hug, and within minutes was snug inside a cocoon of feathers in the four-poster.

She awoke quite naturally to a grey, dismal day with lowering skies. The view was hidden in a mass of clouds, and she wondered how they would cope with travelling north that day. She packed her bag, washed and dressed, so that James was agreeably surprised to find her ready when he called her some half an hour later.

'Slept well … good, so did I. Mrs Muirhead has breakfast on the go and she's packed us a lunch. I had intended stopping in Callander for a meal, but she's advised against that, for we've still a long way to go beyond that. She suggested that we "eat up the miles and her sandwiches …" I must admit it's the best idea, for ferry crossings are much nicer in daylight. I want you to see your first glimpse of Skye before dark.'

They were on the road and making good headway an hour later, and although the weather worsened as they progressed northwards, their spirits were high. Jo requested that they stop in Callander for coffee and was thrilled with the clean, pretty little town.

'If they work hard at this it could become a real tourist centre,' she commented. 'Now that the war is over, more and more people will be taking holidays up here, I'm sure.'

James bought her a bright scarf and also some long warm socks for his aunt, who had requested that he find some on the journey up. They looked like boot socks to Jo, long and cumbersome; James explained that both his aunt and uncle went hillwalking on the island, and needed to be decently and warmly dressed and shod.

Lunch-time found them on the lower slopes of Ben Nevis, where they spread a rug and picnicked. It was rather chilly, but good to be out in the air which, whilst misty and damp, had a sweetness of smell that was new to Jo. 'The smell of Scotland,' James had said when she'd mentioned it to him.

Jo chewed on her sandwiches and thought of their journey through the great glen. The skies had been lowering even more, dark and forbidding, and with the mountains either side she'd felt hemmed in and totally overawed. She had almost asked James to find an alternative route, but as if he read her mind he had commented:

'Strange feeling, isn't it, Jo? Everyone feels like this when they go through Glen Coe for the first time, especially if the weather has closed in, as now. It feels as if we are the only ones about, doesn't it? A magical, spooky place. Dad always used to make it appear worse by telling the most awful stories of the battle, so many years ago. I quite expected all the McDonald Clan to appear fully armed, to chase us away. You'll love it on the way back though. Skye has places like this too, so we'll visit them and get you used to the strangeness.'

James took her up the Mamratagan route and over the little ferry to the south of Kyle of Lochalsh. The road wound round the mountain in a series of hairpin bends; as they climbed higher they were occasionally afforded a view through the trees: wooded hills, rocky crags and fast-running water, all spiralling so far downwards that Jo felt giddy and unsure as she gazed through the car windows. At one point only, the road opened out and became flat before beginning its tortuous path down again; here the view was breathtakingly beautiful, with mile upon mile of open moorland and water. Their hearts were lifted with the majesty of it all.

Skye greeted them with a weak sunshine as they landed on the slipway that had been cut out of granite rock. The road dipped and turned in a frightening fashion. It was narrow, with a deep gully on either side. At times Jo couldn't see over the bonnet of the car, and it felt as if they had taken off, but, bumping a little, the car always found the road again. They passed huge lochs, the water like steel in the late evening sun. The journey was impossibly long; she wondered how James was faring, and wished she could drive to help out. He must be so tired …

Eventually they arrived at the only little town on the island, Portree, where James slowed down in a quiet main street, stopping outside a store.

'Here we are, Jo.' Within seconds he was being engulfed in the arms of the largest man Jo had ever seen. She watched as James was pumped up and down and back-slapped in the most energetic manner. He emerged safely from this embrace smiling, and now introduced uncle Edgar. He was a man of great proportions, well over six feet tall, with a large square head set onto shoulders that seemed to have no neck. He had a shock of white hair above a beaky nose, and the broadest smile she had ever seen. Now he held out wide arms for her. Jo was scared of involvement, but he smiled and whispered in a gentle Scottish voice.

'Nay … I'll not hurt you lassie … Jo, isn't it? I've heard so much about you that I feel I know you already.' She found she enjoyed the hug; heard the strong beating of his heart as she was held close, and there hung about him a smell of newly baked bread.

'Come on in, lass … Kate is longing to meet you.'

As they were ushered into the entrance of the shop, Jo was immediately transported back to her teenage years, when she'd spent some happy summer holiday weeks helping in the local grocer's near to her home in London. The wooden block floor was there, giving off the same slightly pine smell; the counter, fronted by a row of biscuit containers with lift-up glass fronts; a huge bacon slicer was tucked away at one end of the counter, and all over the walls were wide shelves housing brown-glazed storage jars, neatly labelled … dried fruit … peas … haricot beans etc. There was a warmth and welcome in the variety of smells that assailed her nostrils; in the glow of the lights switched on against the gathering dusk outside; in the ordered lines of packages and parcels, neatly labelled for easy use. Against a counter at the back of the shop were little bundles of sticks, neatly stacked and marked 'fire wood'; there were cans of paraffin, tidily and safely tucked under a concrete shelf on a slate slab; candles, matches, bottles of disinfectant, soap and packets of lavender bath-crystals … all adding to the variety of aromas, but over every other smell … was the all-pervading, wonderful smell of newly baked bread.

Aunt Kate arrived from a room at the back of the shop, her face rosy with heat and wiping her hands on a white apron. Jo was entranced – this then was Jane Trevarder's sister. It seemed impossible for two people to be so different, and yet be closely related. None of Mrs Trevarder's elegance of dress was apparent in her sister. She was a short, dainty lady, with dark curls interspersed now with grey. Her face, round and red with her exertions in the kitchen, was happy, her smile wide, and balanced on her nose were the largest pair of steel glasses Jo had ever seen. Underneath the white apron, she wore a dress of light-blue woollen fabric that exactly matched her eyes. Her feet sported flat-heeled walking shoes, not quite as heavy as Mrs Muirhead's brogues, but as serviceable and comfortable-looking. Her legs were plump and solid in appearance, but she walked lightly, with a little bounce, now moving towards Johanna with such a happy, twinkling welcome.

'Jo, how good to meet you. We've heard so much about you from the boys … come in … come in,' and she gestured the way into the back room from whence the bread smell came.

Jo was startled to hear her mention 'the boys' and then remembered that Bryn too had often been to stay in Skye during various school holidays. Her heart gave a little jerk for a moment, and then she was swept along with aunt Kate's enthusiasm.

'Come on, love, tea's ready. Just a quick wash and we'll tuck in. Close the shop now, Edgar. If anyone wants anything they can ring the side bell … it's a special day today.'

The table was groaning with food. Salads, cold meat, various dishes of pickles, jams, buttered tea cakes, hot crusty bread, dishes of real butter and, in the centre, the most inviting-looking fruit cake that Jo had seen for years. James was smiling benignly at her.

'The main aim of a holiday with aunt Kate is to fatten her guests – so be prepared, Jo!'

But that evening Johanna needed no encouragement. She ate the freshly prepared, tasty food with relish, drank copious cups of hot tea that Uncle Edgar poured for her, whilst she listened to the happy chatter from them both, the questions put to James about events at Pensilva, letting the whole happy atmosphere wash over her. What lovely people. She felt she had come home somehow, for nothing felt strange.

From the side window she could see the water, slate-like, polished and deep, still in the last of the evening light. An occasional seagull flew past the window, slowly and without purpose, as if having a last low flight before settling for the night. She heard a clock chime somewhere, probably a church clock, and looked forward to the morning when they would be able to explore what seemed to her to be a very lovely, and decidedly different, part of the United Kingdom.

She was shown to her room by both adults, with James climbing the narrow staircase behind them all, carrying the cases!

'Here.' Uncle Edgar threw the door open on a little blue-decorated room that faced out to the water. 'This was always Bryn's room when he came. He loved it!' There was quiet for a minute. James struggled in with her case and cast a quick look at his aunt.

'Here you are, Jo, get organised and we'll meet downstairs in a moment.' He left the room with his uncle. Aunt Kate looked carefully at her young guest. Jo had leant her body against the wall near to the window, as if suddenly taken faint. She looked pale and strained. 'My dear,' Kate said, 'that was thoughtless of Edgar …

but he just doesn't seem to think … we always loved having Bryn, you see, he was just like family. Would you rather change rooms with James?'

Jo started and looked up, her eyes swimming with tears.

'Oh, of course not aunt Kate … no … I'd love to be here. It's just … oh … it's just so awful – keeps coming back you see – the hurt …' Jo's voice caught on a little sob. Kate took a step forward and clasped her in her arms. She was shorter than Jo, but the hug was warm and comforting.

'I'm all right really,' Jo whispered after a while.

'Of course you are. Now, shall I leave you to settle in? Come down when you are ready, lass, we'll be waiting.' She left the room quietly, but not before she heard her young guest murmur, 'Bryn, oh Bryn … why is it like this … why?' Turning, she saw Jo lean against the window, with such a sad expression on her face, that it pained her.

James found his aunt sitting by the fire downstairs, the table still in disarray, and the kettle boiling over and spitting into the open flames, causing steam to rise.

'Is she all right?' James asked anxiously. He should have been angry with his uncle for mentioning Bryn at that moment upstairs, but then Edgar wasn't to know, and in any case he was such a bombastically happy man James doubted that he would have understood.

'Yes love – she'll do.' He smiled at the familiar comment – just like Mollie, he thought, as his aunt continued. 'But whatever happened is still very painful to her. Were they engaged? If so, why did he marry someone else? She seems a very lovely girl to me.'

'She is, aunt Kate.' There was in his voice a suggestion of despair that made her look at him quickly. 'She is,' he repeated, 'and, yes, they were engaged. Forever, since children, and that's why it's all so awful for her. I'll not talk about it now, in case she comes down, but Jo's hurt to the core. That's why I've brought her here, to help her to cope.'

He gazed into the fireplace, watching the spitting and spluttering of the kettle on the trivet, and then automatically reached out to move it away from the direct heat.

'Please don't say anything to uncle Edgar. Jo doesn't want to forget Bryn. She'd much rather talk about him, for he's not dead, just lost to her, and I'm afraid she'll hurt for a long time yet.'

'Never mind, James. We'll do our best to make this a good holiday for both of you … never mind lad, everything passes … you'll see!' James looked at his aunt a little puzzled, for she seemed to be commiserating with him.

Jo arrived down some minutes later and found them busily washing the dishes; she took a cloth and joined in, asking about the town, about the island, and eventually they sat down at a low table, where Edgar had set out Monopoly.

'We always play, Jo,' James explained. 'Uncle is no whizz kid where real business is concerned, but he's never been beaten at this game. See if you can win!'

The weather held for most of their visit and Jo came to realise why the island was called the Blue Isle. There was so much space … so much sky … so many lovely views, and all the time the sea was just a short ride away. They followed a route around the lochs and inlets one day, searching for signs of seal, and were lucky enough to see them coming in at evening time to a small rocky inlet to the north of the island. They sat in the car watching their progress and listening to them call – that wild sweet, heart-rending call that seemed to echo across the water and beyond. They drove south towards the Cuillin mountains. On this day the sky was dark; short sharp showers occurred every so often. As they passed the mountains, Jo looked back at their grandeur, and was thrilled to see three rainbows reflecting against the black rock: a small shower had coincided with a bright spell of sunshine. As she watched, the rain stopped and the colours faded …

'But how, James … how can there be three?'

'They say it's lucky, Jo, and that it's a welcome. The island likes you!'

They visited a little place called Steen, calling in at a tiny pub set in the middle of some terraced grey houses. Jo ordered a ploughman's and was served with hot crusty bread, with the smallest individual round cheese she'd ever seen. It was sweet-tasting and dry, made locally, and she wished she could take some back with her. They stood on the narrow beach here and watched as the tide lapped lazily along the shingle, where several huge mauve-blue jellyfish had been stranded on the early tide. Finally, they wandered over the moorland, out of sight and sound of the sea, and here experienced a silence so complete that, strangely, it hurt her ears! It was an uncanny feeling, and later Jo was to tell Tom: 'It was as if my ears would burst, it was so quiet. I strained and strained to hear just one little thing ... a cricket, perhaps, or the wind sighing softly through the heather, but nothing, nothing at all ... weird and wonderful at the same time.'

They would chase the sunshine from one side of a loch to the other, always longing to be where the spring warmth added to their pleasure, and in this way travelled many more miles than they'd planned. They were lazy, carefree days, with time to relax, time to be energetic, and with always the comforting knowledge that in the evening they could return to the little shop, and the old stone house at the back, with its wooden verandah facing the sea and tiny harbour, from which boats left for the northern isles.

They stopped to ask advice from the island postman one day, on a lonely road, well in the centre of the moors. James got out of the car, stretched his long legs and then approached the red postal van. A head peered out of the window.

'Hello, sir – how nice to see you!' James's face was unbelievable in its surprise, as the voice went on:

'I thought I'd seen you the other day watching the seals, but couldn't be sure.' A body followed the voice from the post van and held out a hand.

The postman, it appeared, had been a platoon sergeant in James's company. They hadn't met since the war had ended.

'I thought you lived in Essex,' said James in bewilderment. 'What brought you here?'

'Peace, quiet, contentment and marriage. I'm the local postman, handyman, messenger. You name it and that's me. It's a lovely life, and we are quite settled. Come over and meet my wife, she's a wonder with scones and things.'

They found that the postman lived in an old barn that was being converted and modernised. One part had been set aside as a little tea room, and it was here that his wife, Jean, served her cream teas.

'It's taking off a little,' she said in her light liting voice. 'The local people come here at weekends, and the tourist trade is increasing. We are hoping to make it more than a sideline in time.'

James told Jo about Roger Hurst that evening, as they sat quietly on the verandah watching the evening stars appear to twinkle in the skies, and the reflection of them in the still water of the harbour.

'He was a real "townie", Jo. Always ready for a pint and fun with the lads. A noisy man really, and I can't imagine him settling here … what a good woman can do for a man, eh!'

CHAPTER SEVENTEEN

Jo was a little apprehensive at the thought of teaching practice so soon after Easter, for she felt unprepared and still very wrapped up in her personal sadness. The slightly buoyant feelings she'd experienced during the holiday in Scotland with James had vanished; it was as if Skye had been a dream. Now reality was back, and with it had come bewilderment and a sense of loss that was hard to bear.

However, two days back in college and it was as if she'd never had a break. It was 'all systems go' for the six weeks the students were to spend in schools. She had been allocated a place in a junior school roughly four miles from her digs and very easy to reach on a regular bus route. Jo went that evening to look at it, but was surprised to see an old 1930s building, standing high, looking slightly gloomy, and at the entrance to a wooded drive.

The gates were locked, but a large notice read: 'Witherham Infant and Junior School'. Where then was the lovely new building she had been told to expect? The school was set in the middle of a vast estate of semi-detached houses. It was a pleasant area, with each house boasting a front garden, and the roads lined with flowering cherry trees, which were now looking very lovely in full blossom. 'It will do,' she murmured to herself, and found she was reasonably content even with the old building. It looked somehow permanent, a 'forever' building, and she pondered on the number of children who must have passed through its front entrance over the years.

With one week to prepare, she went into a frenzy of activity. Jo had been told at the last minute that she would have either Infant children, seven years or so, or a class of eight- to nine-year-olds. It made planning difficult, and was particularly annoying to her when she knew that fellow students had on the whole been allocated a particular class right from the start, but it appeared that the head of Witherham School felt he ought to see his two students before he committed himself to their placings. Jo was to attend with another girl in her year, Ruth Dangerfield, a prim, soft-voiced youngster, who had come to college straight from school. Johanna wore her years well, but she felt, at 24 rather like an aged aunt compared to her colleague.

The head was not prepared to see either of them before the date their teaching practice was due to start, so it was two slightly apprehensive students who walked through the open gates, round to the back of the old brick building, only to be greeted by the sight of an open field. Set in the middle was a long, low-lying new school. Jo was amazed and pleased, whilst her companion was noticeably relieved.

They were greeted by the headmaster. Mr Brown was a large man, inclined to plumpness, with a round florid face that sported a full, dark beard. He was short and stocky; his grey suit seemed a little too tight for his portly frame, a fact that he made more obvious by his continual tugging-down of the sleeves, and the pulling-over of the jacket. Jo noticed that there were spots down one lapel, and that his large hands were rather sweaty. However, he appeared kindly, his eyes smiled at them behind pebble-glass spectacles, as he said he hoped that they would both have a happy six weeks at his school. Having sat them in his office, both quite expected a welcoming speech with directions as to procedure, but he suddenly looked at his watch, jumped up and vanished through the door! A few minutes later, a small neat lady, whom they later learned was the school secretary, put her head round the door and suggested that they might like to join in assembly. They pushed open the hall door as directed, only to find the first hymn already being sung. No seating appeared available, so they stood as inconspicuously as possible and joined in. Jo's clear rendering of 'Morning has Broken' had several heads turn her way, but she was totally oblivious to them. The hymn reminded her of Bryn, David and James when they used to 'sing to the sea' on mornings like this.

As the children filed out, all very curious at the new, members of staff at their school, the headmaster collected them again, muttered a few words quietly into his beard and then said: 'Come!'

They were taken to the Infant Department which was housed in the old part of the school. The external bleakness of the building was in direct contrast to the sight that greeted them as they pushed their way through a heavy swing door, closed now that the children were safely back from assembly. It opened onto a corridor that was alight with colourful pictures, children's pictures, on both walls and stretching high, right up to the old-fashioned sash windows.

'Oh, how lovely!' Jo commented. Mr Brown nodded his head.

'My staff do well here, there are just two classes and the teachers work happily together.'

'Are we to be here?' Ruth asked in anticipation as her eyes wandered over the bright walls as if mesmerised. Both Johanna and the headmaster watched as she stood, hands clasped tightly together, her straight dark hair falling away from her upturned face, button-brown eyes alight with fervour.

'Are we really to be here?' she asked again.

'One of you,' was the non-committal reply. Ruth shot Jo an appealing glance as they were shown into the classroom. It was a long room separated by a glass partition, the open doors of which afforded a view right through to both classes. They were introduced to the two teachers in charge here, both young and lively-looking, who welcomed them with interest. Mr Brown then turned to say, 'One of you can stay here, it's up to you!'

'Oh, I will, please,' Ruth was quick with her comment. Jo looked round the bright room, at the happy curious young faces, and wished that she'd spoken up first, but it was settled as soon as her colleague had answered.

'Come along then, Miss Dingle.' Mr Brown was off through the swing-doors and charging across the green to the new school, so that Johanna had to quicken her pace to keep up with him. Then proceeded the most embarrassing time for both the headmaster and Jo. She was taken through the Junior School, classroom by classroom, introduced to the various teachers, asked to wait for a while, only to see the head, after a short discussion, accepting the shake of the head from the teacher in charge. It didn't take Jo long to realise that the little talk was about her, or that not one of the staff were prepared to relinquish their class to a student, even for just a few weeks. Finally, with much mumbling, Mr Brown announced: 'Now I'll take you to your class.'

Jo was led yet again back across the green to the old part of the school, except that this time she was guided right to the rear, where a small annexe jutted from a corner of the main building, and so through double doors into a dark cloakroom, which led in turn to the strangest, most depressing classroom she had ever seen. A neat, round, dark-haired lady arose from a desk that faced onto a class of some 20 or so nine-year-olds. All were sitting at old-fashioned desks, two-by-two, with the benches set into an iron framework. The classroom was small, the children seemed a little lethargic, but all perked up when the headmaster told them that Jo was to be their new teacher for a while. Miss Coombes, the charming lady at the desk, was an unqualified teacher, who helped where necessary in the school, much the same as Johanna herself had done at Polruan. The head and Miss Coombes told her the bell would be rung in the playground for playtime and lunch-time; hoped that she'd have a good morning, and left!

Jo stood for a while, staring out of the high windows at the back of the classroom. The children were still, quiet and watching her. Slowly, she moved her gaze downwards and starting at the back, looked along the four lines of faces. Some children ducked their heads, most of the girls gave her a hesitant smile; one dark-haired, blue eyed boy, in the front row, grinned at her, his eyes alight with mischief.

'Shall I tell you what we do today, miss?'

Jo grinned back at him. 'Your name?'

'Trevor, miss.'

'No, Trevor, but you can help me find things, just for today.'

She searched her desk for the register. Trevor located it in the cupboard! She looked for the list of children staying for school dinner; Trevor told her:

'All of us, miss. The meals are smashing.'

In short, for that one day, he was Jo's right-hand man. He was helpful, confident, used to adults, and Johanna knew that after this first day she would have to 'demote' him. He would take over if he could!

The first hour went in a flurry of finding her way and in searching for equipment. She set the main class some work, and then studied the cupboards for stock. Such as there was seemed pretty old and decrepit. The classroom lacked books, pencils, notebooks, paper etc, so with the help of several chosen children she made a list of stationery she would require urgently. The morning break bell rang out clearly. The children stopped what they were doing and, without instruction, clambered over benches and desks in a mad rush to get out. Jo was amazed. She watched them, shaking her head and at the same time making plans for the future. Fortunately she had prepared a flask of coffee which enabled her to stay in the classroom during the break. She sipped her hot drink slowly – her mind racing and thinking!

One minute before the end of playtime, she put on her jacket and placed herself by the outer door of the cloakroom. As the first group of children raced pell-mell round the wall of the annexe, they stopped goggle-eyed, pushing at one another.

'Walk, please.' Jo's voice was clear. 'Walk and line up.' It was a raggle-taggle turnout, but she led them into the classroom, where the obviously usual scramble back to their desks occurred. She noticed one of two of the girls hanging back, as if afraid of the boys' scrum-like tactics to return to their places.

'Don't bother with your books, we are having a special sort of lesson now. Stand up, please. File out …'

The next half-hour was spent with the whole class practising standing up, filing out, walking in line, lining up and returning quietly. She treated them like a miniature army, praising where due, censuring those who were lively and thought it all a great giggle. Over and over again – 'Stand up – file out – stop – back to your desks,' until they managed the whole manoeuvre quietly, neatly and seriously. Then Jo talked to them.

'All right, girls and boys, that will do, and I'm proud of the way you've learnt. In the morning, when we walk to and from assembly in the main school, I shall expect the same behaviour. I intend having the best-behaved class in the school. I want to be proud of you, and, most of all, I want you to be proud of yourselves.'

'Not possible, miss. They say we are just "that lot".' Trevor obviously thought the label was there to stay!

'Then *they* will have to find another name for us, won't they, because we are going to work really hard at making our class the nicest in the school. My children are going to be the most responsible. We are going to be polite, helpful and happy, and will start right now! Any coats or satchels left on the back of your seats, into the cloakroom now, please.'

Johanna felt a little like a sergeant-major, but the children were enjoying it and were very attentive. They discussed what could be done to improve the look of the classroom. What lessons they preferred, and why; which hymns they liked and what sports they did. The morning went by very quickly.

Jo smiled when the bell went for lunch. One or two boys had forgotten the new rules and flung themselves out of their seats, but the main bloc of children took things slowly and quietly, and the recalcitrants soon followed suit. Trevor was the last to leave. 'That was fun, miss … ' Jo wasn't sure that she'd meant the disciplining to be fun, but so long as they had got the message she was happy.

She left her classroom only once that lunch-time, and that was to present the secretary with a list of urgently required stationery. The school cook worried that she'd not appeared for lunch, sent over a senior girl with a covered plate upon which, to Jo's delight, nestled two warm Eccles cakes. They were almost as good as Mollie made!

In the afternoon she stirred the children up with some mental arithmetic and simple punctuation, before selecting a book to read to them for the last twenty minutes. It was a weary Johanna who said a friendly 'goodnight' to her new pupils, and was rewarded with a resounding, 'goodnight, miss!'

With the room empty and quiet it had taken on a new character. The shabbiness was enhanced, the walls, painted a dark cream, had rough patches and broken areas where sellotape hung in ugly little strips. She rose from her chair, where she'd collapsed tiredly a few minutes before, and went to investigate. Fancy leaving a wall like this, thought Jo, as her fingers reached out to peel off the nearest piece of tape, only to find that it brought a whole strip of paint with it, so leaving dark brickwork exposed underneath. This then was the reason for the untidy wall. The building was so old, the wall was crumbling, the windows were high and dirty, but it was to be her classroom for the next six weeks. A soul-destroying thought – she'd just have to make something of it.

Jo poured the remnants of coffee from her flask and sat drinking the almost cold liquid whilst making plans, and then notes. Finally, she made lists on the blackboard, checked that the register was handy in her desk drawer, sorted out various pens and pencils for her own use the following day, and left.

Her teaching practice proved to be an extremely busy, very hard, but rewarding and often funny period. Initially she was left much to her own devices. The headmaster came in occasionally to sit at the back of the class and make notes. Jo never found what these were, because at the end of the period he would get up, squeezing with difficulty from the little bench desk, give her a curt 'thank you, Miss Dingle', and go! She found this frustrating at first, but got used to it.

Some of the other teachers occasionally made an excuse to call in and see her. To begin with they came to complain about various of her pupils, but later to congratulate her on, as they put it, 'taming' them. For indeed it was noticeable that they were a much altered class as far as behaviour was concerned. Jo could even trust them to go to assembly and return without her 'eagle' eye on them. She put them on trust, and they appreciated it.

The classroom itself was fast becoming a colourful home. Some of the children produced work that was worthy of display, and this was put up whenever and wherever possible. With the help of the taller boys, Jo had hung a length of plain blue cotton material she had been using as a bedspread in her bed-sit, taking it from the blackboard to the door jamb. It was a little droopy, but was strongly pinned in and held various pieces of work very well. The father of one of the girls, hearing about her predicament with the walls, had offered to put up some battens. Mr Brown agreed and supervised, so that now she had two lines of firm wood, about an inch wide, that would take drawing-pins. The resulting displays were rewarding, and Jo noticed that the children's work had improved, no slapdash art or careless writing now, each child was aiming to have his or her work displayed. At the back of the room, just below the long windows, was a two-inch ledge which became her place for putting out books that were current, perhaps relevant to lessons she'd taken, or ones that she intended to use in the days ahead. She opened each at a suitable page, using clothes-pegs to keep them open. It worked! Often she would return to the class on wet days before the bell, to find groups of children reading and studying them.

Jo went back to her bed-sit each night, weary, but very satisfied. Happy in the knowledge that teaching was for her! She wrote to James …

'Any classroom situation for me so far has been hand-picked and easy. Mum had the nursery school going neatly before I joined her. The school at Polruan is well-organised as you know, and taking over a well-disciplined class of little ones created no problems. My heart did sink when I saw the situation here, but do you know, James, I would have it no other way. I have the joy of seeing what my efforts have achieved, the joy of seeing the change in the children, in their work and behaviour and, most of all, the joy in their appreciation of me. It's great, and makes me feel good.

'Yes, I'll be back at Widegates for a few days at the beginning of June, just before examinations. I'll be "up to my ears" in books, but we'll do something nice together, won't we, please? Margaret has written twice. I really must "tuck up" my problems and get to see them both when I visit this time. No, I've not been near the river, just haven't had time, with all the preparation for school each day, though often I've had the window open in the evenings and caught for a moment the clear, river smell. It has called me once or twice, just as our headland used to, but I've satisfied myself with just looking. Sometimes the towpath is "crowded" with one or two people, now that the nights are drawing out and the weather warmer. My room remains cool though; how I long for the evening sun to pour in as at home. It does in the morning, but then I'm usually in too much of a hurry to notice ...'

During this time, Jo and other students had been applying for teaching posts. Polruan School had particularly asked her to be free for them in mid-October, when one of the staff was leaving to have a baby. Jo meanwhile had to fill in her time until then, and managed to get a temporary supply job in South Wales that would last into five weeks of the Autumn term. It was ideal.

Teaching practice ended on a high note. All the children shook hands seriously with her, one or two of the girls having a little weep. Trevor spoke for them all when he said how much they'd miss their smashing teacher. She loved them all and was sorry to go! On the walk home – it was sunny and she was loathe to get the bus – Jo remembered an incident that had happened just last week. She had been told to expect a tutor from the college as a form of inspection, and was, with her younger colleague, dismayed to hear it was a Mr Johnson: a fairly old gentleman, set in his ways, and with seemingly rigid ideas as far as handling children was concerned. 'Discipline,' he used to say at the end of each lecture on mathematics ... 'Discipline and firmness. I don't require a child to be happy, just attentive!' Of course it was all a cover-up for a very lovely personality, for a man who obviously loved children and knew how to get the best from them.

For his visit Jo had planned a maths lesson: a measuring exercise, which would involve the class in lots of movement, but also plenty of individual study. At the last moment, her young colleague came into Jo's class almost in tears, to say that she had expected Mr Johnson to visit her first. She had prepared a special lesson and couldn't alter it!

'Why,' thought Jo, 'why does it always happen to me?' She turned to her children, intending to change the lessons round, but decided against it as they were already deeply involved. The class had a marvellous time, worked extremely well, and helped one another quietly and purposefully, but just as Jo said, 'Now clear up, please,' Mr Johnson arrived! He stood smiling at her for a moment, then watched as the children organised themselves, smiled even more broadly when Trevor came near to her and whispered in a voice that could be heard at the back of the classroom, 'Is this the special man you said was coming?'

The bell went. The children filed out beautifully, and Mr Johnson sat down at one of the front desks.

'Enjoying yourself, Miss Dingle?' His smile was friendly, but Jo was wary.

'Why yes, and working hard!'

'May I come back this afternoon, please?' Jo tried not to register the dismay she felt, but he followed with ... 'Oh I know you haven't anything prepared, but from what I've heard that won't matter at all. No, I intend taking the class myself. Would you mind?'

Jo was startled, but nodded her head. That afternoon Mr Johnson took a poetry lesson on 'moving things'. He had selected several lively poems to read himself, and having secured the class's attention with a humorous rendering of a snail moving up a slippery slope, sheets were handed out to the children. He formed the class into groups, told them which poem he wanted them to practise, and then after a few rather noisy minutes each group took it in turns to read. The lesson ended with the class shunting back and forth in the playground in a long train line ... 'My wheels go faster, faster, faster ...' the chorus line was shouted by 23 happy, laughing children. They had never had such a lesson, and Jo was sure that the headmaster, who had watched from his office window, must have wondered at letting 'that lot' get so excited. However, period over, they did remember Jo's schooling and filed back to the classroom in line, and resonably quietly. Mr Johnson and Jo exchanged glances. She was proud of them!

Johanna returned to Widegates as she had told James she would. It was a magical time to be in Cornwall, and now, with perfect weather, the lengthening days could happily be taken advantage of. She helped on the farm when the mood took her, though the aunts insisted she needn't.

'Do your swotting, Jo, and then be free to do what you wish.'

'But this is what I wish!' she laughed at them one day as she whitewashed the barn walls. It was a job the boys had loved to do – a delightfully messy one, which in the past had been made messier by their fooling. James found her there one sultry afternoon, wearing old dungarees, and with her hair and face splashed white.

'Oh Jo – you look about sixteen,' his voice was strangely husky. She studied him quizzically. He was smartly dressed in grey flannels, sports jacket, with his usually unruly hair slicked down neatly.

'Come to help James?' she asked. 'No, of course you haven't, for you're far too neat and nice today. Well, you'll just have to watch me enjoy myself.'

His expression was both tender and amused as he sat down on a bale of straw, well out of reach of Jo's splashing brush.

'I quite thought I'd have to tear you away from your books this afternoon, and here you are having fun. Swotting under control, Jo?'

She turned to him, grinned widely and nodded her head.

'Good. Then go and tidy up, there's a good girl. Polruan have a concert this evening at the Cliff Gardens which you might like!'

Jo was thrilled at the thought.

'Really, James. How nice … won't be long then.' She put her brush into a bucket of water, banged the lid on the tin of whitewash, and sidled past him, hugging her messy dungarees close to her, in a fine show of 'don't worry I won't touch you!'

Edith came into the yard to chat whilst James waited. 'Glad you are keeping her busy,' he commented.

'It's not us, James, she doesn't stop, but Mollie and I do get the occasional laugh and smile these days. On the whole, I think Jo is getting things under control.'

They went on to talk about some heifers that Jim Trevarder had purchased recently, and it seemed no time at all before Jo reappeared. She was dressed in a simple linen dress of cinnamon brown, and over her shoulders had thrown a bright yellow cardigan. The few days at the farm had given her more colour, she looked golden and glowing. James's heart turned over at the sight of her, and lifted at the thought that she might now be making headway and coping with her unhappiness.

Edith wandered off to inspect the barn, only to poke her head out and call … 'Jo, you've missed some spots,' as they strolled off to the car. James had brought a picnic tea. They selected a place on the cliff at Polruan, a high vantage point on some flat rocks, with the sea spread out before them; the estuary to their right, and opposite the coastline stretching in a fading wave of beauty towards Mevagissey. Below them was a small flat grass sward, set out now with chairs for the choir and musicians.

Jo sipped a glass of wine, James's special treat. 'I'll be asleep for the concert if I have too much of this. What's on the programme?'

'Sea shanties – the usual ones; some *Peer Gynt* and *Fingles Cave*. A perfect evening for those two I should say.' James raised his glass to hers. They sat companionably close, listening and whispering together. The evening was balmy, a cool, fresh breeze coming in from the sea occasionally as the sky darkened. Later, a half-moon hung over the water, casting a silver sheen in a long swathe, enhancing each little wavelet near to the estuary with a special light. The stars became bright in a cloudless sky. Johanna breathed it all in; the special coastal fragrance that teased her senses and evoked memories from the past; the quiet sea, lapping only gently over the rocks at the bottom of the cliff; the harbour lights reflected in the water below, spreading out beams of colour, and then the music, stirring her emotions, making her feel alternately happy and sad, pensive and gay.

'Oh James, what an almost perfect evening,' she sighed, as with the concert over, people began to move and talk.

'Yes – wasn't it, Jo,' James replied. His hands were on her shoulders guiding her out along the path, and his gaze rested on the top of her head. For him that one little word 'almost' was not necessary. It had for him been a perfect evening!

They walked the north coast the next day, having driven over early in the Bedford, taking six lambs to a farm at Cadewick. Jo was happy to see them gambol and skip when released from their confined travelling space.

They had breakfast at a small hotel on the main highway, bought a couple of cheese rolls and some fruit at the local shop and made for the coastal path. The footpaths on this side were well-defined and wide. The cliffs were high, the views of the coastline extensive; the sun shone warmly, but a brisk wind buffeted them in a playful fashion, sending Jo's fine hair lifting from her head.

'You look like the snake goddess.' James remarked laughing, as he helped her tie on a small restraining headscarf.

'She used to turn men to stone … so beware!'

As they walked, James talked of the war … his war. He mentioned once more the sight of the dolphins when aboard ship, on his way out to the war zone. How they skimmed the water, leaving streaming wakes behind them, before plunging under, only to return again ahead of the ship: an escort showing them the way!

'They looked so happy, Jo – smiling almost – it made my heart glad to see them.'

He described the hammocks below decks and the impossible overcrowding they had all endured. He spoke of the difficulties in the desert, with the daily ration of just one pint of water, of the close companionship during frightening times, and of how he missed home and Cornwall every minute of every day. Finally, he mentioned his journey back by ship, and the first sight of Dover's white cliffs.

'Not our headland, Jo, but after so long away, just as well-loved, for the first thin white line, as it appeared on the horizon, represented "home"…'

'And now you are happy to be a farmer again,' she teased him.

'Yes Jo, I am. David was right all those years ago when he spoke of war. What youngsters we all were, with our dreams of glory and ambitions. Now, with Pensilva, I've got almost all I want. Dad and mum are quite relieved!'

'I'm glad for you, James,' she answered simply, and wished again that she also could find some peace of mind and purpose. True she was continuing with her course, but the joy had gone, and the sense of working towards a goal. Now her training was something to get on with – a means of keeping herself steady and sane; work to be done day by day. Thoughts of the future she pushed to the far recesses of her mind.

They scrambled down a gully to be nearer to the water, where it sucked, pulled and pushed its way through rock crevasses in a magnificently noisy manner. Jo's bag slipped from her shoulder and fell on the wet rocks below her. Without thinking, she stepped forward to reach for it, just as the incoming tide made another surge forward. As she grabbed the bag, she felt the water round her feet, over her feet, and in a second she was knee-deep in a surging powerful sea, and fast losing her balance in its heaving strength. Automatically she reached up. James was there, his arms stretched out, his hands reached and clasped hers, and she was pulled, lifted high out of danger, to land on a grassy knoll at his side. She looked below at the swirling, white-foamed water and, for the first time in her life, felt not exultation and wonder at its wild beauty, but fear, stark fear! What might have happened had James not been there …

They walked slowly up the grassy path and along the cliff in silence. Jo's feet squelched in her shoes. James held her close, but casually, one strong arm round her waist. Occasionally they stopped and rested, both looking out to sea as always, with Jo being particularly careful to avoid looking down, close to the shore, where the green water continued to suck, pull and push itself over and across the black rocks.

'Sorry, James – I didn't think,' she said, still shivering a little, and was at once rewarded with a hug.

Back in Widegates, Tom had a visitor. Selina's father had called to seek some advice about a small farm he was hoping to purchase.

'It's just at the back of Pensilva land, and being run by two elderly brothers, who want to stay on and manage the place. I thought it might be good for retirement. The farmhouse is beautifully situated and has a view of the sea, not the same as the one we have now, but it will do. James was positive about it, but you know what the young are like, anything new inspires them … I like to take my time. What do you think, Thomas, is it a hare-brained scheme?' Mollie had brought tea in for them and some of her seedy cake. When she collected the tray over an hour later they were still talking.

'Tom's really setting Richard right, Edith,' she commented, when the sisters spent the usual 20 minutes or so over their tea in the kitchen. Edith sipped from her cup. When she looked up her eyes were sparkling.

'Do the old bugger good to have something to plan and think about – he's getting far too introspective.'

'He's not at all well, Edith. I just don't know how he copes.' Mollie shook her head sadly. Tom had found it hard readjusting after his accident with the tractor. He seemed to be weaker generally too, and lately had a frail look about him that worried her. Meanwhile, Richard Williams was preparing to leave. He'd said his good-byes, and then turned at the door ...

'Glad to see your young lass is coping, Tom – she seemed really happy going off this morning.'

'Hmm ... oh yes ... of course.' Tom replied, a little bewildered. He'd quite thought that Johanna was pouring over those books of hers, not gallivanting about, but he was nevertheless pleased for the lass.

'Where has Jo gone?' he asked Mollie later.

'With James to deliver some lambs, and then they intended walking the north coast.'

'Seems James is having a whole lot of time off. It's hardly fair on Jim Trevarder, is it, but the young never seem to think of anyone but themselves these days, or at least some of them!'

'Oh, come on now, Tom,' Mollie retorted. 'We are glad for Jo that she has James right now, aren't we, and in any case they've help at Pensilva. Jim isn't having to cope alone!'

'Help, what sort of help? You never mentioned it before.'

'No, well perhaps I didn't, but Margaret's brother is working there. You know how he loved to come for holidays when Margaret worked at Pensilva. Well, it seems he wants to farm. James thought it would be good for him to see if he really liked it, giving him first-hand experience.' Mollie opened the oven door to check on the bread, which was almost done now, filling the kitchen with a warm, heavenly, homely smell.

'It seems he was in some trouble in London. Got in with the wrong lot – "teddy boys" I think they are called. Anyway, his parents took him up to Yorkshire to start a small hotel, but he hated it ... so here he is. Margaret's relieved to have him near. Why, he cycles past here most evenings on his way to see his sister; there can't be much wrong with a lad like that!'

Tom puffed away at his pipe for a while as Mollie took the hot tins from the oven and tapped the loaves out onto the scrubbed wooden table, just as her mother had done years before.

'Hmm,' Tom kept his eyes fixed on the kitchen window. 'Tell the young lad he can call if he wants to. I don't mind giving him a bit of my time if he's lonely …'

Mollie was not fooled. Tom was curious about Jeffrey. The message was passed, and Margaret's brother presented himself at Widegates one cool July evening. He had come through the yard gate just as Mollie left the dairy. She watched as he set his bike against the low wall, removed his cycle clips, stretching his young body and looked around him. He was tall, wide-shouldered, but slim; long arms, long legs, long body. There was a tinge of colour through the tan of his cheeks, and his short brown hair, damp from the recent exertion, clung to his temples in tight little curls. Mollie started as he moved towards the farm. He had the same casual grace of Bryn, and as he drew nearer, she noticed his deep-set, dark-brown eyes wore an amused expression as she stared at him. Dimples at the side of his mouth came and went as he half-smiled at her.

'Hello, I'm Jeff Wyatt.' He held out a hand. She continued to stare for a moment … 'So like Bryn …' then, remembering herself, reached out a hand of welcome.

'Hello, Jeff. Tom is expecting you. He's in his room watching the sunset. Go straight ahead, last room on the right.'

So began a relationship that was good for both of them. Jeff enjoyed listening to stories from the past, and Tom loved to relate them. Some evenings they sat talking for hours. The girls could hear the rise and fall of their voices. Anything and everything was worth a discussion, but they didn't always agree. Tom loved an argument, as both his sisters knew well and to their cost, and at first Jeff didn't know how to cope with some of the remarks his new companion made, for Tom was often rude and inclined to aggressiveness, but eventually Jeff noticed the twinkle in his eye, for Tom would stop suddenly in the middle of an argument to study his young friend.

'Had enough yet, lad?' he would query … but Jeff never said that he had!

'That's what I like so much about country people,' Jeff said one day, after he'd listened to a particularly interesting story of Tom's grandparents. 'You all have a past, something that is yours alone. It's a thing that I've never had. Here you have a whole community of people, living their own lives, but interacting together. London was never like that – not where I lived in the city.' Jeff continued quickly, seeing Tom's mouth open as if to speak. 'Well, perhaps before the war, but I wouldn't remember really … it was just home. Now the past has been bombed away, people have dispersed and there is no sense of past or future, no continuity, as down here.'

'Your parents are making a future now, Jeff, with their new venture.'

'Not really, Tom. They've moved to Yorkshire certainly, but the hotel is small and right in the middle of Wakefield. It's situated in a narrow, dark road; mum and dad were thrilled when they found it. 'Just like home,' mum said. 'They are both such "townies" – I often wonder why Margaret and I are so different!'

'Lots of people living in large towns belong to really caring communities, Jeff, places where families have lived near one another for generations. They have a past too, you'd be surprised.'

'Well, we never had. No aunts; no uncles; no relatives at all … no past! I want to live here somewhere, and make a future for my children and my children's children … see what I mean?'

'Indeed I do, lad. Yes, I see and I think you'll do it too.'

Tom told his sister of this conversation. 'Not much wrong with a lad who thinks like that, Mollie – not much at all.'

'What's to be your future, Jeff, have you thought about it?' Tom asked of his young friend one day.

'I'd like to farm; to have a farm of my own and somewhere in this area if possible.'

'Dear God, just like Bryn,' thought Mollie as she listened.

'Farms cost a whole lot of money, lad. Had you thought of going to college and taking a farm management course – what do you think?'

'Actually, James has been making enquiries for me,' Jeff replied. 'There's one course that accepts working people. Two days at college and the rest practical. I hope to be accepted for September!'

'Get advice from James, by all means, lad. He's a knowledgeable man, but sort out the course for yourself. Ring the college, or write tomorrow. I shall ask you again!'

Tom puffed at his pipe for a while. 'Now did I tell you about the haunted house?'

'He's good for Tom,' Mollie told Edith one evening as they sat in the garden listening to the distant murmur of their voices through Tom's open window. 'He's filling a little of the gap that Bryn left in all our lives. Jeff's rather like him too. I get a jolt each time he comes through the kitchen door, tall, graceful and slow-moving, with the same quizzical expression. Just like Bryn …' Mollie's smile was gentle as she remembered.

'I hope the lad is all right,' Edith said. They heard an owl hoot in the valley … a weird, haunting, lonely sound. Mollie shivered … 'Let's go in now.'

Early July saw Johanna back at Widegates with her bags and baggage. The course was finished, exams over; she had done well and was now qualified to teach. Jo had felt a little sad at leaving her bed-sit, for the quiet room had become a haven of peace for her, a place where she could shut the door and feel safe. But Widegates, the aunts and uncle Tom welcomed her – she was happy to be back.

Polruan School had requested her help once more for the last two and half weeks of term, so she barely had time to readjust before presenting herself there. It was both new and pleasant becoming involved in the end-of-term activities; sports day, the swimming gala, and then preparation for the carnival, which had been moved forward this year.

The sun shone brightly on the Saturday of her first free weekend. It had been a blustery, stormy night. Jo had watched from her window as dark clouds raced across the moon, their edges caught here and there by its silver light, lacing and fringing them delicately. The wind had come from the land, across the moor, and the clouds broke up as they neared the headland and open sea. It was a spectacular, powerful sight and she longed to be out in it. The strong wind had abated by dawn, but the day was bright, a frisky breeze chased her as she made for the coastal path across the heather-covered moor. She hadn't been this way for ages, and neither had other walkers, for the path was difficult to manoeuvre in areas where the heather had crept over, or swathes of brambles had spread, ready to trip the unwary walker. She had come across a pigeon lying injured, weak and half-eaten at the neck. Jo had killed it with a rock – smashing its head in one heavy blow. The incident had left her shaken and disturbed by what she had done. Restless and unhappy she had walked over to David's cottage, which he now used as an office and base during the day. He wasn't in, but she spotted his red woollen hat below and clambered down to where he sat, on a grassy knoll, so disturbing his after-lunch siesta.

They had been talking for a short while, Jo answering his questions in short, sharp sentences. He studied her for a while, his expression serious and eyes concerned.

'What's wrong, Jo?' Later, after she'd told him about the bird, his words comforted her.

'Better that way. I'm glad that you found him and could save the poor thing from a slow and painful death. It couldn't have been easy for you!' It was always so with David. He seemed to calm her nerves, to set things right, and even when he couldn't do that, just talking to him had a settling effect.

She went out with Mollie to the carnival dance held in the village hall, now decorated for the occasion with streamers, bunting and some wonderful flower arrangements, beautifully created by the ladies from the village. One huge display, set up at the side of the small stage, was comprised entirely of foxgloves, in all shades of mauve and pink. 'Headland flowers,' thought Jo as she danced by and caught their faint fragrance.

James, who had arrived late, having spent the day on Bodmin Moor helping at sheep trials, watched from the doorway. He was chatting to Mollie, who looked hot and flustered after several rounds of the hall with Selina's dad, whose quickstep was known to be quicker than most!

'I shall have to check on Tom now, James. Would you see Jo back for me? She's dancing now and looking happier than I've seen her for ages. I don't want to disturb her.'

James's eyes searched the hall until he spotted her once more. She was dancing with Selina's cousin Victor. James found him easily recognisable, for he had scarcely changed from boyhood. 'Doe' he had been nicknamed because of his large, soft-brown eyes. He was plump still, rather short, and his fly-away, straight mousy hair was smoothed and plastered to his head with Brylcreem. In his pin-striped suit and tightly knotted tie, he seemed strangely out of place. Why he looks like an office worker rather than a sailor, thought James. Victor had been imbued with his family's love of the sea, and had been in the merchant navy since leaving school.

Now, Jo had her head thrown back, hair flying softly about her face, and she was laughing happily at her partner. He was a smooth, active dancer, and looking at them perform, one felt that he was modifying his steps for the jitterbug, to a more sedate fashion than usual, in deference to his partner. Nevertheless, Jo was being flung about the floor in quite a dizzy way. As James watched, the music stopped. They stood talking for a while, and then the band started up once more. The tempo had changed, the song sweet and well known – 'Everything will come right if you'll only believe the Gypsy', a gentle, romantic foxtrot melody. Victor drew Jo to him and they set off across the floor, both dancing well together. As the lights dimmed he held her closer, bent his head, and with one hand reached up to pull hers nearer, so that their cheeks met. Jo acquiesced for a while, then James saw her back stiffen. She pulled away violently, both hands reaching out, as if to ward Victor off. He looked both bewildered and a little amused. Jo raised one hand to her forehead, murmured a few words and made for the doorway. Victor followed, but as James moved forward to intercept her, he noticed Selina take hold of her cousin. 'My turn for a dance, Victor.'

When he remonstrated, he then heard her clear voice say. 'Jo's all right. Goodness, she's just a little hot, and no wonder with the way you've danced tonight.' As they moved off together, amongst the other dancers, Jo was thankful to her friend. She was also unbelievably relieved to see James's tall figure appear from the group of people clustered at the doorway.

'I've been watching you, Jo. Remember how we used to watch Bryn at dances, and how he loved to take the floor? You and I are natural "sitters-out" I think!' He led her out to the quay wall, where they leaned against it in silence, shoulders touching, gazing at the dark water.

'You saw, James, didn't you? It was all right until he got close. I just can't bear to be touched, you know. Other girls don't seem to mind, but I … I hate it! She glanced up at him appealingly.

'But why … why should I show such aversion? Heaven knows, I'm no teenager, and Vic is a sweet kind person.' She shuddered involuntarily, folding her arms across her chest. 'Why, James?'

'Don't be so hard on yourself Jo.' His arm went round her shoulders and he pulled her to him. 'See, you don't mind me …' Before she could answer he went on, his words low and thoughtfully spoken. 'You are not a man-hater you know. It's just that, right from the beginning, since we were kids, it was just the three of us, and then for you, just Bryn. You've never been like other young girls, flirtatious and searching – you never needed to,' James smiled down at her … 'not with two such handsome fellas dancing attendance. Think about it, my dear.'

They were quiet for a while, listening to the dreamy music, and watching the lights from across the river casting shadows on the water.

'It will pass, Jo. You'll find yourself again,' he whispered.

'Oh James. I do hope so. How I hope so! It seems the only times I'm really happy these days is with the kids. Do you know what happened in assembly this week …?' A different girl was showing itself as she regaled James with yet another story of her charges. Within seconds she was the laughing, self-assured, fun-loving girl he had always known.

He left her later at Widegates, where the aunts were struggling in the dark, trying to mend the old barn door. It had been caught in a freak gust of wind earlier, and was flapping noisily. Laughing, he did temporary repairs, and promised to come out the next day to fix it properly. There was no need. The aunts could get one of the farm-workers to do it, but wisely they refrained from saying so. James was good for their niece right now!

'Thanks, James,' Jo said softly as he left for Pensilva, but he knew that her thank-you was for the little episode at the quay, and was happy.

CHAPTER EIGHTEEN

Mrs Dingle stood back to regard the table. It had been set for high tea with the prettiest of lace tablecloths, a gift from Mrs Jackson at Christmas. She felt a little nervous, for Jo was expected home for the first time since learning about Bryn's marriage to Veronica. Earlier Bill had remonstrated with her when she'd confessed to 'not knowing what to say' to her daughter.

'Say nothing, mum. Jo knows we care. She'll speak about Bryn if she wants to, just be natural.'

Now she wondered how she could be 'natural', for since hearing about Bryn her heart had gone out to her daughter. How could the child manage, she thought, over and over again, as she remembered Jo's unhappy restlessness during the years of the war. At least she had her dreams then, but now – Mrs Dingle shivered, and then started on hearing Bill call: 'We are here, mum!'

It was a calm smiling Jo who walked in, her eyes lighting up at the dainty table settings.

'Hello, mum, it's good to be home.' Mrs Dingle hugged her daughter, and as tears came into her eyes, she heard a quiet whisper, 'It's all right, mum, really it is,' before Johanna broke free and called Raymond, who had been standing somewhat sheepishly by the door, teapot in hand.

'Here, Ray, let me take that, it looks hot.

The awkward moments were over, and Bill cast a quizzical look at his mother, before holding out her chair. Very soon they were all chatting happily together.

'We haven't been like this for years,' Mrs Dingle commented, as she looked round proudly at her three young adults.

Bill studied his sister quietly. She was tanned, her hair, newly washed, glistened with highlights from the summer sun. Her smile was gentle and warm as she listened to Raymond talking of his college progress, but when she glanced over at him, aware perhaps of his scrutiny, Bill noticed her eyes … the sparkle had gone from them somehow; they were dull, and her look was so full of appeal and sadness, that he lowered his own quickly, fearful of seeing more.

Mrs Jackson and John Kimber spent part of the evening with them to welcome Jo and congratulate her on becoming a teacher. Mrs Jackson presented her with a neat, black-leather briefcase that had belonged to her husband.

Jo was touched … 'I'll treasure it you know …' she murmured, as she bent to kiss the old lady. John had made a Victoria sponge which they shared for supper. Ray licked his fingers free of jam and asked where the carrot cake was … It was a pleasant, peaceful evening.

Johanna and Bill escorted both visitors home. The night was still, dark and moonless, but the streetlights afforded a pleasant glow to the pavements.

'Let's walk, Bill … shall we?'

They were quiet for a while, each seemingly lost in their own thoughts, but Bill was thinking deeply, wondering how he could find a word, a few words, to help ease the pain that he knew his sister was bearing. In the end she spoke first.

'It hurts Bill … hurts so much, and it's so hard to put up a pretence all the time, for I just can't forget. I crave his voice, his arms, his nearness always!' Her brother put his arm through hers as they walked on through the quiet streets.

'I used to dream, you know, Bill, that one day Bryn and I would have a house, a home and a family. I'd look in windows as we are doing now, and dream my days away. That's the worst part. I've lost the dreams; all those wonderful imaginary moments will never now be real.'

'You've not said what happened, Jo. Did you quarrel? Bryn cared so much for you, he told me … whatever …?' She reached out, putting her fingers to his lips.

'No more, Bill. I will tell you sometime, but not now. It's been such a ghastly mistake – such a waste. If ever you find someone to love, make sure you tell her, over and over again.' Her voice caught on a sob …

'How could Bryn hurt you like this?' Bill was angry now as he watched her try to control herself.

She turned to him swiftly – eyes flashing. 'Don't ever say that, don't be cross. Bryn didn't know … didn't mean to. In hurting me he has hurt himself a whole lot more!' Bill was puzzled by her words, and walked on quietly, his arm still through hers, as he speculated about the meaning of what Jo had said.

Eventually, they found themselves outside an old wood factory.

'Remember, Bill, when we used to tease the old caretaker on the way to school? We were cruel kids weren't we, and all because he hobbled along in those special, clumsy-looking shoes to correct his differing leg lengths. How he used to shout at us!' Jo was laughing now, remembering the excitement, tinged with fear, as they had taunted him: 'Old Mr Hobble ... old Mr Hobble!' The caretaker used to get really irate and chase them from his yard as best he could. Johanna hadn't cared for school very much at that time, but it was infinitely more rewarding than being caught by the caretaker. She went through the gates marked 'Girls' each morning as if it were a sanctuary. Bill chuckled at the memory.

'I met him later when I was first in the services. He was collecting for the Spitfire Fund once when I was on leave, and mum asked him in. We had a long chat – shook hands ...'

Jo interrupted him. 'Did he ...?'

'Oh yes! We recognised one another, but it wasn't until he left that I took in his last comment completely. "Chase the strong ones now, lad!" he said. Made me feel awful for days.'

'He used to look so old though, didn't he, Bill?'

'Yes, and what cruel little blighters we were!'

Jo went on to tell him of her various charges at school. She voiced her misgivings about teaching in Wales and made him laugh at Jeff and uncle Tom's wrangles.

'Oh, I sympathise with that young man,' said Bill. 'I can remember Tom setting me up. I'd always rise to the bait, somehow never learned to count ten. I'm glad he's met his match.'

Just before they went in Bill turned her to face him.

'Remember, Jo, I'm always here if you want me. Mum too you know – she's been absolutely shattered for you. Just felt you ought to know.' She hugged her brother fleetingly.

'Yes, I do know, Bill. I know, and it makes me feel good.'

Johanna had a busy two weeks, initially spending a good deal of time replenishing her wardrobe in readiness for work. Mrs Dingle unpicked an old coat of Mrs Jackson's, a beautiful heather-coloured west of England cloth, and made Jo a simple suit. She found a black jacket in a local shop, which she teamed with a white and grey checked skirt. Several blouses were also made from her mother's now depleted store of remnants, and a special formal, long-sleeved dress in blue linen, which suited her wonderfully well. Mrs Dingle enjoyed 'setting up' her daughter for her new life as a teacher, but her thoughts often wondered over the tragedies of the young when she caught Jo off-guard. It wrenched her heart then to see the sadness of her expression, and the often bewildered loss, reflected in her eyes.

Johanna bought two pairs of wedge shoes, the latest fashion, in red and tan, but discovered that she wouldn't be able to ride her bike wearing them. Both Ray and Bill joined in the excitement that a new wardrobe engendered in their sister, after so many years of 'making do'.

'She looks so lovely,' thought Bill, time and time again … 'Bryn's a fool …'

However, on the whole, Jo's stay in London was pleasant and full. She met Mary, her old school-friend, who had recently returned to the area after spending several years living in Southampton. She was now working for a local solicitor, and was in the process of moving into a small flat at the top of the hill. Jo offered to help with unpacking, and they spend several evenings unwrapping Mary's childhood treasures and laughing over memories of school. It was particularly amusing to read the old school reports.

'Here, Jo, read this, it might come in handy.' Mary tossed her a letter. 'It's one of those awful epistles the head used to write to accompany the report. I used to chew my nails in anguish as my parents read them, just in case … well you know!' Jo did indeed know, for Mary, a quiet obedient girl at home, had always been a leader at school – the first out of class, last in. She found ways of getting out of anything she didn't like and was a master at feigning to be unwell for hockey or any games. She mimicked the staff, and was often seen doing this! The letter read: 'Mary has on the whole worked well throughout the year, but I feel that she could do better, and I would like her to apply her obvious surplus energies to classwork in the future.'

'Mum and dad didn't really understand what that all meant, and I never told them,' she said with a grin.

'One bright-eyed little youngster on teaching practice used to mimic me,' said Jo, laughing to herself about the time Trevor took the class whilst she had watched from the cloakroom. She'd had quite a job keeping a straight face, but by totally ignoring the incident it was soon forgotten. 'I expect all the teachers knew what you were up to, Mary. You were probably the talk of the staffroom. Remember when we were being auditioned for fairies in *Iolanthe*? I scuttled away just as it was my turn to sing on my own. What a scared rabbit I was, and yet how I longed not to be, especially when I saw all you others looking so dainty on the stage. Oh … how I longed to be a fairy!'

'That was Miss Winter. She was just like Puck in *A Midsummer Night's Dream*, with her short curly hair and bouncing little steps. "Windy" we called her – remember?'

'So many years ago, Mary …'

'I know,' her friend replied. 'And so much has happened to us all. I nearly got married, Jo. An air force lad – he was shot down over Germany. Seems like a dream now.' Mary's voice was pensive, as she gazed into the middle distance. 'Did you keep in touch with that Bryn boy, Jo? I've often wondered.'

'He's married and settled in Africa …' Jo's reply was non-committal. 'We do keep in touch vaguely, though.'

Bill called at that moment, and Jo was relieved. She was almost ready to confide in Mary, to see what she thought of it all, and perhaps to find some reassurance that this continual ache would ease. Mary should know, for she'd lost someone very dear … But Bill brought in a change of mood.

'Fish and chips for you both. Mum thought you'd not be bothering to cook, and so here I am. Any plates and things?'

Jo noticed that her brother smiled pleasantly at Mary and his eyes teased her throughout the make-do meal. Of course, they'd known each other years ago, but then Mary had been just his kid sister's friend, someone to be reasonably polite to, and that was all. She watched them both, parrying comments and laughing openly. Wouldn't it be nice if they got together!

Bill joined them for a bike ride to Keston. Jo hadn't been there since that lovely misty day with Bryn so long ago. She hated being reminded of it, but, somehow, and in spite of her memories, she felt peaceful as she wandered down to the little well to make another wish. 'Do you think second wishes come true, Bill?' she queried.

His reply gave her food for thought.

'It's not what you wish that matters, it's more the amount of effort you are prepared to work towards your dream, to make it come true. Nothing comes from nothing!'

'I know that,' she answered a little testily, and moved away to hide the tears forming in her eyes. I know only too well, she thought.

Mrs Dingle was joining Nancy Grant for a holiday in Scotland. It was to be her first real break for years, but she was worried about not being around for Johanna.

'Don't worry, mum. I'd planned to go back to Widegates for my birthday in any case. Most of my school work is there, and it's a promise I'd made to James. The journey to Wales won't be difficult from Cornwall.

'Scotland is heavenly, mum. I loved everything about it at Easter. The wayward skies, the mountains, the distant views ... the lochs, the colour – the people!'

'And the midges, Jo,' Ray interrupted her flow.

'We didn't have any at Easter silly,' Jo retorted, 'but you might, mum ... see you have the Germolene or whatever.'

The sweet, clear singing of the children's voices washed over Jo as she gazed out of the hall window towards the hills. They looked so close this morning, almost as if she could reach out and touch them. The barren cluster of rock and shale caught by the sun looked glassy and cold, in complete contrast to the wide patches of deep red-brown, where the bilberries covered the hills in wild clusters. Jo smiled slightly, recalling how last weekend she had gone bilberry-gathering on the lower slopes with two of her colleagues and the young Welsh couple with whom she was staying. It was a tedious, back-breaking task, for the berries were small and hid themselves well. Later she had watched whilst a pie was prepared and, later still, tasted by them all. It was delicious, with a strange tart flavour, not like anything she'd eaten before.

The singing stopped. Jo turned her gaze back into the hall, where some 150 children stood in lines for morning assembly. Now they were all looking attentively at the headmaster, who was telling them about a festival of song to be held at the school the following week. Their bright, healthy faces reminded Jo of the Polruan children, and she longed to be back there, where everything was familiar and had a pattern to it that she understood.

She had been made welcome in the school, indeed had found the little Welsh town, nestling in the valley, a delightful place to be, and she was more than fortunate with her digs. Even so, Jo felt strange, felt that she did not belong. It's probably because I can't speak Welsh, she mused, for every child and colleague had the use of that extra language and could revert to it at any time.

Jo had no specific class, but was used around the school as and when required. Her immediate task was to take over from the remedial teacher, who was to be absent for three weeks. The little groups of children who came to her for special help were delightfully friendly and most willing to work. Jo was pleased with the way she'd settled into this new field of teaching. She spent a good deal of her time in the evenings thinking of new ways to help her charges, and was rewarded by their interest and progress. Her base was a strange one, in the library area of the main hall. She was well tucked away, with her desk sheltered and hidden between two tall bookshelves, but the hall was situated next to the kitchen, and lessons were taken to the accompaniment of noisy pots and pans, talking, and sometimes laughter from the school cook and her helpers. The hall was also used as a way through to the toilets: in consequence Jo had to get used to the almost continual thumping, as the doors were opened and then swung themselves shut as a steady line of children moved back and forth.

Assembly was over and Jo's first three pupils had arrived, found their folders and were waiting expectantly for her attention.

'What should you be doing?' she asked of them gently, as she struggled to erect the blackboard. One of the pegs was tight and always gave her trouble, but this morning it just wouldn't budge, and she needed to move it one space up.

'Looking at our books, miss,' answered Evan, a dark-haired, dark-eyed nine-year-old, with a bonny round face and rosy complexion that many girls would have loved. There were scrabbling movements as the children opened books and settled themselves.

'I could do that for you, miss!' again Evan's voice.

'I'd like to think that you could,' replied Jo, whilst still struggling to remove the peg, 'but I'm bigger and stronger, and I can't budge it …'

A moment or two passed and then Evan spoke once more.

'But I could, miss … let me try …' and he arrived at her side, reached over for the blackboard rubber from her desk and, with the wooden side, banged the peg so strongly that it fell out. Jo was impressed – why on earth hadn't she thought of that!

'Thank you, Evan.' She smiled at the boy, whose expression was guileless.

'That's all right, miss,' and Evan followed these words with one or two in Welsh that made his two companions snigger. Jo chose to ignore this and quickly set them work using the now firm blackboard.

From that day on, she found the board already erected each morning and shining clean. Her board rubber was banged free of chalk, her chair set behind her desk, and often a small jamjar of flowers had been set upon the low bookcase at her side.

'Your admirer at it again?' commented the headmaster when he noticed the jar filled tight with an assortment of late garden michaelmas daisies.

'Evan – oh yes, he looks after me well.' It was to Evan she owed her contentment for the five weeks of her stay in Wales; his cheeky grin sought her out each morning, and his continual care touched her, particularly as around the school he was known as 'nuisance number one'!

At first, Evan's behaviour was good; he was helpful, polite, and Jo wondered whether all she'd heard about him was true. However, she did become aware of some problems with his behaviour once a short 'summing-up' period was over. She knew that Evan's home-life was difficult. He was an only child, subjected to the varying moods of a bullying father. Techniques of discipline were wrong, in that punishment was indiscriminate beatings by the father, who, on other occasions, could be called over-indulgent. In some degree, his parents were too permissive; Evan was allowed absolute freedom and would often wander off for a whole day without them being concerned. It has been proved, and Jo had learnt on her course, that constant conflict in the home has a worse effect on a child than the actual physical absence of a parent … Its effects on Evan were being slowly revealed to Jo.

He was a solitary child through choice, though he was good at soccer and much sought after for 'kick-about' sessions in the playground. These he resisted, but during games lessons, his skills with the ball drew admiration from all his peers, but, even so, he preferred to remain on the periphery of any group. Jo noticed that often, when he had played extremely well, he would wander in alone to change, whilst the rest of the boys gathered in little groups discussing every move of the game excitedly.

To Jo's small remedial group, and indeed in the main classroom, he was a continual source of amusement, and one sensed that other pupils awaited his every mood. He was popular with classmates, they found his disruption fun, and he played up to this. Evan was a 'magpie' and always had in his pocket some distracting toy or other. He would do wonders with a piece of string and an old bent pin … fiddling with his strong fingers, his face quietly absorbed, as if unaware of the amusement he was affording the other members of the class. Jo puzzled about how to cope with this, and in the end reduced the effects of his fiddling by 'rabbit in the hat' play. A large box was placed at the side of her desk, and with hand extended, without a word being spoken, the 'rabbits' were collected and placed in the box. Evan took a long time with this procedure. It was obviously enjoyable to him and the whole group. He smiled as the last object was removed from his pocket, bearing no grudges. It was understood that everything was returned in the last period on Friday. This ritual became automatic and now never disturbed the even tenor of the class. After a while the children ignored the procedure, though Evan's supply of bits and pieces never lessened. His pockets were always jammed full, and on Fridays his shoulder bag was weighed down with the week's 'rabbits'.

Being late in one morning, after her bike had developed a puncture, Jo forgot the collection. About mid-morning Evan asked whether she had forgotten something. Jo was a little short with him – 'Get on with your work, Evan, I'll see you at playtime.' The brown eyes looked up at her … his hands came out from below his desk, and he held out the day's supply of treasures. Jo related afterwards that she'd had quite a job to maintain a serious expression. That Evan was incorrigible everyone knew, that he had a sense of fun was now obvious. Jo felt that in this instance he was teasing and testing her. She hoped that she'd passed. Certainly things changed a little, for Evan arrived in the hall each morning, made straight for her desk, and with a slight smile emptied his pockets, pulling out the linings and shaking them, just to show that all was well … he had nothing to play with!

Staff room gossip had relayed for some time that 'things' were missing around the school, blame being apportioned to John, an unpleasant, thin-faced, messy boy, with long blonde greasy hair. Several of Jo's groups of children mislaid pens, pocket money and key-rings. When the cook lost the keys to her car, the head felt he ought to bring the matter out into the open and held a special meeting in the hall.

'Children,' he began. 'Children.' His lilting voice was quiet, his look stern as he paced in front of the school, stopping every so often to glare at one particular child or another. 'This is not a pleasant moment for me, no not at all. Some of you have had things go missing. As you know, nothing goes missing on its own. Things don't just walk away and decide they'd rather be somewhere else … no indeed!' He stood surveying the children for some moments; they were quiet and attentive, one or two looking down at the floor as if guilty of something.

'It's my belief,' continued the headmaster, 'it's my belief that someone is helping these things to vanish.' He looked around again at the sea of expectant, worried faces turned up to him. Suddenly he pulled himself up, pointed a long finger round the whole school and, with as fierce an expresion as he could muster, shouted:

'We have a thief in the school!' Johanna was sure that each child in that assembly felt guilty – she almost felt guilty herself, and certainly it was a quiet lot of youngsters who filed back to class with that admonishment ringing in their ears. Class teachers took the matter one step further by suggesting that children should be watchful, that valuables should be left at home, or, if really needed at school, they should be handed to the class teacher for safe-keeping. Cook's keys miraculously appeared in the middle of the playground during lunch-time play, and nothing was said for a while, though occasionally small things still vanished. Evan was the first child to ask Jo to look after his sixpence, and, significantly, money and treasures were left on her desk quite openly and were never touched.

Evan made repeated requests to attend the toilets. His class teacher thought that he had a nervous system due to the troubles at home, and it was agreed that he should never be refused. Jo, concerned about his lengthy absence one day, went in search of him. She was loathe to enter the boys' toilets, which were situated across the playground, but her concern took her in. She heard a scraping sound in one of the cubicles, and when calling 'Evan', he appeared after a moment or two, looking wide-eyed, a little sheepish, and covered in brick dust. She said nothing, settled him down in class once more and then went to investigate. Two whole bricks in the toilet cubicle had been removed, then slotted back into place so that they scarcely noticed. She prised them out and behind found a cache of missing 'things'. Evan was a squirrel as well as a magpie. Very little was said at the time, though he was made to return every last item, going from class to class. It was agreed that the children should think that he'd found them. His parents were sent for. Jo worried about this and the effect it would have on his father, but Mr Jones just smiled … 'Oh, is that all,' he said. 'I used to do that when I was at school.' This comment was rewarded by Evan's wide smile, and relations between father and son improved from then on. 'Things' didn't go missing any more, and Evan's work improved in leaps and bounds so that, just before Johanna left, he was settled in his own class without the need for remedial help.

CHAPTER NINETEEN

The weather had turned. The golden days of autumn were gone, and in their place came wind, rain and cold. Jo had great difficulty cycling to school these mornings, particularly when the wind came from the sea. The road was exposed in all directions and suffered from the full force of gales; even the high hedgerows afforded only scanty shelter.

'You'll have to get a little car, lass,' Tom had said one night, when she arrived home drenched and shivering.

'But I haven't the money, uncle Tom, and in any case the exercise is good for me!' She didn't mention that the journey home was always full of extra trauma, because, sitting high on her bike, she caught odd glimpses of the headland that, even now, after so long, sent her heart racing and began within her an awful longing for Bryn. At school now, her days in Polruan were busy, and she was content, finding the children interesting, demanding, and a constant source of amusement. She didn't have time to think, and that was good! But the journey home was a lonely one, and as she cycled along the well-known road, memories came flooding back. It only needed a seagull to wheel away near to her, or perhaps the wind to catch and fling her hair high up over her head, or, on quieter days, the mere sound of the breeze rustling the dry leaves caught on the hedgerows. She pondered on the advisability of her return to Widegates, where it seemed everything evoked memories of Bryn, of their fun days together, but of course it was here she wanted to be. No, thought Jo, I'll have to learn to cope. In time everything will settle!

Mollie and Edith talked about Bryn and Veronica quietly, wishing that they'd played a more active part in sorting out 'that wicked girl', but, like Johanna, they realised that nothing could be done now, life had to go on, and it seemed that their niece was really happy at school.

'Thank heaven for James,' Mollie announced one day when he'd telephoned to ask Jo out.

Prolonged rain was causing difficulties on the farm. The entrance to the yard from the field was a quagmire. The aunts attempted to keep cheerful, but work was hard under these conditions, even with the help they had.

Edith set about looking for another farm-worker and managed to get a young man in from Polruan. It was a temporary position only for he was due to join the Royal Navy after Christmas. Philip was the son of the local publican, who was also a great friend of Tom's; everyone at the farm knew him. Even though inexperienced in the ways of farming, he was quick to learn, strong and willing. Mollie adored him. 'Such a young gentleman,' she was heard to say, when asked about him.

It was easier for Jo now to have her free time to herself instead of helping out, and consequently Saturday saw her travelling with James to Penzance. They were hoping to see *Odette*, a film about the Resistance set in wartime France. The weather had worsened overnight, and so they were apprehensive about using the car ferry. Theirs was the last crossing because of the strong winds! The road to Penzance was littered with debris from the trees, and often low branches would whiplash against the top of the car. At times they went through stretches of floodwater. James didn't think of returning, they were well-committed to the journey; it would be bad whichever direction they went. Cornwall was caught in the teeth of a real winter storm.

'We'll have to stay the night, Jo. It would be foolish to drive back in this. Can you manage?'

'Yes, I'll be all right if you let me stop off at a chemist for a toothbrush.'

This was developing into a real adventure, thought Johanna. It seemed ages since she'd stayed overnight in an hotel. 'We'll book dinner of course,' she said.

'Hungry already, Jo? You always did like your food. That was one of the things Bryn loved about you. No fads or fancies, just a good healthy appetite. Yes, we'll order dinner.'

Jo was quiet. Mention of Bryn still always upset her. At one period she had wanted to talk about him all the time, and happy childhood and teenage memories had been brought to life again and again. Now though, now that he was married to Veronica, the hurt caused by his absence went deeper. She hugged the pain of it to her, it was part of her life, but a controlled part. Only when, 'out of the blue', his name was mentioned and past memories restored, did the hurt explode, as now. She felt tears start in her eyes and her throat constricted painfully. 'How long?' she thought, as she turned her gaze to the window. 'How long will I feel like this?'

'You all right, Jo?' James's voice was concerned. She nodded her head as she stared out into the grey, stormy scene. They were now crawling along a road awash with flood water. Fountains of spray were reaching up either side of them.

'How do you know where the roadway is?'

'Guesswork really, but if you look carefully, you can see the grass verges. Uphill soon and then a high road all the way, thank goodness.' James's voice was strained as he held firmly onto the wheel of the car, easing it along to safety.

There was no difficulty about booking two rooms in the smart hotel on the front at Penzance, and both were glad to get warm and dry. Jo had a hot bath, luxuriating in the depth of water allowed now after the war austerity of six inches. She had just completed her toilet; her face was flushed, and her hair clung damply to her head in soft curls.

'Ready, Johanna? My, but you look lovely!'

'Thank you, sir,' returned Jo coquettishly.

'We are going by taxi so that I don't have the bother of parking. Pity that it's raining, I was looking forward to walking you along the front!' Penzance sported a wide front facing out to the bay and St Michael's Mount; in the evenings the lights from both the town and the little island made the place special, for the joy of lights after so many years of blackout was still new.

'Perhaps the morning will be fine. We don't have to leave too early, do we?' James would have liked to stay forever. He had Jo all to himself at last, and he knew that every moment would be special.

The film was short. No accompanying programme, just the *Pathé News*. It was an extremely sad film, and Jo's mood was quiet and thoughtful as they made their way back to the hotel. The rain had stopped, so they walked along the front just as James had wished. The wind blew strongly, whilst the sea washed boisterously over the harbour wall; it was an invigorating walk, and served to increase their appetites – they were ready for a meal! The food, a vegetable cobbler, was delightfully warming and filling. After a glass of wine they were both talking animatedly about their plans for the weeks up to Christmas. Jo was deeply involved in children's parties at school, and the usual nativity play.

'Mollie has promised to make some of the costumes for us this year. We've been searching the attic for material and have found some marvellous old curtains that will do for the kings.' She told James about the problems they'd had in casting the production without offending either parents or children. Joseph, the smallest speaking part, had been deliberately built up to be the main character, and this had been given to the most chatty nuisance, a little boy with saucy eyes called Robin. He was tall and held himself erect, almost soldier-like, setting his usually mobile mouth into a firm, grim line. 'He won't bother us now,' Jo laughed, when talking about it in the staffroom. The head raised her eyebrows and made one comment only: 'He's a redhead!'

James was to appear in the local 'rep' production of *The Pirates of Penzance*. He had a beautiful tenor voice. His love of singing had stemmed from those days when, as teenagers, they would spend time with David Grant, listening to music and 'singing to the sea'.

Coffee was taken in the lounge, where they watched the storm raging once more and saw evidence of its fury as wave after wave came high up over the harbour wall, flooding the area where they had walked quite safely just a short while ago. Jo watched amazed as the seas came right over the main road. Bright lines of flags left there from the summer festivities had fractured, and now long strands were wheeling and whipping as the gusts became more frantic.

'The storm must have turned. We are in for a bad night.' James was peering over her shoulder. Jo's eyes were mesmerised by the lashing lines of wind-whipped bunting.

'That's dangerous, James. Bad for any motorist stupid or clever enough to use that road tonight.'

The waiter heard her remark as he refilled their coffee cups. 'Yes, miss. The storm is worse than ever. We've had instructions to batten down belowstairs as flooding is expected at high tide. That low road through town has been closed though, the only way through being from the top and out into the country. Even that's a hazard for there are trees blown down, blocking many of the side roads. A night to be in, sir … miss … a night to be warm and safe!'

They sat for a while, moving away from the window seat to a cosy fireplace area, until Johanna yawned: 'Let's hit the hay!' James stretched his long body and made for the stairs, which they climbed companionably, commenting on various pictures hanging on the stairway walls. Jo thought of the many London hotels that had once housed decor like this, but now were stark and open to the sky. Monuments to war!

They both stopped outside Jo's door, laughing. A moment ago they had been admiring a painting of St Michael's Mount. The sea was out, the causeway clearly visible, with the whole painted in the most bizarre colours. The sea was a bright, harsh green, the rocks more red than black, and the castle itself was a gleaming white, enhanced by an amber sky. The same waiter had passed them on the stairs.

'It's a joke, isn't it?' he commented. 'Painted by one of our regular guests. He left it to us in his will requesting that it hang there … look at the comment!' They leaned together over the bannisters to peer at a line of tiny letters at the base of the picture: 'It was never like this until the day the war ended!'

'He was "sloshed",' the waiter said, as he vanished round the bend of the stairs.

Now they were quietly regarding one another.

'Thanks, James. Thanks for a lovely day,' Jo leaned forward to kiss his cheek. James stepped half back, then reached out both hands to grip her arms. It was a powerful grip and Jo winced a little.

'My darling girl. I've enjoyed it too. You look so lovely Jo – so happy. You are very special to me – you know that, don't you?' His eyes gazed at her with longing. She stared at him for a moment, shook free of his hands and stood facing him, her face troubled, her mouth trembling and her brown eyes wide, as she reached behind her for the door handle. James moved back, leaving a wide space between them. Watching her carefully he noted the confusion, the dismay and the swift light of fear in her eyes.

'Sorry, my dear – wrong timing.' His words were clipped and tense, his eyes wary.

'It's all right, James,' Jo said quietly. 'See you in the morning at breakfast,' and she flung her door open, vanished inside, slamming it with a finality that shook James to the core.

'How stupid of me,' he thought as he let himself into his room and collapsed onto the edge of the bed. 'God, how stupid of me. I should have known she wasn't ready.' He sat, with his head in his hands. 'What a fool I am. She'll never understand. It was always Bryn, and now I've spoiled everything.'

Just a few yards away, Johanna too felt unhappy. She leant against the door – wishing ... oh, what was she wishing? That James was dear to her without a doubt, but as a friend, nothing more! She did love him, loved him dearly, but he was more like a brother to her. Now things could never be the same – this 'something' had come between them. After a while she got ready for bed, only to lie there sleepless, until she realised just how silly it was for her to be either scared or upset. After all, she'd known James all of her life. They were friends ... She'd talk to him over breakfast, act normal, for nothing had really changed, and on that happy thought she slept.

Meanwhile James had switched on the radio for distraction, but found his thoughts still on Jo. 'I'll apologise in the morning. Can't risk losing her – it will be all right.' He too slept, if fitfully!

Jo was already seated when James joined her, clutching his newspaper which he'd collected at the desk.

'Morning, James – a lovely day,' Jo's smile was wide.

'Good morning, pet. Glad it's to be dry for the drive home.' James searched her face uneasily. 'Sorry about last night, Jo. Hadn't meant to scare or offend you. Can we still be friends?'

She looked at him with warmth in her brown eyes.

'I'm not offended James, rather flattered, but yes, let's be friends. It's what I want. Just good friends,' and she reached out for his hand across the table.

Now they were journeying back. She was a chatty companion. Talking about the changes to be made in the school after Christmas; the new toilets and infant class to be built, and about the difficulties they'd all have to contend with until the building work was complete.

She talked of Horse and the gentle life he led on the farm now that he was old.

'He's sort of pensioned off. Sometimes, from my bedroom window, I see him standing high in the corner of the field, head up as if he's sniffing the air ... the sea air. Do you think he misses it like we do when we are away?'

'Probably, Jo. But why don't you lead him. Take him just to the gate at the beginning of the cliff walk. I'll come with you if you like, perhaps this coming weekend.'

'Oh would you, James. Yes, that would be nice.'

Finally Johanna talked about aunt Edith. 'You will have heard about John Ellery, James, and how he's been dating her for ages. It was so good for her. They got along famously from day one. He appreciated her sense of humour, which always did turn the most mundane chores into a pleasure, remember? He was happy to join in her dares; small bets were decided at the length of time it would take them to do certain jobs round the farm, or which ewes would have twins or even triplets. Edith loved the special attention she received, sailing through farm gates that were opened for her; she laughed merrily for days, when he caught her loading bales of hay on the tractor and said: "That's no job for a lady!" She's always been so proud of her strength, and her face was a picture … she didn't know whether to be pleased or annoyed. John liked her company. At odd breaks and during walks on the farm to check what things might need attention, they could be seen, heads together, she talking animatedly, he nodding his approval. He admired her ability to join in with any group of people perfectly naturally; John found it difficult to cope with people generally, and on these social occasions he would stand close, adding the odd "Yes, of course!" when she turned to say, "Isn't that so, John?"

'Edith enjoyed being taken out, and particularly to the cinema. They were always planning their next visit and talked incessantly about future programmes. She confided to Mollie how much she liked John. "He's wonderful company. We are a good team at the farm, but he just can't cope with people. He has a shell of stiffness about him. He's like a hermit crab, Mollie, stays inside where he feels safe. I expect it's all those years living with his mother that makes him so."

'Mollie had been happy for her sister. We all were, that is except for Tom. He teased her unmercifully and was quite rude at times.

' "When's he going to make an honest woman of you, Edith?" Tom took a delight in teasing. He resented John now that he was unable to do much work on the farm himself, and was always jealous of Edith's strength and good health. The farm was being well-run … he knew it and felt useless. To make a nuisance of himself was his way of coping, I suppose.

'Edith took all the leg-pulling in good part at first, but with John so obviously putting pressure on her for commitment, she must have felt that her brother was fanning a fire that just wasn't there. Then, last week, Edith was quiet during a milking session. We thought she might not be feeling well. She left early to go back to the farmhouse, asking if we'd mind finishing off on our own; said she had an announcement to make and needed time to work it out. We were, well, you know, we were all keyed-up. Who'd have thought aunt Edith would have found a beau, and now it seemed she and John were planning marriage – at least, that's what we both thought.

'Everyone was looking at us questioningly as we finally made it for breakfast, nobody had started eating! We'd finished washing our hands at the kitchen sink when Edith came in from the dairy. She stood with her hands on the back of grandma's chair, looking solemn and pale. Her mouth opened and closed again; she just stood there James, looking at us all, until uncle Tom got impatient.

' "Come on girl – what is it you have to say – I'm hungry."

' "John and I," Edith had begun, then stopped, her face going pink. Not pink really, oh James, her face was so red, and I've never seen her so flustered. She looked at John who was staring hard at her. "Well, John and I have talked and we've decided … that is, I've decided and he understands … well, I want to tell you that I have decided to remain single." We were all so quiet. We'd quite thought Edith was to announce her forthcoming marriage.

'Then Mollie got up, went over to Edith and with her arms about her said, "Oh, Edith. I'm so glad. Now we won't lose you after all."

'The warm bread was passed round the breakfast table, and the meal went on as usual, though we all noticed that John ate very little, until with a wry smile at Edith he left early. "Got them sheep to get to market," he said by way of explanation.

'Tom left the table soon after in his wheelchair, and bumped his way to his room. Mollie heard him mutter. "Damn silly girl – I was only fooling."

' "The thing is, James, Tom will now be looking for someone else to tease. I can't see a leopard changing its spots.' But in that Jo was wrong, for from that weekend Tom began to ail.

James was quiet, concentrating on his driving. All that talk about Edith and John was pretty ill-timed, he thought, bearing in mind last night, but he was glad that Jo could chatter, and that they were back on their old friendly footing.

When later he dropped her at the gate of the farm, refusing an invitation to come in and see the aunts, he noticed John in the yard, fixing his cycle clips. He waved to him, then moved off, thinking that there were two chastened and saddened men in the area that night!

Mrs Dingle had to wait until the new year before she saw her daughter. Tom developed pneumonia after a particularly heavy cold which went to his chest and wouldn't budge. He was whisked away one damp, dark night in early December to hospital in Plymouth. His sisters were devastated, for the doctors gave little hope of recovery. However, two weeks later he was still holding his own, a little better, but still giving cause for concern.

'It's as if he doesn't want to live any more, Edith,' Mollie suggested fearfully to her sister, as they travelled back from visiting him. 'He's not interested in anything – not anything at all, is he?'

'You can hardly blame him, Mollie. Since his accident he's been very restricted in movement. Maybe he has had enough. We ought to think of things from his point of view. I mean, what has he got to live for? A farm he can't run himself, no wife, no future – only to get more and more incapacitated … poor old lad. I'd understand if he gave in, really I would!'

Her sister made no reply. Mollie knew she was right. How unfortunate Tom had been, she thought, recalling the bright, happy young man on the day of his wedding. Since then, ill health had dogged him, ruined his marriage and conditioned his life.

'Tom set such store by Jo and Bryn, Edith … they were his future, and it's as if a light went out in him when Bryn married Vee. He sort of lost hope. Oh, how I wish we could start again – all of us!'

'Not possible,' returned Edith. 'None of us can take back time or alter what has happened, unfortunately.' She was quiet for a while as she manoeuvred the Bedford round a difficult bend near to the river at Looe. 'No, what we've got to do is look forward. Why don't we get Jeff to visit Tom now? He comes into Plymouth twice a week for his college course, doesn't he?'

'Jeff has asked to, Edith, but Tom's been so ill, I thought ...'

'Well, we can suggest that he does visit now,' Edith interrupted. 'See if that will pull Tom out of ...' she paused for a while, her face unusually sad, 'out of wherever he's almost gone,' she concluded.

So Jeff walked into the hospital ward early the next morning, with his arms full of books and papers for college, and in one hand a small bunch of early daffodils.

'Hello, Tom. I've missed you,' he said, trying hard not to register his feelings on seeing his friend so wan and ill. 'I found these under the hedge at Pensilva. Spring is on the way even before Christmas. Lots more budded and waiting to open! Don't forget that trip to Scilly that you promised me. How about the daffodils in the spring there?'

It was a small joke with them. Tom had once expressed a desire to go to the Scilly Isles again and wished he were fit enough to do so. Jeff had dismissed every reason he gave for not being able to cope, and for some time 'See you in the Scillys' had been a farewell for them ... a sort of password, almost like 'see you tomorrow'. Now Tom's eyes lit up, his hand reached out and feebly clasped Jeff's.

'Good to see you, lad – where've you been?' The old teasing expression was back, and from that moment Tom began making progress.

Jo stayed at Widegates over Christmas to help, leaving for London two days before the new year.

'It's all right at the farm for a while now, mum' she reported, when questioned about events there. 'Tom's back. The nurse comes in every day and Aunt Mollie has her friend coming from Swindon for a while. She says you'll remember her – a Fiona someone ... oh, I can't think!'

'Fiona Harris,' her mother blurted out. 'Oh yes, I remember her! She was the most awful girl, an outrageous flirt. Set her cap at Tom, but he had other ideas. I hope she's still as lively, it will be good for that brother of mine.'

'I did think it strange, the way Tom answered, when Mollie said she was coming. He looked up startled somehow, then grinned wickedly and said. "I wonder if she's as difficult an old lady as she was a gal?" Mollie just patted him on the head and told him he'd have to "wait and see". Well, of course they've not met for years and years – not any of them, though Mollie and Fiona have always corresponded.'

Her mother was gazing into the middle distance, still in the past, and sat there waggling her head a little.

'Yes, she was quite a girl, our Fiona; your father was nearly swept away by her charms ...' Johanna was immediately curious, but her mother chose that moment to rescue the dinner.

A surprise party had been planned for Jo on New Year's Eve. Old friends from the road came, her mother's colleagues from school, one or two of Raymond's young friends, and Mary. Bill went up the road to escort her back; they came in laughing, Bill's arm affectionately around her waist. Jo was intrigued as she watched them. It looked serious. How lovely to have Mary for a sister-in-law ... they looked so happy! As she watched them, her heart lurched suddenly and a feeling of jealousy overtook her. She stepped out into the passageway to recover her composure. 'Why ... why ... why ...?' Jo felt stifled; a cold spasm reached from her chest to her throat, threatening to choke her. She put her hands up, as if to ward off some invading foe; then suddenly she found strong arms around her and a soft voice speaking gently.

'It's all right, Jo ... it's all right. Let it go, pet, you'll feel better if you do!' Bill had seen her swift departure and guessed the reason for it. Now, as he held her, realising again the depth of her despair, he felt regret that he was the cause of her immediate breakdown. How thoughtless of me, he mused ... but Jo, now recovering a little, knew her brother well and guessed his feelings too.

'I'm so glad about you and Mary, Bill, really I am.' She was tearful and breathless. 'But I get so angry at times ... it's just me! Sometimes I just can't cope.'

Slowly the sobs subsided, and her breathing became easier. Bill waited for her whilst she rinsed her face and brushed her hair. He would talk to Mary, they would be careful not to show their feelings whilst Jo was at home; she would understand. Mrs Dingle had noticed their absence and her keen eyes watched Bill's solicitous gentleness with his sister. 'How like his father he is now ...' she thought. Her eyes turned to her daughter now talking in the corner to John Kimber, noting how tired and pale she looked. She needs a good holiday. I'll have a chat tomorrow and see whether we can plan something together for half-term. I seem to be losing Jo to Widegates, and that just won't do!

The party went well. The new year was greeted in with a hearty rendering of 'Land of Hope and Glory'. Jo hugged her mother and wished her a happy new year.

Mrs Dingle took her daughter's face in her hands … 'You too, pet. A very happy new year.'

'Mum, let's go shopping tomorrow, shall we? Just the two of us.'

The following day was fun for them both. The shops had gradually filled with new stock over the past months. It was a joy to actually search through a line of clothes for something special. Jo found herself a navy woollen dress that had an unusual side opening, with cloth-covered buttons in gold across one shoulder. The skirt was straight, and it made her look taller. She felt very adult and sophisticated as she preened in front of the mirror.

'Do you know, mum – this is my very first bought dress. Incredible, isn't it?'

She persuaded her mother to buy a wine-coloured suit. Mrs Dingle remonstrated at first. 'It's extravagant, Jo. What I need are school clothes.' But Johanna was adamant.

'You can always make those, mum. Come on, my treat. Bill says he'll take us out for a meal tonight. Let's surprise him and get really smart.'

They spent hours in the shoe department without buying. Pleasingly Mrs Dingle located some tea towels selling at a special price and swiftly bought a dozen.

'You're more thrilled with those, mum, than with your suit, aren't you?'

'Oh Jo, just look at these lovely bright colours. Drying dishes will be a treat after managing with our old thin tea towels for so long.'

Johanna returned to Widegates in time for the new school term. Margaret met her at St Austell and answered Jo's first questions about Tom with some amusement.

'No really, Jo, he's fine. I've never seen such a change in anyone since Fiona came. Mollie and Edith are so happy that he's back to normal.'

On reaching the farm, Jo was welcomed by her aunts and ushered very quickly into Tom's room, where he greeted her with outstretched arms and a hug that was proof of his increasing strength and rising spirits.

'Come to save me, lass ... I'm absolutely hag-ridden, and if it weren't for young Jeff, I think I'd have taken myself off to Scilly or somewhere.'

'What an awful liar you are ...' The voice came from the corner of Tom's room. Jo turned round to meet the laughing eyes of a lady of some sixty years. She had a duster in her hand and was obviously in the process of getting Tom's room dust free.

'Introduce me then Tom – or do you want to brush me under the carpet as if I don't exist?' Her tone was bantering. Jo glanced from one to the other – noted the twinkle of fondness in Tom's eyes and her heart lifted for him.

'This is my niece, Johanna. Jo, meet Fiona, the most devastatingly beautiful creature it's been my luck to have contact with for a very long time.' He paused, sucked in his lips and then smiled, a wide happy smile ... 'And also the most crabby, organising female I've ever known. Why, she's even worse than my sisters!'

Fiona let out a sharp laugh. 'You old bugger,' she said with relish. Then held her hand out towards Jo.

'I've looked forward to meeting you. Everyone here has missed you. Welcome home.' Fiona was a graceful woman, tall and slender, with straight blonde hair, now turning a silvery grey. She had coiled it fashionably into a soft bun at the nape of her neck, and curly little wisps fell around her face and ears. Her mouth was wide and generous ... her cheeks youthfully rosy, and she moved with a sinuous grace that made Jo think what a startlingly lovely girl she must have been.

Mollie bustled in as they smiled at one another. 'Have you told her, Tom?'

'Hush now, Mollie – you'll spoil my fun. Come here, Jo lass. I've something for you,' and he passed her an envelope. 'Go to the barn. Edith will show you, you'll need this,' and he pushed the envelope tight into the palm of her hand. As she left the room Jo heard him say wistfully ... 'Wish I could be there to see her face ...' The envelope held something hard ... Jo squeezed it tight as she followed Edith across the yard.

Inside the barn was a neat blue car, not new, but it had been lovingly cleaned, so that the chrome fittings shone and gleamed in the wintery sun that now poured through the open door. A large label was tied to the bonnet. 'For Johanna. A happy late Christmas

– with love from Tom'. She was thrilled. No more cycling across the top in the wind and rain, no more being blown along, or having to fight the gales to reach the shelter of Widegates. She rushed inside. 'Oh Tom, what a lovely surprise, and thank you, thank you over and over again.' He was rewarded by her happy face, seeing again the girl in her, the girl that they'd all thought they'd lost completely.

'Now that's enough, lass. I just got fed up with seeing you come home looking like a drowned rat. Got the key safe?' and he pointed to the envelope still clutched in her hand.

Johanna asked James to help her to learn to drive. He was a diligent teacher, so that within three weeks she was able to take herself to school. She didn't, at first, go all the way, preferring to leave the car at the top of Polruan hill, not daring to venture down that steep road trusting on her brakes. The hill led directly to the harbour, and the thought of rushing, tumbling down into the water was very real to her for some time. James, though was patient and took her on practice runs most evenings in the dark; true, she couldn't see the water clearly then, but she knew it was there. However, all things are overcome and soon Jo was driving the car halfway down, turning to the left where the little school stood facing the estuary and where a widening at the side of the narrow road afforded her a parking space. The only time she didn't use the car was during rare snowy days. There was only one all that winter, towards the end of February. The snow came softly and silently during the night, making the world a wonderland by morning. Jo got a lift with the postman who had chains on his van, and by midday the white covering had all disappeared!

The daffodils that had made great headway as Jeff had envisaged lifted their heads from the weight of snow as it melted, as if announcing 'that was that'. Winter was over and gone. Primroses hiding in the banks and hedgerows straightened their stems and showed themselves to the world. Spring really was here. The snowfall seemed to have cleansed and invigorated growth. Now buds grew fat and burst; Cornwall blossomed into a beautiful April.

Jo's spirits were not always high at this time. School continued to occupy her days fully. Her car was a boon, and with the lighter evenings she was able to get out and about more. Occasionally she would leave school and drive out to the moor, park her car overlooking the cliff edge, where she would gather her pupils' books onto her lap and mark their work to the accompaniment of mewling cries from the gulls and the chatter of the braver little chiffchaffs, as they searched for food on the short gorse bushes. Often she just sat and thought. Recalling the past, and the many happy times she and Bryn had shared on this wonderful part of Cornish coast; then she would go home for her meal, contented and relaxed. At other times though, the old feelings of loss still assailed her, and she began, more and more, to blame herself for the break up with Bryn. To blame herself for not being totally honest with him, for sharing his dreams, but never writing about them, for not saying that she loved him! Why oh why had it seemed so impossible to just say: 'I love you, Bryn.' Now, now that it was too late, she saw the folly of her pride, for that's all it had been, foolish pride.

She thought of several of her mother's charges when Pendower House was opened to them. How lost they had seemed, how bewildered. Jo had seen at first hand the effect that the loss of one's parents had on the young. Mollie had always said that Bryn drew back from commitment because of the early loss of his beloved mother and father … why then hadn't she helped him …? Sometimes Jo felt that she hadn't deserved him. What a poor thing her love had been if she couldn't declare it, not even to her beloved aunt. How many times had she said to Mollie: 'We're just pals …' Hard to believe that almost a whole year had gone by since that awful day she learnt of Bryn's marriage to Vee. The children and school helped her. Life was hectic mostly and busy always. Jo hadn't time to feel lonely during the day, and at night she often planned future lessons, becoming totally absorbed in her work so that, on the whole, she hadn't time to think. Her loss was now just a dull ache, an emptiness that awoke with her in the mornings and kept her wakeful at night, but gradually the restless longings had eased, threatening to flare only occasionally at a stirred memory, or sometimes by a cheeky, bright-eyed little boy at school.

She wondered constantly how Bryn was. James, who wrote regularly to him, told her little bits of news that he thought might interest but not hurt her. It was from Mollie that she learned Veronica had given birth to a baby boy.

'They've called him Bryn after his dad, Jane Trevarder told me. I wonder if they'll visit. It's time they came back to see us all.' Mollie's expression was guileless. Jo merely smiled and continued with her meal, but her aunt was not deceived; she knew this news would hurt her, that's why she had made sure that she was the one to give it.

Later, sitting on her favourite rock at the headland, Johanna dwelt on the news ... a little boy, he could so easily have been hers! She felt the tremor of unrest begin in the pit of her stomach and spread to become an ache of emptiness. Her throat tightened, and her chest hurt, all the old feelings of loss returning. She sat on for a long while, finally finding peace in the thought of Bryn's happiness at having a son. He had always wanted children – they both had!

James called that evening and told her of his impending visit to Africa.

'Veronica and Bryn have been asking me for ages, now they have asked if I will be godfather to young Bryn. I'm to go out for the christening in about a month's time.'

Jo felt relieved to hear this. Now she would learn that all really was well in Africa, then she would 'let go' – really let go, pick up the pieces and get on with her life.

'How lovely, James. You'll take a little gift out from me, won't you?' She turned wistfully to him. 'I'd love to go too, really love to go and see that all is well with Bryn.' Then, being as honest as only she knew how. 'Emotions are the cause of lots of strife, aren't they? We were all such good friends, so why am I not included in this invitation? Doesn't Bryn want to see me, not ever again?' She turned away, but James reached out to hold her close, and Jo took comfort from his nearness.

She spoke to Mollie of this later, and of how great her loss was; the Bryn of her dreams and also her dear, loved friend.

'I feel no bitterness, aunt. I know I'm mostly to blame. You were right about going to Africa – I just left it too late. But after all those years of sharing, to have nothing, not a crumb. It's not right – it's foolish, and it hurts!'

Aunt Mollie sniffed. Her lips set tight. 'Veronica won't want you there. You are her only threat.'

'But ...' Jo began.

'No, Jo, it's true. She knew what you and Bryn were to each other, she broke that relationship. It's no good you saying otherwise. She'll not want you there. Accept it love. Start again. It's the only way.'

'But Bryn …' Again Mollie interrupted her.

'Bryn must make the best of things now. She's his wife, the mother of his child. He too has to make a new life.'

The words twisted in Jo's heart, but she knew this was true. Bryn was not hers. He had chosen his life, rightly or wrongly. What Mollie said was true, the past was over and only 'today' counted now.

'I love you, aunt Mollie,' she said, as she made for the door.

'I know you do, lass. It's the first time you've said it though.'

'Lots of things I've left unsaid …' Johanna's expression was unutterably sad as she stood by the back door, the egg basket on her arm. 'Come and help me with the eggs, aunt Mollie, please!'

CHAPTER TWENTY

Three years had gone by and Johanna was quite settled now with her life in Cornwall. The effects of the war were lessening as each month went by. Food and clothing were more plentiful; farming restrictions had eased and everyone was working towards a peaceful and prosperous country. That things were slow-moving in London was obvious to Jo when she returned home for holidays. It was still looking careworn and war-scarred. Some clearing of wrecked homes had taken place, but evidence of war was still to be seen in the stark and damaged buildings, colourful weed-filled bomb sites, and particularly in her home area where there was much devastation, rock-strewn and desolate ground that had once housed people's homes.

Polruan seemed to remain untouched, though various clubs were reopening, and carnival week was discussed with more relish now that a life of complete austerity was easing.

Selina's husband had returned safely and was now training to be a river pilot like his father-in-law. They had bought a small cottage at Pill, a romantic place with roses and honeysuckle round the door, and Selina was expecting their first child. Margaret and David had permission now to extend their cottage on the hill. Tom had once suggested that they might like to rent Trenorwin, his old grey house down the lane from Widegates, the previous tenant, a strange artistic gentleman, having returned to his home area in the north, but they loved Polruan and their open view of the estuary.

James was slowly taking more and more responsibility for the farm at Pensilva, but Mr Trevarder was not yet ready to relinquish his hold of things entirely. He acquiesced to most of James' more modern methods, and was heard to complain laughingly to Tom.

'I've two forward-looking youngsters to cope with now that young Jeff comes back from college with all these newfangled ideas as well. I can't fight them both.' For all his disability, Tom was always interested in anything new and often wished that he could alter some of the practices around Widegates. He had heated arguments with Edith over this, and, in spite of his failing health, she gave him no quarter, but usually acceded when John Ellery put much the same proposals to her. Mollie often wondered if she argued with Tom deliberately, for once she heard her mutter … 'That stirred the old bugger up. He'll have something to think about for a while now!'

Mollie continued her daily round in the farmyard, dairy and kitchen. She became an active member of the Charity Club, formed by a group of women from the village. Its purpose was to collect money for the war homeless; fêtes were held, dances organised, concerts arranged, and it seemed that nowadays Mollie was always dashing here and there to see fellow-members to discuss and organise events. She and Edith shared a little car, a noisy thing that belched fumes and ran erratically, but they were proud of it, resisting any mention of a newer one.

Jeff had finished his course and sadly was now looking for a definite placement as farm manager. Tom was proud of his achievements, but devastated at the prospect of him moving away from the immediate area. They had remained the best of friends. Jeff had taught Tom how to play chess, and they would sit for hours pondering over various moves, an incongruous sight, with Jeff's dark head and straight back in complete contrast to Tom's now feeble rounded shoulders, covered with a shawl, and his grey thinning hair. The old twinkle was there at such times though, and they kept up a lively banter. Jeff arrived one night with a young, dark-haired girl whom he introduced as 'my future wife'. He had met her at college in Plymouth. Her home was in Yorkshire, quite near to Wakefield where his parents lived and where he had finally found a place on a large farm nearby. They were an excited happy couple when they called at Widegates to break the news to Tom and the aunts. He took it well, but there was a glint of tears in his eyes when they left. Within the space of two weeks Jeff had left the area, and Tom turned his face to the wall. A light had gone out for him once more. He repeatedly asked James when Bryn was coming for a visit, and when the answer was a vague 'soon', he murmured to himself, 'Soon might not be soon enough!' His health was failing in earnest now, and he remained cloistered in his room day after day.

School remained Jo's lifeline. It was a busy place to be. She loved all the children, relished various difficult moments with the saucy or downright naughty pupils and spent hours thinking up new ways of introducing her lessons. Bryn entered her thoughts during some part of every day, but not as a torment any more … rather as a remembered and very dear friend. She recalled often the gay times when the three of them had spent so much time together. She gleaned news of him from James, and on her wall had placed a photograph of the bungalow that had been sent to Mollie. It was long and low, set on a small mound of hill, with an area of plain stretching into the far distance where dark mountains formed an arc on the horizon. The ground looked dusty and bare, but the bungalow sported a colourful garden at the front, which was obviously cared for by the 'boys' … the natives who worked for Bryn on the farm.

Jo had finished school and was spending a few quiet moments sorting through the children's books, arranging blackboard work for the morning, putting some bright pictures on the walls and, finally, feeding the fish. The aquarium had been a gift from one of the parents and afforded the whole class so much pleasure. It was heated and housed bright tropical fish: little striped ones that darted to and fro and the beautifully graceful angel-fish, who seemed to swim their own ballet through the water. There were also small dark, shark-like fish, that mostly hid in the weeds, and many other bright, colourful specimens who paraded up and down the face of the tank, like a flock of flamingoes. Jo was talking quietly to them when she sensed someone behind her. A shadow fell over the tank and she turned. It was Bryn … an older, severe-looking Bryn. His deep tan suited him, but he looked cold somehow – cold and bleak.

'Hello, Jo,' he said quietly, a half-smile hovering on his lips.

'Bryn,' Jo breathed, before holding out her arms and hugging him. They stayed still for a while, then, embarrassed, she pulled away and looked up at him.

'We didn't know … is everything all right?'

He smiled at her now, that same friendly close smile.

'Hey – hey. Of course everything is all right. I had to come over for an appointment at Plymouth – so I came here, came here to see you.'

She smiled readily, catching the light friendly banter of his words; this she could cope with, and soon they were sitting on her desk, legs swinging and sipping from steaming mugs of coffee that she'd produced from the staff kitchen. Bryn had refused a comfortable seat in the staffroom.

'No thanks – I want to see where teacher operates from,' and he now proceeded to study the classroom, every nook and cranny, every wall space colourfully filled, the view from the window and the placing of her desk. He noted that the window afforded a narrow view of the estuary and far, far below, the little quay at Polruan, where they'd said so many goodbyes.

'I shall think of you here, Jo,' Bryn said, and then quickly added … 'I'm to come to dinner. James will be there too. He's putting me up at Pensilva for the night, and then will take me to Heathrow in the morning. It will be grand for us all to be together again.'

'It's been such a long time, Bryn.' Her voice was wistful, but she swung her legs down off the table, reached for her jacket and turned to him with a smile.

'Come on then, we've time for a walk before going home.'

They didn't make for the headland, but chose instead a river walk, taking a path through the lower slopes of Polruan, and then following the little tributary to Pont, and so on round the wide grassy pathway above the estuary. It was an easy walk, and a familiar one, for they had often wandered it when young, but it wasn't special like the headland. Jo was so full of emotions that she was sure she'd have burst if they'd gone seawards, for it was the headland path that still evoked sweet, but painful memories – impossible now!

They talked and talked. Of Africa, the bungalow, the vast dry lands of the farm. Of the African people, of the animals, and finally of Veronica and young Bryn.

'I hope she's happy,' Bryn had said. 'Though I don't think farm life really suits her. Fortunately, the bungalow is large and we are able to have regular house guests. I'm always working, you see, and she gets lonely.' His voice dwindled away to a murmur, leaving Jo to speculate on Veronica … she hasn't changed at all!

'And your son?' she asked quietly.

Bryn's voice was louder, firmer. 'Oh he's great, a real little charmer and fast becoming the boss. I'm looking forward to teaching him about the land when he's older. I hope he'll come to love it as I do!'

She hugged his joy to her. 'Bryn will be all right,' she thought. 'He'll make his son his life and find true happiness that way.'

They had almost reached the end of the path and stood for a moment looking at the view before turning down the hill to the Bodinnick car ferry. The sun was sinking beyond the headland at Gribbin, casting an orange sheen over the water. Gay little sailing boats jostled and bobbed at their moorings as the pilot boat made its way out of the harbour to guide in a clay-carrying vessel. They could just see the passenger ferry in the distance, with it's flags flying high, and beyond it the white cloud of gulls, wheeling and dipping as they escorted in a small fishing-boat.

'It's a dream,' Bryn whispered. 'Pinch me, Jo!' But she didn't. Tears filled her eyes as she turned towards the car ferry, but they were tears of happiness. They had talked without saying anything – yet both knew that now they could go ahead, get on with their lives. The dreams they had shared must lie dead forever – to reawaken them now would mean disaster for them both.

'Thanks, Jo ...' Bryn began, but she shook her head at him so vehemently that he didn't finish what he'd intended to say. The car ferry was empty except for just one car and themselves. The breeze blew Jo's hair back from her head and cooled the nape of her neck. It tossed Bryn's about his forehead in such a familiar way that she caught her breath. Remembered sights were commented on as they stood close to the rail, both knowing that although, hopefully, they would meet again and again, this was their real and final goodbye – a goodbye to youth, to dreams and to love!

They walked quickly through the narrow streets of Fowey, and out to the passenger ferry, recrossing the river in the crowded little boat, and sought out Jo's car in the school yard.

'How did you get here, Bryn?' she asked.

'Oh I got a lift. Pure luck really. I met a chap in Plymouth who lives in Fowey. That's how I was able to visit you at school.'

'I'm glad that you did.' Jo replied quietly as she manoeuvred the car round the narrow winding lanes of the village, and out onto the high road, where glimpses of the sea teased them through gaps in the hedges. She pulled into a little lay-by when the sweeping curve of the headland path came into view. They sat for a long while, not talking, just drinking in the view and reliving memories that now must be put away forever.

'Thanks, Jo,' Bryn said quietly again, as she eased the car out onto the road, turning left towards the church and the winding, familiar lane to Widegates.

Before the evening meal Bryn spent some time with Tom, who was now completely confined to his room. It was a gentle, friendly reunion, and Bryn spent a whole hour sitting by his bed and telling him about Africa, the farm and his life there.

'Are you all right lad?' The blue eyes were questioning. 'Does that gal of yours help you?'

'I've plenty of help, Tom. That part of it is fine, but the actual management is still strange. Everything is done on such a large scale, but I'm adjusting and I'm in control. Wonderful climate, but oh how I miss our cold, windblown days here. There is a freshness about England that one never finds elsewhere.'

'Now, lad – what's this I hear about hospital tests?' Tom had heard the aunts talking to James earlier that day and now wanted to find out about this for himself.

'I don't know the results yet, Tom – just haven't been feeling right, though this visit has been like a tonic to me. I wish it could be for longer.'

'Have you seen Jo?' Bryn nodded his head and sat looking out of the window to where the honeysuckle hung over the adjoining barn wall. Tom watched him for a while.

'Has to be said lad, … we thought you and Jo …'
Bryn's eyes flashed in his direction and were eloquent in despair and appeal – their eyes held for a moment.

'All right, Bryn. I'll not say more. We will take good care of her, don't fret.'

Later in the evening, Bryn dropped in to say good-bye. Tom reached out a palsied hand, pallid now and liver-spotted. 'Good luck, my boy – good luck.' They hugged one another strangely and briefly, and as Bryn turned to go, Tom called him back. 'Never let go of the land, Bryn – the land is all important, guard it well.'

'I'll see you again when I visit.'

Tom shook his head. 'Maybe, lad, maybe, but "Old Father Time" is feeling my collar. Have a good life, Bryn.' There was a brightness to Tom's eyes as he shook the hand again of the young man he'd always thought of as one of the family and indeed had hoped would be in the real sense of the word. 'Take good care of the young one.' Tom turned his face to the window, and Bryn watched him for a while before leaving the room. 'Tom has been like a father to me,' Bryn thought. 'I must try and get back to see him somehow.'

The evening was a happy one. Jo was bright-eyed and talkative, telling them of amusing incidents that had happened at school. James and Bryn were both rather quiet and watchful at first, but soon both responded to Edith's natural ability to charm and laughed readily at some of her memories of them when young. Mollie watched Jo, happy that she was coping so well with this reunion and admiring the way she parried their teasings. The men left just before midnight. Jo and Mollie walked through the farmyard with them and waited while James turned the car in the narrow lane. Bryn stood with his arms around them both. His tall frame was trembling slightly as if he were caught suddenly in a cold wind.

'Look after each other you two, won't you?'

'The little one,' Mollie said, her face turned up to his. 'Next time, bring young Bryn – Veronica too, of course.' Bryn smiled down at her fondly.

'Of course I will, just as soon as I can. You and Edith are the nearest thing he'll know to a grandma – he'll love you both!'

It was time to leave. Bryn's arm tightened for a while round Jo's waist. 'Keep up the good work, little teacher,' he whispered in her ear. 'God bless,' … and he was gone.

Jo could hardly believe it all. For Bryn to have come from nowhere like that, without warning; for them to have spent precious time together. She was filled with a sense of joy as she turned to her aunt, only for that joy to fade and leave her with a feeling of unutterable sadness and loss as her eyes caught the tail-lights of James's car as it turned the corner at the top of the lane and then vanished out of sight. She turned away … seeking Horse.

'I'll be in shortly, aunt Mollie.' Her aunt understood … it had been a poignant moment for them all. She pondered too on the hospital tests. Was Bryn telling them the truth? Were things really all right with him? Slowly she made her way back to the house. The yard was dry and dusty, each step threw up familiar smells of hay, cattle and the hen-feed that she threw out so liberally in the mornings when her feathered friends squawked and gabbled for her attention. She remembered days, so long ago, when Jo and the boys used to tease the chickens … throwing small handfuls of feed here, and then racing across the yard with the swarm behind them to begin the game again. 'What a pity one can't take back the years,' she thought as she joined Edith, laughing, smiling, happy Edith, as they set about clearing the remains of the meal and settling Tom for the night.

Only James had known of Bryn's visit to England. He had flown over secretly two weeks before, having been told by his doctor to see a specialist.

'It's your blood,' Dr Simpson had said. 'Things are not quite right and we need to do more tests. I'll make arrangements for you to be seen in London immediately.'

James had received an urgent call from Bryn.

'I'm in London, James – I need to see you, can you come?'

So he had taken an overnight train, confiding only in his father until he knew what was troubling Bryn or the reason for his visit. Bryn looked pale when James joined him for breakfast in a small hotel in central London. It was rather shabby, but warm and near to the hospital. As they shook hands, James noticed Bryn's palm was clammy and became alarmed … 'What's wrong, Bryn?'

'I've got leukaemia.' It was out, just like that.

Practically every moment since he'd been told the day before about his illness, Bryn had practised how he would tell James. He had worried and fretted about it, and now it was done – so simply. James was staring at him …

'My doctor in Africa thought that there was something wrong with my blood – it's leukaemia, James, they told me yesterday. I think I'm scared and I needed someone … thanks for coming.'

They talked the morning away, initially over breakfast, and then, when the sun came out, they sat in the small garden opposite the hotel. Bryn told James that his illness was treatable, that he would return to Africa for this treatment once a routine had been established for him over here, that he was determined to get better and, finally, that he didn't want anyone to be told.

'I hope to get down to see them all at Widegates, and I'd like a happy visit, James, and it wouldn't be if they knew. I'll just drop in, out of the blue as it were – no plans, so please don't say I'm around, will you?

'Does Jim know about this?' James asked.

'Yes, he does … just the two of you, and I want it to stay that way.'

'What do they say at the hospital, Bryn?'

'That I've a good chance of recovery. I'm young, fit and strong – at least I was, but I will have to adhere to certain rules. No work – no worries, plenty of rest, and of course the medication. I think Vee has a fair idea of what is wrong – she'll cope. She's really quite a strong person, you know!'

'And the farm?' James was wondering how Bryn could rest whilst at home with that vast estate to manage.

'I've some wonderful boys and a good farm manager. It will run itself and I'll be able to keep an eye on expenses and the books from my 'wheelchair'. Bryn gave a wry grin.

'I'm so sorry old chap … so sorry,' James said quietly as they prepared for Bryn's afternoon session at the hospital.

'Thanks, James. You don't know how much better I feel already, just having you here with me.'

James's stay was short. Bryn travelled with him by train as far as Taunton, where he was to join Jim and begin his first treatment. As the train drew into the station, Bryn turned and asked how Johanna was.

'She's fine.' James's reply seemed curt somehow.

'Good,' said Bryn as he raised his hand in salute. 'See you soon then.'

Some two weeks after Bryn's return to Africa, Mollie asked James if he knew how Bryn was. James told her simply how things were, and Bryn's reasons for not wanting anyone to know.

'We wondered, Edith and I,' Mollie answered.

'There was a lethargy about him, a stillness that we'd never known before. Will he be all right?'

'God willing,' was James's reply.

Jo was told and she wrote to him immediately, the first letter since hearing of his marriage. She too had sensed he wasn't well, but had put it down to travel weariness. Like her aunts, she wished she had known, but respected and understood Bryn's reasons for the secrecy. It would indeed have put his visit on a difficult footing.

Tom never knew about Bryn's illness. He had been saved the worry and sorrow of that. After saying goodbye to the man he had loved as a son, he had turned his face to the wall and just faded away. Within a week he was dead. Mollie found him one morning, lying on his side as if still gazing out of the window at the fields of the farm he'd loved so much. It was as if he'd waited for Bryn's visit before letting go.

'My dear Bryn,' Jo wrote. 'James has told us of your illness, and I hasten to send you all our loving thoughts and wishes for a speedy recovery, and for years of good health in the future. We all had thought you looked tired, and now this explains it.

'Tom died in his sleep about a week after you went back and is now laid to rest in St Lowell churchyard in a plot overlooking the fields of Widegates and the headland beyond. Don't be sad about him for his life had been meaningless for some time, and he suffered a good deal. We all felt that he was holding on just to see you. Your visit made him very happy, as it did all of us.

'I heard today that he has left Trenorwin to me. Dear Tom, he spent such a short time there. I'm going down the lane this afternoon to see its potential and can't help thinking how very nice it will be to have a place of my own.

'The day is blustery, the winds are from the west, and the air is fresh and sweet. We send some to you, Bryn, to help with your recovery. It was lovely seeing you … our love to you, Vee and little Bryn – God bless …'

Bryn read the letter over and over. Her simple comments about the weather painted a picture of that part of England he loved so well, as she knew it would. He was resting on the verandah of the farm one afternoon and closed his eyes as a cooling breeze blew across the plain. Bryn imagined for a moment that he was back on their headland – it was as if, somehow, Jo had really sent some of England's sweet fresh air to help him. He sat there dreaming of carefree younger days spent at Pensilva; of his boat now used and cared for so lovingly by old Ben and awaiting his return. He resolved then to take his son back to Cornwall regularly, to teach him to sail, to walk the headland paths with him and to introduce him to all at Widegates. He would get better – he knew!

'Shall I come with you, lass?' Mollie asked when Jo mentioned she would visit Trenorwin.

'No thanks, aunt. I'd sooner have a first look on my own. I'll come to you later for ideas about it all, but right now, well, I'd like to be on my own.'

'I quite understand,' Mollie replied. 'And Jo, you know we love having you here … we are not sending you away, not at all. We just thought, Tom thought …'

'Yes Mollie, I know, but it might be just what I need right now – a place of my very own. If it's suitable I could take a lodger. We've a new teacher coming from North Wales next term and she has already asked for somewhere to stay!' With a wave of her hand she was gone, up over the home field and out onto the familiar high-hedged road. Mollie mapped her progress for a while as crows lining the telegraph wires massed in flight at her approach.

Jo walked with her head up, breathing in the tangy air that this morning blew straight from the sea. There was a sparkle about the day, unusual for August, and she could imagine that, just over the hill, the sea would be a picture of white-tipped waves and feathery spindrift.

The banks were high either side of her and, as the road dipped steeply, she lost the view of the wide uplands towards Pelynt. The hedgerows wore their summer splendour. Delicate bindweed trailed its pink and white flowers at all levels; the fluffy white seeds of willowherb blew in the wind. Dainty thale-cress and the odd sunbright Welsh poppy were a delight amongst the straight stems of pennywort, and the red berries of the trailing woodbines offered bright jewels of colour that caught and glowed in the sunshine. Fronds of calico-bleached grass waved their heads against the sky. Wild scabious hung in drifts down the bank sides and occasionally joined the grasses at the top, the clear mauve blooms lending an extra dimension of colour, as they danced and weaved against the azure blue of the heavens. Small wild thistles hugged the side of the bank, whilst new growth of hawthorn and frond of hazel spread arks of green upwards. The air was fresh and clear and perfumed once in a while with the honey fragrance of heather.

Johanna reached the old grey house and just stood for a while. 'It's mine, all mine,' she thought, as she gazed round with a smile of complete satisfaction on her tanned face.

Trenorwin was placed well back from the road and half-hidden by shrubs and rhododendron bushes that had been neglected for some years. They were colourful now, but overlarge and straggly. A path ending in two large steps led straight up to the front door, which was placed in the centre of the house and flanked by two wide bay windows. She searched for the key in her pocket, caught the wild smell of the sea once more and turned. A wide sweep of the bay was visible from the top step, and as she'd thought, the sea was a mass of white water. 'So beautiful,' she murmured softly.

The key turned readily in the lock, but the door was stiff and heavy. Jo had to exert all her strength to push it open. How on earth Tom's lodger had managed she would never know. A musty smell greeted her, a hint of mothballs. Tom had always smelled of mothballs, especially when he wore his Sunday suit. She remembered now how the boys had teased him about it.

'You can stop laughing and pointing, you two. I'll not let those pesky moths lay eggs in my best suit … no, not ever!'

'Oh Tom,' breathed Jo. But of course the mothballs must have belonged to the lodger – her uncle hadn't lived at Trenorwin for years!

Jo went through the house opening the heavy-framed windows. Some were difficult and inclined to stick, and all were cumbersome, but she flung them wide, with purpose, and let in the clear unsullied air. The views from the top windows were even more wonderful and offered a wider expanse of sea. Jo thought of stormy days, when the water would be whipped up into tumultuous waves; of moonlit nights, when the radiance would reflect on the water like silver skeins of wool. She thought too of the still summer days, when the sea would be quiet and dreamy. Now, so much churning, bubbling water filled the bay, and yet the sun shone warmly, the sky was blue and to her left, the heather-covered moor offered its special beauty of mauve and yellow.

She leant against the window jamb … 'Oh thanks, uncle Tom. Thank you for this!'

After a while Jo went from room to room. It was a light house, with some of the rooms having two windows each which afforded views of both sea and countryside. There were three bedrooms and a bathroom upstairs, a wide square landing, and a comfortable shallow staircase led down to the ground floor and large hallway. Either side of the hall were twin rooms, equal in size, and each with a bay window facing directly out to sea. There was a small room at the back that had obviously been used as a study, whilst the rest of the ground floor was taken up with kitchen space. This comprised one long room which had been sectioned off into a series of small bays, and near to the back door was a deep, marble-shelved pantry. Jo was pleased with it all.

She took a cursory look at the garden and shuddered, for it was a jungle of old vegetable plots and tumbled fruit cages. A few ripe blackberries tempted her to pick and taste. They were sweet and firm, just like those Mollie grew at the farm. 'I'll have to ask for help to get this back into shape,' she thought, and made up her mind that she'd ask for advice from the aunts as soon as she got back to Widegates.

To the left was a wide lawn, bordered with flower-beds. Several overgrown shrubs grew near to the house, and in the middle of the lawn was an old oak-tree, affording shade to a wide area of the grass. 'What a wonderful climbing tree,' Jo thought, her mind flashing back to the tree at Widegates and the day she had first met Bryn. Was it really so many years ago?

She closed all the windows; had one last look round and left Trenorwin. Her step was light as she made her way up towards the wide path that led to the open moor. Jo stopped to gaze around her. The cliffs here, so wild and rugged, were softened where the sunshine caught the dry blooms of thrift and lichen. Dandelion heads shed snowy clocks, which danced away in the breeze. Heather, ling and short yellow gorse spread a carpet of yellow and mauve around her, the blooms tipping over the edge of the cliff top in places, like soft icing on a cake. The path led inland and upward and became more rocky as she struggled to the top of the hill. Jo sat here for a while, loathe to leave the beauty around her and the honey smell of the heather, that was more pronounced than before. She could see the farm in the distance spread out before her, the outbuildings shining newly white where John Ellery and Philip had painted them recently. The old farmhouse looked comfortable and solid in its hollow, and further on, the tower of St Lowell looked tiny and distant. She walked slowly down the path, smoother now, and as she drew nearer to Widegates she noticed Mollie in the fruit garden, her blue-clad figure bending and stretching as she picked blackberries. Mollie sensed Jo's presence on the hill and waved. Laughingly Jo called to her aunt, her voice carrying on the now soft wind.

'I'm coming aunt … I'm coming to help …' She cast one last look around her and ran down the path, across the field to the farm. Blackberry pie for tea!

While they were enjoying its crusty sweetness, the telephone rang. It was Bob; Selina's baby had arrived: a girl weighing seven and half pounds, mother and baby both well. Jo went to see her than evening and was touched by the beauty of the new baby. She was sweetly pink, compact, with rounded limbs and a small well-shaped head covered in a mass of brown curls. A rosebud mouth, button nose and dark-blue eyes, fringed by long lashes, completed the picture.

'Oh Selina – she's beautiful!' Jo breathed … and indeed she was.

Jo moved into Trenorwin during the long summer holidays. The day after school finished in mid-July she went down to the old grey house to clean up. James helped transport her personal bits from Widegates and to re-arrange the furniture. She discarded some pieces, painted others, replaced most of the curtains with spares from the farm and generally freshened the whole place. Decorations were on hold, for certain internal structural alterations were to be carried out first. Mollie fretted that she couldn't get these done sooner, but the builder had said, 'In the new year, miss,' and Jo didn't want to wait that long before moving in.

'Well, at least wait until your lodger arrives,' her aunts had said. 'No sense in your staying in that big house all on your own!'

James had been voicing his misgivings about this too, so Jo conceded. 'I'll move in when she arrives. All right?'

Bethan Jones chose a blustery wet day at the end of August to make her acquaintance with Cornwall. Jo met her at the station, where she alighted from the train in a flurry of colour, like a huge butterfly amidst the grey of the day. She was a vital, dark-haired and pale-faced girl, long of limb, slender and extremely graceful in her movements. She wore an ankle-length dress in pink and mauve cotton, and a bright shawl hung loosely round her shoulders; she seemed to float towards Jo, one shoulder weighed down with an enormous suitcase, and tucked under the other arm was an assortment of rectangular boards that proved to be canvas mountings. Her smile was warm and friendly, and Johanna knew she need have no worries about sharing her house with this colleague.

Jo took some of the parcels from her and they made their way along the platform towards the exit. Jo was striding ahead, but Bethan called her back.

'I've some things in the guard's van as well, just a minute whilst I get help.'

To Jo's amazement, several wooden boxes were taken from the van. Bethan made a plea to a young porter, who deposited them and the suitcase onto a trolley and wheeled them to the station car park.

'My painting stuff,' Bethan explained to Jo, in between flashing encouraging smiles and keeping up a light bubbly conversation with the helpful and rosy-faced young porter.

Bethan settled in well at the house. Her artistic temperament loved the situation; she went into raptures over her room with the wide bay window and scenic view. She sighed with relief when Jo said she would give her a lift into school and made herself so at home at Widegates that the aunts were completely bowled over.

She was a gifted painter and set up her easel whenever time allowed, so that within a couple of months she had completed several pictures of the local area. Seascapes, some peaceful and calm, others wild and stormy, just as if she'd put her own moods into them. She did a watercolour of Lansallos church, high in the folds of the headlands; the clay hills towards Bodmin, impressive on a summer evening with a stormy sky as a background; foxgloves on the headland with carpets of thrift on the cliff edge.

Bethan was creative at cookery too. They took it in turns to prepare meals and Jo was delighted with the light new dishes her lodger introduced to her. She would raid, with permission, Widegates' vegetable garden, producing thereby some mouth-watering salads and light soups, all strangely flavoured with herbs and spices.

As the days grew shorter and the weather became colder, they would light wood fires and sit curled up on Tom's old fireside chairs, chatting about school; of Bethan's home in North Wales, and sometimes of the war years, when Jo spoke quite freely of her two lives – the one in London and the other at Widegates. Jo had never had such a close, continual relationship with a girl of her own age before. She found it pleasurable, a comfort and a continual source of amusement, for Bethan was a 'laughing girl'.

'That young lass is a tonic!' Mollie had been heard to say on more than one occasion.

Sometimes now the house would echo with merry voices and much laughter, when Margaret, David and James joined them.

'Tom would have liked this,' James commented on one such occasion, and was rewarded with a special smile from Jo.

CHAPTER TWENTY-ONE

Johanna spent the middle two weeks of the summer holidays in London. She left Cornwall during a particularly wet and savage spell of weather, but as the train progressed eastwards, the skies cleared and the rain stopped. She found Paddington station awash with evening sunshine and crowded with happy, excited holiday-makers, parents and children off to spend a few short weeks in fresh air and beauty. Normality once more after the bleak war years! As she stood waiting for Bill, she watched with amusement the hustle and bustle of it all. Mothers restraining toddlers, children racing here and there in a frenzy of excitement, bags spilled, bags lifted onto trolleys, whole families laden down with parcels of necessities to ease their holiday along. One young mother had been particularly hard-pressed, endeavouring to control four lively youngsters, and now, having settled them all into a carriage almost opposite to where Jo stood, she was waving frantically – gesticulating through the open train window … 'Please, please …' she mouthed above the din of the station activity. 'Please …' as she pointed at a small card attaché-case near to Jo. As the mother reached for it through the long, low window, she called to Jo. 'Thanks, dear … sandwiches … just imagine taking this little lot to Cornwall with no grub!' Jo waved and smiled at four cherubic faces as the train moved slowly out, all eyes, wide with excitement and wonder.

Bill and Mary arrived laughing, excusing themselves for being late.

'It's the buses, Jo. We had to see three go by absolutely full up. We thought we'd never make it. I can't think where everybody is coming from.'

'It's school holidays,' said Jo. 'It seems everyone is thinking of getting away by what I've seen here this evening.'

They hurried through the barrier, then chased a 47 bus as it began to draw out, and finally landed in a muddled heap on the top, breathless and laughing, all clutching bits of Jo's baggage.

'This reminds me of the war years when we used to chase the buses from Waterloo.' Jo's eyes were distant for a moment, as she remembered the awful times when the flying bombs were landing. No such trauma now though. She sat behind Mary and Bill telling them about school, giving them news from Widegates, and, eventually, quite naturally, of Bryn's visit and his illness.

'He's doing well – all the news from Africa is good.' she said. Bill's eyes were troubled as he looked back at her, but she smiled readily at her brother. 'It was lovely seeing him, Bill. We had a long time together and said our good-byes. It's all right ... really it is!'

Mary changed the subject, chattering about the changes to her little flat. Jo too had been working on ideas for Trenorwin, and soon they were comparing colour schemes and discussing building problems, so enabling Bill to really study his sister. She seemed well. Her colour was good; her mouth smiled readily. No falseness about that, he thought. Jo really did seem all right. She was not fooled and gave him a steady glance; her eyes were bright, slightly teasing, and he could see no underlying sadness there to make him want to hug her close. Yes, it seemed Jo was taking up her life once more.

The short holiday went in preparation for a wedding. Bill and Mary had decided on *the* day. They had given no warning, just announced one evening that they would like to get married in August and requested a quiet wedding with no special plans. Mrs Dingle was surprised at first, but realised that Mary was still mourning her parents. They had died just before Christmas, within one week of each other.

'I don't want a fuss,' she told Bill's mother. 'No cars, no reception – just a simple wedding ... just us!' Mary's face was crumpling and she was near to tears. 'That way,' she added. 'That way, I shall feel they are both with us!'

'I understand, dear,' Mrs Dingle had felt so sorry for her. 'We'll make it a quiet wedding, I promise.'

It seemed the right time for the flat was almost finished and Mrs Dingle could find time for the simple wedding plans during her school holiday. They had wanted Johanna there to complete the family.

It was a warm still day in mid-August as they all walked together along the high street, beautiful once more with small plane-trees and sunken colourful gardens, to the family church set back from the main road, the same church that Jo had passed night after night in the blackout.

Mary wore a neat, pale-blue dress and carried a bouquet of late pink roses. Their fragrance hung about her as she walked. Jo had bought a new buttercup yellow suit, and her mother was splendidly smart in her favourite wine colour, a dress that fitted her closely at the waist and hung neatly below her calves in the fashion of the day. She looked younger and happier, and was heard to murmur several times … 'He's so like his dad!' Raymond acted as best man. Jo noticed how adult he appeared, especially so when he rather shyly introduced a bright, fair-haired lass of about nineteen years to his sister. 'This is Helen … we've known each other for ages.'

'It looks serious, mum, Ray and Helen,' Jo commented later in the day. Mrs Dingle smiled fondly at them as they sat in the bay of the window, heads together and talking animatedly.

'Yes, how lucky I am that both my boys have found such lovely partners. Just you …' But Jo had turned away, sad for the first time that day … sad that her life was still on hold.

Throughout the autumn, news of Bryn continued to cheer them all, and James made plans to visit before Christmas to check for himself. Once again, Jo wished that she could accompany him, but although Vee did write to her occasionally, telling her about life on the farm, about her son, and how Bryn was progressing – she never, ever, suggested a visit or invited her. Jo tried hard not to mind, but she felt a shrinking dislike of Veronica at times, a dislike that surprised her, but made her understand more and more her aunts' spicy comments on 'that wicked girl!'

School was gradually winding down for Christmas as James left for Africa at the beginning of December. He flew out and was expected to be gone for two weeks. Jo missed him badly, but her days and evenings were full, coping with all the trauma, anxieties and hard work needed to put on a school play. They had decided on a south-sea island theme. Grass skirts were made from coloured raffia for the girls, and the boys were dressed in white shirts, navy school trousers, with square neckerchiefs of various colours that gave them a nautical air. The school stage was set up with John Ellery's help. It was a 'make-do' thing, consisting of large square wooden blocks, in front of which he fixed a curtain rail. Old sheets were painted with poster and powder paint to resemble exotic south-sea scenes, and fronds of greenery were gathered from every possible source, splashed with colour and entwined with flowers of tissue paper. These were hung around the side and the back of the stage. It was all beautifully colourful, and quite out of season, for outside the wind blew, gale after gale coming in from the west. Practice sessions, when the girls danced lightly in their swaying, colourful skirts and the boys stomped their feet on the stage blocks, doing a lively hornpipe, were accompanied by the sound of lashing rain on the hall windows, and a wild keening from a wind that seemed determined to get in on the act!

The show was for one night only. The hall was packed with parents, young children and friends. Wet mackintoshes were packed underneath the seating and umbrellas left dripping in the corridor. The scene was set and the hall quiet, when one boy found that he'd left his neckerchief in the classroom. He rushed across the playground, getting back just in time to join the line of dancing hornpipers. A couple of steps into the dance, he slipped in his wet plimsolls and shot right off the low stage to land almost in the vicar's lap. To his credit, he climbed back up on stage and completed the dance with a certain flair. He was rewarded with enthusiastic clapping from the audience. Jo couldn't mind; it set the scene on a light-hearted evening. A touch of summer to lighten the dreary winter days.

James returned with excellent news of Bryn and had much to relate about life on the farm. It seemed Bryn was well enough now to take on full management once more and was able to ride over the vast acres, which he loved. He had taken James out one morning, before dawn, to experience the delight of the special coolness of that time, and the beauty of an African sunrise. James's face was red with sunburn, and his nose peeling, something he had never experienced before.

'It's so very hot, Jo,' he complained. 'Hot and enervating. I was happy to laze the afternoons away on the verandah, just swinging back and forth in a hammock. I didn't read, just dozed, talked and dreamed. We both did! Your ears should have been burning for we spoke of you incessantly. Here – Bryn sent you this ...' James put a photograph into her hand. It was a family portrait of the three of them. Young Bryn, central to the picture, but caught close in his father's arms. Father and son so much alike. Vee – a grown up mature Vee, with her hair set high on her head, fuller in face, and perhaps a little severe-looking. Jo studied it carefully before passing it to Mollie, who, after several nods of her head and comments on Bryn and his son, tucked the photograph on the mantelpiece, wedging it behind the clock so that Vee was out of sight!

Christmas came and went with Mrs Dingle and Raymond joining them on the farm. It seemed strange without Tom somehow. Jo took her brother for long walks round the headland. The wet and windy weather had gone, leaving them with a grey, but calm spell. The sky was grey, the sea was sluggish and grey, the landscape was grey, and everywhere had a stillness that made Johanna long for the return of the blustery days. David heard her complaining and, in-between puffs on his pipe, promised a boisterous January and February.

'It's a pattern I've learned to recognise Jo. The gales will be back, you'll see!'

They returned with a vengeance on the afternoon she saw her mother and brother off at St Austell station. The sky had darkened after lunch and a skittish wind was teasing out light debris and leaves from under the rails, as they waited for the London train.

'Mind how you go back, Jo,' Mrs Dingle was concerned as she hugged her daughter goodbye. 'This is to be no ordinary storm. Put your lights on and drive carefully.'

It began with snow, blinding snow that covered the windscreen and blotted out the road. Jo had almost reached Fowey when gusts of wind shook the Bedford truck.

The road was high and exposed, but the wide view was quite obliterated, as she struggled to keep the vehicle straight. The road to the ferry dipped now and afforded her some shelter. The snow seemed to ease and she relaxed a little at the wheel, so was totally unprepared for the sight that met her eyes as she drew up at the ferry crossing. The wind had reached gale force, blowing straight in from the sea, whipping the water into wild, white waves. The empty car ferries were both moored tightly, but the chains groaned and fretted with each new gust of wind. The trees were being lashed this way and that, and then, as she watched from the shelter of her van, the ferry notice-board was torn from its mounting, to go sailing

away across the water. Everywhere was noise – rushing – tearing
– clanging noise! Jo thought of her mother's words of warning and
turned the van quickly round to seek the shelter of the ferry road.
Here though, the wind pulled and sucked at her vehicle. Some
slates crashed down onto the bonnet, torn from the roof of a nearby
garage. The sheltered road became a danger to her now, as the slates
continued to fall and tree branches whipped on the roof of the van.
Jo hugged the wheel and eased the vehicle up the hill and out once
more onto the wide exposed highway. Here she felt vulnerable in
a different way, for the gale buffeted against the side of the van,
threatening to tip it over. Sometimes small woodland areas afforded
her respite from the wind, or the road dipped low into pockets of
stillness. Eventually, she turned right to take the winding narrow
road through Lerryn. It was always a long way round for Widegates,
but today the journey seemed to take hours. Debris carried by the
wind fell on the roof of the Bedford, but high banks either side
of the lanes once again gave her shelter from its rushing madness.
Her arms ached with trying to manoeuvre the vehicle round tight,
narrow corners; her eyes stung with the concentration required to
see the twists and turns of the road through the swirling whiteness.
All the time she worried that the snow might become too deep, that
she would be stuck! Jo was more than glad when she finally reached
the main road. Lights flashed ahead of her, bright in the white mist
of snow. She stopped the van as a figure emerged by the side door.
James had come to find her! Edith and Mollie, who were expecting
Jo back at the farm, had become worried, particularly when they
heard that the ferry crossing had been cancelled.

'She'll never make it through Lerryn,' Edith had said. 'Stop
fretting now, Mollie. She'll wait somewhere.' But Mollie knew her
niece well. 'Jo will try to get through so that we don't worry …
don't you see? I'll ring James.'

Both father and son had gone in search of her, and it was Jim
Trevarder's idea to wait on the highway.

'She'll manage the lanes, lad,' he consoled his son. 'But she'll be
tired. We'll wait here.'

Now James climbed into the van on the driver's side, as Johanna
eased her tired body over. They made the journey back to Widegates
in silence – listening to the roaring of the storm and the struggling
of the engine to maintain its dominance over the deep, snowy lanes.

Only when they finally drew up in the yard of the farm did James reach over for her. His arms enveloped her in a warm, strong hug.

'I was so worried Jo.' She nestled happily against him.

'And I was never so pleased to see anyone in my whole life. Thanks, James, for coming …'

Mollie and Edith welcomed them both and fussed over them with warm soup and hot-water bottles. The gale worsened, and James stayed the night, stayed at Widegates for the first time ever. The aunts went to bed leaving them pouring over plans Jo had worked on for Trenorwin.

School started again, but the inclement weather continued. There would be one or two days' respite, and once, in early February, they were blessed with several sunny days, but each time the storms returned, pouring a fury of wind and rain over the land.

Lambing had started, and still there was no abatement.

John Ellery and Edith brought all of the ewes into the lower fields, and penned them in. Gradually, the bleating of the new-born lambs could be heard above the roaring winds. The barn was penned out with straw bales for the new arrivals, and because of their careful management, John and Edith got through the two week lambing period without mishap.

Things at Pensilva were not so good. Here the sheep were normally kept well away from the farmhouse and outbuildings, shelter being provided for them in the form of wooden huts, long, low buildings that had been erected originally by James's grandfather. They had stood the test of time for many years, but finally succumbed to the gales just before the lambing started; the side walls gave way one wild night, and they collapsed inwards. In consequence, James had to find alternative shelter for his animals. The sheep were brought nearer to the farm and settled in a large rectangular field, ringed on all sides by deep ditches. Not an ideal situation, but a small barn in one corner would afford them shelter. It was penned out in readiness, but the lambing got underway one stormy evening; James went in search of ewes and lambs to bring them into the shelter. He had been gone for some hours. Jim Trevarder had searched for his son, getting increasingly worried as the hours went by. Eventually, he telephoned Trenorwin for help. A sleepy Johanna was jerked awake.

'I just can't find him, Jo. I've been round and round the field. Could you get someone to help me search?' She dressed hurriedly, phoned John Ellery and arranged to pick him up, then she rang Widegates.

'Contact us soon,' Mollie had said. 'If you've no sign of him by daylight, then we'll ring the neighbours and get lots of help in.'

It was early dawn before they found him, lying still and deathly pale, his body half in a flooded ditch. He was pinned by the branches of an old oak-tree. The tree was not completely uprooted, but rather had keeled over in a quiet, tired way, its roots tugging gently from the softened bank, much the same as a loose tooth is extracted, with roots intact. He was well hidden amongst the tree debris and had obviously been trying to rescue a lamb that had got caught in the flooded ditch. It was still held tightly in his arms, its little body wet, cold and still; quite dead!

Jo flew to James, grabbed him by the shoulders and tried to pull him free.

'Steady, lass,' John's voice was quiet, but firm. 'We must think this one out!' He bent down as James moved his head slightly and groaned.

'Oh God,' thought Jo, as she bent down to cradle his head.

'James, we are here, we are here. John will soon get you free.' He moaned once more, turned his head towards her voice, but with eyes still closed, and his mouth formed a strained tight smile.

'Hello, pet, knew you'd come.'

There was nothing they could do. James was held fast.

'I'm going for help, Jo. A doctor too, will you be all right?'

She nodded her head, her eyes fixed on James's pale features. He seemed to be unconscious now. He was breathing shallowly, but he was breathing. She stroked the wet, matted fair hair from his forehead, as John removed his old oilskin and wrapped it round the top half of James's body. Jo turned her back to the wind to afford them both a little more shelter from the cold blasts.

'Be quick, John,' she called, as she heard his feet squelching in the muddy field behind her.

Help came quickly in the form of tractor, doctor and ambulance, and soon James was being transported to hospital, conscious once more and in evident pain. Lengthy examinations showed extensive leg injuries, where a splinter of wood had gouged a deep wound from knee to ankle, taking whole shards of shin bone. He had bruising to his rib cage and a slight head wound.

'He'll live,' Jim Trevarder reported to a worried Jo, 'but it will take some time before he's on his feet once more.'

James proved a bad patient. He fussed and fumed at his forced inactivity. His father coped with the farm, and was secretly happy to be 'back in harness' once more, reporting back each day to his son. It was three weeks before James became even a little mobile, then he would hobble around, leaning heavily on his walking stick, one leg still encased in plaster.

Jo would spend every free moment with him. She helped with the farm administration by becoming his part-time secretary.

'It's a job I do for all the men I like,' she teased, remembering her time with Bryn in Beckenham. James looked for her always … counted the hours until she would be free to visit, and if at times she got held up at school, or with jobs at Widegates, he demanded of her angrily, 'where have you been … I've waited ages.' Jo remained patient, understanding his frustrations, even smiling a little at memories of Bryn when he had pneumonia. When eventually the plaster was removed and James became more mobile, she asked if he would give advice at Trenorwin, to help with the workmen there. So it was James who organised the alterations, James who chose new glass doors for the kitchen and dining-room, selected tiles and working surfaces. James who saw to the positioning of power points, and finally James who organised two young lads from the village to begin a dig-over of the raggle-taggle garden and to clear the swathes of bramble from the once colourful flower-beds.

His leg healed slowly, but cleanly, and by late March he was moving more freely, but always with the aid of a stick. Mollie teased him about his 'war wound', and swooned playfully at the picture he presented with his 'attractive' limp! Inwardly James resented the need for the continued use of this aid to full mobility. He had been told by the doctors that he would always need its support, and somehow it made him feel less of a man. He watched Jo, to see whether it had any effect on her, but she remained her usual friendly self, happier now perhaps than she'd been for years, content to talk about and to hear about Bryn … and quite wrapped up in her teaching. Like Bill, he could see that now she was getting her life together once more.

James visited Scotland for two weeks in April. Johanna had been at Pensilva finishing the accounts on the morning of his departure, and had watched from the small office window, as he packed the car with farm produce for his aunt and uncle on Skye. Jo remembered their visit together, of the peace it had given her during her traumatic time over Bryn, and wished that she could join him now.

James's limp seemed more pronounced as he struggled with packages to the car. He had flung the stick down in annoyance as he'd tried to carry a tray of eggs safely, and was now on his knees trying to retrieve it. Every part of her being wanted to go and help, but she knew how much he would hate that help. So she watched his struggle, feeling tense and a little sad. James hugged her tight before he left. He didn't speak at first, but gathered her up into his arms in a bear-like embrace. With a deep sigh, he buried his face in her hair, breathing in its own woodland fragrance.

'Miss me Jo,' he said. 'Miss me.'

She stood with his parents waving him off and watched as the car turned the corner, to dip out of sight as he drove towards the highway. Suddenly she felt desolate.

Jo did miss him. Missed him more than she had thought possible. Without realising it, she had begun to rely on him, accepting his loving gentleness. She looked for him always and was disappointed if he didn't call. She discussed her life with him; decisions she had to make with regard to both her school and the aunts were made with his help. She telephoned him when happy – sought his companionship and ready ear when sad or lonely. James had become, without her noticing, a complete part of her whole life.

Johanna never thought beyond friendship. That was until one night in early June when they had visited Margaret and David. They had sat out after supper on the small patio, listening to a new recording of *Madam Butterfly*, and both were transported to realms of delight with the music. They stayed late and were loathe to go back to Widegates. Jo was staying the night to keep Mollie company, as Edith was visiting her friend in Penzance. The evening was bright with moonlight, and without discussing it with her James set the car into the lay-by near to the headland and helped her out.

'Let's walk over to the top of South Down.' he said. Jo acquiesced – she wasn't sure what she would have done had he suggested a walk out to Mr Pencarrow, which still for her somehow was wrapped up in special memories of childhood and Bryn.

They walked slowly, drinking in the peace and beauty of the area. The grass was cool underfoot and Jo could feel the sweetness of it through her fine sandals. Little rustlings could be heard from the hedges, and, nearer to the cliff, the sea, far below, was slushing easily back and forth across the shingle beach. It was a still night, a gentle night, and it seemed perfectly natural for James to pull her to him, to lift her chin with his long fingers and kiss her. It was a long kiss, increasing in intensity as the moments passed. Jo didn't draw away. She found the experience remarkably lovely – she was drawn to him by a gentle calmness, a secure, safe feeling, by a need to be loved, to know that she was loved and to love back. The kiss was long. They drew away, and James enclosed her in his arms so that they both looked out across the moonlit water, his chin resting on the top of her head.

'My girl?' The question was a whispered one.

She nodded, then added quietly. 'Yes, James … your girl!' He turned her swiftly, gathered her up into his arms once more and kissed her yielding mouth, one hand all the while caressing the lobe of her ear. As they drew away, she looked up at him and their eyes met and held for a long moment. Jo reached up and ran her fingers gently over his lips; his grip tightened as he crushed her to him. He was trembling slightly; Jo felt a little dismayed, realising that he was holding himself in complete control. She reached out for him once more, anxious to feel again the sweetness of his kiss, but he held her arms tight to her sides.

'Good,' he said. 'Good.'

She shivered, and he helped while she slipped her arms into her cardigan, which had been slung casually over her shoulders. She struggled with the buttons as he pulled her close once more and pressed his face into her hair.

'Mine, Jo – really mine?' he whispered huskily.

'Always,' she answered clearly, as he relaxed his grip and she turned to face him. Their gaze held again for timeless seconds. Jo could feel a soft breeze caress the back of her neck as she smiled up at him, her eyes alight with joy. James grinned down at her as they clung together, both feeling now the wild beating of their hearts and listening to the soft splash of the waves as they rolled in, far below them into the wide bay. They stood for what seemed hours, her thoughts in a turmoil … and yet at peace at the same time, until eventually, they made their way back to the car and Widegates, where James held her close once more, kissed her gently, and with a whispered 'goodnight pet, love you, see you tomorrow,' he got back into the car and drove off down the lane towards Pensilva.

Mollie had heard them come, and was at the back door to welcome her.

'What a beautiful night, Jo. Did you enjoy your visit to David and Margaret, and are they both all right?'

Johanna would much rather have been on her own for a while, alone there in the moonlight, to think over her new found happiness. James and Jo ... Johanna and James ... her mind was going over and over, but Aunt Mollie had waited up.

'They are fine. Margaret is well and both are looking forward to next month and the baby's arrival. David takes such tender care of her. It's quite lovely to see.

'Has James gone? He was quick,' Mollie said. And then she studied her niece. 'Is everything well with you, Jo?'

'Yes, aunt – everything is well with me, James is fine. Let's have some cocoa before bed, shall we?' Later, as they sat at the kitchen table sipping their warm drinks, Jo began to talk in quite a feverish fashion of James.

'He's so much better, Mollie, changed somehow; is walking well now and planning all sorts of things for the farm. I think that he's really back to his old self. He had an assertiveness about him this evening that I've never seen before.'

Jo was quiet then, deep in her own thoughts, and so was startled to hear her aunt say:

'He loves you, Jo, did you know? He always has.' Johanna looked long at Mollie and felt a flush come to her cheeks.

'Yes I know, Mollie, but I didn't really want to until this evening. I think I love him too ...' Her aunt reached a hand across the table and tapped Jo's lightly as it lay relaxed by the side of the mug of cocoa.

'So glad, darling,' she whispered. 'So glad for you both.'

They were married that autumn in the little church of St Lowell, along the lane from Widegates. Margaret and Selina spent long hours decorating it with seasonal flowers and greenery, and it was aglow with autumnal colours, bright berries standing out from garlands of differing shades of leaves. The aunts prepared food for the reception to be held at the farm afterwards.

Jo had wished for it to be a quiet occasion, but she had by now become a part of the community and a well-loved teacher, so the church was full when she arrived on Bill's arm, dressed in a voile suit of autumnal colours. It had a neat waisted jacket, a narrow belt, and the skirt was full and floated as she walked. With the flower arrangements everywhere, she resembled a 'nymph' of the forest, as she moved slowly between the pews, her face composed, and glowing with an inner peace and happiness. 'She'll do,' thought Mollie.

James stood, tall and proud, watching her move towards him. The sun was streaming through the high window to his left, brightening the spot where he stood, and as Jo reached his side, he took her hand, gazing down at her for a long while, both now bathed in the warm, gentle rays. It was a special moment for them, and for all who watched.

Johanna had no attendants, but after a moment had turned to hand her bouquet of autumn berries and some late honeysuckle from the farm to Margaret, who waited nearby before returning to her place beside David.

Mrs Dingle was resplendent in a wine-coloured suit, her hair, now almost entirely grey, caught into a coil at the neck and topped by the sweetest cloche hat covered in flowers. She was a perfect bride's mother, her face suffused with pride, joy and happiness for her only daughter. Ray stood next to her, having completed his job as usher. He was unrecognisably smart in his new grey suit. Mollie and Edith stood together, a delightful contrast in their wedding finery, for Mollie had chosen a subtle tan shade for her simple button-through dress, complete with a small straw hat which, in turn, sported a light-beige chiffon scarf round the brim. The scarf trailed down her back a little, giving it a youthful appearance, and the whole blended beautifully with the autumnal colours in the church, so that Edith's bright pink outfit came almost as a shock. She was pink from head to toe and wore the colour well. Jo had been with her when she'd shopped for it. The suit was severely tailored, and yet managed to soften and curve her angular frame. The hat was plain: a boater, which she wore perched on her head and slightly forward over one eye. It made Edith hold her head high. She looked very handsome and stately.

Bill took his place next to Mary. She wore a bright lemon dress and was hatless, her dark hair gleaming from the brushing afforded it that morning. Bill, in a brown suit, was attentive, but his eyes caught and held Jo's for a moment as she half-turned at the end of the service. She smiled at them all … yes, they were all there, all there to wish her well on this happiest of days!

Edith had been studying her niece. Jo looks young for her twenty-eight years, she thought, and noticed for the first time how like her mother she was. She recalled another wedding years ago, when Lillian had stood at that same spot in a flood of bright spring sunshine. Hers had been a good marriage until the war had come along to spoil things. Edith hoped that Jo would have the same happiness as her mother. She glanced across at her sister now, smart in her dark red suit and flowered hat; she caught a glint of tears in her eyes and turned away.

'I'll not cry for Jo today – she's happy now, bless her!'

An early morning mist had been a promise of a fine day, and none were disappointed. Mollie had, for the first time, shut her 'quackers' out of reach in the home field, where they had set up a distant racket for some two hours before quietening. When back at the farm, she sent various children to feed them, so that they would be included, giving each child a small container of grain.

The verandah doors were opened onto the garden, and guests wandered about, or sat to enjoy the warm sunshine and dramatic views of the mauve, heather-covered moors, and distant glimpses of a calm untroubled sea. That was how everyone remembered the day … it was calm, untroubled and very beautiful.

The newly weds went to St Ives for their honeymoon, going by car and driving slightly north of Penzance.

'Remember the last time we came here?' James asked. Jo was quick to reply. 'Of course I do. We had all that flooding, didn't we?'

'Yes, we did …' he laughed aloud and hugged the wheel. 'You turned me down, Jo, didn't you?'

'What a silly I was,' she answered, light-heartedly, 'and so good of you to wait!'

Margaret's baby had been born in the early hours of one Saturday morning in July; a beautiful boy and some eight pounds in weight.

He was put into her arms, rosy-cheeked, firm of limb, and with a mass of dark curly hair, to lie there with a placid contentment that was to belie his first months in the world. He looked at his mother with seeming approval. David said you could almost imagine him saying – 'That was a job well done!'

It was love at first sight. Margaret's face was gently possessive as she gazed at his perfection. They had a stream of visitors to the cottage at the top of the hill, and women from the village rallied round to give what help was necessary. David used to look back from one part of the cliff at South Down and locate his garden by the line of snowy nappies, now fluttering daily there.

Young John was a sick baby right from the start. The midwife had been troubled by his projectile-type vomiting immediately after each feed. He would scream with the shock of it, and then stuff one whole little fist in his mouth as if hungry once more. He could not and would not be placated, and with the four-hourly feeding rule being rigidly adhered to, he spent most of his time in an angry rage at a world that refused to nourish him. When Margaret, ignoring the advice of the nurse, fed him once more, the same violent sickness occurred, and it was mentioned that he might just be a greedy baby and taking too much too quickly. She was torn … not knowing how, and yet wanting to do the right thing for her new charge. David bought a dummy, a horrid rubber thing, and this they dipped into Nurse Harvey's Mixture, obtainable from the chemist; it soothed him a little, but feeding and subsequent vomiting remained a problem.

John's weight loss was pronounced and giving cause for real concern, when early one Sunday afternoon he had a convulsion and was rushed to hospital. He was barely three weeks old! Here he was test fed and found to be losing most of each feed. Margaret had to relinquish him to the hospital or risk losing her bonny, but unhappy little boy. Tubes were inserted into his nose for drip-feeding, his little hands were tied to the side of the cot by soft bandages to prevent him tugging at these tubes and pulling them out. He lay there, so tiny and defenceless, in a huge hospital cot, secured tightly and deprived of the natural comforts a baby needs, the arms and presence of his mother and the ability to suck.

Margaret watched through the glass partition – she was not allowed in, as he sucked and sucked on nothing, his little mouth moving constantly, and his eyes sad and lost.

David worried about his wife and his baby son. Margaret had changed, gone was the merry, laughing companion. She was quiet, withdrawn almost and completed her chores about the home with a restlessness alien to her. Every morning she visited the hospital, asking lifts from whomever might be going that way, and, failing that, she would trudge down the hill, cross on the passenger ferry, and catch a bus from Fowey. She lost weight, her once rosy cheeks were pale and her eyes red-rimmed with tears that she shed, day after day, week after week.

John made no progress for some four weeks, and she watched hour after hour from the glass partition, as his weight remained static, and his little face became pinched-looking.

David lost his temper on one visit to the hospital, when the Sister told him that she felt John liked being sick. He was white with rage and frustration and the hospital's inability to tell them what exactly was wrong with their son. Margaret, who had never seen him like this, was a little frightened.

'We'll take our baby then, sister, now. Get him ready, please.' His voice was ice-cold. He turned a strained face to Margaret.

'Don't fret, we'll go to London with him. They are doing no good at all here.'

The hospital was in a dilemma, not wanting to relinquish John. Doctors were called to explain things, but David was adamant, until finally it was agreed that they would arrange for a child specialist from London to see John the very next day. Phones buzzed, a time was fixed, David making arrangements for both Margaret and himself to be there when their baby was examined. The specialist was a charming, caring man of about David's age. He talked to them quietly about what he proposed to do, and so finally the tubes were removed and John was fed with Bengers Food, a thick gruel-like mixture that necessitated larger holes being made in the bottle teats.

John 'grabbed' at this way of feeding and although he was still very sick, managed to absorb enough nourishment to begin a slight increase in weight. Progress at last, but oh so slowly!

Margaret's continued presence at the hospital was frowned on by Sister, who suggested frequently that she 'go home – have a shopping spree, make the most of this freedom, for you'll not have it when baby comes home.' She turned a deaf ear to all of these suggestions. How could she go and leave John … why, oh why wouldn't they let her in to help; help in the ward in any way they thought fit. Just to be near him, to touch him, to whisper to him once more. Oh, but they were so cruel!

Her patience was rewarded one day when John was taken for an X-ray and the young nurse suggested she might like to carry him back to the ward. She held her son for the first time for six weeks – held his little body close and gazed down into his eyes … eyes that once were dark-blue and now were brown. He held on tightly to her finger and seemed to smile a little as tears started in her eyes. She whispered tremulously. 'Hello, my baby … I love you.'

'I don't know how I managed to hand him back,' she told Jo later. 'It was as if he knew who I was, and his little smile was a comfort for me … and Jo,' Margaret sobbed quietly, 'his eyes have changed, they are dark-brown now, and I've missed all that.' Johanna held her close and wondered at a system that denied a mother like Margaret access to her sick child. She was incensed about it, not realising that, in a few short years, parents would be made welcome at such times and would be able to afford, not only comfort to their children, but care as well!

John continued to gain weight. Margaret was at last encouraged to enter the ward to bath and feed him for the two days prior to discharge. She left the hospital one bright morning with a sleepy, contented baby, complete and happy for the first time since his birth. But one more obstacle had to be overcome! John, on waking, refused to be comforted. Mollie came to talk to him softly, even Edith 'shushed' him gently in her strong arms, but he screamed and cried at any close human contact. Margaret woke exhausted the first night to cradle and feed him. John was quiet in the darkness. No struggling, and then it hit her … he had been used to nurses wearing face-masks for about the whole of his young life! She rushed to the chemist the next morning, bought one dozen washable masks, and anyone wishing to come near had to 'mask-up' first.

About two weeks later he playfully pulled hers off and then chuckled at his mother, as his tiny hand reached up to caress her mouth.

CHAPTER TWENTY-TWO

Johanna and James returned from their short honeymoon and set up home at Trenorwin. Most of the work had been completed by now. The garden was flourishing, nicely planted out with some new shrubs, a honeysuckle bower and fruit garden. The rhododendron bushes at the front had been carefully pruned, and now a wide view of the bay was exposed to be admired all the time. That same view came into the house through the bay windows, welcomed them on the square landing and increased in width and distance when they were at the top of the house. Both pondered on the sense of changing the name of the house, but Ocean View, Seascape, Widebay, all suggested names, lacked in the end the magic and mystery of its real name – Trenorwin!

Bethan, who had lodged with Jo through all the mess of renovations, had now moved to Widegates and was a great help and comfort to the aunts. She took over Tom's room, with the distant sea views, as her studio. Both Mollie and Edith were thrilled when, during a small exhibition she had at Polruan, they found that many of her paintings were of views from the farm. Johanna bought one of the headland. It caught exactly the magic of a bubbly spring day. It was a light-hearted, gay picture; she hung it over the mantelpiece in the front room. 'So that Mr P can look out at his real self!' she laughingly told them.

Once settled, their evenings were often spent at the small house on the cliff with Margaret and David, and of course the new baby. John was a happy little chap now with his feeding problems resolved, but Margaret was so careful of him, and loathed to let him out of her sight. Often, after supper with them, Jo and James would walk home the two miles or so down the lane, occasionally, when the summer days permitted, going the long way round, over the headland and across the high moor, their minds recalling the joys and memories this lovely part of the coastline evoked in them both.

'I want to stay here forever, James,' Jo would breath. 'Forever and forever!'

'Well, I'm not going anywhere, and you can't because you're mine!' was the laughing reply.

The days were peaceful and busy. The aunts watched over them both in simple ways, making the odd batch of Eccles cakes or presenting a rabbit pie for the evening meal. On fine, late autumn days, Jo often found Mollie busy in the front garden, when she herself had been particularly tied to school, and James worked on late at the farm.

The winter was long and hard, but cold and dry! Lambing at Pensilva had presented no problems this year, and Jo was made aware of the arrival of spring in the nicest possible way, when a jar of primroses was set on her desk one morning. She handled the flowers fondly, touching them lightly and breathing in their special fragrance. Outside the schoolroom the day was bright and she yearned to be free, to be out there in the fresh spring air.

'Don't overdo things, Mollie, will you?' Jo admonished one day on finding her aunt on her knees chasing some early bindweed from the shrubs.

'I'm happy, lass – didn't you know?' Mollie said, as she struggled to her feet. 'So happy that you and James …' Her soft voice faltered, and Jo linked arms with her affectionately, as they stood together facing the view. They watched as the gulls weaved high in the sky, watched the larks dipping into the field adjoining them, and heard the distant thunder of an incoming tide. … 'happy that you're here and settled, Jo,' Mollie finished.

That Johanna was happy with this her first real home was evident. She was delighted with all the improvements and thrilled at the way the garden was shaping up, but was anxious to have more time to herself to really enjoy it all. She spoke to Mollie tentatively of leaving her school job.

'But how will you manage, Jo, without your children?'

'That's exactly what James says,' she laughed. 'Oh, I'd miss them, of course I would, but I could always return after a year if it didn't suit. Tom always said there was a time and place for everything, and I feel, Mollie, that now is the right time for me to leave teaching. And in any case,' she added rather shyly, 'in any case, we are hoping to start a family of our own before we get too old!'

'And so you should,' Mollie's voice was bright with laughter. 'After all you are very, very ancient!'

The decision was taken from her by events at Pensilva. James's mother had a slight stroke, and his father was diagnosed as diabetic all within two short weeks. James needed help, so Johanna gave in her notice to leave teaching at the end of the school year. She took over various tasks at Pensilva immediately and, with Margaret's help, managed the dairy side of things until James could get extra staff.

Jo had never completely relinquished the administrative duties she had undertaken after James had had his accident. The office was moved to Trenorwin, and they spent the evening hours together, sorting, planning, filling in forms and writing letters to keep this side of the farm together.

James found a wonderful helper from the village. Janet Coombes was a tiny stick of a woman, a widow with no dependants. She had a bright bird-like face, wispy brown hair, rosy cheeks, large gentle brown eyes, and an energy that would put most people to shame. She was more than happy to leave her small flat and take up residence in the cottage that Margaret had once used. She took over Pensilva in the nicest possible way and did all she could to help James's mother cope with her disability. Jane Trevarder had lost the use of one arm, and her mouth now had a sideways tilt. However, she remained totally elegant, but was now fragilely so, and it suited her.

Work on the farm was eased by the introduction of two students from the college at Plymouth. They were very agreeable, hard-working lads, both anxious to learn and they formed a good relationship with James. His strong laugh could often be heard ringing out when he worked with the boys. Pensilva was a happy place to visit in spite of the recent traumas.

Bryn's leukaemia returned after two years. It attacked without warning one sunny spring morning with none of the previous experience of weeks of tiredness and lethargy, loss of appetite and slight infections that had warned him before of something being not quite right.

He had been riding the perimeter of the farm with his neighbour's son, a sunny-haired boy of some fourteen years, when he had keeled over from his saddle and lain on the ground as if dead. His young companion packed a jacket under his head, cooled his forehead with a soaked neckerchief, using water from the bottle Bryn always carried in his saddlebag, and wisely waited for Bryn to recover from his faint. He assisted him back into the saddle and, holding the bridles of both horses, slowly guided him back home.

The doctors at the local hospital ordered him straight back to England for specialist treatment. Vee phoned James to tell him and to ask whether he could meet them and make arrangements at his end. Medical appointments were made and flights fixed, and then Bryn telephoned his friend fleetingly on the eve of their departure. His voice was clear across the miles, though he sounded tired and worried, but said how much he was looking forward to seeing England and all of them once more.

'What of young Bryn?' James asked. 'Mollie has said she'd love to have him at the farm if that will help.'

'We are leaving him here, James. Vee's aunt is coming up from the south, and he knows her fairly well. I shall miss him. He's a spunky little chap – always up to something or other.'

'Well, so long as he's all right, but I promised I'd ask. They are longing to see him, Bryn.'

'I know – perhaps next time.' The phone went quiet for a while, then Bryn began talking again. His voice seemed distant now.

'James, if anything happens to me … to us, you'll take him for me; raise him well, good schools, everything, won't you?'

James was shattered. Bryn must be in very low spirits to talk like this.

'Of course, Bryn, but nothing is going to happen. You'll get fit again. Now rest and we'll see you very soon. Take care, old chap.'

'Yes, I'll take care … but you will remember what I have asked of you … good. My love to Jo – good-bye!' The line went dead, leaving James perturbed at his friend's comments. Later his father reassured him.

'Bryn's feeling low, that's all. He'll soon perk up when he gets here. Awful to think he has to undergo more of that miserable treatment. He's entitled to be in low spirits I should think.'

It had been arranged that Jim would meet his nephew in London, so that initial examinations and treatment could be carried out there. He had booked accommodation for all three of them and would, as soon as the specialist cleared him, bring Bryn and Veronica back to Taunton, where he could attend the local hospital as before.

James was anxious to see his friend, and had persuaded Jo to join him for a weekend in town as soon as Bryn was settled. Mrs Dingle was looking forward to seeing them both, but apprehensive about the trauma she knew Jo would have to cope with by seeing Bryn once more, especially as he was so ill. But it was the thought of Veronica that bothered Jo. She just didn't know how she'd cope with meeting her again. Memories of her betrayal came flooding back, threatening to destroy her recently found peace, but she said: 'Yes James, of course I'll come,' though inwardly her whole being shrank from involvement; but Bryn would need to see her, she knew that for sure, and she couldn't let him down!

Jim reached Heathrow on a warm summer day in June. He had arrived early by hire car, which was also to take them straight on to the hotel. He wore a light-grey suit, his thin wispy hair was combed close to his head, and his face had what his friends called his 'Taunton' tan. He walked briskly to the barrier, a sprightly, slightly bent figure, swinging his cane nonchalantly.

The plane was late. Enquiries received only reassurances that the flight was slightly delayed. So he sat near to the barrier watching people arrive and leave, pondering on their lives and trying hard not to nod off! He had missed out on his usual midday sleep and felt weary and a little disorientated. The loudspeaker drew him back from his reverie, and he heard – 'Information on flight number two, nought, six'. Why that's Bryn's flight, he thought. It went on – 'Please report to the desk if you are awaiting flight two, nought, six. There has been an accident'! He followed a small group of people, who like him had been sitting near the barrier, his legs feeling weak and his heart racing madly. They all then learned of the plane crash … 'There are no survivors' – rang in his ears. Jim's head became muzzy. He heard a roaring sound and for a while knew no more! He had fainted for the first time in his life!

Later, back at the hotel, he put through a call to Pensilva hoping to catch James. Jim Trevarder answered the telephone, and the two elderly men spoke for a while.

'Shall I come up for you? Are you sure you're all right?' Jim Trevarder was concerned at Bryn's uncle's weak breathless voice.

'I'm leaving now by hire car. Will you tell James please, and be careful with Johanna. I'll phone from home … so sad, poor lad.' His voice sounded raw as he placed the phone back on the hook.

Jo was in the front garden when James arrived home early. She was on her knees, layering the shrubs, and called out happily to him.

'I won't be a minute, James; my, but you are early!' He didn't answer, just stood looking down at her, until she turned, sensing that something was wrong. His face was pale, his expression grave, and his eyes were deep pools of hurt.

'My dear, what is it?' She was on her feet in an instant reaching for him, but he held his hands out, as if to push her away.

'He's dead, Jo – Bryn is dead. The plane crashed … Jim just phoned …' His voice sounded harsh, the words were cruelly forthright, and Jo scarcely grasped what he was saying. James reached for her then as she looked up into his face bewildered … 'James? …' Her voice was small and tight.

'Oh, Jo – it's true. A terrible accident – no survivors, both of them … dead.' His arms tightened round her seeking to give and receive comfort. Jo was still for a while and then suddenly tore herself free. She stumbled to the roadway as if drunk, looking back at him wildly for a moment, and then ran, tripping and almost falling, down the road towards the gully, where her feet slithered and slipped, as a huge, hard lump formed in her chest and grew and grew, threatening to choke her. She gasped for breath, but didn't stop her flight. She reached the gate to the wide moor, and flung herself along the path, her arms flaying wildly in front of her, as if pushing something away, and her lips forming the words: 'No … no … no!' She thought she heard James calling, she didn't turn round, but continued her mad flight until her feet suddenly slipped beneath her, and she collapsed onto the long grass, the coolness soothing her face, but not the burning, tearing pain in her chest.

James found her there and reached down, pulling her up and into his arms; he turned her to face him, holding her gently, but firmly, forcing her to look at him.

'I loved him too, Jo,' his voice was raw with feeling. 'We share the pain. Don't turn away from me now. We were always together, we three. I know how you feel.' His speech now was tender, softening the cold hard lump inside her. Jo's breath caught on a sob as he drew her closer. They stood then for a long while, listening to the surf breaking on the shingle beach below and hearing the soft sighing of the wind through the tall gorse bushes that shielded the path to their left. Jo's gaze fell on the headland. Mr Pencarrow rested proudly in the late afternoon sun, some mile away along the footpath, and, as she watched, a feeling of peace came over her, and she saw, climbing up his noble forehead, two boys and a girl. They were laughing together, chasing, talking …

'He'll always be here with us, Jo,' James whispered, as if he too had seen the same trio – the same glimpse of the past!

There was no funeral. The plane had seemed to explode over the sea; no bodies were recovered. Jim arranged a memorial service at Taunton, and a little group of friends set off from Cornwall to attend. Johanna felt that she just couldn't go, but instead spent the day on the headland, sitting with her back against the warm rocks, seeing and yet not seeing the beauty of familiar scenes around her; remembering the past days, childhood days; fun times and quiet times; and finally, remembering the last time she and Bryn spent together on the headland, just before he went to Africa. She cried softly then, her heart still breaking a little at the hurt they had both had to suffer because of their inability to say those three special words. Now she whispered them … 'I loved you Bryn … I loved you, and I'm so sorry … so very, very, sorry.'

David came to sit beside her as the afternoon sun became weaker and the air grew chill. His look was tender as he said, 'He wouldn't have wanted a long illness, Jo.'

She squeezed his hand. 'I know,' she said, and reached into her pocket for a handkerchief to wipe away the tears still welling from her eyes. Her hand discovered a letter. The postman had given it to her as she'd left Trenorwin that morning. She turned it over.

'An official one,' David said. 'Why don't you look?'

'It's from Africa.' Jo's voice was a little incredulous. 'Probably the solicitor.' Two letters were contained inside. She spread one sheet on her knees and read.

'Mr Brynmau Vaughan asked me to forward this letter to you in the event of his death. It's self-explanatory, but I would add that the contents are being worked on even now, and, if you are agreeable, I could bring young Bryn over myself early next month.'

'Whatever does it mean, David?' Jo was excited.

'Read Bryn's letter and find out, my dear. I would,' and he sucked and puffed at his pipe, gazing all the while out to sea, as she tore open the other envelope and began to read. He glanced sideways at her when she'd finished. She was so still, but he could feel the excitement buzzing through her, and as she glanced up at him, he caught an expression of such happiness and joy in her eyes, those same eyes that a moment ago had been so sad. She passed the letter to him and he read:

'My dear "you two". I hope this letter never reaches you, but I feel somewhat compelled to write it now. Firstly to thank you both for all the lovely times we've spent together in your beautiful part of the world. We've been blessed with a very special friendship, and I am proud and grateful to you for allowing me to be part of it.

'I hope to bring young Bryn over again and again, so that he will learn to love Cornwall as I do.

'My second reason for writing now is to say – if anything should happen to us, would you have Bryn for me, please? Bring him up as your own, show him our special places, teach him to swim, to sail, and to have the same carefree growing up that you had, James, at Pensilva, and allowed me later to join. I'd like him to go to school at Taunton and, if he's clever enough, to university. How I'd love to share these days with him, but as you know, it's not likely to be …

'So, I give him to you both – part of me, so that our trio will be one again! Good-bye – God bless, and I love you both. Bryn.'

Johanna watched as he read, her eyes shining with unshed tears and her mouth tremulous as they tried to form words, to make some sense of Bryn's wonderful gift.

'Steady, my dear,' David said, pulling her to him for a brief hug before helping her to her feet.

'Come. We'd better get back and plan a bedroom for a boy, hadn't we?'

David stayed with Johanna until James arrived back from Taunton. He looked pale and weary, but both noticed an excitement in his manner.

'Jim heard from Africa today,' he said.

'So did we, James – look!' Jo held the letters out for him to read. He sat for a long time when he'd finished, staring out of the window, so they couldn't see his face.

'James,' Jo's voice was soft. 'James, it is all right, isn't it?'

He turned then. Their eyes met in deep understanding, and Jo sped across the room and into his arms. David watched for a while, then let himself quietly out of the house.

Later that day they visited Widegates together and told the aunts their news. Mollie shook her head.

'The poor darling boy, whatever must it be like to come to strangers in a strange land.'

'I'm not altogether a stranger, Mollie. We did quite a lot of things together when I visited.'

'Oh I know, lad, and we are happy for you, aren't we, Edith? Bryn's boy, just fancy, and living here. Do you think he'll mind if we say we are family?' Mollie was remembering what Bryn had said about grandmothers when he had visited.

There was so much to talk about, so much to plan, and the next few weeks went in a buzz of preparation. They decorated the back bedroom for him. It looked out over Pensilva land, but had a small side window that afforded a glimpse of the sea and the cliffs off the high moor. Ben brought up a model boat. A small replica of Bryn's, in blue and yellow, which they placed on a shelf in his room, together with some African statues that James had brought back with him on his last visit.

'Tell the lad that his real boat is ready when he is,' Ben said, as he prepared to leave.

Johanna put the photograph Bryn had sent her into a small frame and hung it near to the bed, and Mollie unearthed from the loft at Widegates several books that had belonged to Tom when a child. There was an illustrated edition of *Peter Pan*, *Just So Stories* and some young poetry books, also a beautiful pictorial copy of *Robinson Crusoe*.

'They are a bit grand for a five-year-old, but he will soon grow into them, I'm sure,' Mollie set them onto a bedside table. 'Tom would have loved to have met the boy. He'll be happy for him to have his things – the loft is full of them.'

Finally, everything was ready. They had done all they could to make Bryn's little boy feel welcome and at home. Each day, James hurried out to meet the postman, and each day they were disappointed, but it was only a slight dismay that they felt, a slight chagrin maybe at the delay.

Jo had spent a good deal of her young life waiting, but this time it was different, this time she was sure of the outcome; the papers had been signed, forms completed, and soon Bryn would come to them.

So they went about their daily tasks with an inner excitement and were content.

Johanna was out of breath by the time she reached the lychgate. Her hands were trembling slightly as they wrestled with the rope that looped the top bar and prevented it swinging open. She glanced back to the road … a lonely, empty road, devoid of traffic and with no sign of the usual walkers, backpacked and laughing, ready for a tramp around the headland and coastal path. Not a day for the faint-hearted, just right for me though, she thought.

It was now very windy, with low clouds almost hugging the cliffs and promising rain. Closing the gate, she stopped for a moment to still the inner excitement that this morning's news had precipitated, her hand rustling the letter in her pocket! She gave a moment's thought for her kitchen … had she left everything safe? Then she turned to plunge down the covered walk towards the open moor and the sea. The walkway was slippery from overnight rain. Her feet slithered frequently, and often she only kept her balance by reaching out for exposed tree roots or a low-lying bush to cling to. The gully was rocky underfoot. The continual damp of late summer had formed moss, which made her hurrying footsteps even more difficult to control. She scarcely noticed how deep the channel had been cut overnight, for the rain had been heavy and prolonged. The culverts that converged at the top of the leafy path had disgorged their overflowing contents, gaining force until the whole of the walkway had become a running river. She felt her feet slipping repeatedly, but her eyes were focused straight ahead, to where the bright clear path for the headland began. The few chirrups and scurries from nearby birds didn't stop her flight. Usually, Jo would have walked the leafy lane, stopping to talk to anything she heard rustling. The bramblings had become quite tame, used to hearing people in this confined space, and could be encouraged to come near for titbits. She had nothing for them today though. Johanna was not even thinking of them, until one bird gave out such a sweet shrill song, right over her head. Then she paused in her flight for a moment, gazing skywards through the branches of the overhang to see the little songster.

'Oh yes …' she breathed. 'Oh yes!' Her heart felt like singing too, singing like the bird. Her steps were light now, she could feel her heart pounding in her chest.

Her breath caught again, and she stopped, folding her hands tightly together in front of her. Jo thought she'd burst with happiness, and yet this overwhelming feeling of joy was almost like a pain. As tears formed in her eyes and ran slowly down her cheeks, she turned to the open gate, gasping as the full force of the wind off the sea caught her. She faced the view now revealed, the wide sweep of the bay, and then she threw her head back and laughed, laughed at the sheer joy of being alive … of being alive on this special day … this very special day!

Jo crumpled the letter again, as if to reassure herself it was really there. Her features softened as she thought of the day ahead, and her eyes were distant as they gazed towards the horizon, seeing and yet not seeing the pitching and plunging of the white horses stretching away into the distance. Some strands of her fair hair had escaped from the wide comb controlling it; she put up her hands to tame them. Strong capable hands, square almost, but with tapering, well-cared-for fingernails, and browned by the summer sun. Jo stood still, leaning into the wind, enjoying the buffeting. Her slender body still girlishly rounded, brown eyes clear, and a face as unlined and smooth as a teenager's.

She lifted her face to the wind and stepped out towards the headland path, as memories came flooding back – back to the long hot summer of 1939, before the start of the second war, and when it had all begun. She had been fifteen years old then; happy and carefree, and spending the holidays in her favourite place in Cornwall. Fourteen years ago, she mused … such a long, long time!

Jo walked slowly now, towards the cliff path, rereading the letter in her mind.

'We will reach Plymouth at noon. Can you meet us there?'

She recalled the excitement they'd both felt when she'd read those words aloud that morning. How she had fussed James … 'Hurry now, please hurry. You mustn't be late!' And now he was speeding on his way to Plymouth.

'Oh hurry, James,' she whispered again.

Jo had reached the cliff edge now and could see the waves coming in strongly on a turning tide, speeding over the rocky shore of the little bay, far below her. Something at the back of her mind troubled her. What was it? Had she forgotten something? A picture of a young boy flashed before her eyes. A laughing boy, with dark curly hair, climbing a rope-ladder into a tree to retrieve a kite for her. That was it … the rope-ladder! She must get it from Mollie.

She fled back up the gully path and on to Widegates. Mollie was sitting in the warm kitchen listening to the radio. Her calm and gentle face was attentive as Jo asked about the ladder.

'It's in the barn, Jo. We salvaged it when the old oak fell down, remember? You'll find it behind the door, but check mind … it's pretty old now.' Her keen eyes studied her niece. 'Why, you're as taut as a telephone wire, come and sit down for a while.'

'Oh I am, Mollie. Excited, anxious, happy, impossibly happy – all those things.' Her face softened as she sat down at the table, leant her elbows on the surface, and cushioned her head in her hands. She was still and gazing towards the fire.

'What is it, lass – can you tell me?' Mollie asked softly. Jo flashed a wide-eyed look at her aunt.

'I dreamed of him last night, Mollie.' Her voice was soft as she began. 'I was in a small walled garden. High walls covered with creepers that hung waving fronds in the mist. It was warm and evening time; the garden was full of people … everyone was there. Friends from our childhood, you Mollie, Edith and Tom, even people from the village. I remember standing close to the house. A tall house, like the London one … red-brick, with wide bay windows, and the gables that reached high seemed lost in the swirling grey of the mist.

'I felt peaceful as I watched; small groups of people were chatting, mixing and mingling; I was at peace with myself and not at all bothered that I was alone. I felt truly alone, as if I was watching and yet couldn't be seen … watchful really. I was watchful! Almost without noticing that feeling of peace and gentle contentment changed. I found my whole being taken over by a restlessness – a fearful expectancy. I wanted … I wanted. I didn't know what I wanted, but I felt this awful longing turn my heart into a painful tight lump, as if all the blood was being squeezed out of it. My throat ached with a sadness that I just couldn't bear. The feeling increased, and I heard a sob tear itself from my throat, a sob that rose and hurt as I tried to stifle it. My hands reached out for the comfort of the house wall behind me. I felt the warmth of the wall, and then noticed, through my anguish, that the mist had cleared. It was a fine warm summer evening, and the smell of the honeysuckle falling off the nearby arbour was sweet and cloying. My breathing slowed – I turned my head, and he was there! A young Bryn as we remember him. Young and vital, and smiling that strangely twisted smile of welcome. You remember how he used to look; his whole body tall, straight and yet casually relaxed as he leaned against the wall near to me. Our eyes met and held for an endless moment. He shrugged his shoulders at the company, as we've seen him do so many times before.

'Just then, just as it seemed natural for him to be there, a group of people came between us, and when I sought him once more – nothing – nothing. The anguish returned, but this time more severely, accompanied by a longing again, a desperate longing for him as he was then, for myself as I was then … for someone to take back the years – for us all to begin again!

'I went inside and made my way up through the house to a room at the back. It was small and square, darkly furnished, a study perhaps, and the bay windows overlooked the garden. I leaned against the window frame, my hands clutching the curtains. People were milling about below. It was like many parties we have been to, with groups forming and reforming, lots of chatter; quiet voices though, as if in a dream – as if everyone was far away.

'As I watched, I saw him again – near to me, just under the window, and he was with a frail little lady. He put his arm gently round her shoulders and his face was oh so tender! He looked up at me. Whether he could feel the intensity of my gaze, or whether he'd known I was there … well I don't know, but it all seemed inevitable, natural somehow. His glance was warm and compelling, and as our eyes met, time stood still. We were both young once more, I felt it, I noticed it, for my hands that held onto the fabric of the curtain, were a young girl's hands. All work marks gone – slender fingers, and on the nails the transparent varnish that I'd always used. Our look held, his tender teasing eyes sending a shudder through my wilting frame. It seemed as if the whole world contained just him and me. Every other figure milling down below was a shadowy one. It was then I heard Veronica. She was with a group of friends quite near to Bryn. An argument was in full swing, and now her voice rose loud and clear.

"But surely," she said. "But surely, in this day and time, there is hope still for us all!"

'I don't know to what she was referring. I scarcely took in what she had said, but caught the word "hope", and in my dream I heard Bryn say to me.'

"Yes my dear, there's hope, always hope – hope!"

'I immediately responded to him with a smile; a feeling of complete and overwhelming understanding relayed itself back and forth. I saw his eyes darken, and felt myself young and impatient, with wild dreams in my heart. We stayed like that forever, or that is how it seemed. Then he smiled, a loving smile – a teasing smile – oh, all the ways he had of smiling, and I heard his voice say again: "there's always hope, hope, hope!"

'I woke to hear that well-loved voice still speaking and wondered, Mollie, at the inward joy I felt, even through the loss of my dream on the wakening day. Six times he said it, and I knew he was right, for a younger generation is giving us hope. A letter came this morning from the solicitor. Now I feel that all will be well. James has gone to Plymouth. Bryn has entrusted him to our care, and everything will be all right. I know it will!'

Some minutes later Jo returned to Trenorwin, walking quietly and with purpose down the lane, the rope-ladder folded under one arm. On reaching her garden she set it up in the lower branches of the oak tree, twisting it a little so that one end was caught untidily. It was two-thirty by the time she'd finished. They would be here soon. She stood in the doorway, awaiting their arrival.

The clouds had lifted and given way to a sunny day. The wind was blustery still, and over the bay she could see that the waves were still being whipped into white foam. There was a strong smell of seaweed, unusual for these parts, and the sky was a deep azure blue. A perfect day to say hello to Cornwall, she thought. Jo watched as the sheep moved in a line across the field opposite, and her eyes looked upwards, following the tumbling black specks in the sky as the rooks were disturbed in the corner copse.

She saw James's car appear over the brow of the hill in the distance, and then dip out of view. Jo traced in her mind its journey along the winding Cornish lane, hearing occasionally the tight little 'hoot' as it rounded each blind corner.

Finally it drew up outside Trenorwin. Jo's heart was thumping nervously, but outwardly she appeared totally calm.

James emerged from the car and waved to her, and then she saw a young boy standing on the gravel drive, scuffing his shoes in the small stones and glancing up shyly. He was dressed all in grey, rather like a school uniform, and she noticed that he was tall for his age.

'Come and say hello to Johanna, Bryn,' James put out his hand to the boy, and they both advanced to where she stood – waiting. Jo found herself looking into the past … looking into two questioning blue-grey eyes, but these were wary and tired, not bright and sparkling as his father's had been on that first day.

'Hello,' she said. 'You are just in time. I need help with the rope-ladder. Can you climb trees?'

The boy looked up, a straight direct look, and said seriously:

'I'm very good at climbing. Dad said I take after him.'

'Come along then,' Jo replied, and her eyes met James's over the boy's dark curly head. She nodded to herself before hurrying with him to the huge old oak-tree, set in the middle of the spacious lawn … Bryn had come home after all!

Lightning Source UK Ltd.
Milton Keynes UK
UKHW02f1808160218
318009UK00005B/34/P